Matt &

May Shadows of War serve
as a lasting reminder that
heroism often doesn't make
headlines. Instead it often
results from what could be
termed quiet courage — courage
that often goes unnoticed or
noticed not at all except by
those closest to the hero.

Savor the journey with
WWII heroes and heroines
from Ohio to Romania
to Singapore.

Mike Johnsen

Shadows of War

Mike Johnson

AuthorHouse™
1663 Liberty Drive
Bloomington, IN 47403
www.authorhouse.com
Phone: 1-800-839-8640

First published by AuthorHouse 10/30/2010

ISBN: 978-1-4520-9433-5 (hc)
ISBN: 978-1-4520-9434-2 (sc)
ISBN: 978-1-4520-9435-9 (e)

Library of Congress Control Number: 2010916004

Printed in the United States of America

This book is printed on acid-free paper.

This is a historical novel. The story combines real-life historical figures (roster shown at book's rear) with fictional characters. All names of ships and planes are historically accurate. All locales are authentic, and cited statistics are accurate in so far as my research shows. References to actual historical events and real people as well as locales are intended to give the fiction a stronger sense of authenticity. The chronology of the story is historically accurate.

Also by Mike Johnson

Warrior Priest

Fate of the Warriors

God's Perfect Scar

Mascot, Minister, Man of Steel – The Final Reunion

For

Alexandra Dinita
Lynne Haley Johnson
Oon Soo Khoo
Bill Miller
Pat Shedenhelm Papenbrock
Azizah Sidek
Keat Fong Tan
Poh Hong Tan
Grace Thong
Prasad Varaprasad
Dianne Haley Vots
Chin Chuan Yit
Nancy Nicholson Yoder

More can be learned about why this book is dedicated to them in the
Acknowledgements section.

CHAPTER 1

"Where was he killed?"

"In Belleau Wood," Marie Hughes replied softly after a slight pause, eyes downcast. "He was with the Fourth Marine Brigade. They were attached to the Army's Second Infantry Division. They stopped the Germans on the road to Paris. We lost almost ten thousand men in that battle. Nearly two thousand killed, the rest wounded. Marines and soldiers." She sighed deeply. "The battle lasted nearly three weeks."

In fact, that crucial battle raged from June 6-26, 1918. It earned the Marines the sobriquet Devil Dogs. A battlefield report transmitted on June 26 read: "Woods now U.S. Marine Corps entirely."

"Do you know how?" Joe Barton asked in a near whisper.

"Not really. But knowing what I know about World War One and Belleau Wood, probably machine gun fire. At close range. Perhaps by rifle or shrapnel from a mortar. Not likely by falling bombs. Airplane pilots tossed down the occasional bomb, but they mostly fired machine guns and flew reconnaissance. To take Belleau Wood our Marines had to charge across a wheat field. There was no cover and the Germans cut loose with machine guns." Her head shook. "It was sheer incompetence by senior officers."

Marie Hughes knew plenty about World War I. She also knew much about all the wars in which Americans had fought, died and been maimed. Miss Hughes taught American history at Shelby High School from which she graduated in 1908. That was 25 years before her conversation with Joe Barton that was taking place in early November 1933. In between, she had earned a bachelor's degree at Ohio Wesleyan University in Delaware and then returned to Shelby to begin a teaching career that would end 47 years later when she retired in 1960. Afterward she substitute taught for several more years before dying in 1974 at age 83.

Joe was a strapping 17-year-old who stood six feet tall and weighed 185 pounds made hard through a daily exercise regimen that included 200 push-ups and 50 chin-ups. He wasn't Hollywood handsome, but two facial flaws lent his countenance a certain magnetism. One was a half-dollar size birthmark between his right eyebrow and temple. The other was an inch and a half-long jagged scar below his right sideburn. The latter was courtesy of a fall against a row of red bricks bordering a flower garden in a neighbor's backyard. Said bricks met Joe's face during a rousing game of neighborhood football.

"Were you engaged?" Joe asked.

"Yes. He was my fiancé."

"How did you learn about it? His death, I mean."

"From his mother." Miss Hughes sighed again. "I haven't talked about it much. Actually, hardly at all, just with my mother." Her eyes were gazing past Joe's left shoulder as though peering back through the years, 15 of them.

"Why are you telling me?"

"A good question, Joe. The answer is I'm not sure," Miss Hughes replied, lips pursing and redirecting her eyes toward Joe's. "Sometimes I just get to reflecting. Armistice Day is next week. November eleventh. And maybe because you are fond of history. And maybe too because I sense you have a spirit of adventure. Somehow I see your future taking you far from Shelby."

She was right about Joe's zest for history. From early childhood he had been lugging armloads of histories and biographies from stately, columned Marvin Memorial Library on North Gamble Street to his home on East Main Street. Benjamin Franklin. Daniel Boone. General Mad Anthony Wayne. Blackjack Pershing. They all had accompanied Joe on the half-mile trek from the former mansion of one of Shelby's earliest families turned library.

A smile creased Joe's face. "I've never been outside of Ohio."

Miss Hughes was Joe's favorite teacher. She was a whisper of a woman, barely five feet tall. Petite, her weight barely nudged the scales to 100 pounds. Miss Hughes dressed smartly. She favored navy blue and black dresses, usually accented by a single strand of pearls. When she wasn't smiling her visage was mildly haunted, eyes sad and lips curling slightly downward. Although only 42, her hair was graying, fetchingly so. Her movements – walking, bending, stretching to chalk names, dates and places at the top of her classroom blackboard – were unfailingly graceful, much like a cat leaping effortlessly from floor to window sill. She maintained discipline equally gracefully. Her favorite technique was turning a yellow

#2 pencil eraser down and tapping her desk. Sometimes a penetrating stare accompanied the tapping. It was unfailingly effective. Occasionally she invited her girl students to her home for formal afternoon tea.

"Time, Joe. Give yourself time. For the young it's a precious gift."

"Have you ever been to France?"

Miss Hughes shook her head and sighed shallowly. "I've thought about it. Often. I guess I don't want to go alone, and I'm not sure if anyone would want to go with me." She removed her wire-rimmed glasses and with left forefinger and thumb rubbed the bridge of her nose between her Aegean Sea-blue eyes that seemed made to complement her graying hair. "Besides it would be a long and expensive trip. A train to New York, the long voyage across the Atlantic, another train ride." A pause. "But I'm saving money, so Europe might find me paying a visit one day."

"Is he buried there? In France?" Joe watched Miss Hughes reposition her glasses and nod. "I'm only a kid but I think you should go."

The fifth period bell – each of the six periods lasted 56 minutes – had rung, and Joe and Miss Hughes were chatting in her third floor classroom with windows overlooking a parking lot and a slender tributary of the not-much-wider Blackfork River that flowed between the school and Skiles Stadium and sliced Shelby into nearly symmetrical east and west sides. Miss Hughes was standing beside her heavy rectangular wooden desk, and Joe was sitting at his front-row desk, the kind that combined writing surface, storage space and chair into a single unit. He was leaning forward, elbows on desk.

"Sometime. Perhaps," she smiled down at him. "Why do you think I should go?"

The word closure hadn't entered the everyday vocabulary of 1930s Shelbians, but that was the concept that shaped Joe's reply. He breathed deeply and his eyes closed momentarily. "I think you are still mourning him. Maybe if you stood at his grave, you could say goodbye, and you wouldn't feel so heavy."

Miss Hughes shook her head almost imperceptibly. "You see things very clearly, Joe. Remarkably for one so young."

Joe's face reddened, except for the brown birthmark and jagged scar. He glanced up at the large round clock above the blackboard. He began easing from his chair. "I have to get to football practice."

"I know. Go." A pause as Joe stepped past her. "Thanks for listening. And, Joe…" He stopped and pivoted. "Look beyond Shelby and Ohio. I believe you have much to offer the wider world."

CHAPTER 2

The rider flicked the reins twice and the coal black mare with a large white circle on her snout, whimsically named Pearl, easily ascended the last few feet of the trail leading to the summit of the hill that crested some 600 feet above the meadow below. The rider tightened the reins and the obedient mount stopped and stood virtually motionless.

"What do you think?" asked the rider, Gabriella Balas.

From behind her a little girl's voice replied, "It's so very pretty. I've never been this high." The voice belonged to Laura Ramaschi, age seven. "Can we stay a while?"

"Certainly," said Gabriella. "Take my left hand and slide off." Laura did as instructed and Gabriella held her hand until the girl's foot touched the ground. Then Gabriella removed her brown-booted right foot from the stirrup and dismounted quickly and gracefully. In 1933 she was 18. Lustrous black hair, falling to her shoulders, crowned her five feet seven inches. Her brown eyes sparkled with intelligence and wit. She jokingly ascribed her slightly olive complexion to her ancestors – a mix of gypsies with ill-defined roots and Roman conquerors of what was called Dacia when Emperor Trajan and his troops arrived in A.D. 101.

Gabriella was slender with uncommonly small breasts and narrow hips. Her lithe build enhanced her athleticism. She eschewed sidesaddles as too delicate for the Romanian equivalent of a tomboy who didn't confine swimming to the pool at her father's club. She exulted in taking plunges into a small pond near her home.

Romania was a poor nation but Gabriella's leather boots, black riding pants and black leather jacket were items her parents could easily afford. Cornel, her father, oversaw the nation's prosperous petroleum industry. Gabriella's mother Elena managed the household. The family lived in Ploesti

(pronounced Ploy-esht in Romanian), center of the petroleum industry and as an oil boomtown the nation's most affluent city. The horse belonged to friends of Cornel with whom Gabriella and Laura were spending an autumn weekend.

"Look," said Gabriella, extended right arm and forefinger pointing toward the distant horizon. "That's Peles Castle."

"It's very pretty too." Laura's countenance clearly reflected her ancestry – Sicilians who had made their way to Dacia with Trajan's powerful legions. Black hair, long and curly, wide-set eyes, dazzling smile and strong chin. Her parents were close to Gabriella's. In fact, Laura's father was a senior member of Cornel's staff.

Peles Castle, flanked and backed by majestic fir trees, sat atop a rise in the foothills of the Carpathian Mountains near Sinaia, population about 10,000, and some 30 miles north of Ploesti. Peles was never intended to be a fortress. In reality, it was a 168-room palace. Still, it had been called a castle since its construction began in 1875 and was completed in 1914.

King Carol II was born at Peles in 1893. Peles incorporated a mélange of architectural styles – neo-Renaissance, Gothic Revival, Saxon, Baroque. Wood, stone, bricks and marble all could be seen in the exterior. Asymmetrical towers, the taller soaring 180 feet, dwarfed the rest of the four-floor structure. A decorative heavy stone balustrade extended across the castle's front. The mish-mash design perhaps was explained by an entry in the journal of Queen Elizabeth, wife of King Carol I. "Italians

5

were masons, Romanians were building terraces, the Gypsies were coolies. Albanians and Greeks worked in stone, Germans and Hungarians were carpenters. Turks were burning brick. Engineers were Polish and the stone carvers were Czech. The Frenchmen were drawing, the Englishmen were measuring, and so it was then when you could see hundreds of national costumes and hear fourteen languages in which they spoke, sang, cursed and quarreled in all dialects and tones, a joyful mix of men, horses, cart oxen and domestic buffaloes."

"It looks like an exciting place to live," said Laura, wearing a brown cloth jacket over a white blouse, blue ankle-length skirt and brown leather shoes. "Such a big house and no neighbors."

"I don't think the king wants neighbors."

"Why?"

"Probably so his guards can see anyone coming. Kings worry about things like that."

"Why?"

"Kings often have enemies. People who want a different king – or no king at all."

CHAPTER 3

The plane soared gracefully, first gaining altitude, then turning upside down before swooping and beginning a quick descent to a smooth landing on the long grass.

The craft was only 12 inches from nose to tail and, made of balsa, weighed only a few ounces.

Jefferson Davis Wolfrom, age 10 in 1933, had launched the tiny plane from a second floor window of the boarding house his mother Iris Ann operated at 305 East Martin in Pine Bluff, Arkansas. The boarding house stood just east of Main Street and on the "right" side of the Union Pacific Railroad tracks that bisected the city, running southwest to northeast. West of the tracks lived most of Pine Bluff's poorer residents including virtually all its blacks, commonly and not always maliciously spoken of as niggers. Jeff's hair was the gold of wheat ready for harvesting, and his eyes were as blue as Pine Bluff skies on an autumn afternoon. He inherited his coloring from Iris Ann. She stood a trim five feet four inches but radiated a presence that caused others to see her as taller. In 1932 at the fairgrounds outside Pine Bluff, Jeff saw a troop of barnstorming stunt flyers. They seemingly defied all of nature's immutable laws and still kept their planes safely airborne. Jeff was smitten. Soon he was making and sailing paper planes from second floor windows of the boarding house. He often fell asleep imagining himself at the controls of one of the aerial dervishes.

Iris Ann had more earthbound concerns. Her husband Wilfred had been killed in a logging accident in 1930. He had been crushed by a falling pine tree. Wilfred had seen the magnificent tree toppling toward him but had tripped and was unable to scramble from harm's way.

With his death went his wages, leaving Iris Ann to eke out a living for her and Jeff from the boarding house. That required no mean financial management ability. The house, built in the mid-1880s, was two stories with enough triangles in its design to suggest Grecian influence. On the left side of the façade a large triangular gable enclosed a pair of small attic windows. In the façade's center a smaller triangle crowned another attic window. A wide porch with a red tile floor spanned the entire front of the house and wrapped around to the right. Above the porch's center a wide low-slung triangle capped four Corinthian-style columns, two each flanking five concrete steps. Anchoring the façade's right side was a six-sided cupola capped by a six-sided cone-shaped roof.

The house sat on high ground. Before reaching the porch steps, an arrival first had to ascend five wide concrete steps and walk several more paces.

Inside, the house sprawled. There was no foyer; the front door opened immediately into a large living room. To its left were two bedrooms, the first of which had begun as a library and included built-in bookshelves, and the second of which was Jeff's. Beyond the living room was a hallway with a staircase on the left to the second floor. The hallway led to a large dining room and then a breakfast room that boasted a built-in china closet that covered an entire wall and a ceiling fan that battled Pine Bluff's sauna-like summers. To its left was Iris Ann's bedroom that adjoined the floor's lone bathroom. The kitchen occupied the rear and was huge, including a pantry. To the kitchen's left was an enclosed back porch.

The house's second floor included three spacious bedrooms, each furnished with a pair of double beds and with space for a cot. The single bathroom's floor was tiled in black and white.

No boarder enjoyed a private room. As a result, the four bedrooms easily accommodated eight boarders and sometimes as many as 10.

In the 1930s Pine Bluff's population hovered around 21,000. The Great Depression hit hard and two local banks failed. One of the failures wiped out Iris Ann's small savings account.

"Thank God for the railroads," Iris Ann said often enough for Jeff to regard it as something of a mantra. The railroads central to her survival were the Union Pacific and its grand station built in 1906 and the Cotton Belt with its sprawling complex on the city's far east side that included a roundhouse, switching yard and repair shops. The Cotton Belt was the town's largest employer and supplied most of Iris Ann's roomers and boarders who easily could walk back and forth from 315 East Martin to their jobs. Other large employers included area paper mills, and some of their workers were among Iris Ann's "drop-ins" for dinner for which she charged 25 cents.

Later, in 1936, a stockyard would be built in Pine Bluff, and in 1941 a military arsenal and Grider Field Airport which would include the Pine

Bluff School of Aviation that would train some 10,000 pilots and crew before closing in 1944.

Iris Ann worked hard to make ends meet, and Jeff helped as best he could. Mornings she arose at 4:30 to fix brown bag lunches for boarders who started work at 6:00. With no refrigeration available at the rail complex, Iris Ann had to prepare lunches that could withstand several hours of Pine Bluff's stifling summer heat and humidity. Those lunches included such staples as a white bread meatloaf sandwich, a piece of fruit and a slice of cake or a couple cookies. Lunches also tended to consist of leftovers from the previous night's supper and baking. She inserted a napkin in each bag and wrote boarders' names on the bags.

Some early rising boarders ate breakfast and favorite dishes included Iris Ann's biscuits and cornbread, sometimes crumbled into fresh buttermilk. Iris Ann served small glasses of orange juice and if time permitted cooked eggs to order. Her coffee was fresh and made as needed in round glass pots that she also used to serve coffee at all meals. Her pride in her work was obvious.

In addition to Jeff, Iris Ann's help included black women, mostly young, who bussed to 315 East Martin from the west side of the Union Pacific tracks. Some worked harder than others and some were smarter than others, but all heard the same message from Iris Ann: "You must be friendly, helpful and amiable with my boarders as well as folks who come in for supper." She also was a thoughtful boss; she gave workers an extra 10 cents if they needed daily bus fare.

She equipped her front porch with several lightweight chairs as in evenings many of her boarders enjoyed sitting there, chatting and reading newspapers. Generally she was too busy to join them.

Within two years of Wilfred's death, the resulting loss of his wages and the Great Depression were conspiring to push Iris Ann to the brink of insolvency. Her hard work alone, she knew, wasn't going to save the boarding house. After much agonizing and a silent conversation with God, she decided to supplement her meager income by renting her lissome body. As insurance against unwanted pregnancy she urged partners – her most trustworthy boarders – to withdraw before ejaculating. That they didn't consistently succeed caused her no small measure of anxiety. She also insisted on quiet couplings. "I will brook no noise beyond heavy breathing.

And there will be no picture frames rattling against the walls. I simply will not embarrass my son that way. He is not to know about this. I also do not want my reputation sullied around town. There will be no second chance." Her horizontal customers acceded – or they knew they would lose the opportunity to purchase her favors. Iris Ann accepted men into her bed only after she was sure Jeff was asleep or when he was in school. An unexpected benefit from this side venture: reduced turnover among her boarders.

She also didn't delude herself. With Wilfred more than two years in his grave, her couplings satisfied physical urges while keeping her boarding house a going concern. She enjoyed intimacy with two of her boarders in particular and didn't try telling herself otherwise.

When Jeff wasn't in school, launching his balsa planes from upstairs windows or playing baseball, he was tramping the thick forests around Pine Bluff. His frequent companion was a .22 rifle that had been a prized possession of Wilfred. With no formal instruction – and no hunting license – Jeff quickly achieved remarkable hand-eye coordination. Small game within 20 yards of his trigger finger seldom escaped his aim. He became equally skilled with a hunting knife – a four-inch Remington steel blade attached to a four-inch steel haft wrapped tightly in leather. With quick, economic movements, young Jeff could gut, clean and skin cottontails and squirrels that Iris Ann invariably welcomed in her kitchen.

CHAPTER 4

On a summer day in 1933 in Vienna, Austria, sweat was drenching the 17-year-old girl as a fever raged. Marie Caradja lay in a hospital bed, groaning lowly, curled into a fetal position. Her appendix had burst and poison was spreading.

Her mother, Princess Catherine Caradja, took the phone call from her husband in the manor house on their 1,000-acre estate near Nedelea, a village 10 miles northwest of Ploesti.

"I – we – the doctor, we fear the worst," said Prince Constantin Caradja. "Marie looks so white and her forehead is so hot."

"I will get there as soon as possible," Catherine replied. She returned the heavy black phone to its cradle and went sprinting for her black Plymouth. She started the engine and went tearing down rutted dirt roads, at one point billowing dust that enveloped a horse-driven cart and its cursing driver. She swiftly traversed the 40 miles to Otopeni Airport, just six miles north of central Bucharest. "Dear God," she prayed aloud, "please spare my daughter. And if that is not your will, then let me see her while she still lives."

In Vienna, Marie's breathing was becoming worrisomely shallow. The attending physician told Catherine's husband that earthly hands could do nothing more for Marie, the couple's second of three daughters.

Flying was hardly new to Catherine. In 1916 while pregnant with Marie, she had flown with her husband and their year-old daughter Irene from Bucharest to Moldavia to escape invading German troops. Born on January 28, 1893, Catherine at age 40 possessed a face best described as motherly with underlying grit. Golden hair complimented her intelligent ice blue eyes. Her chin jutted slightly and she smiled easily and often. Her robust frame didn't slow her movements or sap her energy.

At Otopeni, little more than a clay runway with a tiny terminal and two hangars, Catherine had only to ask the airport manager, and a Ford Tri-Motor and crew were quickly at her disposal. The plane bounced down the rough runway and lurched into the air. The 530-mile fight northwest to Vienna was underway.

While sitting alone in the cabin, Catherine had ample time to reflect. If I don't arrive in time, I must not blame anyone – not my husband, not myself. That would achieve nothing. I encouraged him to vacation with the girls in Vienna. Develop their appreciation for fine music. Is there any city on earth where a person can listen to more wonderful music? Every day it seems there is a concert. I had to stay behind to take care of matters at the orphanages. So many children with so many needs.

Catherine's early years enabled her to empathize with orphans and their plight. In 1896 at age 3 she found herself a pawn in a financial struggle between family factions. Her father, Prince Radu Cretulescu, abducted the tot, spirited her to England and placed her in an orphanage under a false name. Catherine's mother, Princess Irina, divorced Radu, married another prince and kept searching for the child until Irina died in 1906.

In 1908, then 15 and detained in a French convent, one of Catherine's aunts found the girl, helped her escape and brought her back to Romania where she was put in the care of her maternal grandparents.

Catherine's odyssey led to a major advantage: She was conversant in five languages – Romanian, English, French, German and Dutch. In 1914, just before the outbreak of World War I, Catherine married well – to Prince Constantin Caradja, a year her senior.

While in refuge in Moldavia during Germany's occupation of Romania, Catherine began working in a 30-bed hospital for typhus patients. She contracted the disease herself. After the armistice of November 11, 1918, Catherine and her family returned to Bucharest. Though a young mother of two, she immediately plunged into social work, most notably with a complex of orphanages begun by her mother and called Saint Catherine's Crib. Financially underpinning the enterprise were rent from leased properties and oil well holdings. Eventually Catherine would find herself overseeing the care of more than 3,000 orphans.

Aboard the noisy plane Catherine closed her eyes and prayed. Please, Lord, let me see Marie again while she still breathes. She was depending on God and the Ford Tri-Motor to answer her supplication. The plane, nicknamed *The Tin Goose*, had been introduced in 1925 and soon was selling the world over. King Carol II was one of its buyers. The monoplane's length was 50 feet and its wing span 77 feet. Maximum speed was 150 miles per hour and typical cruising speed was 90 mph. Its range was 550 miles. Crewing the craft were a pilot, co-pilot and stewardess. Depending on seating configurations, the plane could accommodate from eight to 15 passengers. King Carol's model seated eight.

Six hours, Catherine reflected. From takeoff to touchdown, that's how long I'll be in the air, and that plus a little longer and I can see Marie. Catherine's left hand pushed back through her golden hair.

Because pressurized cabins hadn't yet been introduced, the Tri-Motor cruised at under 10,000 feet. That required a flight path that evaded the highest peaks between Bucharest and Vienna. The low altitude and less than 100 mph speed afforded Catherine ample time to observe doings on the ground. It all looks so peaceful, she mused, so serene, so full of life. Wagons and carts drawn by horses and oxen lumbered along narrow dirt roads and among fields rich with grains. She could see women hanging laundry and children helping with chores and gamboling along streams. Will my daughter live to play like that again?

Half a world away, Sister Regina, a ward sister, was cleaning a newly born, squalling girl at Singapore General Hospital. She was smiling and humming while working. "You are a beauty," the nun murmured. Then she handed the infant to her mother. "I'll be back soon to collect your daughter and show her to your husband."

Sister Regina headed the maternity ward nursing staff and relished working there. Unlike other wards, maternity was generally a joyful beehive of birthing, feeding, diapering, cuddling and cooing. Often Sister Regina acknowledged to herself that caring for infants was satisfying her own maternal instincts, never to be satisfied by a virginal nun but certainly virtually.

She was born in 1908 in Petworth, a village about 45 miles southwest from London. The village lay on rolling terrain not far north from the South Downs, the line of high hills stretching across West Sussex. Petworth had a small Roman Catholic church and Regina's family members were pious parishioners. Her parents nudged her toward a convent and Regina didn't resist.

13

By the time Regina took her vows, her face resembled more that of a Parisian runway model. Indeed, she had acted in school plays and dreamed occasionally of life as a thespian. Her blond hair complimented a creamy, flawless complexion accented by blue eyes capable of fluttering male hearts. Regina wasn't blind to her beauty but during her convent years didn't see it in terms of snaring romantic interest. Nor had she since.

Now she was carrying the newborn down the maternity ward hallway to the waiting room. Her light gray habit was swishing at her shoe tops, and her wimple was gently pinching forehead and cheeks. The equatorial heat and humidity notwithstanding, Sister Regina didn't appear to be perspiring.

Her left hand pushed open the waiting room door, and a slightly built, bespectacled young man with a narrow face and gentle eyes leaped up from a wicker chair.

"You must be Lim Bo Seng," Sister Regina smiled. "Let me introduce you to your new child."

Lim smiled wanly but extended his arms with confidence. This baby was his second child and first daughter. "Thank you, Sister. How is my wife?" he asked as he cradled the baby in his left arm and stroked her cheeks with his right hand.

"She is fine. Tired, as you can imagine and needing rest. Please, sit down. I'll be back in a while to collect your beautiful daughter and return her to your wife."

Lim was born in 1909, the eleventh – and youngest – child but first son of a wealthy businessman, Lim Loh, who owned a rubber plantation, large bakery and brick-making operation in Singapore. Lim Bo Seng first studied at Raffles Institution and at 17 had left Singapore to study at the University of Hong Kong, a natural choice given England's colonial influence in the region and Lim Loh's seeing advantages for his son in studying in a British-ruled colony. Returning to Singapore, in 1930 Lim married Gan Choo Neo, a pretty and petite, bespectacled young woman.

Catherine pushed through the heavy doors of the Vienna hospital and went striding briskly to the reception desk. "I am here to see my daughter," she said in German. "My name is" – from the corner of her right eye, Catherine saw Constantin approaching the desk from a long hallway. His pace – slow, more like shuffling – and downcast eyes rendered the verdict as loudly as would a pompous judge banging his gavel and shouting for order before bleating a death sentence. Trailing two steps behind was Irene, eyes reddened and sniffling.

Catherine had taken barely three steps toward Constantin when tears began coursing down her face. Caring as she did for hundreds of orphans, many chronically and acutely sick, Catherine knew well the fragility of life. Death visited her orphans too often and the losses – each of them – tore at her heart. Still, those losses hadn't prepared her for losing a daughter and, as strong as she was, Catherine knew her grief would endure.

CHAPTER 5

The two horses were cantering spiritedly across the expansive pasture, and their riders were hatless, faces glowing in the warmth of early spring sunshine.

"It's so nice of Mr. Dawson to let us keep riding his horses," said Maureen Alston. "I can't think of a nicer way to spend this afternoon."

"Not even two seats in the back row of the State Theater?" Joe Barton teased.

"Only if it was a double feature," Maureen replied with mock wickedness. The State, along with the Castamba, were Shelby's two theaters, both located on the south side of Main Street and only two blocks apart.

"I think today was a cowboy movie and lots of cartoons," Joe said mischievously. "Plenty of noise to muffle any sounds we might make."

"That tree," Maureen said, pointing to a lone oak near the pasture's south end, "let's head for its shade."

"Let's race," said Joe, and Maureen grinned her agreement. She shrieked delightedly as the two teenagers kicked against the horses' flanks and flicked their reins. Within seconds their mounts, manes and tails streaming wildly, went thundering across the pasture. Pounding hoofs were kicking up clumps of rich earth. Approaching the tree, Joe and Maureen pulled back forcefully on the reins, bringing the horses to a sharp stop.

"Not bad for a couple of city kids," Joe said dryly.

"Do this often enough and I might want to become a farm girl," Maureen laughed. "You could become the next cowboy movie star. Your scar would make the girls swoon."

"But not my birthmark."

"The makeup artists would take care of that."

She and her family lived on South Gamble Street, atop a rise that overlooked the high school baseball field, the football stadium, the Blackfork and the school beyond. Her father was an executive at the Shelby Mutual Insurance Company, housed in a handsome three-story, half-block long building on Main Street. His office was on the top floor, and he provided well for his family. Maureen was short, five feet three inches, pretty with blond hair, blue eyes that nearly always seemed to be laughing, and an infectious can-do spirit. Her legs were slightly bowed and she was the most athletic girl in the senior class.

She and Joe hopped down from their saddles and merely let the reins drop, brushing the grass. They saw no need to tether the horses in the fenced pasture. They stepped into the shade of the oak, about 30 feet high, embraced and kissed with passion, lips parting and tongues darting.

"Umm," Maureen cooed happily, "that tasted better than a chocolate sundae at Isaly's."

"But it didn't last as long. Another?"

"Do you think anyone is watching? Besides the horses?"

"We're a long way from the barn and even farther from the house."

They kissed again and this time as their lips parted Joe's hand gripped Maureen's bottom and squeezed. She moaned and the two of them sank to their knees.

Maureen pulled back. "I don't know, Joe. How far do you want to go with the horses standing there?"

"One's a stallion and the other a mare so they probably have a good understanding of certain things."

"But there's no blanket and-"

"And you don't want to get your pretty butt scratched." Maureen laughed. "Okay," said Joe, "then let's sit and talk a while. We need to anyway."

"Oh, that sounds serious."

"I think it is." A pause. "You know, Maureen, graduation's just a little more than two months off."

"I know."

"And then?"

"What do you mean?"

"You know I'm going to college."

"I thought maybe you were just talking. You know after we're married Dad could get you a job at the Mutual." She extended her right hand and lightly fingered Joe's birthmark and scar. "You wouldn't have to worry about supporting us and we could be happy."

Joe sighed and looked up through the oak's branches. Spring leaf buds were swelling. "I really feel a need to try someplace besides Shelby." Joe had taken to heart his conversation the previous autumn with Marie Hughes.

"And where might that be?" Maureen asked, clasping her fingers together in her lap.

"I've been accepted at Ohio University."

She studied Joe's face for a long moment. "What about us? What about marriage and family?"

"They would have to wait."

"I see. What would you study?"

"I'm planning to major in history and government."

"Sounds boring."

"Not to me."

"Why?"

"Because I enjoy history and a combination of history and government might open certain doors."

"To where?"

"The Foreign Service."

In that instant Maureen could sense Joe slipping away from her and the future she wanted. She also sensed that objecting or complaining would only hasten the slipping. "Do you think it's too late for me to get into Ohio University?"

"I don't know," Joe said, his surprise obvious to Maureen. "Is that what you really want?"

"I'm not sure but what you said about seeing someplace away from Shelby makes sense. Where exactly is the university?"

Joe smiled. "I understand from Shelby to Athens is a scenic train ride. About three hours south in Ohio's hill country."

CHAPTER 6

Gabriella Balas was riding her own horse, Rainbow, a gentle, dappled mare – gray and black – named after her hometown of Ploesti which means "rainy town." This time Gabriella was riding alone, slowly, in a meadow not far from Ploesti. The wild grasses, made lush by heavy spring rains, were brushing Rainbow's belly.

But hardly pastoral was what lay between her and her home on a cobble-stoned street shaded by a leafy green canopy – the ring of oil refineries with their soaring smokestacks and huge storage tanks surrounding the city that made it Romania's most prosperous.

"This is what Father wants for me," she murmured to Rainbow, "a life spent here in Ploesti. It wouldn't be so bad. A good marriage. A job in the oil industry if I want it. Father might like that. Mother wouldn't. She wants her only daughter to give her lots of grandchildren." Gabriella chuckled at that thought. "Mother would live for her grandchildren, Rainbow. Father might have to fend for himself. Well, not really. I am pretty sure he has a mistress in Bucharest. That's what I've heard. Ploesti isn't so bad."

The city was founded by Michael the Brave in 1596. On this decidedly unrainy spring afternoon in 1934, Ploesti's population totaled about 78,000. Oil was first refined there in 1857 – two years before the world-changing petroleum strike in Titusville, Pennsylvania. By the 1930s, Ploesti boasted 11 refineries that annually produced 10 million tons of oil, including 90-octane aviation fuel, the highest quality in Europe. Trains moving through the city's noisy rail yards transported the black gold that accounted for 40 percent of Romania's exports.

18

The sprawling complex was not unnoticed in Berlin. Back in 1916 Germany invaded Romania to satisfy its military thirst for oil. But British engineers, employed by companies that owned and managed the refineries, dynamited the complex. After World War I, though, thanks to burgeoning demand resulting from a growing fleet of cars, ships and aircraft, the complex rose like a phoenix.

Ploesti's prosperity enabled it to boast of a first-rate philharmonic orchestra and several fine museums including one dedicated to oil.

Gabriella's family lived in an acadia-shaded white villa with a Roman-style center atrium open to the sky and adorned with profusions of flowers from early spring well into Romania's mild autumn. The villa was mid-way down Margelelor, a street redolent with lilacs and roses and that contrasted sharply with the smoking stacks.

Rainbow stumbled but regained her balance before toppling. "Are you all right, girl?" Gabriella asked softly. "Step on a rock or in a hole? This grass is so high it's impossible for you to see the ground. Seeing is my problem too. I'm not sure if the life Father and Mother see for me is the life I see for myself. Can you understand that, Rainbow?" She patted the horse's neck. "I'll bet you can, better than they can. I'm not sure what that other life might be, Rainbow. We will have to think about it and take another ride. How does that sound, girl?"

CHAPTER 7

The Thames at London Bridge is about 250 yards wide. Some 25 miles farther east at Gravesend, the river widens to about 700 yards. On a June morning in 1934 it looked considerably wider to 14-year-old George Britton.

"You say you're such a strong swimmer, swim the Thames." The challenge came from one of George's schoolmates, Oliver Needle.

George's Adam's apple bobbed up and then down and his right hand pushed back a shock of sandy-hued hair from his forehead. "The water's still not very warm." It also looked forebodingly gray.

"It will never be quite warm enough for you to swim," snickered another friend, bespectacled Malcolm Goode. "Maybe you should just stick to wading streams."

Gravesend sits on the south bank of the Thames. In the Domesday Book of 1086 the town was recorded as Gravesham. With the fast-flowing Thames as fuel, mills prospered along the banks. Near the river's mouth and the North Sea, Gravesend also spawned numerous fisheries. Seldom, though, did it make history. Pocahontas, the legendary Indian bride of colonist John Rolfe, took ill after arriving in England and died at Gravesend at 22 in 1617. She is buried in the parish churchyard of St. George's. But a church fire and subsequent reconstruction in the early 1700s rendered unknown her precise resting spot. In 1834 Gravesend built a cast-iron pier, and that's where Oliver Needle and Malcolm Goode were goading George Britton.

"I'm our master fisherman," boasted Oliver whose eyebrows seemingly were as thick and impenetrable as hedgerows. Depending on his mood they had him looking either sinister or swashbuckling. "You're our best swimmer."

"I could be our best fisherman," Malcolm grinned impishly, "if I didn't turn queasy putting hooks in squirming worms."

George tried swallowing his fear. "All right, I'll give it a go," he said with forced bravado.

"If you jump in at the end of the pier," Oliver said puckishly, "you can shave a few yards off the distance."

"You're quite the helpmate, aren't you?" George replied caustically.

"One thing, George," Malcolm said quietly. "You might want to remove your shoes."

"Yes, of course."

"Your trousers too. You wouldn't want waterlogged trousers dragging you under."

"I might as well go bloody naked," George complained, forcing a half-smile.

"Any birds about, you can give them a thrill," Oliver chortled.

"Question," Malcolm said, nudging his eyeglasses higher. "If you make it across how will you get back?" A long pause. "Didn't think of that, did you?"

Before George could reply, Oliver said, "We can borrow a dinghy and row across. Give you a head start. Perhaps I'll drop a line in the water on the way across. Catch supper."

George unceremoniously plopped down on the pier and began removing his shoes. "Yes, well, you might want passengers – my shoes and trousers."

Oliver and Malcolm laughed. George stood, loosened his belt and pushed down his trousers. He handed them to Oliver, turned and stepped to the end of the pier. He looked down, 10 feet to the surface of the gray Thames. He hesitated only a moment before leaping artlessly, arms and hands locked beneath his knees. The splash was high and the water every degree as cold as George had imagined.

Oliver and Malcolm went running back to the pier's shore end while George began stroking strongly. Midway, the cold water and strong current were tiring George.

Not far from the pier Oliver and Malcolm saw several dinghies with no owners nearby. They looked at each other and shrugged. "It's only borrowing," Malcolm said. They picked a blue one, 12 feet long, stepped in holding George's shoes and trousers, sat, picked up the oars and began rowing. Against the strong current they were struggling to maintain course.

I don't think I can make it, George was thinking nervously. Not another 300 yards. He rotated his body, attempting to rest while floating on his back. He could feel the current carrying his almost motionless body down stream and toward the North Sea. Stupid. That's what I am. I'm going to have to try swimming again before this cold water does me in.

Oliver and Malcolm could see that George was in trouble. "We were foolish to dare him," Oliver said.

"We?"

"Row harder," Oliver commanded.

George had swum only a few more strokes when he heard a plop. Looking to his right he saw the end of a rope.

"Grab it," a gruff voice ordered.

George complied and immediately felt himself being pulled back upstream. He looked up and saw a long black barge, a crewman standing on its prow and pulling hard on the rope. Moments later the barge was along side George and the crewman and the pilot were pulling him aboard.

"Damned foolish stunt," muttered the pilot, a gray-flecked black beard framing his mouth. "Are those your mates in the boat?"

George, shivering, lips bluing, only nodded.

"Thought so. We'll leave them to their own mindless devices. As for you, I can't take the barge ashore. We'd be grounded. But I'll maneuver close enough for you to jump and swim in. Think you can manage?"

"Yes, sir. Thank you."

"Whose idea was this?" the pilot asked.

"My friends."

"Some friends. And you were too weak to say no. Almost cost you your life. Try not to throw it away again."

"I was lucky you came along. Bloody lucky."

"That you were. Now do yourself a favor. Don't rely on luck. It's a wretched bet."

"Yes, sir."

"Get the lad a slicker," the pilot instructed his crewman. "Get him warmed up."

George was looking out over the broadening Thames. "Do you mind if I ask you a question, sir?"

The pilot grinned. "As your manners are good, go ahead."

"What about risk? Men who make their living on water take risks."

"That we do, lad. But the vessels we work on are designed for certain waters. They are equipped with safety features – lines, vests, inflatables, small boats. And we are properly trained. But I will admit that luck sometimes proves our savior. But it's not the kind of luck you needed, now is it?"

"I guess not, sir."

"You guess correctly. Luck without preparation is courting disaster. Sailors and soldiers, luck sometimes spares them. But you could argue – and I would – that training and proper equipment betters their luck."

George nodded thoughtfully. The barge was nearing shore. "Stand and get ready to jump," the pilot told him. "This will be a shorter swim and you've had time to rest. In a word, you are prepared."

George stood and smiled. He extended his right hand. The pilot took it and they shook.

"If ever I'm a sailor or soldier, I will try to remember this day – and our conversation."

"For someone who's a brain, you have your share of gray matter cramps," Oliver teased. "Trying to swim the Thames. Mad."

"What on earth makes you think I'm a brain?" George asked, shivering as he pulled on his trousers.

"I fish. You read books. Ones you don't have to read for school."

"That makes me a brain?"

"Well, you know more stuff than we do. Or ever will."

"I concede I like to read books, especially histories and biographies. They make me think about things. Issues."

"See?" Oliver cried. "That's what I mean. You see things differently from us blokes. I think it's a gift you have."

"If it is," George grinned, "I gladly accept."

CHAPTER 8

Gabriella and 21 other students were standing around the perimeter of a classroom at Ploesti's Oil & Gas University. They were taking a test – examining and trying to identify rocks of varying sizes, shapes and hues arrayed in a series of low-sided wooden boxes.

Gabriella was experiencing difficulty concentrating on the rocks. Learning about them was central to the introductory geology curriculum. Boring, actually stultifying, Gabriella was thinking, that's the only word to describe how I feel about geology. My eyes are in danger of glazing over. I'm here for one reason and one reason only – Father. He wants me to be a petroleum geologist, and this course is telling me that I want to be anything but. I'm twenty-one and it's time I stood up to Father and let him know that his precious daughter simply cannot get excited about geology much less spend her life studying core samples of rock formations or managing a tank farm. Or worse, sitting in a stuffy office worrying about oil prices in Persia or Texas.

A bouquet of purple lilacs and pink rhododendrons picked from the atrium garden served as the delicately scented centerpiece. Cornel, Elena and Gabriella were finishing a dinner of pork roast, sweet potatoes and green beans with vanilla cake for dessert. Cornel reached to the center of the dining room table for a bottle of plum brandy, poured about three ounces in his large snifter, swirled it and sipped. He sighed contentedly and passed the tip of his tongue between his lips.

Gabriella breathed deeply and forced a thin smile. "Father, there is something I would like to discuss."

Elena had listened to Gabriella earlier in the day and knew what was coming – an explosion that could dwarf that of a newly tapped oil well.

"Go ahead," said Cornel. He pulled a cigar from his suit jacket breast pocket, lit it, puffed languorously and reached again for the brandy.

"I am not suited to become a petroleum geologist or engineer. I – it's boring." She paused, expecting in the next moment an oral eruption.

"I know that," Cornel replied benignly. "I realize geology isn't for you. Have known it."

"How?" Gabriella said, her astonishment evident in widened eyes, a reaction duplicated by Elena.

"Fathers aren't totally blind or entirely insensitive. Surprised, aren't you? You've talked about this with your mother, haven't you?" Gabriella nodded. "You both thought I would throw a tantrum."

In that moment Gabriella's love and respect for her father went soaring to new heights. "The thing is," Gabriella felt unexpectedly comfortable admitting, "I'm not sure what I want to do or where."

Cornel puffed on his cigar, gray smoke curling toward the ceiling. "The best ones come from Cuba, you know. Well, I've got an idea I've been thinking about," Cornel said pensively. He puffed again.

"You do?" Had Gabriella not been shocked she would have been suspicious. Heretofore he had been the iron-willed father who seemingly viewed changing his mind about the most mundane matters a sign of abject weakness. He was more likely to thump a table to underscore an opinion than accommodate even a hint of contrarian thinking.

"Full of surprises today, don't you agree?" Cornel was hugely enjoying this exchange.

Gabriella's head swung in time to see Elena's lower jaw drop. Gabriella nearly spluttered when her next words escaped her mouth. "What is your idea?"

"Indulge your father for a couple minutes and he shall explain." That Cornel was savoring this moment wasn't lost on daughter and wife. "Today nations view the economy as *their* economy. For example, in 1930 the United States, the world's richest and most powerful nation, passed an abomination called the Hoot-Smalley Tariff. It makes it virtually impossible for other nations to export many of their products to the U.S. because of strangling import duties. Small-minded," Cornel growled, shaking is head in disgust. "Other nations have been retaliating and economies around the world are suffering for lack of trade. But I believe there is silver lining to Hoot-Smalley. It's teaching a bitter lesson, and it's going to end these nationalistic views of economies. Why do I predict this? I am in the oil industry, and it is perfectly clear that oil will become a global industry. Even with the U.S. mired in its Great Depression you can see the worldwide growth in cars, trucks and airplanes. They all need oil and lots of it. The change won't happen in the next year or two, but oil will become an industry without borders. It will be shipped from country to country, and it will lead to the birth of an interdependent global economy. Only governments acting stupidly will resist."

Gabriella leaned forward, elbows resting on the table, right forefinger and thumb cupping her chin. "You are a wise man," she said quietly and slowly. "And how does that wisdom relate to an idea you have for me and my future? You've admitted that you know the oil industry isn't for me."

Cornel sipped his brandy and smiled warmly. "I'm not thinking of you and oil. But I am thinking about you and a global economy, a worldwide perspective. People who have one will enjoy an advantage. I have contacts, good ones, at the United States Embassy in Bucharest. It's on Strada Tudor Arghezi. A handsome edifice. I made a phone call. A tactful one."

At that both Gabriella and Elena couldn't resist chortling. "A new talent, Father?"

"An old one rediscovered," he said dryly. "You have studied English – in high school and at university – for how many years?"

"Six."

"I learned that the American embassy could use someone who would work as a translator and clerk."

Gabriella was peering intently at her father. Elena was staring at him wide-eyed and with new admiration. "Just when I regard you as entirely predictable," she said, shaking her head in incredulity, "you spring a surprise."

Cornel shrugged. "Merely working at being predictably unpredictable, my dear."

"I could probably do translating of documents," Gabriella said pensively, "but as you know I've never spoken English with an American."

"My dear daughter, if you are sufficiently motivated, I think that is a skill you would master quickly."

CHAPTER 9

Four Japanese soldiers – all young and all privates – were about to taste combat for the first time and they were nervous. Etsuro Yamada, Kai Hata, Kazuo Hoshi and Takuma Matsui were in China among troops poised at the west end of the Marco Polo Bridge about nine miles southwest of Beijing. The bridge, an architectural masterwork, spanned the Yongding River. Eleven granite arches supported the 874-foot-long span that was begun in 1189, completed in 1192 and restored in 1698. Adorning granite balustrades on both sides of the bridge were handsomely sculpted lions, some depicted with mates and cubs – 490 lions in all.

In the predawn of July 8, 1937, the darkness was too opaque for Yamada, Hata, Hoshi and Matsui to appreciate the bridge's architectural and artistic splendor.

Matsui was the tallest of the four at five feet seven inches. He was thick-chested, broad shouldered and strong. The others each stood about five feet five inches. All four were unmarried, although Matsui had left behind a girlfriend, Shuri, in his hometown of Yokohama. He carried with him a wallet-size school graduation photo of Shuri. The four soldiers had pledged fealty to Emperor Hirohito but none was eager to sacrifice his life for the bespectacled deity safely ensconced inside the moat and walls of the Imperial Palace in Tokyo.

Before midnight a small firefight had broken out, and it resulted from a series of classic military mix-ups. Japanese forces already had conquered Manchuria in 1931 and subsequently had gained control over much of northern China. Now only an uneasy truce was keeping Japanese troops from sweeping aside resistance throughout central China. On that night of July 7, Japanese units, in knowing violation of their understanding with China's leaders to forego after-dark exercises, were conducting maneuvers near the bridge's west end. About 11 p.m., gunshots rang out and Chinese troops east of the bridge mistook them for an attack. A Chinese soldier – later no one could say which one – opened fire and before a counter order was issued, more Chinese fired a few ineffectual rifle rounds across the river.

Reflexively, Matsui, Hata, Hoshi and Yamada, bunched with fellow soldiers, squatted. Soon afterward a Japanese soldier was reported missing, and Japanese senior officers brazenly demanded permission from the Chinese to cross the bridge, enter the nearby village of Wamping and search for him.

The Chinese doubted the Japanese account and refused.

A quiet interlude ensued. Then at about 3:30 a.m., the Japanese, concerned that the numerically superior Chinese might attack, brought in reinforcements, including four small artillery pieces, a company of machine gunners and two infantry companies. The additional firepower buoyed the spirits of the four young privates, but it also heightened tensions.

Then came a loudly barked order that tightened young stomachs. "Fix bayonets and prepare to storm the bridge," a disembodied voice commanded them. They obeyed and were relieved that the darkness hid their trembling hands. Matsui nearly dropped his bayonet before locking it in place.

On the other side of the bridge, the Chinese were defending with 1,000 men.

The Japanese commenced firing the four artillery pieces. Then their machine gun company, supported by riflemen all shouting battle cries, went surging onto the bridge. To Yamada, Hata, Hoshi and Matsui, the cacophony was unnerving and an order of magnitude louder than anything they imagined or experienced in training.

The fighting didn't last long. To the four soldiers' relief, casualties were few and to their surprise they soon took the bridge. But not for long. The Chinese brought forward their own reserves and soon Yamada, Hata, Hoshi and Matsui were among soldiers backing across the span, firing as they retreated. A Chinese bullet grazed Hata's left thigh, but dawn would arrive before he realized he'd been hit. And he found himself the butt of teasing from his friends.

"A little to the right and your family jewels would be worthless," Yamada chortled.

"I doubt if they were worth much to begin with," Matsui needled Hata.

What was no joke was the reality that this nearly comic incident would eventually come to be regarded as the real beginning of World War II in Asia.

In short order, Japanese troops captured both Beijing and Shanghai, long a bastion of British influence. The loss of Beijing caused the government to flee hurriedly about 600 miles southeast of Beijing.

CHAPTER 10

The silver-haired man waited patiently for his chauffeur to exit the gleaming black Cadillac, circle around the car's rear and open the passenger side rear door. Well-worn brown leather briefcase in his left hand, he eased out, stood and nodded thanks to his driver. Then he shrugged and stretched his five feet ten inches to relieve kinks in his shoulders and back. It was July 31, 1937.

The two Marines flanking the entrance and standing rigidly at attention saluted him and opened the double doors.

Inside at the massive, ornate reception desk, a young woman was intently studying a sheet of paper in her left hand. Her right hand was holding a black fountain pen and poised over a second sheet of paper.

The man approached slowly and stood quietly in front of the desk. He could see the woman was preoccupied. She was taking no notice of his looming presence. He stood motionless for nearly a minute then cleared his throat. "Ahem."

The woman looked up. "Oh, I am sorry, sir. I was – never mind. How can I help you?"

The man smiled slightly and lowered his briefcase to the marble floor and extended his right hand. The woman took it and they shook hands politely.

"Well," he said, smiling more warmly, "I suppose you could ask someone to show me to my office."

"Sir? Oh. I am so sorry. You must be-"

"Franklin Mott Gunther."

"Of course. Forgive me, please. America's new ambassador. I mean our new ambassador."

"No need for awkwardness. As you can see, no flourish of trumpets presaged my arrival."

"We were expecting you but, well, I am not the regular receptionist."

"By your accent – a lovely one – may I conclude you are Romanian in the service of the United States?"

"Yes, sir. My position is translator and clerk, but occasionally when our receptionist is away I am asked to substitute."

"And I can see why, miss. Your English is very good, better than many of my fellow Americans."

"Thank you."

"Your name?"

"Certainly. I am Gabriella Balas."

"I am very pleased to make your acquaintance, Miss Balas. As you are a translator I expect we will be working together often."

"That would be my privilege, sir."

"Likewise. You can also expect me to ask you questions about your country and its people. I am a curious man."

"Very good, sir."

Gunther was born on February 28, 1885, in New York City. Many ambassadors, especially to nations politically important to the U.S., were plucked from civilian life and given ambassadorships by presidents grateful for their financial support during campaigns. By contrast, Gunther was a career State Department field service officer. He was both respected and liked by a series of Secretaries of State, and he saw the Bucharest posting as more evidence of his competence.

Gabriella was reaching for her ringing phone when she hesitated. "Sir, if you will give me a moment to answer this call, I will be pleased to show you to your office."

"By all means."

"If you do not object to me leaving this station for a few minutes."

"Not at all. Take the call and then lead the way."

CHAPTER 11

The road from Shanghai west to Nanking snaked 150 dusty, rutted miles. Along the way every few miles were villages not shown on any Japanese Army map and with names known to few beyond local residents. The streets were narrow ribbons, mostly not named. But villagers knew each other and infrequent mail reached intended recipients.

A Japanese rifle company was trailing the vanguard of the advancing army. The company including Yamada, Hata, Hoshi and Matsui was marching unhurriedly and approaching one of the hamlets. It was atypically quiet. The company commander was Lieutenant Haruo Wada. He was intelligent, introspective and enjoyed the respect of his men. Like Matsui he stood five feet seven inches. Wada raised his right hand above his head, signaling the men to halt. He turned to face them. "Weapons at the ready," he instructed. Chinese snipers were a continual threat. As Wada raised his right arm again to signal follow me, the troops heard a baby's cry of distress.

The lieutenant decided to follow the baby's sound. He pointed to four men including Hata and Matsui to follow him. "Fix bayonets," he ordered and four clicks were soon heard. The men advanced a few paces farther along the village's main street and then turned right into an alley. Several corpses littered the narrow passage. Men and women were among the dead. A few more steps and they were standing outside a home that was little more than a hovel.

Lieutenant Wada motioned to Matsui to open the crude wooden door. Uneasily, Matsui used his bayonet to push open the door. Inside, his eyes required a few seconds to adjust to the dimness. He could see the baby. A woman, likely the baby's mother, Matsui quickly concluded, was cowering in a corner and holding the infant against her left shoulder. The woman was naked. Her lower lip was trembling. Her clothing, torn and soiled, was lying beside her.

Wada and the other three men eased inside. Matsui turned toward Wada with a questioning look. Wada stepped past Matsui for a closer examination. He stood silently, his mind processing the situation. Should we kill this victim of an atrocity by our soldiers or spare her? She was a witness to her own degradation but who could she tell? If there are other survivors, they can't be many. Forward units are several miles ahead of us and more units are following. If we kill the mother do we also kill the baby? It wouldn't survive without her. When other units come through here, will she be raped again? Will she be murdered? Wada closed his eyes and let his chin droop. Then he turned away from the young mother and motioned to his men to exit. Why, Wada asked himself, did our men do all this killing and raping?

The answer to Lieutenant Wada's question resided in two messages that had reached forward units but not yet his company. On August 5, 1937, Emperor Hirohito, at the urging of senior Japanese Army commanders, had ratified their recommendation to remove the constraints of international law – the Geneva Convention – on the treatment of Chinese military prisoners. Under Bushido, the Japanese code that formulated warrior attitudes and behavior, prisoners were unworthy of respect. In addition, Army leaders knew that well-treated prisoners could more easily escape and lead resistance movements. Subsequently the imperial family's Prince Yasuhiko Asaka signed a directive to "kill all captives."

Together those two messages, once communicated to Japanese units, were increasingly interpreted liberally or purposely distorted. They were giving license to go beyond the intended meaning of the directives and were fueling a lust for murder and rape that was spreading with the contagion of a lethal virus. In other words, Chinese civilians as well as soldiers were becoming frequent prey.

As Matsui departed the hovel, his head pivoted for a last look at the woman and baby. This will bring shame on our Army and our nation, he was thinking. Enemies made today will remain our enemies for many years in the future. Perhaps decades – or even longer. My fellow soldiers are sowing seeds for lasting hatred and mistrust. Where will it end?

CHAPTER 12

"You know, in the early years of this century, some philosophers were making the case that mankind had changed for the better. That peoples would treat each other more humanely." Ambassador Gunther was seated at his desk, thoughtfully puffing on a Macanudo cigar and talking with Gabriella. They had finished discussing a translation of a report she had completed on oil production at Ploesti when Gunther shifted the conversation to war news from Asia. Gabriella's competence and English speaking ability had quickly earned Gunther's respect, and he enjoyed chatting with the intelligent young woman who seemed eager to learn and take on responsibility.

"They were wrong," Gabriella observed softly.

"Yes. World War One shattered their beliefs. They saw that men – nations bent on conquest – were still eminently capable of slaughtering each other. Today, if one needed additional confirmation of man's capacity for wantonly violating human rights, he need only consider Japan's actions in China."

"What do you think is Japan's ultimate aim?" Gabriella asked the seasoned diplomat.

"Empire. A big one. Certainly China and Southeast Asia. They've ruled Korea since 1910. Ruthlessly, I might add. No doubt the Japanese want to control western Pacific islands. Japan needs oil and rubber and other raw materials, and it doesn't have them at home. So it's hell bent – excuse me – on conquering countries that do have them. Along with controlling those nations, Japan sees the need to control Pacific shipping lanes. If you think back to 1904 and Japan's victory in its war with Russia, it likely wants to occupy eastern Siberia. For raw materials, yes, but also because the Japanese loathe the Russians. See them as the ultimate barbarians. There are some westerners who wouldn't disagree with that view. To them Stalin and Lucifer could well be blood brothers."

Gabriella chuckled lightly. Then becoming serious again she asked, "Do you think anyone can stop Japan?"

"I'm not sure," Gunther said. "Perhaps a more fundamental question is, Does anyone want to or have the will to?"

December 13, 1937. Chinese troops had stiffened their resistance, but the Japanese captured the provisional capital of Nanking, forcing Chiang Kai-Shek and his administration to flee once again.

December 14, 1937.

"The Chinese weren't able to stop the Japanese from taking Nanking," Gabriella observed somberly. She was holding a cable from the State Department in Washington.

"I don't think anyone expected them to," Ambassador Gunther replied softly.

Gunther had asked Gabriella to come to his office to provide a quick, summary translation of a newly arrived document from Ploesti. Once finished, as had become their custom, wide-ranging conversation followed.

"Sir, what have you found most satisfying in your career?"

"Good question. May I assume you have a particular reason for asking?"

"Yes."

"Thought so. Well, I'll answer your question, and then you can tell me why you asked." Gunther drew in a deep breath and let it out slowly, gathering his thoughts. "Certainly it has been satisfying to know I've been of some service to my country. Not great, mind you, but still satisfying. And I would like to think I've helped the countries where I've been posted. Helped them increase trade with the U.S. Strengthened relations. Then there are the people I've met and the friends I've made. Like you. But the most satisfaction? I think that's been broadening my own perspective on the world and its people. To deepening my understanding of different beliefs and cultures."

Three times Gabriella nodded pensively. "You should be proud, Mr. Gunther, and your country should be proud of you."

"Thank you, Gabriella." He puffed his Macanudo and leaned forward, elbows resting on his desk. "Now, the reason for your question?"

"I enjoy working here at the embassy. I have learned so much. About America. About government and politics and trade. Much of what I have learned, it has come from you. You have been kind, actually incredibly kind, to give me your time for these conversations. You also would have made an excellent professor."

"Thank you," he smiled, "but I don't think you've yet explained the reason for your question to me."

"I love Romania. We are a small country. And poor. Yes, we have oil and, yes, some men have made good livings, like my father."

"A good man."

"Yes. But I want to do more for my country. Perhaps become a member of our country's diplomatic corps. Be posted in another nation. What do you think?"

Now it was Gunther who was nodding thoughtfully. "I think your country would do well to send you abroad. You would make an exceptional representative."

The same day Japanese troops took Nanking, what came to be known as the Rape of Nanking began. As horrific as that term seemed, it still sanitized what for the most part were atrocities committed by soldiers acting alone, in pairs or small groups. One of those pairs was Kazuo Hoshi and Takuma Matsui.

By the time their rifle company entered Nanking, the most frequently heard sounds weren't rumbling military vehicle engines or the neighing of packhorses. Instead they were single gunshots, brief bursts of machine gun fire and anguished screams.

Lieutenant Wada and a squad of eight, including Hoshi, Yamada, Hata and Matsui, followed the sound of a rifle shot and a ragged chorus of youthful screams into a cement-block elementary school. The soldiers began easing down a narrow hallway. At the first door on the left, Wada stopped and looked in. A male teacher's corpse lay sprawled on the floor beneath the blackboard. He had been shot between his eyes that lay open in shock. The shrill cries were emanating from a cluster of boys and girls, as another girl, appearing to be about age 12, was screaming her terror and agony. She was supine on the teacher's desk, and a soldier was raping her. Blood was spreading between her legs and staining the desk.

The lieutenant and his men squeezed through the doorway. Wada was disgusted but obedience to the apparent wishes of Emperor Hirohito and Prince Asaka, combined with a gnawing fear that intervening could cost him his life at the hands of crazed troops, caused him to turn and shoulder his way through the men and into the hallway.

Without hesitating, six of Wada's men went farther along the hallway, looking for more young prey. Hoshi and Matsui exited the classroom but turned the other way and left the school with Wada. The lieutenant saw a playground swing, went walking unsteadily toward it and sat.

"Let's go this way," Hoshi said to Matsui, "and see what we can find." Hoshi surprised Matsui when he removed his bayonet from its scabbard and locked it in place. "Best to be prepared," Hoshi said. Matsui nodded and fixed his bayonet.

About 30 yards ahead, Hoshi saw a young woman dart into a small house. "Come on," he said.

"What?" Matsui hadn't seen the woman.

Less than a minute later, they were standing in front of the house. "We're going in," said Hoshi. He pushed hard and the door swung back easily. Hoshi stepped inside, bayonet at the ready. Matsui followed.

No sign of life in the room. Hoshi stepped toward a curtained doorway. Using his bayonet he pushed aside the curtain. Standing stone cold terror-stricken was a family – the young woman, perhaps 20, her father, mother and a younger brother, maybe 14 in Hoshi's eyes.

Hoshi saw a rear door and began stepping toward it. Without looking back, he said, "Watch them."

Hoshi pressed down the handle of the door that opened into an alley no wider than Hoshi's outstretched arms. He looked each way and saw nothing.

Hoshi stepped back inside, closing the door behind him. He stood in front of the family and positioned his bayonet between the young woman's right shoulder and her mother's left shoulder. "Move those three into that corner," Hoshi said to Matsui. "I'm taking this one."

"What?"

"I want her and I'm taking her."

"Here?" Matsui didn't try to mask his surprise and disgust.

"Why not? I want this family to see me mount the girl."

Matsui lowered his bayonet and placed his hand on the mother's left shoulder. Gently he began nudging her against her husband, and both began inching toward the corner. Their son, standing in front, moved with them.

Hoshi backed the young woman against an ornate chest of drawers, red with blue trim and brass handles. He lowered his bayonet and used its tip to begin lifting the hem of the woman's long skirt. Reflexively she pushed down on the bayonet with her right hand. Hoshi fiercely twisted and raised the blade, slicing the woman's palm. She winced and blood immediately began dripping onto the black linoleum floor. Hoshi then shifted his rifle to his left hand and with his right viciously slapped the woman's face. Her bleeding hand flew up to her reddened cheek. In the next instant Hoshi, eyes blazing contempt, whirled and confronted the family. He raised his rifle and took aim on the mother who flinched.

"No!" the young woman screamed.

"Down!" Hoshi commanded, pointing to the floor.

The woman began lowering herself, her back sliding against the chest of drawers until she was seated on the floor.

Hoshi placed his rifle on the floor, reached for the woman's ankles and dragged her until she was supine. Next Hoshi removed the bayonet from the rifle and shoved its point against the woman's neck. With his left hand he pulled her skirt above her waist and began pulling down her white cotton panties.

The father, anger at the boiling point, took a half step toward Hoshi, but Matsui blocked his way with his rifle and bayonet.

Hoshi loosened his belt and unbuttoned his fly. The woman, seeing his erection, whimpered.

"A virgin," Hoshi muttered. "Better yet." He then mounted and penetrated and the woman cried out.

After what seemed like an eternity to all except Hoshi, he pulled back and smiled contentedly. Still kneeling between the woman's legs, he reached for his bayonet and positioned it, poised just inches from her labia. Hoshi looked back over his left shoulder at Matsui. "I'm going to make sure no man ever wants her." As the tip of his bayonet neared the labia, a single image flashed through Matsui's mind – the photo of Shuri in his wallet. In the next instant, he found himself reacting more swiftly than he would have imagined possible. In a fluid series of moves that seemed a blur to the young woman's family, Matsui shot across the room, simultaneously raising his rifle above his head, bayonet pointed downward. With a fierce thrust the bayonet plunged between Hoshi's shoulders.

Hoshi bellowed and then grunted and the bayonet slipped from his hand, falling between the woman's thighs. He collapsed, near death when his face struck the floor.

Matsui placed his booted right foot on Hoshi's back and applied pressure. He waited a few long moments then pulled the bayonet free. It was dripping blood. Matsui laid his rifle on the floor and then pulled Hoshi's corpse away from the woman. That he had killed a friend and comrade had not yet consumed him with guilt or regret. He returned to the woman, reached down, pulled her skirt low and then offered his hands. She took them and with help slowly regained her footing.

Matsui released her hands and peered into her dark eyes for a long moment. She was Chinese; Shuri was Japanese but Matsui saw haunting similarities. Then slowly he turned to face the family. They were numb with relief and beginning to feel a rush of gratitude.

He moved toward them. Pausing, he closed his eyes and pressed his right thumb and forefinger against the lids. He was asking himself: How can I communicate with these people? He decided to try pantomiming that he knew would appear farcical and hoped would prove effective. First, he pointed to Hoshi's body, his uniform trousers bunched at this knees. "We cannot leave him here. We must move him. If he is found here, no one can save you." Using his arms, he pantomimed shoveling and pointed toward the rear door. He looked at the family and thought he detected a glint of understanding. Then, again using his arms, he pantomimed digging a hole – a grave. "Is it possible to move him" – he pointed again at the corpse – "after dark?" He pointed to his wristwatch and using his right forefinger slowly moved it around the edge of the timepiece.

The father smiled weakly and nodded. Then he bowed. Matsui paused – and did likewise. Looking around the room he saw a round stool, no more than 14 inches in diameter and 18 inches high. He stepped toward it and using his right boot edged it toward the room's rear wall. Then he turned and sat. I am exhausted, he thought. I need to rest.

The family – father, mother, son – now moved to the young woman. The mother extended her arms, and the daughter collapsed into them, burying her face against her mother's neck.

Matsui closed his eyes again and lowered his chin to his chest. Can this family survive, even another day? We need to move the body if they are to have any chance at all. Then I will try to let them know that I want to march them away from here. Pretend they are my prisoners. If possible I will get them to the countryside. If I am stopped or questioned, I will say they are mine to kill, that they murdered one of my friends and I intend to execute the father and son, make the wife and daughter watch and then stab them with my bayonet. Am I a good liar? I hope I don't have to find that out.

The Rape of Nanking would continue until the end of January. During those six weeks an estimated 300,000 Chinese civilians were murdered and upward of 20,000 – some historians think the total reached 80,000 – women and girls were raped. Soldiers continued going door to door, hunting for young women and girls. Frequently the victims were killed immediately after being raped – often with a bayonet, sword or sharpened bamboo stick shoved into and through the vagina. Males who tried to intervene were shot. Sons were forced to rape mothers, fathers their daughters. If those men and boys, under extreme stress, couldn't achieve an erection, they were shot. Monks who had pledged to remain celibate were forced to rape women – and shot if they refused or couldn't.

That night Matsui experienced an epiphany. If one Japanese soldier marching a family to their execution was believable, two would be more convincing. With help from the father he stripped the corpse. Then he gestured, urging the father to strip himself and don Hoshi's uniform. The bloodstain on the back, Matsui was thinking, shouldn't be visible at night. Using pantomime, he told the mother to prepare a small pack with her husband's clothes and some food. Then he gave the father a short lesson in how to hold a rifle when escorting prisoners. Next he grasped Hoshi's corpse by the armpits. Father and son each gripped an ankle. Together they carried the corpse into the alley.

Then the father had his own epiphany. Instead of trying to bury the corpse without being seen or heard, why not make it disappear entirely? He motioned his son and Matsui to help him carry the body deeper into the alley. They did so for about 70 yards when the father signaled them to stop. Carefully they laid the corpse on the hard clay.

Softly the father tapped on the rear door of a small shop. Nothing. He tapped again, still lightly. The door cracked open. The father smiled. So did the man inside the shop. He was the neighborhood butcher.

CHAPTER 13

Christmas season, 1937.

The Baltimore & Ohio train was gliding north from Athens to Shelby in the gathering dusk. Steel wheels clicking across the seams of steel rails had proven a strong sedative for Maureen Alston. Her head was resting against Joe Barton's left shoulder. Her mouth was agape.

If she's dreaming, Joe was reflecting, it might be about a wedding and getting pregnant. If we got engaged over the holidays, she might quit school to begin planning the wedding. Air inside the train was warm but Joe shivered slightly at that thought. I could afford an engagement ring – with Dad's help – but that's not the kind of shopping I want to do in Shelby. Joe yawned and smiled tiredly. I know I can find something Dad would like at the Western Auto or Shelby Sporting Goods. I love walking Main Street at Christmas. All the colorful lights and window decorations. Almost enough to make me want to believe in Santa Claus again. Mom's more of a challenge. I'll have to ask Dad for suggestions.

Maureen stirred but didn't wake. Her lower jaw remained slack. Joe's mind turned to Miss Hughes. It would be nice to see her over the holidays. Maybe I'll phone her.

Sister Grace Ann was gripping the sides of her light gray habit, hoisting it a few inches above her ankles. She was skipping a rope held by Sisters Caroline and Augusta. They were on the lawn outside the nurses' quarters across narrow Hospital Drive from Singapore General Hospital. Their quarters were situated on a small rise, about six feet higher than the hospital grounds. Beside the entrance to their quarters was a large umbrella tree, so named for the parasol-like canopy formed by its branches and leaves.

Grace Ann's face was locked in concentration as she tried to maintain timing with the twirling rope. Caroline was giggling.

Equatorial heat and humidity soon had sweat cascading beneath Grace Ann's habit and leaking from the edges of her tight-fitting wimple. After six minutes of skipping, she yelled, "Stop!"

Caroline and Augusta let the rope fall limp against the grass.

With her habit's right sleeve, Grace Ann brushed sweat from her flushed forehead. "Your turn," she said brightly.

"All right," said Caroline, "but don't twirl the rope too fast. You are younger than I am."

"Only four years," Grace Ann replied with mock haughtiness.

Grace Ann and Augusta began twirling the rope, and Caroline giggled despite herself. After only three minutes she was gasping. Caroline laughed and cried, "Enough!" Grace Ann and Augusta laughed with her.

"It's too bad Sister Regina isn't here to see her nuns as athletes," Grace Ann laughed.

"Oh, but she is." The voice accompanied footsteps as they emerged from the nurses' quarters. "And she is suitably impressed."

"Sister Regina!" Grace Ann cried in pleasant surprise. "You should try skipping rope."

"Try?" Regina replied puckishly. "What are you implying? That your superior has grown old and unathletic? Physical training wasn't part of the convent curriculum, but that doesn't mean I've fallen apart."

"You are younger than I – by a substantial margin," Augusta interjected.

"But you still look fit to me," Regina said impishly. "Perhaps I should order you to take a turn."

"Then," Augusta replied merrily, "you'd better send Grace Ann and Caroline to prepare a bed for me in the hospital."

They all laughed heartily.

The family was seated around the dining room table. Six white Christmas candles, each with a red wax "bow" near its top, flamed the season's joy. Gabriella had returned from Bucharest to Ploesti for the holidays.

"Do you know what I would like for Christmas?" She directed her question to her father. "What I would like more than anything else?"

Cornel's eyes narrowed in suspicion. "How expensive is it?"

Elena didn't reply to either Gabriella's or Cornel's question, but she sensed something extraordinary was coming. Reason: Several years had passed since Gabriella had asked for anything in particular.

"A one-way passage to America."

Elena felt her lower jaw slackening and made no effort to close her gaping mouth. Then she began feeling motherly hurt.

Cornel's eyes narrowed still more. "One way?" His eyes then widened as fatherly concern began displacing suspicion.

"I want you to arrange a posting for me in our embassy in Washington, D.C. Once I am there and working, I will save enough to pay for my eventual return."

"Your mother..."

"Mother," Gabriella said, shifting her gaze away from Cornel for the first time, "I hope you can understand. And support me in this. I will need frequent letters from you or I know I will go mad with homesickness."

Elena's mouth closed, but her only reply for the moment was a series of quick blinks.

Cornel was more composed. "What makes you think I can get you that kind of posting?"

"Father," Gabriella said, eyes rolling upward with daughterly exasperation.

"Has anyone seen Private Hoshi?" Lieutenant Haruo Wada asked his men at morning formation.

For several seconds no one spoke. Then Etsuro Yamada said, "The last I saw him he was with Private Matsui."

"When was that?"

"Yesterday afternoon," said Yamada.

"Does that sound right?" Wada asked Matsui.

"Yes, sir. We left the elementary school together."

"And?"

"We began walking. After a few minutes, maybe three hundred meters," – a lie – "he saw a girl. Actually a young woman. She walked into a shop." Another lie. "Private Hoshi followed her inside."

"And?"

"I heard screams."

"From the woman?"

"Yes, sir. It was a woman's voice."

"You didn't see him again?"

"No, sir. I kept on walking."

"You didn't come back to see Hoshi?"

"No, sir. I found my own woman."

Sister Regina and Lim Bo Seng were walking the grounds of Singapore General Hospital that had been founded in 1821 just south of the Singapore River. In 1882 a new Singapore General was built just south of Outram Road and about two-thirds of a mile south of the river. To some it looked more like a fortress than a medical facility. Its main entrance was flanked by 12 20-foot-high white columns and was crowned by a four-sided clock tower. In 1937 the hospital held 800 beds. Plentiful trees shaded the grounds. A banyan, its roots emerging from the rich earth and entwining its trunk, towered over all others. Beds of purple bougainvillea contrasted with all the greenery.

"A Christmas baby. How absolutely special!"

Lim smiled. "Yes, Sister, especially in view of the Christian religion."

Regina reddened. "Ah, but not in your Taoism."

Lim merely smiled again. He and Sister Regina had come to know each other well. This baby was Lim's fifth, and eventually he would father eight children, one of whom would die in infancy. That tragic death would lead to closer ties with Sister Regina who would comfort Lim and Gan Choo Neo.

Thanks to his father, Lim had been living a life of privilege. He looked more like a mild-mannered professor than a budding business executive.

His frame was slender, his glasses were wire-rimmed and his black hair was neatly trimmed. His face seemed to reflect perpetual serenity. But the inner Lim was a man of principles and he backed them with actions. By 1937 he already had begun raising money to help his ancestral China resist Japan's relentlessly spreading invasion.

"Actually, Sister Regina, I have been meaning to ask you about that."

"About what?"

"Converting to Christianity."

Regina's widened eyes showed her surprise. She swallowed. "I would be pleased to speak with you about it. And to put you in touch with a missionary priest."

"Thank you. I've watched you and the other nuns closely. You seem to have a sense of peace that I admire. And your virtue is easy to respect."

Regina blushed anew. "Thank you."

Taoism then was Singapore's most popular faith. It provided spiritual support and moral guidance. Its central tenet was wu wei which advised adapting to change and not working to create change, thus maintaining harmony. Increasingly, Lim was becoming disenchanted with Taoism, realizing that it didn't mesh with his action-oriented philosophy. Christianity did.

Lim and Regina continued strolling the hospital grounds, umbrella, banyan and palm trees providing interludes of shade from the searing sun.

"I have another concern," Lim confided.

"Oh?"

"I worry for my wife and children."

"Why? You are a good provider. You are successful and should be proud of your achievements – in education and business."

"It's their freedom that I worry about."

"The Japanese?"

Lim nodded. "You might have heard that I have been helping fund China's resistance. It's no secret. But I am not all certain that money can stop the Japanese."

"Do you fear they will invade Malaya? Even Singapore?"

"I can't be certain but, yes, I worry that they will want to control our port and England's naval base here. Enough to fight for them. Fight hard."

"My knowledge is narrower than yours and certainly no match for your knowledge of politics and war. But wouldn't the Japanese have to fight their way across the mountains and through hundreds of miles of thick jungle?"

"Yes, but if they invade they might choose more than a ground operation. They also have a strong navy and expanding air power."

Regina shook her head sadly. "Britain regards Singapore as her Gibraltar of the East. I can only pray that it is as strong as the real Gibraltar."

Breaths – human and horse – were crystallizing in the brisk December air. Maureen and Joe were once again riding on Mr. Dawson's farm. A thin blanket of snow lay atop the stubble of a cornfield.

"It's been a wonderful Christmas day," Maureen smiled warmly. "Church, the tree, opening gifts, brunch, visiting your parents."

"I enjoyed seeing your parents too," Joe said.

"Can you believe we only have another five months till graduation? I can't believe how fast the years at OU have gone by. Positively flown! That makes me sound old, doesn't it? My parents are always saying how fast time flies."

"I'll bet both our parents will come down to Athens for commencement."

"They wouldn't miss it," Maureen said excitedly.

"And you're all squared away to student-teach next semester."

"Yep. In Logan." Logan was a small community about 25 miles north of Athens. Nestled between two lines of ridges, the town was several miles long but only three or four blocks wide.

"We won't be seeing as much of each other," Joe observed evenly.

"Not during the week, but I'll take the morning train down on Saturdays."

"Yeah. Hey, it's getting to be dusk. We'd better be getting the horses back to the barn. They aren't equipped with headlights."

Maureen laughed at Joe's little joke and looked at him lovingly. A few minutes later they arrived at the huge L-shaped red barn. They dismounted, opened one half of the double doors and led the horses to their stalls. Joe and Maureen uncinched their mounts and removed saddles, blankets and bridles. They patted their horses, rubbed them down, exited the stalls and secured each gate with a loop of rope over a large hook.

By the time they reached Joe's parents' 1937 sleek, black Hudson Terraplane – named by aviatrix Amelia Earhart – winter's early cloak of darkness had descended. Joe started the car's engine and began easing down the narrow, winding quarter-mile lane lined on both sides by a mix of mature maple and pine trees.

"Stop, Joe," Maureen said after they had rounded one of the lane's curves.

"Forget something?"

"Just stop."

Joe braked. Maureen slid across the seat and absent hesitation kissed him passionately. Joe was slow to respond but within moments their probing tongues found each other. When they pulled apart, Joe tried joking. "I hope the Dawsons aren't expecting company tonight."

Maureen's reply was her right hand reaching into Joe's crotch. "Maybe you should turn off the headlights," she whispered.

"I didn't expect to see you until after the first of January," smiled Franklin Mott Gunther. "Simply couldn't stay away from the office?"

"I was too excited to wait until after the holidays to tell you," Gabriella said, eyes beaming.

"Uh oh. My sixth sense is telling me big news is coming, and I'm not sure I'm going to like it."

"Father said yes! He is going to put in a word for me in the right place and get me a posting in our embassy in Washington."

Gunther didn't want to deflate Gabriella's exuberance so he said what he knew he must. "Congratulations! This calls for an early New Year's toast. I've no iced champagne so could we settle for a sip or two of cognac? Martell VS."

"That would be perfect, sir. Thank you. I knew you would be glad for me."

Gunther was. He also was saddened to be losing an able translator, clerk and fill-in receptionist – and a young woman for whom he had developed fatherly warmth. At a side table he opened the Martell and poured slowly into a pair of expensive snifters. He lifted both and swirled the cognac. Then he handed a snifter to Gabriella. "Liquid gold," Gunther smiled appreciatively, "and I can't think of a more suitable occasion for consuming some."

They each extended their right arms, and the snifters clinked softly. With the first sip, Gabriella murmured, "Oooh, this is sooo good."

"I am glad you came to tell me, that I'm the first here to know."

"I owed you that much and more," Gabriella replied. "Your work here and your thoughts on foreign service inspired me."

Unexpectedly, Gunther found emotion thickening his throat. His head shook. "Normally I'm not exactly speechless. But I don't know what else to say."

"You need not say anything more." Gabriella placed her snifter on a corner of Gunther's desk, stepped forward and hugged him. He lowered his snifter to the desk and returned the hug. "I don't want to embarrass you," Gabriella said, backing away and looking into Gunther's damp eyes, "but I see you as a very wise and kind man. Like my second father."

It was the morning of January 2 and the official end of the Christmas season for Ohio University students. Joe and Maureen were among a sizable group boarding the early Baltimore & Ohio train at the small, yellow wooden station off Broadway Avenue in Shelby's north end. Most of the boarding passengers would be disembarking in Columbus and Lancaster or well before the train reached Athens.

Joe and Maureen settled into a pair of seats, Maureen at the window. Joe had bought a Cleveland Plain Dealer and was leafing through the sports section. Within 10 minutes Maureen was gazing out the window, her eyes seeing nothing, her mind immersed in a recurring daydream. In this reverie Joe was on bended knee, proposing marriage. Maureen accepted – almost giddily – and Joe stood. He reached into a tweed sport jacket pocket and extracted a small black case. He removed the engagement ring. Maureen's hand was trembling as Joe slipped the ring on her finger.

Maureen sighed deeply. If it wasn't such a mortifyingly deplorable breach of convention, she was thinking, I would kneel in front of Joe and ask him to marry me. Then I would reach into my purse and hand Joe the ring that I already had bought at Armintrout's. (Armintrout's, Shelby's leading jeweler, was located in a handsome, three-story yellow brick building adjacent the Blackfork on the south side of Main Street.) He would have no choice but to slip it on my finger. I would then tell him that I'd scheduled the wedding for the Sunday after our graduation. Joe would make a great husband and a wonderful father, just like my dad.

Maureen shifted her gaze away from the window and looked up at Joe. She snuggled her five feet three inches against his left arm and shoulder. He glanced away from the paper and smiled, then returned his focus to the Plain Dealer. Maureen could see he was reading an article by Gordon Cobbledick.

She looked back out the window and smiled as the train passed a large herd of Holsteins, chewing contentedly on a haystack. Spring break, Maureen was hoping, maybe that's what Joe has in mind for giving me a ring and popping the question.

CHAPTER 14

June 1938.

"I don't know," Oliver Needle said dubiously. "It smells a trifle rank to me – like rotting fish heads."

George Britton looked away from The Daily Telegraph, his conservative newspaper of choice, and chortled. "What about you?" he asked Malcolm Goode.

"Job prospects are dreadful," Malcolm said somberly. "I've heard it's that so-called Great Depression that the yanks have exported all around the bloody world. My old man reads The Telegraph, and that's all he seems to talk about. Somehow their problems leaped over three thousand miles of sea and crossed from Land's End to here in Gravesend."

The three young men were relaxing on a bench on the cast iron pier, lazing away a sunny afternoon.

"You're serious about this, aren't you?" said Oliver.

"As serious as that failed banker who took a header from London Bridge last year."

Oliver and Malcolm both chortled. "Served him right," Oliver said snidely. "He ruined enough other blokes' lives."

"The thing is," Malcolm said thoughtfully, pushing his glasses higher on his nose, "your decision could prove just as fatal. After all, soldiers, British soldiers, have this tradition. They go where people are shooting at each other. America, India, Afghanistan, Africa. Been that way for centuries so I don't see it changing much. Except possibly for the worst if some pompous ass becomes our next prime minister."

"Well," George said, grinning mischievously and folding his newspaper, "at least you'd be getting paid for your troubles."

"Not nearly enough," Oliver said, spitting into the Thames. "What's a Tommy make? Barely enough to buy a floosie once a month, I've heard."

"That should be more than enough for you," George teased.

"Shut your bloody yap," Oliver snapped, trying to sound testy but unable to keep from grinning his appreciation at George's wit.

"So, gentlemen," George intoned with exaggerated solemnity, "it's the Army for me."

"I've heard the training is bloody rigorous," Oliver said, uncertainty elevating his voice's pitch. "Perhaps I should concentrate on remaining our master fisherman."

"That's what I've heard about the training too," George said. "But if I can survive trying to swim the Thames, basic training shouldn't be a problem."

"You survived because you were lucky," Malcolm said.

George shrugged his shoulders. "Point well made, mate. In the Army I wonder if my luck will hold."

What in 1938 was called the College Green at Ohio University was a community cow pasture when the school was founded in 1804. The university was chartered in Boston in 1787 as part of the Northwest Ordinance and was to be called the American Western University. The name soon was changed to The Ohio University but the school's first president, William McGuffey, thought that pretentious and dropped the The. Even after the university began classes the community continued using a strip of the green 94 feet wide along its northern border. Horses and oxen were hitched there, other livestock roamed freely and circuses erected their tents. As late as 1810 Indian hunting parties used it to rest feet and legs weary from tramping the steep hills of southeastern Ohio.

By 1938 the university's enrollment had grown slowly to some 1,200 students, with women outnumbering men four to one. Early on the first Sunday morning in June, Joe Barton walked from his room in a house on East State Street to Howard Hall. The stately three-story red brick dormitory, crowned by a single brick chimney, had been built in 1896 and named Ladies Hall. Soon it became Women's Hall and in 1916, Howard Hall. It sat at the corner of East Union and College Streets and had been Maureen Alston's home away from Shelby for four years.

Joe rang the hall's doorbell and soon a coed pulled open the door.

"Hi, Joe," the woman said brightly to the frequent visitor.

"Good morning, Janice."

"I'll see if Maureen's ready."

"Thanks."

As Maureen and Joe stepped outside, they looked across East Union at College Green.

"I wasn't expecting you this early," she said.

"They've already got the folding chairs set up for commencement," Joe observed.

Maureen looked at her petite wristwatch. "The ceremony begins at eleven. We've got three hours. Well, not quite. We've got to get into our caps and gowns and be ready to meet our parents."

"What time did you tell your parents you'd meet them at the Berry?" Joe found it amusing to think of his parents' surprise on learning they were staying in a hotel owned and operated by a black couple, Edward and Mattie Berry. Shelby had not a single black resident. The Berrys built the hotel in 1907, and it had become Athens' most fashionable inn. Edward Cornelius Berry was the son – one of eight siblings – of free black parents. He and Mattie, area natives, first built a structure with 20 guest rooms and later expanded it to 55. Located on North Court, the town's main street, the Berry stood three stories and was chiefly red brick. Accenting its façade on the second and third floors were four sets of bay windows set in off-white wood frames. The hotel boasted an elevator and rooms included built-in closets. The Berrys were the first hoteliers to place bibles in every room, and they provided guests small kits with needles, thread, buttons and pincushions.

"Ten thirty," Maureen answered.

"I told my mom and dad ten fifteen. But once we have our caps and gowns on thirty minutes will be plenty to walk them to College Green and get ourselves in place for the procession."

"Agreed. Besides, when you consider how hot and humid it's going to be, no one will want to get there earlier than necessary."

By now Joe and Maureen were strolling north on College Street. Maureen took Joes left hand with her right and squeezed gently. "Do you have a destination in mind?" she asked.

"Not really," Joe said, barely more than mumbling.

"Then why this early walk? And why so somber? This is graduation day. Ours. After four years. You should be feeling chipper."

Joe looked down at Maureen. "I wanted to talk about the future."

At those words, Maureen's heart seemed to swell and skip a beat. "Our future?" A ring, she was hoping again, is he going to give me a ring on graduation morning?

"I'm thinking about what's next – for me."

Not us? Maureen thought. Her heart seemed to shrink as fast as it had swollen. She could barely get her next words through her lips. "What do you mean? For you?"

Joe stopped where College Street met Washington Street to form a T. "I've never forgotten what Miss Hughes said about seeking my future beyond Shelby. I liked the sound of it five years ago. I still do. Even more after being in Athens these last four years." A pause.

"Go on." Her anxiety was increasing by the second.

"I'm going to apply to the Foreign Service."

Maureen blinked and forced a swallow. "You could be sent anywhere. Right?"

"Yes. That's right."

"What about us? What about getting married? Starting a family?"

"Not yet," Joe said softly. "Like you said, I could be sent anywhere in the world, and your heart is set on living in Shelby. Teaching school there. I just don't think it would work. Not now."

"Not work?" Maureen nearly shrieked her incredulity. She pulled her hand from Joe's and struggled to calm her emotions. "You don't want to marry me, do you, Joe? Not now. Not ever."

"I didn't say not ever."

"You told me you love me."

"I do."

"Yes, but – oh, my God," she blurted, feeling panic rising. "I'm not a virgin. I gave myself to you. What other man would want me?"

"Pregnant?"

"I don't think so."

"Your periods?"

"I haven't missed one."

Joe's relief was visible. For an instant he had seen his dreams vanishing in the dense clouds of parenthood.

Gabriella Balas stepped outside Union Station onto Massachusetts Avenue on that same Sunday, a sun-splashed afternoon. Crowds swarming sidewalks on a Sunday surprised her. Then she took note of the large numbers of children with parents and smiled. Tourists. Visiting their nation's capital.

A taxi driver loaded her luggage into the trunk and on the rear seat and floor, leaving Gabriella to sit in front. "Romanian embassy," she told him. The taxi sped straight on Massachusetts Avenue and scant minutes later braked in front of 1607 23rd Street N.W., around the corner from Massachusetts and only a few paces from Sheridan Circle. Gabriella paused before entering the building and marveled at its elegance. It had been built in 1907 as a mansion in the style of a Parisian townhouse. A gleaming white marble façade sheathed all three floors. It had been Romania's embassy since 1921.

Gabriella insisted on helping the driver carry her luggage inside where she was struck by the foyer's stylistic purity – white walls with gold trim, a white settee flanked by a pair of white 18th century Spanish wing chairs and a coffee table with a white marble top. Off to one side was a fireplace, also framed in white marble.

Cornel Balas had acceded to his daughter's wish and used his influence to secure a job for her. Nothing bureaucratically pretentious, just an entry-level clerical position – where her bilingualism would prove an asset.

Gabriella approached the reception desk where a matronly, smartly dressed woman, eyeing the luggage, stood and greeted her. "Hello, Miss Balas. Welcome to your new home, a little corner of Romania in these huge United States. We have been expecting you."

"Thank you," Gabriella replied, glancing down at a name plaque, "Miss Manescu. I am very happy to be occupying an even smaller corner of Romania."

"In our little Romanian community, I prefer Alice."

"Very good, Alice. Thank you."

As Gabriella was to learn moments later, her "little corner" was more the size of a monastic cubicle. When the building had functioned as a private residence, she surmised her quarters had been those of a lowly servant.

After her bags had been brought to the room, Gabriella succumbed to exhaustion. She let her body flop backward onto the narrow bed. The journey had been grueling. Trains from Bucharest to Paris, switching whenever track gauges changed, and south to Marseilles. A ship to New York and the train to Washington. Almost immediately she began dozing.

Seventy minutes later, to Gabriella's surprise, she was awake. She lay staring at the 12-foot-high ceiling for a few minutes and then remembered the tourists. She rose from the bed and made her way down to the ground floor and the reception desk.

"Alice," she said, "I would love to take a stroll. But I can easily imagine getting lost. Is there a map I can use?"

Alice looked at her watch. "We can do better than a map. If you can wait about forty minutes, my shift will end, and I would be delighted to be your guide."

Gabriella marveled at the whiteness of governmental and monumental Washington. The White House, the Washington Monument, the Lincoln and Jefferson Memorials. When she first gazed at the Capitol, it brought to mind her own country's capitol in Bucharest – six columns supporting a portico topped by an ornate dome encircled at its base by small, circular stained glass windows.

"I am glad to see so many tourists," Gabriella said to Alice. "It tells me they are proud of their nation and what it stands for – independence and freedom. I hope Americans never forget they are a beacon of hope for people around the world."

Alice smiled maternally. "You already are reaping the benefit of a posting here."

"Seeing things more broadly?"

"Precisely."

"How long have you been here, Alice?"

"Not long enough. Oh, I still love my beautiful homeland, but I have this intense love affair with America, and I don't want it to end."

"You have asked to stay longer?"

Alice laughed. "Twice. Staff call me the Romanian Yankee."

"Do you mind?" Gabriella at five feet seven inches was looking down at her five-feet-one inch companion.

"It is hard to object since it is true."

Gabriella chuckled. "Maybe I'll have my own love affair with America."

Jeff Wolfrom at age 15 already had reached his ultimate height of five feet seven inches. He was slightly built but strong. In addition to fishing, he had grown fond of hunting and become a crack marksman. Stalking prey with a .22-caliber rifle, he had shot cottontails and squirrels at 40 or more feet. When Jeff wasn't hunting or casting baited hooks into the Arkansas River, he often could be found reading about the exploits of American flyers who were achieving legendary status - from Jimmy Doolittle to Amelia Earhart.

On this June afternoon in 1938, Jeff was hunting for small game. Anything with edible meat would do. If his aim was true, he could supplement Iris Ann's supper menu. He eyed a squirrel perched on its hindquarters, surveying for signs of danger. Slowly, Jeff brought the rifle to the firing position. The stock fit snugly against his right shoulder. His left hand cupped the barrel. He sighted, inhaled and exhaled slowly. His right forefinger was poised against the trigger, ready to squeeze.

In the next sliver of time, without warning, a low-flying plane flashed past barely above tree top level. It passed so quickly over the canopy of green that Jeff didn't see the craft. The noise frightened and spared the squirrel, and Jeff smiled.

CHAPTER 15

Joe Barton was standing on Park Avenue. He had just exited his parents' Hudson Terraplane and was looking at the main entrance to Shelby High School. It was the first full week of classes in September 1938, and the air still held the heat of summer. He shifted his gaze upward to certain third floor windows that were open to create ventilation and keep drowsy students from nodding off after lunch.

Joe advanced and was smiling as he pulled open a door and began ascending marble steps. From outside an open classroom he could easily hear the teacher's words. "If you don't remember anything else from this course, boys and girls, remember that history is much more – so much more – than dry recitations of names, dates and places. It is about people, real people, who make decisions and take actions that sometimes change the world we live in." Miss Hughes paused, looking for signs of inattention. Well, she self-deprecatingly told herself, I've not lost any of them yet. "History," she continued, "is about people who take risks and make sacrifices. Sometimes their decisions and actions are big and noisy and the kind that make front-page headlines. Just as often, though, they are quiet and private and little known and long forgotten. But their stories are nonetheless ones that deserve to be told. Why? Because they impart lessons that we all should use as guideposts for life and living. As we proceed during the coming weeks, we'll-" From the corner of her left eye she caught movement in the hallway. She pivoted. "Joe," she murmured, smiling warmly. With her left arm, she beckoned her former student.

He stepped into the classroom and looked at the faces of 26 students. None knew him personally, although some remembered him for his exploits on the Skiles Stadium football field. They look so incredibly young, Joe thought, more like junior high students. Is that the way I looked when I sat in this classroom? Then he focused on Miss Hughes. He found it somehow comforting to see her in a familiar navy blue dress accented by the strand of pearls. She's a reminder that not everything changes, he reflected.

As he neared Miss Hughes, Joe extended his right hand. She reached for it and they shook hands.

"Boys and girls," she said, "this is one of my former history students, Joe Barton. Joe just graduated from Ohio University last June. He majored in history and government."

Joe gave a small wave, right arm barely raised. "Nice to be back here." A pause. "You'll never have a better teacher than Miss Hughes. You're lucky to have her." Joe had everyone's attention. Some of the girls, their eyes riveted on his birthmark and scar, were developing instant crushes. "She just might inspire you to go places and try things you've never imagined." Miss Hughes blushed at the unexpected encomium.

"Thank you for those kind words, Joe. Please," she said, gesturing toward her desk chair, "sit until class ends and then let's talk."

Joe did what Miss Hughes' students were conditioned to doing: He listened and followed her instructions.

"Joe, it's so good to see you." The last student, a girl studying Joe's visage, had departed the classroom and Joe was standing.

"I wanted to see you and thank you and let you know what I'm doing. So, first, thank you."

"You are most welcome. Now, what did I do to earn your gratitude?" As Miss Hughes spoke, she looked up at the clock atop her blackboard. Only four minutes separated classes, and a new group of students soon would begin entering her room.

"You encouraged me to think widely. To dream dreams that go beyond Shelby."

Tiny Miss Hughes was gazing up intently at Joe. "It's always so nice to learn that one of my students was listening and absorbing. Believe me, Joe, I don't think it happens often."

"You are way too modest, Miss Hughes."

"Just realistic. Now tell me. What's next in store for Joseph Barton?"

"The Foreign Service. I've been accepted and I'm to report to the State Department in a couple weeks."

"Oh, how wonderful!"

"Agreed. First I'll go through orientation in Washington."

"And then you'll be assigned."

"So I'm told."

"Do you have any preferences?"

"Not really. Well, I guess I'm hoping for someplace exotic or exciting or both."

Students were entering and tentatively taking seats. Miss Hughes was oblivious to them. One of the girls saw Joe's birthmark and scar and immediately wanted to know more about the man who was holding her teacher's rapt attention.

"Joe, I have this feeling that wherever you are sent will be exciting."

"Why?"

"Because you will make it so." On impulse Miss Hughes closed against Joe and hugged him, her arms around his chest. Then, reddening and now looking at assembling students, their eyes wide in surprise, she stepped back.

Joe was smiling. "I should be going, but I do have one last thing to say."

"I think I know what it is."

"Right, but I'll say it anyway. I still think you should go to France."

CHAPTER 16

Christmas season, 1938.

Joe was sitting at his spartan, gunmetal gray desk in the massive State Department building that occupied a block between 23rd and 21st Streets. A secretary approached and handed him a cream-colored, embossed envelope that was secured with a wax seal and addressed to the State Department's Foreign Service.

"What's this?" he asked.

"Open it."

Joe cracked the seal and extracted a single sheet of parchment. The lettering was in gold-colored ink and embossed. It was an invitation to a holiday party at Romania's embassy. "Why me?" Joe asked.

The secretary smiled knowingly. "We get lots of these invitations to Christmas parties. Senior officers accept the ones from countries like England, France and Russia."

"I see. As a junior officer – the most junior – I draw one of the, shall we say, nations less crucial to our own country's security."

"Delicately put, Joe. Glad to see you're absorbing the orientation."

"It's been a challenge for a small town Midwesterner," Joe said self-deprecatingly with the straightest of faces, "learning Foreign Service lingo. Delicate is something I'm not used to being."

The December air in Washington was brisk but not northern Ohio cold, Joe reflected, as he walked toward Romania's embassy. He had eschewed wearing a topcoat over his rented tuxedo. From what I've learned winter here is more like Romania's mild climate, at least the southeastern part of the country near the Black Sea.

On entering the foyer Joe handed his invitation to a smartly dressed woman.

"Welcome, Mr. Barton. I am Alice Manescu. We are delighted to have you join us and hope you will enjoy a splendid evening."

"Thank you. I'm certain I will." Joe couldn't help thinking of Marie Hughes as he looked down at Alice. Both small, both graying, both favoring simple, elegant dresses.

"The ballroom is on the second floor. Use that staircase," Alice said, pointing to a curving set of carpeted steps.

Joe surveyed the ballroom that occupied virtually the entire second floor. A handsomely attired servant stepped in front of Joe. "Care for champagne, sir?"

Joe removed a fluted glass from the proffered tray and sipped. First this Ohio boy has ever tasted, Joe mused. Not bad.

About 30 feet away Joe spotted a young woman chatting with an older man. She was tall and slender with black hair that was brushing her bare shoulders. She was wearing a pastel green gown that extended to just below her knees. Two thin shoulder straps secured the bodice. She was wearing white gloves. "Here goes nothing," Joe muttered to himself.

As Joe approached her, the older man nodded to the woman and stepped away. Good, Joe thought, go mingle. Make this a little easier for me.

"Hello," he said, holding his champagne glass in his left hand and extending the right.

A gloved hand accepted it. "Hello. Welcome to our embassy."

Joe smiled. "Your embassy. You are, may I conclude? on the staff here."

"You may do so, sir, and correctly." She smiled warmly. "I am Gabriella Balas."

"Nice to meet you, Miss Balas," Joe replied, releasing her hand. "I'm Joe Barton and I might as well confess. I'm new here and this is my first diplomatic party."

"We have that in common, Mr. Barton."

"Well," Joe brightened, "perhaps as we Americans say, we can learn the ropes together."

Gabriella chuckled. "Learn the ropes. I must remember that." In Joe's imperfect features – the birthmark and scar – Gabriella thought she detected a genuineness that was appealing. "Perhaps we can begin by sampling some hors d'oeuvres. We could wait for a servant to circulate our way, or we could make our way there," Gabriella said, smiling and pointing to a long, gaily decorated table on the far side of the room.

"My appetite is telling us to make our own way."

Joe didn't do much mingling. Nor did Gabriella. They were finding each other's company and conversation much to their mutual liking.

"I must admit," Joe said, "I wish I had the command of a second language that you have."

"Thank you. But remember, you Americans live in a huge country. Most of your citizens have no need to speak any but your native tongue. Many have never been outside the borders of the U.S. In our smaller – much smaller – European nations, we are much more likely to find ourselves in the company of people speaking other languages. And often we don't have to cross borders to do so."

"You chose to study English."

"From secondary school. French too."

"I'm studying French now," Joe said. "But I would be embarrassed to try my elementary French on you."

"What better way to practice it, Monsieur Barton."

Joe laughed. In the next moment the orchestra began playing a waltz. "At least that's something I knew how to do before coming to Washington," said Joe. "Dancing, that is. May I please have the pleasure of this dance with you?"

"You may – if you try saying please in French." She smiled mischievously.

"Oui, madame. S'il vous plait."

"Enchante."

Gabriella, at five feet seven inches and two inches taller with heels, was by far Joe's tallest-ever dance partner. In seconds she proved to be the most fluid.

"You are a very good dancer, Mister Barton."

"Thank you. As long as something doesn't overly tax my brain, I'm fine."

Gabriella laughed. "Self-deprecation. Is it part of your State Department training?"

"In my case," Joe grinned, "it comes easily because it suits the man." They both laughed. "You know, Miss Balas, you possess a unique combination of qualities."

"Oh?"

"You are both light on your feet and eminently holdable."

"And you have your own unique combination."

Joe narrowed his eyes in mock suspicion. "Yes?"

"Your mind and your tongue are both quite facile."

As the evening wore on, Joe felt compelled to seek other dance partners. One he had no difficulty asking was Alice Manescu who had ascended to the ballroom after checking that all expected guests had arrived. She proved an expert partner who followed Joe easily despite appearing a miniature next to his strapping presence. This must be, Joe mused, what it would be like to dance with Miss Hughes.

Later, when the orchestra leader announced the last dance, Joe quickly found and took Gabriella by the hand. It was a slow tune and as they swayed to the music, Joe said, "Do you think it might be possible for me to see you again?"

"It might be," Gabriella smiled.

"It would have to be something very informal. The State Department pays us junior staffers something less than munificently." Joe's left hand separated from Gabriella's and fingered the lapel on his rented tuxedo. "It will be a while before I can afford to buy one of these."

"My embassy doesn't reward its new clerks with riches. But," Gabriella smiled, fingering one of the thin shoulder straps, "I could afford to buy this gown because I have a father who can afford to dote on his only child – and does so, although sometimes only after a little urging from my mother."

As the last notes of the song were being played, Joe twirled Gabriella and her gown swirled slightly above her knees.

Sister Grace Ann's only gown was her gray habit, and it often was swirling although never far above her ankles. She seemingly remained in perpetual motion despite the December air in Singapore that reflected the virtual absence of seasons. The climate was singular and unvarying – steamy and sticky. December did bring with it an additional meteorological element – the annual monsoons that often arrived in November.

She burst into the parlor of the nurses' quarters, and her colleagues could immediately sense her excitement. Absent any prefatory comment, Sister Grace Ann exclaimed, "Let's make a crèche!"

To a woman the other nuns were smiling, unable to resist Sister Grace Ann's infectious enthusiasm for all activities religious and secular.

"Wonderful idea," replied Sister Augusta. "What sort of crèche do you have in mind?"

"One for the lawn. For the joy of everyone. We can design the figures on paper and ask the hospital's custodians to cut some figures out of wood. Then we can paint them."

"We could save them from year to year," added Sister Caroline. "A perennial nativity scene. It could outlast us." She chuckled at her own small joke.

"What about the monsoons?" Sister Regina asked. "They will shorten the lives of both wood and paint."

"A manger!" all but cried Sister Grace Ann. "We can design it and ask the custodians to build a wooden frame. Then we can cover it with palm fronds or even red tiles if some can be found."

"You know," said Sister Augusta, "that might be the way the actual birthplace of Jesus was built. With wood and palm fronds. Red tiles," she smiled wryly, "not so likely."

"I'll bet all of Singapore will want to come and see it," Grace Ann enthused. "Christian and non-Christian alike."

"We must take pictures," said Caroline, "and send them back to our families in England. Won't they be surprised! Of course," she smiled gleefully, "we might have to explain palm fronds."

"Speaking of our families I have another idea," Grace Ann exulted. "After the frame is made, let's carve our names and this year on one of the pieces of wood. It can be our legacy. A lasting one."

CHAPTER 17

"Is this informal enough to suit your taste, Mr. Joseph Barton?"

"It is, Miss Gabriella Balas, and it equally suits my thin wallet."

They both laughed and clasped hands.

"They are so delicate, Joe. So beautiful, don't you think?"

"They are as beautiful as anything I've ever seen in nature. Millions of them but each one, in its own way, is perfect."

It was after working hours on a Tuesday in late March 1939, and Joe and Gabriella, wearing light jackets, were joining thousands of other strollers, Washingtonians and visitors alike, in marveling at the annual profusion of white cherry blossoms.

The trees could be seen throughout Washington. Joe and Gabriella were walking around the west end of the Tidal Basin where had been planted the original Yoshino cherry trees donated by Japan to the United States in 1912. The young couple – along with other pairs, solitary men and women and families – was gazing up in wonder at the fragile symbols of earth's annual awakening.

"It's ironic," Joe observed. "These trees are meant to symbolize peace and hope, and at this very moment Japan is destroying much of China and continuing its brutal rule in Korea. The Japanese conquered Korea in 1910, two years before they gave us these trees. But who in America really cared what Japan was doing in Korea? I'll bet most Americans couldn't find Korea on a globe. The Japanese are still there, and everything I've learned says their occupation is heavy-handed at best. They invaded Manchuria, on flimsy grounds, in 1931 and never left."

Now they were nearing the Jefferson Memorial that anchored the Tidal Basin's south shore.

"If the Japanese eventually conquer all of China," Gabriella asked, "do you think they will stop there?"

"I'm not smart enough to answer that," Joe admitted. "Who's calling the shots in Tokyo will be a big factor. The biggest. If their so-called divine emperor has any spine, if he has any compassion, he'd order an end to the massacres and repression. But then I'm not at all sure how much he knows about what's going on outside his palace. If the generals and admirals continue to hold sway, maybe one day Japanese troops will be marching through Red Square in Moscow." Before Gabriella could say anything, Joe added, "Yes, I know that seems far-fetched. But the Japanese whipped Russia in 1904 and given their successes in China they can't be hurting for confidence."

"We – Romania – were invaded in World War One. Whatever Japan has in mind, let's hope it doesn't result in another world war."

"Agreed. My high school history teacher lost her fiancé in World War One."

Gabriella tugged on Joe's right sleeve and they stopped beneath the last cherry tree. "How many times have we seen each other since the Christmas party?"

"I haven't been counting. Lots."

"That is close enough," Gabriella smiled. "Lots of walks, lots of conversations, lots of getting to know each other."

"Your point being?"

Gabriella's right hand reached up and out and touched Joe's scar. "My point being that I think I love you."

"Think?" Joe's effort to lighten the moment was a lame one. Their intimacy hadn't advanced beyond end-of-walk kisses, and Gabriella's declaration startled Joe.

"If I let myself go beyond thinking to concluding, the situation could become complex."

Joe was regaining his composure. "I've heard that love is like that."

Gabriella laughed. "Complex. That's what we are, Joe, you and me. I suppose I could arrange to stay here indefinitely. But not you. Your State Department is going to send you somewhere, and that will be the end of us."

"That might be better for you."

"What do you mean?"

"Look at me. I'm not exactly God's gift to womankind. The birthmark. The scar. And even if you can look past those, no talent agent is likely to send me to Hollywood for a screen test."

Gabriella shook her head. "Joe, I have looked beyond your face – which by the way I find most appealing. I have looked inside you." Joe's eyes widened in surprise then quickly narrowed in dubiousness. "Yes, Joe, it's true. I can see inside you and I see substance. I see passion and compassion. I see a man worthy of a woman's love."

Joe's next words were uttered barely above a whisper. "I'm not sure your vision is all that accurate."

"What do you mean?"

"I've already disappointed a woman who loved me and wanted to marry me."

"Why did she love you, Joe?"

"Why?"

"Yes, why? Did she love you for who you are? Or for what you could do for her?"

CHAPTER 18

"Are you hearing what I'm hearing about Romania?" Joe asked.

"Yes," said Gabriella, "of course we saw the cables from Bucharest in our embassy. And my father managed to telephone me."

It was late on the afternoon of April 13, 1939, and Joe had walked the mile and a quarter – about 20 minutes at a brisk pace – north on 23rd Street from his State Department desk to Romania's embassy. Now he and Gabriella were strolling hand-in-hand toward Rock Creek Park, an expansive green oasis only a half-mile from the embassy. It had become their favorite destination for what Gabriella had taken to calling "our walking dates."

The news was big. Great Britain and France both had signed a pledge to guarantee the independence of the Kingdom of Romania.

"King Carol is worried," said Gabriella.

"He has good reason to be," Joe replied. He stopped, picked up a couple small pebbles and tossed them in the creek. "Romania has lots of oil, and King Carol no doubt believes Hitler would like access to it – or better yet, control of it."

"And of course Great Britain and France don't want Hitler to get it. They have a sense of urgency that few Americans appreciate or understand.

We Romanians will never forget that Germany invaded us during World War One."

King Carol II had tried to win a similar pledge from Russia but backed away from a deal when Russia insisted that its pledge be supported by the presence of Red Army troops in Romania.

"King Carol was wise not to sign an agreement that would permit Soviet forces from walking into Romania," Joe said. "He no doubt foresees Russia doing to Romania what Hitler has done to Austria and Czechoslovakia. Once in, the Reds could mount a takeover, seize the throne and never leave."

"The United States is fortunate," Gabriella observed. "To be so large and to have lots of resources and two oceans serving as defense zones or buffers. As far as I can see, there is no reason for America to become involved in another war in Europe."

"I'm not sure President Roosevelt could persuade Americans to rescue France again. It might take an attack on England."

"Or perhaps," Gabriella suggested, pausing to admire blue wildflowers blooming near the water's edge, "an attack on American interests. But," she shrugged, "where? And would American retaliate and risk involvement in a broader war?"

CHAPTER 19

Hans Mueller pushed his helmet up and used the sleeve of his left arm to wipe perspiration from his forehead. Then he drew in a deep breath. It doesn't seem right, he was thinking, but what choice do I have? Any of us? Our fuhrer has ordered us to take over another country, and I have heard of no general with the courage to oppose Hitler. No balls. That leaves it to us enlisted men to execute the orders.

Hitler says we need more living space. I think we have more than enough. But Hitler has a loud voice and the only one that matters. Hans looked across a wide expanse of plain at waiting enemy cavalry. At least, he tried to reassure himself, we have more men and more modern weapons. But some of us are going to be killed or wounded. Not the most pleasant prospect for a lovely summer day.

It was September 1, 1939. Hans was a young infantryman who recently had celebrated his twentieth birthday. Today he was among German soldiers assigned to support a battalion of tanks that were poised to lunge into Poland. Their idling engines were emitting anticipatory growls – ominous to the Poles, comforting to Hans and his comrades.

Then came the order to advance and Hans stepped forward across the border into Poland. His tongue licked sweat from above his upper lip. He was marching beside one of the menacing panzer tanks. This earth is so flat and hard, he mused. We should be able to gain ground fast.

Almost 300 yards to the east Hans was watching Polish cavalry. What beautiful horses, he thought. All white. It looks like one or two hundred of them. Why don't they turn and run? They are holding lances. My God, they have no chance. Not against our tanks and machine guns. Either they are very stupid – that's what we have been told about the Poles – or very brave.

The tanks accelerated and the Polish lancers wheeled their mounts and began riding eastward. Not so stupid, Hans mused. The tanks opened fire and nearly simultaneously Stuka dive-bombers began swooping low and creating a terrifying roar thanks to whistles affixed to their wings.

Hans saw two things happening. Some of the escaping lancers were falling, and the distance between Hans and the panzers was widening.

They are going too fast for us to provide support, but it looks like they don't need us. It won't bother me if I don't have to fire this rifle.

In the next instant, Hans heard a scream of terror. He knew it had come from one of his fellow soldiers, and he looked to his left for its source. That's when he saw them and that's the moment he knew he might be in trouble. Emerging from a large copse of thick forest and thundering toward him was a force of lancers. My God, Hans realized, they are many more than the other group. A regiment. Then it occurred to him. The first, smaller group of lancers had been serving as a diversion – a temptation to separate the panzers from infantry. Their plan is working perfectly. So much for Polish stupidity.

Hans, like many of his fellow soldiers, was awestruck. The oncoming lancers – at least 1,000 of them – all were riding white horses. It was the custom of lancer regiments all to ride the same color horse. They are attacking our flank so it will be more difficult – almost impossible – for many of us to get off a clear shot. We could end up shooting our own men in the back.

The lancers were shouting unintelligible but blood-icing battle cries. He watched transfixed as the forest of upright lances simultaneously were lowered – he was admiring their precision and discipline – and now looked like nothing so much as monsters eager to impale waiting victims. Will I be one? Hans felt his gut tighten.

Hans knew his fate would be settled soon. The straining warhorses, nostrils flaring, had accelerated from a spirited gallop to an all-out charge. They were kicking up clumps of Polish earth and swiftly closing the gap between them and the Germans on the infantry's far left.

Hans quickly selected a target – a lancer with blond – Aryan – hair peeking from below his helmet. Hans pulled his trigger roughly – too roughly he knew instantly – and his shot missed. The rider's long lance didn't miss, and Hans fell screaming, the first German to die in Poland.

The lancers' discipline didn't falter. After their initial contact with their enemies, a Polish bugler sounded retreat. The lancers, knowing they couldn't long engage the better weaponed Germans, wheeled their mounts and dispersed, to the north back into the woods or east behind the panzers, still unaware of their role in creating opportunity for the Poles. As the lancers riding east closed on the tanks' rear, they wheeled their horses to the south, hoping to escape and fight another day.

Overall that day the Germans won much the better of combat. Their 250,000 infantry, battalions of panzers and squadrons of Stukas overwhelmed Polish opposition. The Poles had been able to defend with only 10 regiments of lancers, outgunned infantry, outmoded and outnumbered tanks and a few obsolete planes, most of which never left the ground. Still, as the world soon would learn, the Poles were as stubborn as they were courageous. They held on for 28 days before surrendering. And then to the world's amazement some 165,000 Polish troops would manage to escape to the west where later they would distinguish themselves again and again, fighting in France, Netherlands and Italy.

Two days later, September 3, England and France declared war on Germany.

"There is but one question to be answered," George Britton said to his friends Oliver Needle and Malcolm Goode during a break in their army training. "Where and when will I be fighting?"

"I can think of a second question," Oliver said morbidly. "Will we all three survive?"

"In one piece each?" Malcolm added. "That's a grim thought."

"We must," George said, trying to lighten the moment.

"Why?" Oliver asked.

"Because, master fisherman, I want to try swimming the Thames again – at Gravesend. And I'll need you two to man the escort boat."

Gabriella had suggested to Joe that they try a departure from one of their walking dates.

"Have you ever ridden?" she asked. "Horses?"

Joe's reply had been a wide grin. After he'd described his equestrian experiences, Gabriella had suggested going to stables she'd heard about across the Potomac River near Alexandria.

"I really can't afford it," Joe had lamented.

"Thanks to Father," Gabriella grinned, "I can. Enough for both of us. And we'll hire a taxi to take us to the stables and bring us back after we ride."

Joe and Gabriella were relishing their time on horseback in the gently rolling countryside. Clouding their joy, though, was the news coming from Europe.

Joe tussled his horse's black mane. "Where do you think Hitler will stop?"

"Not in Poland," Gabriella replied with certainty. "He has demonstrated ambition that is endless. Moscow. I feel certain he will try to accomplish what Napoleon and Germany in World War One couldn't. Take Moscow. Crush the communists."

"Miss Hughes would enjoy listening to our conversation."

"You have mentioned Miss Hughes before. Who is she?"

"My high school history teacher. She encouraged me to think more broadly about the world. To try living and working away from my hometown."

"I now have immediate and immense fondness for your Miss Hughes."

"She would like and respect you too. After all you are living and working far from your hometown."

"Is she a woman of prayer?"

"I'm sure she is. I know that she is a regular churchgoer."

"Then you might want to write and ask her to remember Romania in her prayers. Because I wouldn't be surprised if Hitler decides to visit my country. And stay."

"Your oil?"

"Precisely. And what really worries me is that our oil industry is centered in my hometown. If Hitler does invade Romania, I might need to return."

King Carol II was viewing the unfolding war with clear-eyed realism. "We must remain neutral," he told his prime minister, Armand Calinescu.

That was the course King Carol set and tried to keep steady. But events were undermining his efforts. First, he granted refuge – albeit temporarily – to Poland's fleeing government leaders who eventually would establish a government-in-exile in England. Next, on September 21, Prime Minister Calinescu was assassinated. Lastly, Ion Antonescu, an army general, was itching to join the Axis and attack the communist-controlled government in Russia. Antonescu was enjoying support from the Iron Guard, a fascist force that was rising in popularity and urging rapprochement with the Nazis.

"We will keep trying to remain neutral, to continue neutrality as our official position," Carol told his son Michael, then 18. Carol, born in 1893, had ruled since 1930 and was acutely aware of the precariousness of the royal throne and his seat on it. "But each day that becomes more difficult. I fear for our country and our people if we take sides against the Allies. Even if the Axis Powers win, the price in Romanian blood will be expensive to the point of ruination. And if the United States would be tempted to enter the war, well, history provides an object lesson. Remember what happened when the U.S. joined the Allies in World War One. The Central Powers – think Germany most of all – had no chance. Does any rational leader think the Axis could defeat the Allies with the U.S. as a partner?"

Michael paused thoughtfully before replying. "Let me answer your question with a question, Father."

"All right, go ahead."

"How rational do you think Hitler is? Mussolini?"

CHAPTER 20

At age 18 Prince Michael was a striking figure. Blue eyes, wavy brown hair, strong jaw and Romanesque nose hinted at lineage dating from the time when his land was called Dacia and even earlier when Greece was seeding western culture and learning.

Michael was born on October 25, 1921, in Peles Castle. His mother, Queen Elena, had arrived in Romania as a princess from Greece. England's Queen Victoria was his great-great-grandmother.

Although a prince in 1939, Michael already had occupied Romania's throne – as a boy from July 20, 1927, until June 8, 1930. He had ascended after his father, Carol II, had eloped with his mistress Elena and renounced his royal rights. On taking the throne Michael appeared on the cover of TIME magazine as the world's youngest monarch. Actually, governing during his brief reign was a three-man regency that included Michael's uncle, the church patriarch and the nation's chief justice.

After three years Romania's parliament had grown dissatisfied with the regency's work and invited Carol II to retake the throne. Michael was proclaimed crown prince.

Now, in November 1939 when Michael had passed his 18th birthday, in accordance with the country's 1938 constitution, he took a seat in Romania's senate.

Michael loved and respected his father but from early on recognized that he, the younger royal, was the stronger-minded of the two. And at this juncture, with Europe seemingly being torn apart at the seams, he knew Romania required strong leadership.

Is it possible for Romania to remain independent? Michael asked himself. Will Father be able to retain his throne? It's impossible not to hear the rumors. General Antonescu. The Iron Guard. Can Father trust any of them? What if there is a coup? If Father is overthrown, what will happen to him? What would become of me?

On this Saturday afternoon in 1939, on an occasion when Maureen Alston's laughing eyes could be expected to be radiating undiminished joy, they were instead reflecting serious thoughts. Maureen was grateful for what had become of her. She had learned a lasting lesson from her romance with Joe Barton and had put it to use continuously. It was called abstinence.

Maureen was standing beside Sam Nelson in Shelby's Methodist Church on South Gamble Street, and the minister was addressing the guests.

Sam was two years Maureen's senior and half a foot taller than her five feet three inches. The two had begun dating after Maureen's graduation from Ohio University and her return to Shelby to begin teaching third grade at Grant School, built in 1896 at the corner of Broadway and Whitney Avenues. Sam had not gone to college. Instead, immediately after graduating from Shelby High School, he had secured a job at the Shelby Mutual Insurance Company. His work had impressed Maureen's father and he had arranged an introduction.

Although the couple had been engaged for nearly a year, Maureen had refrained from intercourse with Sam. Occasional petting was as far as she had let him – and herself – go. She was taking no chances with becoming pregnant. Maureen was determined to wear white at her wedding and with no unseemly midriff bulge. During the ceremony, her mind wandered. I was lucky, she reflected, not to already be a mother to a child by Joe. If I'd gotten pregnant he would have married me. I think. But would the marriage have lasted? I don't think Joe would have been happy with me. Not in Shelby. I wonder how long he will remember me. I know I'll never forget him.

The vows having been exchanged, the minister was intoning, "I now pronounce you husband and wife."

Maureen lifted her veil. She looked dreamily at Sam and they kissed tenderly. While guests were applauding the couple, Maureen couldn't help thinking, mission accomplished.

CHAPTER 21

Christmas season, 1939.

"I'm new at this," Gabriella said nervously.

"I'm no expert either," Joe replied.

"That's very reassuring," she replied with mock sarcasm.

Joe laughed. "I know you have a spirit of adventure or you wouldn't have left Romania for Washington."

"If you say so. But our Romanian winters are too mild for this. At least winters on the plain from Ploesti south to the Black Sea. In the north in the Carpathians we get snow, but there is no ground in the mountains that is flat enough for this."

"This" found them sitting on a bench by the long, narrow reflecting pool that stretched between the Lincoln Memorial and the Washington Monument.

Here," said Joe, "let me lace these up for you. Sharp blades and tight laces, that's what we need."

A lingering cold snap had frozen the pool's surface, and ice skaters were taking advantage.

"What if I fall?" Gabriella asked, her tone combining petulance with plaintiveness.

"You probably will," Joe laughed. "Up we go."

They stepped tentatively onto the ice. Joe was far from expert, but his balance, honed by years of playing sports, was sound. His right hand grasped Gabriella's left arm to steady her. It wasn't enough. She hadn't glided more than 20 feet when her skates flew out in front, Joe lost his grip on her arm, and she landed gracelessly on her bottom. Her knee-length skirt was gathered around her waist, and his first move was to bend and use his hands to push the garment lower.

"Are you all right?"

Gabriella blew out a breath that crystallized in the sub-freezing air. "I don't think anything is broken. I do expect to have a bruise where no one will see it. You might have noticed that I don't have a lot of padding back there."

Joe smiled. "Your slender behind is one of your more endearing features."

"I am glad to know it is appreciated."

"Okay, we gave it a try. Now let's get you off the ice." He braced himself, hoping his skate blades would keep biting the glassy surface, and lifted until Gabriella's skates were beneath her where they remained until they maneuvered slowly off the ice. Skates removed, they were sitting on the first step of the Lincoln Memorial.

"You realize this is a memorable way to celebrate the first anniversary of our meeting," Gabriella said.

"It was part of my plan," Joe said, managing to keep a straight face. "Cold temperatures, frozen pool, ice skating, you falling. I had it all mapped out."

Gabriella turned her head to look up at the statue looming above them. "Well, we certainly gave President Lincoln some entertainment."

"He's no doubt seen a lot."

Gabriella's mood shifted. "When I first arrived here, the whiteness of your capital amazed me. I was touched. Buildings and monuments so white. Now, with snow covering the ground, everything seems so pure, so clean."

"Your capital?"

"Bucresti. Or Bucharest as Americans call it. It is also beautiful. Many of our buildings have stood for hundreds of years. But our capital is not so white as Washington. Not as clean."

"I wish our politics were as clean as our buildings."

"Ah, Joe. Don't despair. I think politics everywhere must be at least a little dirty. Don't you? They are so competitive. Everyone wants to win, no one can stand losing. People hunger for power. They bend rules. Or break them. Not all. Let's keep hoping that there are more good people than corrupt people holding the public's trust."

"I'll tell myself to keep hoping."

"Good. Now let's get these skates back to the vendor and figure out another way to celebrate our anniversary and Christmas."

Sister Regina was watching with pleasure as the other nuns were setting up the crèche on the hospital grounds for the second year. Dear Lord, she prayed silently, thank you for letting me be here. Yes, I am far from England and my family, but I am so grateful to be here with these wonderful sisters. They are my dearest friends. When I was a child in Petworth, I never imagined such a place existed. So much sun and so much warmth. She smiled inwardly. Quite a difference from Mother England, so wet and so often gray. We have rain here in Singapore but even it is warm and comforting. Well, except for the monsoons. I am not naive, Lord. Lim Bo Seng thinks it's possible war could reach this earthly paradise. I beseech you that it doesn't. But if it does, I ask for mercy for my friends and all the people here on the island.

Sister Regina made a quick sign of the cross, sighed and went walking toward the nuns. They were chattering and so obviously happy with their work. "Sister Grace Ann," she said, "the crèche looks absolutely lovely. Your creativity is an inspiration to all of us."

"Thank you, Sister. Do you want to help?"

"You don't need me. I'm happy to watch. Do you have any other decorating plans for this season?"

"Of a sort," the young nun replied while placing a white wooden lamb in front of the sturdy manger. "I am thinking we could bake cookies. Christmas cookies. We could ask a custodian to make metal cookie cutters in the shape of stars. Then we could decorate the cookies. With icing or red and green sprinkles. Or both. We could treat our patients and children in the neighborhood."

Sister Regina smiled warmly. "Excellent idea, Sister. I truly believe you are one of a kind. Certainly not the product of a cookie cutter."

"Thank you," Grace Ann blushed.

"But I am attaching a condition to your idea."

"Oh?"

"I get to eat the first cookie, straight from the oven."

All laughed heartily.

CHAPTER 22

King Carol II was pacing back and forth on the long veranda – stone-paved and bordered with an ornate stone balustrade – that fronted Peles Castle. He was feeling pressured and increasingly insecure. He was giving serious thought to confiding in Michael, away in Bucharest tending to senate matters. *I think my son would be the better king. I wonder if he realizes that. He is more decisive and if I'm honest with myself, more intelligent.*

Carol's chief concern at the moment: Great Britain and France, the two main guarantors of Romania's territorial integrity, were weakened. The British evacuation at Dunkirk shook Carol badly. And France's quick capitulation both unnerved and saddened him. Two great powers rendered impotent. Carol now regarded as meaningless earlier British and French assurances to protect Romanian independence. Worsening his anxiety was the little hope he held that Russia would serve as a faithful ally. In fact, he feared that Russia would see his nation's weakness as an opportunity to gain revenge for face lost to Romania at the end of World War I when it was awarded Transylvania, Banat and Bucovina. Those three territories had nearly doubled Romania's size.

A few minutes later Carol returned to his office inside the castle and summoned his secretary. "I want to send a cable to Berlin." *It pains me,* he thought, *to seek a similar guarantee from Germany, but at the moment that seems the best of bad choices. I wonder if Michael would agree.*

Joe and Gabriella were standing in the lobby of the Washington Monument, 555 feet below its pinnacle.

"It's high time – pun very much intended – that you see Washington from above," Joe said.

"I could use a view from the top," Gabriella said somberly. "I have a lot on my mind. Maybe the view from above will clear my thoughts."

"Or at least lighten them for a while. Do you want to walk up?"

"How many steps?"

"Take a look at that sign," Joe said, pointing to a small plaque.

"Eight hundred ninety-eight," Gabriella read aloud. "We'll take the elevator."

Moments later the elevator door opened. They were the only passengers and silent for the first moments. Then conversation, spoken quietly, ensued.

"You know, Gabriella, your king is feeling squeezed. Between Russia and Germany."

"That is our history. Being squeezed by bigger countries. I am beginning to feel guilty."

"About what?"

"About being here. In this big, free nation."

The elevator door opened.

"You think you should go back?"

"Father believes I should stay here. He thinks it is safer."

"You don't disagree?"

"No. He's right. But I still think Romania is where I belong, especially if the situation worsens. As I believe it will. Germany or Russia. One of them will do us evil." A pause. "Joe, you were right. The view up here is fantastic. Every American should see it. You can see so far. I hope none of those skyscrapers I saw in New York are built here. They would ruin the view. In fact, they would ruin the whole atmosphere of Washington."

Joe was barely listening. He was thinking ahead to his next words. "I have news."

"Oh?"

"I'm being assigned – to Singapore."

"Oh, Joe. I…I knew a posting was coming but…so far."

"It presents a problem. A big one."

"That being?"

"I've reached a conclusion, Miss Balas. I love you."

Gabriella wasn't surprised to learn that Joe loved her. She had long sensed his love; it showed in his attentiveness, his obvious joy in being with her. What surprised her was his declaration, hearing him speak those three words, words with the power of magic. She reached for and grasped his hands. "I am touched, Joe. Truly. Washington has all these beautiful blond women. Young, single, available, looking for the right man. And you fall in love with an olive-skinned, black-haired Romanian that some people probably see as a gypsy. A tall gypsy."

Joe laughed and squeezed her hands. He leaned forward and they kissed tenderly. "Gypsies have a reputation for stealing, and you have stolen my heart."

"But you are still going to Singapore." He nodded. "Perhaps that is a sign for me to return home."

"I think you should wait a while."

"For you to come back?"

"That would be nice. But, no, to heed your father's counsel. In Romania you could find yourself in danger."

"And how about you in Singapore?"

"It's a small island. Japan might covet it, but if they do try to take it, by the time they arrive I might be returning stateside. Besides, the U.S. only has a consulate there. If hostilities broke out, I expect our staff would be among the first evacuated."

"I hope you are right. I would hate to think we won't have a reunion."

CHAPTER 23

As the summer of 1940 wore on, mini-earthquakes struck England daily as German bombs shook the ground and blew apart buildings and citizens during the Battle of Britain. In Pine Bluff, Arkansas, Jeff Wolfrom couldn't help imagining what it was like to be waging dogfights in English skies against determined Luftwaffe fighter pilots.

September 7 brought the first major Luftwaffe assault on London proper. Previous attacks had been confined largely to port facilities, rail yards and airfields. Although Jeff was itching to fly, he was grateful his hometown was safe from German bombs and strafing runs.

Of the 2,365 pilots who flew for the British during the battle, 348 were killed in action. About 80 percent of all the airmen were British. The rest were volunteers from 13 nations, including Poland and the U.S.

In Romania a political earthquake was about to shake the land. King Carol awoke with a start. He heard footsteps. Many of them. Loud ones. Boots running on the castle's hard floors. Rapidly climbing stairs.

"Elena." He grasped his wife's shoulder and shook it. "Wake up." His pulse was racing and his heart tightening.

"What is it?" she mumbled, sitting up. "Oh, my God!"

The footsteps were nearing their chamber. Both were fearing the worst. They held each other tightly.

"I love you," Carol said.

"I love you too."

"Try to stay strong."

"I will – try."

The door to their chamber burst open. Twenty soldiers armed with rifles and submachine guns entered the room and surrounded their bed.

Elena couldn't control her trembling.

The last to enter the chamber was General Ion Antonescu. "You are under arrest," he announced officiously. "Get dressed."

"Why are you doing this?" Carol asked plaintively.

"You are anti-German."

In an instant, Carol's fear gave way to a surge of anger. "I am pro-Romanian."

"That," the general bristled, "is not sufficient."

"Germany is no friend. It occupied us during the first world war."

"That was then. Old history. Now, get dressed."

"Our son, Michael…" Carol said.

"He won't be harmed. Not unless you cause trouble."

The coup was bloodless. That was the only consolation for Carol and Elena. They were taken to an apartment in Bucharest and guards were posted outside the door around the clock.

Antonescu wasted no time imposing his will. In a matter of hours he ordered the constitution suspended and dissolved Parliament. His next move surprised all but his cronies: He re-installed Michael as king. Antonescu forbade Michael from taking a formal oath of office, but he did have him crowned in the Romanian Orthodox Patriarchal Cathedral that sits atop Dealul Mitropoliei, a hill in central Bucharest.

After the ceremony and before exiting the cathedral, Antonescu took Michael aside. "You will be the supreme leader of our army – in name only. I am now marshal and will make all decisions. Clear?"

"Very." Michael's eyes were cold, nearly dead cold, and Antonescu didn't miss the seething anger.

"Your father is weak and you know it. Romania needs strong leadership."

"You didn't need to humiliate him. There were other ways."

"Those other ways would have been cumbersome and slow. We needed swift surgery."

"What if Germany loses this war? It lost the last one."

"Germany, Italy, Austria, Romania. All committed to defeating Russia. The West is already firmly under Hitler's heel. There can be only one victor."

"England still stands."

"Only because of that blowhard Churchill. How long do you think it will take Hitler to cross the Channel? You will get up one morning soon, pick up your newspaper and see a headline: Churchill Sues For Peace."

"Your confidence matches Churchill's."

Antonescu's eyes narrowed, searching Michael's for evidence of whether the marshal had been complimented or skewered. He saw none.

"One last thing," Antonescu said lowly, "tell your father that if he is smart he will find another residence."

"Go into exile?"

Antonescu nodded.

King Carol was considering more than his own safety when he and Elena began their flight to Mexico via genuinely neutral Switzerland, then south to Marseille and across the Mediterranean and the Atlantic. Elena was part Jew, and Carol foresaw her possible fate under the virulently anti-Semitic Antonescu. Carol did not depart Bucharest empty handed. In a secretive move that earned him the enmity of most Romanians and deeply distressed Michael, Carol arranged to leave in a nine-car train filled with much of Romania's gold and many of its art treasures. Once across the seas and in Mexico, Carol and Elena moved farther south to Brazil. Later, yearning for Europe, they would seek refuge in neutral Portugal, settling in Lisbon where Carol would die in 1953. Elena would pass away at age 77 in 1982.

Catherine Caradja showed spine. Within days after of the coup, she confronted Antonescu at his office in the Royal Palace on Calea Victoriei.

Even before Catherine uttered her first words, the fire in her cheeks told Antonescu she had arrived in high dudgeon. He tried clumsily to defuse her anger with deference.

"Please sit here, Princess Caradja," he said, pointing to a royal blue overstuffed chair. "It is the most comfortable chair. May I offer you tea?"

"You may but I would decline."

"Another beverage? Coffee? Plum brandy?"

"Look at you," Catherine said, throwing her shoulders back, forefinger pointing accusingly. "You are taking this country – my country – down a road to ruin. And for what? So that you can sit here in the Royal Palace and plan war that could destroy us."

"Careful, Princess."

"Princess Caradja," she tautly corrected him.

"Your title means little to me." He was asking himself how much longer he should contain his anger. Royalty and their airs are insufferable, he seethed.

"It means something to my fellow Romanians because they know – and you know – that it symbolizes love of country and its people. Our people know that I am not another duplicitous, power hungry despot."

The truth of her words caused Antonescu to think it wise to again try soothing the angry woman. "Your work with orphans is admirable and widely respected."

"And if you take our country to war I will have many more orphans to care for."

"If we go to war, it will only be when I know we are ready and certain of victory."

"Ha. Now that you have deposed Carol and spoken openly of your fondness for all things Nazi, do you really think Hitler will permit you to act independently?"

"We have a large army. We soon will have more than five hundred thousand men under arms."

"And fighting for what? The Russian steppes can make a dubious prize."

"We have strong leadership."

"Strong leadership? The Iron Guard are thugs. If you trust them you are even more of a fool than I thought."

"That is enough!" Antonescu barked, slamming his right fist on the ornate desk used by both King Carol I and King Ferdinand before him. "You are mired in our past. Crowns and the trappings of royalty. I see the future and I see greatness for Romania. Expanded borders, richer resources, a hand in remaking the world order."

"You, Marshal Antonescu, are delusional."

In less than a month, on October 8, Nazi troops began crossing into Romania. They soon numbered more than half a million and were well equipped and trained. Hitler hadn't waited for a formal invitation and Antonescu, although ambivalent about their arrival, didn't openly object to their presence or even question it.

To Catherine Caradja, the presence of German forces confirmed her suspicion: Hitler would treat Romania as another of his personal fiefdoms.

"Father!" Irene's terrified scream was Prince Constantin's first inkling of disaster. The floor in his bedroom began undulating, and in the darkness he could hear walls and ceiling cracking. Shaking off the fog of heavy sleep, he threw back a multi-hued quilt and swung his legs over the bedside. For an instant he considered going to his armoire for his bathrobe but dismissed the thought.

"Irene, Father, are you all right?" Constantin recognized the voice of Alexandra, at age 20, his youngest daughter. Irene was the oldest, age 25.

A chandelier crashed beside him on the hardwood floor, and Constantin knew that time for escape was slim. "Get downstairs and outside!" he bellowed. "Now!" For a sliver of an instant, he thought of Catherine and was glad she was at their villa near Nedelea and hoped she wasn't endangered.

Alexandra was the first to react. Wearing only a beige flannel nightgown with a red rose print, she sprinted from her room into the hallway. She paused briefly to look at the door to Irene's room and then went dashing for the staircase. From its top she descended two steps at a time until she was three from the bottom when she leaped to the floor. In the blackness she could hear sections of walls and the ceiling beginning to collapse, and she went running through the foyer to the home's front entrance. Fighting off panic she slid the bolt on the heavy wooden door, pulled it open and lunged into Luterana, a short street some 200 yards long that ran north-south immediately behind the Royal Palace.

Two electric street lamps at either end of the street scarcely pierced the darkness. From every direction came screams and the sickening sounds of sundering buildings. The ground continued to heave beneath Alexandra's bare feet. She didn't notice the cold.

She turned and looked at her house. Inside Constantin and Irene had met in the darkened hallway. Irene froze. "Move! Now!" Constantin commanded sharply. Though unable to see her eyes he knew that terror was paralyzing his daughter. With his right hand he grabbed her left arm and pulled hard. They reached the top of the staircase and Irene hesitated. Constantin jerked harder and they took one step down. Then the staircase collapsed. As they went plunging, Constantin held his grip on Irene's arm. Neither cried out.

It was 3:39 a.m. on November 10, 1940, when Bucharest residents began awakening in panic. The city sits atop a major seismic fault line, and the earthquake that was killing and maiming was registering 7.7 on the Richter Scale.

The earth's convulsion awakened Catherine, but Nedelea was nearly 45 miles northwest of Bucharest, and she felt no urgency to evacuate her home. Methodically, she arose from her bed, slipped on a robe, descended stairs and stepped onto the broad veranda. In the darkness she looked south and prayed that the earthquake, wherever it was centered, wasn't claiming lives.

Flames began leaping from fires sparked by overturned candles and ruptured gas lines. A cold rain began falling and, numbly, Alexandra hoped it would extinguish the blazes. She took a few steps and thought the better of it. Sharp edges of bricks and glass shards are probably littering Luterana, she thought. I don't think I'm bleeding. I'll wait for first light before moving.

Then she turned back to the house. Squinting as her eyes adjusted to darkness, she could make out only rubble. Not even the outline of their house.

"Father," she called out. "Irene. Can you hear me? Please say something. Father."

Silence. Then Alexandra realized that the ground no longer was shuddering. "Father!" she cried out again. "Irene!"

Slowly Alexandra lowered herself to the cold, damp cobblestones. The rain was wetting her hair and gown. Squatting, she placed her palms against the pavement. Then she eased into a sitting position and began her solitary wait.

The tree, some 70 feet high, stood alone on a knoll about 100 yards east, across a narrow stream, from Catherine's manor house. Its long limbs, leafless in November, hovered over three graves. One served as the resting place of Marie, Catherine's second daughter, dead now for seven years. The other two were freshly dug and held the caskets for Constantin and Irene.

Only three people were there. Catherine was wearing a black veil and dress covered by a long gray coat trimmed with black fur at the collar and cuffs. At her left was Alexandra. She too was wearing black – both her dress and coat.

The third person was Nedelea's Romanian Orthodox priest. Tall and rugged looking with a gray beard that descended to his chest, he wore black vestments trimmed in gold.

No representatives of Ion Antonescu's administration were present, and Catherine didn't count their absence as a loss or insult. She hadn't invited them and they hadn't inquired about the burial's location or date.

Just as the priest elevated his arms to begin praying, a strange caravan came driving up the dirt road toward the villa. In the lead was a black Packard. Following were a blue and white Bucharest city bus and a small white delivery truck.

"Wait," Catherine said to the priest.

"Do you know who they are?" Alexandra asked.

"I have no idea."

The three vehicles stopped. A moment later a man exited the car and Catherine blinked in surprise. "It's King Michael," she murmured to her daughter. Catherine wasn't easily astonished but this occasion was proving an exception. Michael was wearing a black suit, white shirt and black necktie. He wore neither topcoat nor hat. Seeing Catherine in the distance he waved gaily. She acknowledged his greeting with a tentative half-wave.

Michael walked to the bus's door and signaled the driver. Within seconds a young girl, appearing about age 12, emerged and stepped to the roadside. Following in quick succession were more girls and boys, ranging in age from three to 14. In all, 23 youngsters. Michael waited for the last to alight, then motioned to them to follow him to the gravesite.

"Alexandra tugged at the mother's sleeve. "Do you know what's happening?"

"No, dear."

The children followed closely at Michael's heels. Their discomfort was visible. Some wore clothes that were soiled and torn. A herd of 80 or so sheep that kept the wild grasses short parted as Michael and his herd approached. He led them across the narrow bridge and toward the towering tree. He stopped in front of Catherine and bowed. "Please accept my sincerest condolences on your tragic loss." He then bowed to Alexandra.

"Thank you, Excellency," Catherine replied, eyes glistening, smiling royalty to royalty. She hadn't regarded Michael as a friend, merely a seldom-seen occupant of the throne. But his unexpected arrival impressed and touched the princess. Perhaps, she was thinking, the day will come when he will be more than a figurehead. "The children?"

"Bucharest's newest orphans," he replied. "Their parents were killed in the earthquake. I found them at hospitals, churches, police and fire stations. I hope you don't mind. I thought you might possibly find space for them somewhere in Saint Catherine's Crib."

Catherine felt a lump swelling in her throat. "Of course, Excellency," she said, brushing away a tear. "Our crib has been shown to be flexible. Your thoughtfulness is remarkable and your quick action commendable. And your timing is exquisite. Their presence here today changes everything. These lovely children are lifting my spirits."

"I was hoping they might help brighten your day – and your daughter's. I must admit, though, I didn't know we would be arriving during the burial service."

She cleared her throat and forced a slight smile. "Please stay for the service. The children too. Afterward I would like to feed them, but I'm afraid I am unprepared. We'll have to – "

Michael pressed his right forefinger against his lips. Then he pointed to the small delivery truck. "Food. More than enough. Pork, dumplings, vegetables. Also clatite (crepes), papanasi (doughnuts with jam and sour cream) and tortes (creamy cakes). Milk for the children and we brought coffee and plum brandy." At that an appreciative grin creased the priest's heretofore sober visage.

Catherine's smile reflected her utter amazement and delight. "You seem to have thought of everything." Then, on impulse she reached for Michael's hands, took them and squeezed. In the next instant she rose up on tiptoes and air-kissed each of this cheeks. "Constantin and Irene no doubt approve. On their behalf and Alexandra's, thank you." A pause. "I must ask you: How did you manage all of this?"

"As you know, I am but a figurehead king. I know that. But Antonescu really sees me as a harmless lackey. Ever ready to do his bidding. He misreads me. I have friends who are willing to do me favors and ask nothing in return. These last few days" – he turned and pointed to the bus and truck – "I asked for some."

"Remind me," Catherine smiled wryly, "not to misread or underestimate you."

CHAPTER 24

A third earthquake, another political temblor, shook Romania on November 23. Ion Antonescu, after exchanging cables with Berlin, announced with pomp that Romania had joined the Axis Powers. His hubris – characterizing Romania as a partner with Germany – didn't go unnoticed by King Michael in Bucharest, Catherine in Nedelea and Gabriella in Washington.

Four days later, November 27, before other Romanian influentials could mount a protest, Antonescu ordered arrests and summoned Horia Sima to his Royal Palace office.

"Here," a grim-faced Antonescu said to Sima, a cabinet minister and Iron Guard leader, "take these." Antonescu reached across his desk and handed Sima two sheets of ordinary white paper.

Sima scanned the sheets. "How many names are on these?"

"Sixty-four."

"They all appear to be former government officials and dignitaries – professors, artists."

"Yes," said Antonescu, "and they all are now in Jilava Prison awaiting trial for crimes against the state."

Sima nodded. "You don't want those trials to take place."

"We know they are guilty of being pro-monarchy and anti-German. The trials aren't necessary. We need to take strong action that will serve as a deterrent to any would-be opposition."

"When?"

"Today."

"How?"

"That's up to you. Shooting, hanging, strangling."

Later that day, the 64 saw guards approaching their cells. They were guilty only of being Jewish or men of principal and loyal to a constitutional

91

government and an elected parliament that worked in concert with their king. Keys were inserted into locks and barred doors pulled open. The men were dragged from their cells and herded into the prison courtyard. Greeting them were Sima and a contingent of 50 Iron Guardsmen armed with submachine guns. Immediately, the prisoners sensed their fate.

Sima acted with dispatch. "Prepare to fire," he ordered. Some of the victims stood firm while others flinched and cried out. Sima's men leveled their weapons. "Fire."

Shots rang out and echoed in the courtyard. Some bullets pinged as they ricocheted off stone walls. The carnage didn't take long. A few bursts from each gun and all 64 were on the ground. Most were still. A few were writhing and moaning. Blood was seeping from bodies and staining the cobblestones.

At a silent signal from Sima, six of the Iron Guardsmen walked among the bodies. At each sign of life they fired another burst.

Sima's work that day wasn't complete. Later, a squad of Guardsmen assassinated Nicolae Iorga, a historian and former prime minister, and Virgil Madgearu, a former cabinet minister.

At his home that night Sima poured five ounces of plum brandy into a snifter. Jews are scum, he reminded himself, and we would be better off without them. Hitler has made it clear beyond all doubt that dispatching Jews will be regarded as virtuous. But the murders of the others? It's also clear that Antonescu is insecure. He fears anyone he regards as a potential threat. That could include me. Probably does. Sima sipped the brandy. So do I follow his orders ever so meekly and wait for my turn at execution? Or do I follow my instincts and organize a pre-emptive strike?

In Nedelea and in Bucharest, Catherine Caradja and King Michael reacted identically. They were aghast at Antonescu's atrocities. Michael sensed, though, that the better part of valor was holding his tongue and biding his time as long as Antonescu's blood was up. Why give him even the slightest excuse to rid himself of me? Catherine's concern was less for herself and more for Alexandra and her growing brood of orphans. With those worries uppermost, could she refrain from upbraiding Antonescu? Even privately? As yet she didn't have the answer to her questions.

In Washington, Gabriella's worries centered on her father. Could he survive an all-out purge? Antonescu, if he was thinking rationally, would spare the man leading Romania's most crucial industry. But if Antonescu is beset with paranoia, then no man might be above suspicion and liquidation. As bad as things are, she was thinking, they could get much worse.

On the platform for Union Station's track number nine, Joe Barton motioned to a porter to handle his bags and tipped the black man generously. Five dollars. Gabriella, both hands clasping his left arm, already was sniffling. Joe's throat had swollen so fast he wondered whether he could swallow, let alone speak.

"I think your tall gypsy is out of words." Tears now were streaming down her cheeks.

Joe cupped her chin with his right hand. "For the first time I think I really understand how Miss Hughes felt."

"Your history teacher?"

Joe nodded. "When she learned her fiancé had been killed, I think I now know the pain she felt. God, the hurt is so physical." He shook his head. His left hand brushed his own tears.

Gabriella pressed her face against Joe's chest. Her lips barely moving she murmured miserably, "I love you."

"I love you too," Joe whispered, nearly choking on the words.

Both knew this might be the last time they would see and hold each other. Both were feeling an urge to say as much. Both also were fearful that saying so could lead to a self-fulfilling prophecy, and the words remained unspoken.

CHAPTER 25

The taxi inched along the stone-paved quay and braked when the driver spotted the proper address ahead on the left.

Joe exited the black, British-built taxi that had transported him and his luggage two miles east from the pier at Keppel Harbor to Collyer Quay where he would be living and working in the United States Consulate.

The consulate was housed in the Union Building, a columned five-story, stone office block squeezed among others along the quay. Their architecture could best be described as British colonial. That is, they all were grim and gray with seemingly requisite gingerbread at the roofline. Crowning the Union Building was a stately cupola with its own small columns. Atop it from a pole flew the union jack.

The quay itself bordered Marina Bay just east of the mouth of the winding Singapore River. To the north and east of the bay was Kallang Basin, formed by the confluence of two other rivers, the Geylang and the Rochor.

Collyer Quay was built securely about six feet above the water's surface. The retaining wall was constructed of stones quarried in the island's interior.

The long journey from Washington – train to San Pedro, Los Angeles' port city, and then a spartan cabin on a slow freighter to Singapore – had been largely boring and unutterably lonely. Many of Joe's waking hours had been spent longing for Gabriella and trying fruitlessly to keep suppressed the stabs of pain in his torso. At many moments, some unexpected, his throat had swollen shut and his eyes leaked tears.

Now, as he stood on the quay, those pangs had abated, at least temporarily. Joe felt exhilarated. He would be serving as a junior officer – in actuality a staff clerk – for Assistant Trade Commissioner Charles Thompson. Heading the mission was Consul General Kenneth Patton. His area of responsibility embraced Singapore, the Straits Settlements, the Malay states, North Borneo, Brunei and Sarawak. Soon, Joe would learn, Patton resided not in the Union Building but in a colonial-style cottage called Spring Grove, pleasantly situated in a leafy park-like setting farther inland. From Joe's earliest days at the State Department, he knew that rank had as companions privileges.

From his reading during the long sea voyage, Joe had learned, to his amazement, that the United States had established a consulate in Singapore more than a century earlier – June 1837. The first consul was Joseph Balestier. He took office fewer than 20 years after Sir Stamford Raffles, an agent for the British East India Company, had first visited the island on January 29, 1819, and immediately seen its potential. A scant eight days later, February 6, Raffles negotiated an agreement with the sultan of Johor, the southern portion of the Malay Peninsula just north of the narrow strait separating it from the island. As a result Raffles was able to claim Singapore for Great Britain and establish a trading post. In return the British East India Company would pay the sultan the equivalent of $3,000 a year.

Balestier, a New England native, would remain in Singapore for 18 years. His wife Maria was a daughter of Revolutionary War legend Paul Revere. Eventually Singapore would name a district and a street after Balestier.

Before Raffles' arrival Singapore was a sparsely populated island with overgrown jungle and scattered fishing villages. At his initial landing site at the mouth of the Singapore River, Raffles found swamps, jungle and a lone village of some 100 Malay huts.

Historians believe Singapore was settled around 1390. Initially, the island and the city were called Temasek or "Sea town" in the local language. Later, a visiting prince saw a lion and anointed Temasek with a new name – Singa Pura – "Lion City" in Sanskrit.

Joe motioned to the taxi driver to carry his bags inside the Union Building. Before following, Joe smiled ruefully and wondered, Will I ever get used to this heat and humidity? I've been told all days are pretty much alike – tropically beastly. Which stands to reason given that Singapore is only about 70 miles north of the equator. And these smells. Salt water is okay but the fishy smell. Whew. That'll take some getting used to.

New Year's Day morning, 1941.

Joe awoke before dawn and decided to take a walk before the sun began its daily broiling of the island. He pulled on lightweight beige cotton trousers and an equally light, collared shirt. No socks, he thought, not today. He slipped on brown loafers. Joe glanced at the cigar on his chest of drawers. The Macanudo was a gift from Consul General Patton who had hosted consulate staff and spouses at a New Year's Eve party at Spring Grove. Joe had appreciated the invitation, but thoughts of Gabriella dulled his enjoyment of the festivities. After the mantel clock chimed midnight, Joe joined Patton and his wife and the other guests in renderings of *America the Beautiful* and *Auld Lang Syne*. Then he shook hands with the Pattons, claimed residual fatigue from his journey to Singapore and returned to the Union Building and his small room.

Now he was strolling along the promenade on the north bank of Marina Bay, just past the Singapore River's mouth. Joe paused and removed the cigar from his shirt pocket. Therapeutic, Joe mused. Puffing on this cigar – my first one – just might be a dandy way to begin my new posting in a new year in a new part of the world. He slid the cigar beneath his nose and smiled. Rich, was his assessment. This should do a good job of counteracting the sea smells – temporarily.

He fished in his pockets. "Crap," he muttered. "No matches." Joe didn't own a lighter.

"Need a light?" The voice asking the question was British-accented.

Joe looked around and saw no one.

"Down here," the voice said pleasantly.

Joe looked down and saw a brown-skinned man lithely stepping up stairs from a sampan onto a 14-step, gently inclined wooden godown or ladder.

"Good morning," Joe greeted him.

"Good morning. And a fine one it is for a good cigar." The man handed Joe a tiny box of wooden matches.

Joe struck one, placed the flame at the cigar's end and began drawing breaths. Within moments smoke began curling skyward.

"Smells good," said the man.

"Tastes good," Joe said. "First time I've smoked a cigar. Or anything for that matter."

"Well," said the man, "you shouldn't smoke it alone. Give me a minute." He descended back onto the sampan. Moments later he was climbing back onto the promenade. A stubby cigar was clenched between his teeth. "Lion City. Not fancy or expensive but a reputable brand in these parts." He accepted the return of his matches, struck one and lit up. Both men flipped their matches into the bay.

Joe waited for the man's cigar to absorb the flame. "My name's Joe Barton. I work at the United States Consulate. Or soon will."

"New here?"

"Very."

"Welcome to my city."

Joe chuckled. "Yours?"

"As much as anyone's." The brown man chortled. "Sir Stamford Raffles' ghost might dispute that claim, but I stand by it – sir."

"You are?"

"Duane Hurd."

Joe offered his right hand. Duane hesitated before grasping and shaking Joe's hand.

"This is new to me," Duane said. "Don't know if I've ever shaken a white hand before."

Joe smiled. "Yours is my first brown one."

They released each other's hand.

"American?"

"By way of Ohio and Washington, D.C."

Duane nodded. "I am by way of an unusual pairing." He puffed his Lion City. "My father was a seaman. African by way of Britain. He landed here and found Singapore to his liking. A certain Chinese woman in particular."

"Your mother."

"Quite right. And there in lies my coloring – what you get when black mixes with yellow."

Joe puffed his Macanudo. "Where do you live?"

Duane pointed toward the bay. "There."

"On the water?"

"On that boat."

"A bit snug for a big man."

97

"Big enough for me. I'm at home on the water."

Duane's home was a sampan. It had been built to his specifications. At 22 feet it was five to seven feet longer than most such boats. From the start he had intended it to serve as his home. While most sampans were propelled by oars or poles, Duane's was roofed and equipped with an outboard motor.

Joe was right, though, about Duane's size. He was a big man. Born in 1910 he stood six feet one inch and was as lean as he was brown. He was handsome, and to Joe, his dark eyes were exotic, just hinting at the Asian half of his parentage. He was wearing a collarless shirt with black and blue horizontal stripes tucked into black trousers. His feet were bare.

"I'm curious," said Joe. "Living on the water, how do you tolerate…"

"The smell?" Duane nodded and puffed. "What to you are dead fish and brine are to me perfumed freedom." Both men laughed. "Besides, it keeps me close to my parents."

"They are?"

"In Chinatown. Father is Clayton. Mother is Su Mien. Been there yet?"

"Afraid not. Just arrived before Christmas."

"Well, Joe Barton, consider the first brown hand you've shaken and the rest of my anatomy to be at your service."

"Thank you." A pause. "Your father. Does he still work as a seaman?"

"A trifle old for that," Duane said. "He and Mother have a tea room, and Father does a little trading. No, not opium if that's what you are thinking. Although as a Chinatown man he knows how to obtain it." Chinatown's narrow streets were known widely for their opium dens.

"I'm a curious man," Joe smiled. "Educate me."

"A customer," Duane grinned, "goes to the door of a den. He knocks twice. When the door cracks open, he asks for two grasshoppers. Then he hands the dealer the equivalent of two of your American dollars. He's not allowed to enter the den though. Strictly off limits."

"Your father's trading specialty?"

"He buys some of your American cigarettes. Camels if he can get them. From deck hands who are willing to make side sales. Father has ready customers at the tea room." Joe cocked his head to the right. New as he was to Singapore, he caught Duane's gist. Smuggling on a small scale. "Do you object?" Duane asked.

"I admire entrepreneurs and I favor low taxes," Joe grinned. He puffed the Macanudo.

"British port authorities here would prefer to collect duty on every pack. But," Duane grinned, "they know if they stop in my parents' tea room, they'll get some of my mother's delightful British biscuits at a favorable price."

"Your Chinese mother bakes British biscuits?"

"Cookies as you Americans call them. Lovely creations. Father taught her the art. Her tea room is popular with all the races here – Chinese, whites, Indians, Malays."

"And you?" Joe asked.

"What do I do?" Joe nodded. "My needs are few and simple. I do a little fishing. No surprise there, right? I work on coasters – vessels that deliver cargo to Malay ports and Sumatra. On occasion I still get a yen for the open sea and will crew on a voyage to Hong Kong or Manila."

As Joe listened to Duane, memories of conversations with Miss Hughes popped into his mind. Think broadly, Joe, she had urged him. "I'd like to meet your parents."

"They are used to whites visiting their tea room but not accompanied by me."

Joe blew smoke from his mouth and shrugged slightly. "If you – and they – would feel better about it, you could introduce us at their home."

"You would visit their home?" Duane's incredulity was evident.

"Why not?"

"Well, actually, their tea room is their home. It's called a shophouse. Business on the ground floor, home on two floors above. On Trengganu Street."

Joe's lips curled down thoughtfully. "I'd like to visit Trengganu Street."

CHAPTER 26

Humiliation. In early 1941 it was a common emotion among Romanians, none feeling it more so than Ion Antonescu. In openly siding with the Axis Powers, he had effectively ceded Romanian sovereignty to Hitler. He proceeded to name Alfred Gerstenberg, a red-haired, 48-year-old Wehrmacht colonel, soon to be promoted to general, to serve as air attaché at the German embassy in Bucharest. In fact, Gerstenberg's charge was to lead implementation of the Nazis' military policy in southeastern Europe. As to international policy, Antonescu's power had been rendered nominal. It soon eroded further. Gerstenberg nationalized Allied-owned oil operations, appointed new boards of directors with membership limited to compliant Romanians, and staffed refineries with German technicians. Cornel Balas hadn't been sacked, but his authority had been extinguished.

Russia – Stalin – saw Antonescu's weakness and demanded the return of territories lost to Romania after World War I. Bulgaria and Hungary made similar demands. Antonescu acquiesced to all, and his countrymen's disdain for the usurper grew more by the day.

What little respect Antonescu held among Iron Guard leaders evaporated. Horia Sima called them to his home. "Let me be clear. I still detest the monarchy. I regret we failed to assassinate Carol before he fled. And Stalin and his communist cronies, they are a political cancer and should be eradicated. We were correct to align our interests with the Nazis. But Antonescu was shortsighted. He completely sold out our nation. He has relegated us to the status of a Nazi colony. We have no honor in the international community. None."

"I take it you have a proposal," one of the Guardsmen said dryly.

"Antonescu knows of our disdain for him," Sima said calmly. "I wouldn't be surprised if he is plotting action against us. We put him in power but he would turn against us if he felt cornered. Which he likely does."

"So you are thinking we should strike first?"

Bullets began shattering windows and pocking the Royal Palace façade. "Hold your fire. Let them get closer" was the command spread throughout the building.

It was January 20 and some 10,000 Iron Guardsmen were launching a coup attempt. In predawn hours they had begun closing in on the Royal Palace. Treachery would thwart their efforts; an informant had alerted Antonescu to impending danger, and he still controlled the Romanian Army, at least inside the country's borders. He had installed well-armed soldiers inside the palace, and he called in tanks and troops to pounce on the Iron Guardsmen from the rear.

The Guardsmen scattered. Fighting continued in Bucharest streets for four days before Antonescu's forces prevailed. More than 6,000 Guardsmen were killed. The dictator wanted to summarily execute all remaining Guardsmen, including those who had not participated in the attempted overthrow. But he was persuaded that doing so would turn all of Romania against him and lead to his ouster.

He settled for removing all Guardsmen from governmental positions and imprisoning others. Sima and many of his closest colleagues eluded capture and made their way stealthily to Germany where they found refuge.

Sima had been right about the international view of Romania. The next month, February, Britain broke off diplomatic relations with Bucharest. The Black Sea nation was now completely isolated from the West and entirely a pawn of Hitler.

At her villa Catherine Caradja opened the front door for King Michael. In her parlor she poured brandy.

"Much as I detest Antonescu," she was saying, "another coup attempt is out of the question."

"For now, yes," King Michael agreed.

They were sitting in overstuffed chairs near the fireplace. A crackling fire and the plum brandy were keeping winter's chill at bay.

"Only two things exceed my love for Romania – my love for my daughter and my orphans."

"That is precisely why it would be to your benefit – and theirs – to limit your energies to protecting them. Antonescu is like a cornered animal. If he was insecure before, he must be completely paranoid now."

Catherine sipped and smiled warmly. "For a young man – a young king – you have managed to accumulate considerable wisdom."

"I have tried to absorb lessons taught by others."

"You have succeeded where others have failed."

Both knew she was alluding to Michael's father and his unseemly flight with the country's riches.

"I don't know if I'll ever be more than a king in name. But if the opportunity presents itself, I hope I have the courage to act. Or, should I say? – the courage to act wisely."

Catherine chuckled softy. "Let's hope that applies to me as well."

CHAPTER 27

"If I was in Washington, I would probably be looking at cherry blossoms."

"Cherry blossoms?" Duane Hurd asked.

"Sorry. Cherries are a fruit," Joe Barton explained. "Small and red. Some are tart, some sweet. Their blossoms are white and bloom in late March or early April. There are many cherry trees in Washington, and people enjoy strolling and looking at the blossoms."

"Sounds like a pleasant way to spend a Sunday afternoon."

"Or any afternoon after work."

"As you know we have many fruits here, but no cherries. But I am thinking I could show you something else, something new for you."

"Oh my," Joe exclaimed a few days later. "This is fabulous."

"Thought you might like it. But as you now know, seeing it requires more than a casual stroll. One must exert oneself." Duane was grinning impishly. "But that's part of the reward."

"I'll say. I don't know if I'd've tried this if you hadn't suggested it. Too much heat and humidity to make the effort. If I removed my shirt and rolled it up, I think I could wring sweat from it."

"Go ahead. Take your shirt off."

"I think I will." And he did.

Joe and Duane were standing atop Bukit Timah, a hill reaching 537 feet and the highest point on Singapore island. The hill is located near the center of the island that, at its longest, stretches some 26 miles from east to west and, at its widest, 14 miles from north to south. In Malay, Bukit Timah means tin-bearing hill. The path to the summit was narrow, winding and steeply inclined. Monkeys foraged and cavorted in the trailside jungle.

Surrounding the hill was a nature preserve that was established in 1883. Nearby was a thoroughbred horse racing course that had opened in 1933.

"There's something ironic about standing up here, Duane."

"Yes?"

"Those cherry trees in Washington, the original ones, were given to the United States by Japan. Almost thirty years ago as a sign of friendship and peace. From up here I can look through the trees and see across the strait into Malaya. I can't help thinking about the Japanese. They are continuing their conquest of China. They keep pushing south. They are relentless and they are confident. It seems inevitable that they won't stop until they've taken all of China and continued onto the Malayan peninsula and perhaps across the strait and into Singapore."

"You could be right but I'll try not to think about that," said Duane. "We've heard stories of how they have been persecuting – slaughtering – Chinese. There's no reason to think they would treat the Malayan and Singaporean Chinese any differently."

"Including," Joe murmured, "your mother."

Duane's cheeks ballooned as he blew out a breath. He nodded. "My mother migrated here in the early years of this century, but she still is Chinese. And people of color – our dark-skinned Indians and Malays, my father – who knows what evils the Japanese might inflict on us?"

Joe slowly turned 360 degrees, taking in the vistas. "Water on all sides. A natural barrier. Yet from up here the island seems so small. So fragile. I wonder if the British are seriously considering the possibility of a Japanese invasion this far south – the peninsula and maybe the island?"

Later that month, April 28, England's War Department would write this assessment of Japanese military intentions in South Asia:

Japan is unlikely to enter the war unless the Germans make a successful invasion of Great Britain, and even a major disaster like the loss of the Middle East would not necessarily make her come in, because the liberation of the British Mediterranean Fleet which might be expected,

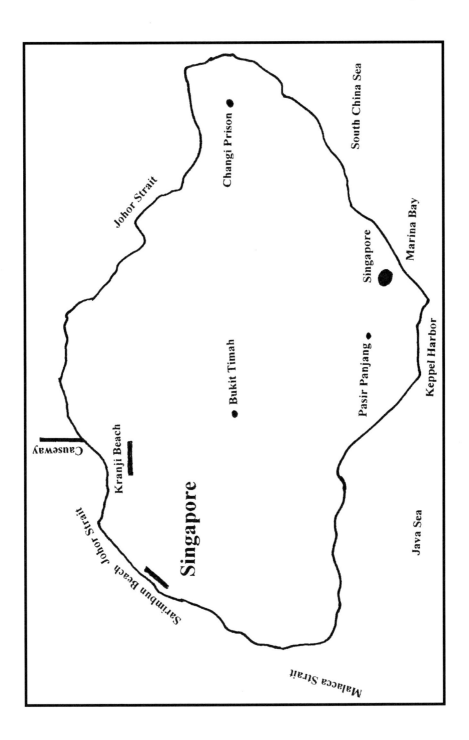

and also any troops evacuated from the Middle East to Singapore, would not weaken the British war-making strength in Malaya. It is very unlikely, moreover, that Japan will enter the war either if the United States have come in, or if Japan thinks that they would come in consequent upon a declaration of war. Finally, it may be taken as almost certain that the entry of Japan into the war would be followed by the immediate entry of the United States on our side. There is no need at the present time to make any further dispositions for the defence of Malaya and Singapore, beyond those modest arrangements which are in progress, until or unless the conditions set out are modified.

As Joe and Duane were slowly descending Bukit Timah, warm rain began pelting them. It felt mildly refreshing. Far below and to the south, Sister Regina and Lim Bo Seng were chatting in the shade of the towering Banyan tree outside the nurses' quarters across the drive from Singapore General Hospital. No rain was falling there. Romping on the grass, jumping rope, chasing each other in a game of tag were Lim's children. His wife, Choo Neo, was watching, refereeing disputes as they arose.

"If the Japanese were to attack…"

"They will, Sister. I am certain of that."

"You and your family…"

"As Chinese we would be certain targets for persecution. Probably execution, given my known support of Chinese resistance."

"I will pray daily that nothing remotely resembling that situation comes to pass," Sister Regina said sadly. "I think it might be too much for my heart to bear."

"Sister, please don't worry about us. If the Japanese look like they are nearing Singapore, I should have enough time to evacuate my family. You and the other nuns as well."

"Your concern for us is genuine and sweet. But as nurses I think we would stay. Our work would be more sorely needed. And I would like to think the Japanese would respect our habits." She looked at Lim. "Do you think I'm being naïve?"

Lim shrugged. He used the middle finger of his right hand to nudge his glasses higher on his nose. "Sister, I think I should be praying daily for you." Lim smiled and at that moment felt more strongly than ever that he had made the right choice in converting to Christianity.

CHAPTER 28

"Hey, Mama!" Jeff Wolfrom's shout startled Iris Ann who at that moment on a Friday afternoon was in her room and augmenting her boarding house income beneath a husky resident of one of the upstairs bedrooms.

"Wait here," Iris Ann whispered sharply, "and don't make a sound."

"Mama! You home?"

"Just a moment, Jeff," she called out, trying not to sound distressed.

"I'm not finished," the railroad worker protested.

Iris Ann pushed hard against his thick shoulders. "You are for today."

"I should get a discount the next time."

"You should pay extra because of the quality."

The worker couldn't, in honesty, claim otherwise. Iris Ann serviced him like no other woman. He pulled away and rolled onto his back.

Iris Ann swung her bare legs off the bed, stood and brushed her palms against her dress. Quickly, she examined herself in the dresser mirror and, using her hands, patted her hair.

"You're home early," she said to Jeff who was entering the kitchen.

"I've got news," he said excitedly.

"Really. Well, before you tell me, let's each get a Dr. Pepper from the fridge and go out on the front porch. Big news deserves a Dr. Pepper."

Jeff laughed. "You're funny. I'll get the bottle opener." He pulled open a drawer next to the sink while Iris Ann opened the refrigerator door and removed two small seven-ounce bottles. Jeff used an opener with Dr. Pepper in red letters on the white grip to remove the two caps.

Mother and son then headed for the porch, passing through the breakfast room, dining room, hallway and living room. Seconds later the railroad worker followed, tiptoeing to the hallway and the staircase and ascending stealthily. He was remembering Iris Ann's standard warning: no second chances.

Seated comfortably on two white wooden porch chairs, Iris Ann was first to speak. "Well, tell me your news before you bust a seam or two," she said in her maternally soft Arkansas accent.

Jeff took a quick sip of his Dr. Pepper then breathed deeply and exhaled strongly. "I'm going to join the Army."

Iris Ann blinked and, for the moment, forgot the bottle in her hand. My only son, her mind raced, in the Army. At least there's no war. "Are you sure that's what you want?"

"Yes, Mama. I'm going to the recruiting office tomorrow and sign up."

"Why the hurry?"

"Graduation's on Sunday. Job prospects aren't the greatest."

"You could get a job with the Union Pacific or Cotton Belt. Or at a paper mill. I'm sure my boarders would speak well of you." She was indeed certain of their willingness to put in a good word with potential employers if she asked. And if it came to that, she knew too that she could leave unsaid the penalty for declining.

"Those aren't the kind of jobs I have in mind."

"Oh? And what might those be?"

"I want to apply to join the Army's Air Corps." Before his mother could say anything, Jeff rushed on. "You know I love flying." He reddened. "Well, at least flying my model planes. I've been dreaming of flying real ones for as long as I can remember."

Iris Ann remembered the bottle in her hand and raised it to her lips. She sipped deliberately, trying to slow her speeding thoughts. She shifted in her chair. "You're my only child and, well, I would probably worry myself sick if you were flying around up in the clouds."

Jeff laughed. "You might even be able to watch me."

"Huh? What do you mean?"

"You know. The Army just finished building Grider Field." Jeff was referring to the newly constructed Army Air Corps base located four miles south of the boarding house. Eventually it would train some 10,000 pilots and crew for duty on bombers and fighters. "If I qualify for the Air Corps, my training might take place there. Wouldn't that be wonderful?"

Iris Ann forced a bright smile. "Yes, Jeff, it would. But how would I know when you're flying?"

"That's easy, Mama. I'd buzz our boarding house and wiggle my wings." Jeff laughed infectiously and Iris Ann let herself laugh with him.

Two days later on Sunday evening, Iris Ann and Jeff were strolling the three short blocks from their East Martin Avenue home to Beech Avenue and Pine Bluff High School, a gothic, three-story red brick structure. Even though it was early June, the Mississippi River valley was already hinting at the heat and humidity that annually turned Pine Bluff summers into one long sauna bath. Drenching was a word used often to describe Pine Bluff in July and August.

Jeff's black graduation gown was draped casually over his left shoulder, and he was holding the mortarboard with tassel. Iris Ann would have loved to be holding his hand but felt such public intimacy would embarrass her son.

Other soon-to-be graduates and their families were converging on the school. Smiles abounded, many parents were beaming and happy greetings were being exchanged.

Jeff and Iris Ann ascended the wide cement staircase. Inside, a younger female student handed Iris Ann a program and said, pointing, "That way to the auditorium, ma'am."

"Thank you," Iris Ann smiled. "I remember." She was a 1922 graduate of the school.

Jeff smiled. "We are forming up in the cafeteria. See you soon."

Iris Ann walked slowly along the hallway, letting memories of her own four years in the building come bubbling to the surface.

At the auditorium entrance, an usher, another younger female student, greeted Iris Ann. "Welcome, ma'am. We hope you enjoy the ceremony."

"I'm sure I will."

"Are you a parent?"

"Yes."

"Then please take a seat in the center section."

At seven o'clock the graduating seniors began their procession down the auditorium aisles and onto the stage. Mortarboards in place, their gowns were swishing as they moved into rows of wooden folding chairs. Iris Ann could see the youngsters were arranging themselves alphabetically, with Jeff among the last to be seated.

The Army Air Corps, Iris Ann found herself musing. Flying military planes sounds so dangerous. I've already lost the most important man in my life to an accident. I'll be praying daily that I don't lose another. God, please forgive me my sins and protect my son. And please, God, no wars.

A week later, June 12, 1941, Ion Antonescu exercised another in his ongoing series of flawed judgments. Now officially in the Axis camp and feeling an urge to taunt Stalin, he windily proclaimed, "When it's a question of action against the Slavs, you can always count on Romania."

Ten days later, June 22, Hitler abrogated his August 1939 non-aggression pact with Stalin by launching Operation Barbarossa. His aim was clear: crush Russia and communism.

For Romania the consequences were immediate: It began providing equipment and oil – tons of it – to the Wehrmacht war machine. Romania had under arms more than 685,000 men. Most were poorly equipped and ill-trained. That didn't give Antonescu pause. He ordered the men into a hastily formed Romanian Third Army and hurled 500,000 infantry and cavalry troops into Russia. Hitler gladly used them as fodder, and 50,000 were killed in taking one city, Odessa. Thousands more fell at Sevastopol and Stalingrad.

The early advances brought out the worst of Antonescu's anti-Semitic proclivities. At Odessa his troops massacred some 100,000 Ukrainian Jews. He then turned his troops loose in wholesale, systematic slaughter of Jews in the territories to Romania's east and north. Forward units of the Romanian forces quickly set up the only non-German-run extermination camps. Some 185,000 Jews were dispatched. They were stripped and most were shot. In a few instances when ammunition supplies were running low, only adults were shot. Children were buried alive.

None other than Adolf Eichmann, Hitler's Holocaust architect, asked Antonescu to suspend the executions until Eichmann's mobile SS murder squads could complete the mission less ghastly. But Antonescu's blood was up and he ignored the request. What finally would cause Antonescu to order dismantling the extermination camps and halting the murders was his sensing as early as September 1942 – as the siege of Stalingrad was unfolding – that the Nazis might not prevail in Russia.

Word of the atrocities was slow in making its way back to Romania. When Catherine Caradja first heard the rumors, she wrapped herself in denial. Romanian men, perhaps including some young men from Saint Catherine's Crib, simply couldn't be a party to slaughtering innocents. Certainly not women and children. Yes, Romanians have been devoutly Christian since antiquity and have little fondness for Jews. There have been persecutions. But nothing like this, she told herself. Not genocide.

A visit to her villa by King Michael persuaded her otherwise. He had heard Antonescu boasting of "cleansing Greater Romania of Jewish contamination."

Catherine might have wept had anger not so consumed her. "He must be stopped, Michael," she bristled. "He is killing wantonly, unjustly, and he is forever besmirching our national honor."

Michael sighed. "May we both live long enough to witness his end."

Late in June, George Britton, Oliver Needle and Malcolm Goode were among troops who had completed their military training. They had received their travel orders and been given brief leaves to visit families before embarking.

"Somehow the Thames doesn't look as wide as it did before our training," George observed as the young men, all in uniform, were standing on the Gravesend iron pier.

"I think things seem to look smaller as we get older," Oliver said, eyes gazing thoughtfully beneath his thick eyebrows.

"And shorter," Malcolm added.

"This is the last time we'll stand here for the next four years," George said. "Do you think we'll miss it?"

British Army enlistees were committed to five years of active duty, including training, plus a seven-year reserve requirement.

"Well," Oliver grinned, "your master fisherman will miss casting from this pier. But from what we've been told, Gravesend will never be as exotic as Singapore."

"Or," added Malcolm, "as exciting."

CHAPTER 29

"Mr. Barton," said the consulate receptionist, Rosalie Reynolds. "Letter for you."

Joe's heart leaped.

Rosalie, like Joe, was young and adventurous. She was 24, five feet three inches, blond, blue-eyed, vivacious and, in Joe's eyes, cute. Her hair was cut short, pageboy style. Rosalie conducted herself professionally, seldom letting surface a delightful sense of whimsy. Unlike Joe she had departed Washington unattached romantically. More than once she had considered signaling Joe her interest in him. What had stopped her was his evident love for a woman left behind. Rosalie didn't regard herself as an intruder, and Joe didn't attempt to mask his excitement at letters from the States, especially ones bearing the return address of Romania's United States embassy.

It hadn't taken long for Joe to grasp why the U.S. had a strong consular presence in Singapore. Trade between Singapore, Malaya and the U.S. was sizable and expanding. Numerous U.S.-based companies had a presence in greater Malaya. Among them were Ford, General Motors, General Electric, Singer Sewing Machine, National City Bank, Goodyear and Firestone. Issues were plentiful and they kept Joe busy. A highlight each day was mail call.

At his desk Joe reached for a dagger-shaped letter opener and sliced apart the envelope. It was postmarked June 23, 1941. Today in Singapore the date was July 30. Five weeks to get here, Joe thought, not too bad. He unfolded the letter. Before beginning to read, he stood and walked past Rosalie's desk to the consulate entrance and stepped outside onto the quay. He began reading slowly.

June 23, 1941

My Dearest Joe,

Where to begin? So many questions. As you know Germany has attacked Russia. So has my country. Madness. Utter stupidity.

My Romania, I fear, will be devastated. Yes, we are on the side of Germany which seems all-conquering. For now. But even if Hitler's Reich does endure for centuries, what will it mean for a small nation like mine? And, Joe, if America decides to fight Germany, would that relieve pressure on Russia? And what would that mean for nations like Poland and Romania? So many questions. The answers I can imagine are not good ones. Certainly not good for Romania's future. Perhaps I should go riding. It won't put my mind at ease, but it might clear it for a couple hours.

I miss you terribly, Joe, but then you know that because I say it in every letter. I hope you don't get tired reading it. It's my favorite sentence next to I love you. Which, of course, I do. Madly.

Your Romanian gypsy,

Gabriella

Joe nearly stepped off the quay into the bay. He had been concentrating so intently on reading the letter that he was startled to realize he was only a half step from a soaking. Wouldn't that take some explaining? he teased himself. I can just hear the story making the rounds. Consular official can't read and walk at the same time. Send him back to Washington for remedial training. Wouldn't Miss Hughes get a huge laugh if she saw an item like that in *The Daily Globe*?

As Joe entered the consulate, Rosalie asked, "Good letter?"

Joe stopped at her desk. "My girlfriend is worried for her country. Romania. But you know that from the envelopes." Rosalie nodded and smiled understandingly. "I worry that she might decide to return there."

"Not a good choice," Rosalie said softly, shaking her head.

"Not by any means."

Joe continued to his desk. He sat, picked up a bulky black fountain pen and paused. His first inclination was to reply to Gabriella's letter. He decided to wait a day, allowing time for sorting and organizing his thoughts. Instead he dipped the pen in a well of black ink and wrote:

July 30, 1941

Dear Miss Hughes,

I hope receiving this letter doesn't knock you off your feet. I just want you to know that I keep following your advice to keep thinking broadly and looking toward distant horizons. I guess you also can regard this letter as a reminder to keep preaching your own "gospel" on the values of history and looking for futures outside Shelby.

You might be interested to know that I have met a most interesting man. He is half Negro. His father is African and his mother Chinese. He lives on a small boat and has been showing me around Singapore. Bukit Timah – a hill, the highest point on the island – and Chinatown. His name is Duane Hurd and we have become friends. Imagine that. A boy from all-white Shelby makes a brown friend on the other side of the world.

By the time this letter reaches you, summer will be over and you'll be back at SHS.

Joe put the pen down on his desk, closed his eyes, rubbed them and pondered. He was thinking of asking Miss Hughes if she had heard anything about Maureen Alston. He was curious more than anything else and admitted to himself that he missed Maureen's zest for sex. In the next moment he shook his head, pushing those memories away. He picked up and dipped the pen again and resumed writing.

I can imagine you having conversations with other boys like the ones we had. I wonder if you've told any of them about your fiancé and Belleau Wood. You should. It's a story lots of young people should hear. They should know about sacrifices and what is required to preserve precious freedoms. But what am I saying? You know that.

Have a great school year, Miss Hughes.
Your devoted former student and continuing admirer,
Joe Barton

At five minutes before 5 p.m. that day, Rosalie Reynolds was straightening the papers on her desk. She saw the consulate door opening and looked up. For an instant her face registered surprise and just as quickly masked it.

"May I help you?"

The man was dressed dapperly – white-collared long-sleeve shirt, white linen trousers, black belt and black loafers. He was brown-skinned with features vaguely both African and Asian. His black hair was cut so short as to appear nearly shaved. He smiled cordially, revealing perfectly aligned white teeth.

"Yes, miss. I am here to meet Joe Barton."

"Your receptionist was surprised to see me," Duane said as he and Joe began walking the approximately three-quarters of a mile west from the Union Building to Trengganu Street in Chinatown.

"I'm not surprised. Most consulate visitors are whites. She's seen a few darker-complexioned Indians. But you probably are the first man with African ancestry she's seen since arriving here. Did she treat you kindly?"

"Oh, she was very professional."

"That sounds like Rosalie."

As the two men entered Trengganu Street, Joe saw he was a target of stares. Duane saw them too. "Not that many white civilians are seen here – especially in the company of a brown man."

"They don't bother me," said Joe.

"My parents were delighted when you came to meet them in their tea room. They are thrilled that you are going upstairs to visit their home. A little nervous too."

"Why? They needn't be."

"I know but they really want you to like their home, and they know it is small by western standards.

"I'm sure I'll like it, and I'll do my best to put them at ease."

"I know."

"And I hope you made it clear to your mother that I am looking forward to authentic Chinese home-cooking."

"I did," Duane laughed. "But I did advise her not to prepare anything too exotic or mysterious."

The dinner was delicious and Joe didn't stint on lavishing praise on Su Mien Hurd's culinary efforts. The menu included steamed rice with pork and steamed pork dumplings nicely seasoned, boiled seaweed soup and a simple lettuce salad with ginger sauce. Dessert was delicate, small round cakes served with strawberries. Duane had told his mother that Americans were known for their hearty appetites, and she had plied Joe with generous servings. She poured green tea in his small china cup several times.

What Joe admired equally was Su Mien and Clayton Hurd's family altar. It was flush against the rear wall of the shophouse's second floor front room. Scarlet and gold were the dominant colors. Included were porcelain statuettes of gods, brightly robed, fiercely posed and wielding swords, axes and hatchets. The altar centerpieces were statuettes of two laughing, paunchy Buddhas. At both ends of the altar were lighted red candles.

Joe expressed his admiration and asked the Hurds to explain the altar's significance. Clayton nodded to his wife and she began speaking. "The altar is a tradition among us Chinese. It reminds us to pray each day – for blessings and to give thanks. It is also meant to welcome good spirits and protect our family and guests – like you – from evil spirits."

"Very nice," said Joe. "It's a tradition that the rest of the world would do well to copy."

His words, sincerely spoken, warmed the hearts of all three Hurds. What was left unspoken was Su Mien and Clayton Hurd's curiosity about

Joe's birthmark and scar. They took them as mysterious, outward signs of his inner goodness.

Darkness had descended before Joe and Duane left Trengganu, typical of Chinatown streets. Shophouses, two and three stories in a rainbow of colors with red tile roofs, lined the narrow byways. The Hurds' was mint green with red shutters. The two men began making their way home, Joe to his Union Building room and Duane to his sampan.

"Know what would taste good now?" Joe asked.

"What?"

"A cigar."

Duane's eyes brightened. "Think you could try a Lion City? I have some at the boat."

"Lead on."

Duane chuckled. "We'll sit on the edge of the promenade and pierce the night with the orange ends of two Lion Cities."

"Let's hold them in our hands," Joe chortled, "and rotate them in wide circles."

"Ho, ho," replied Duane, "you can be the devil's own. Other boat people will wonder what signals are being sent."

"This was a wonderful night," Joe said, "the best I've had here."

"May there be many more like it."

"The world seems so at peace here tonight."

That night in Bucharest's ornate National Theater on Nicolae Bakescu Street, the final curtain had just fallen. Laura Ramaschi, now 15, knew her mother had thrilled to the artistry of the ballet troupe. She was applauding exuberantly. Her father, Laura was equally certain, had only tolerated the performance. He was clapping politely. As was Laura. She had been daydreaming, recalling fondly her horse rides with Gabriella. Laura missed her friend and their outings.

Thirty-four miles north in Ploesti a convoy of Wehrmacht trucks had formed and was beginning the drive south to Bucharest. The trucks were loaded with anti-aircraft guns that General Alfred Gerstenberg planned to use to strengthen air defenses around the capital city.

A few rows behind the Ramaschis, Catherine Caradja and daughter Alexandra were standing and lustily applauding the dancers. If only I could move as gracefully and athletically as they, Catherine was musing. But even in my youth, she smiled inwardly, my body wasn't built for ballet. Too wide in the hips and legs too short. She nearly chortled.

Outside the theater the Ramaschis walked briskly two blocks to their car. Mr. and Mrs. Ramaschi opened the front doors to the unlocked car and eased themselves in. Laura opened a rear door and entered gracefully. Mr. Ramaschi started the engine and the car crept away from the curb and headed north toward Ploesti.

A few minutes later a valet arrived in front of the theater with Catherine's 1939 black Plymouth. She would be piloting the car herself to their home near Nedelea, some 10 miles northwest of Ploesti.

As cars and trucks had become more numerous in Romania, the highway connecting Bucharest and Ploesti had earned a sobriquet – Death Road. It was flat, virtually straight, nearly devoid of curves, narrow and poorly paved. No traffic lights burdened drivers with the need to depress brake pedals. The road carried a mélange of motorized vehicles, both civilian and military, slow-moving horse-drawn wagons and bicycles, some carrying three people. Pedestrians, some leading cows to and from roadside communal pastures, walked along Death Road's edges. Accidents were frequent and corpses not an uncommon sight. No statistics were kept.

Darkness had fallen and traffic was heavy and slow. Laura had stretched out across the rear seat. About 10 minutes into the drive home, her mother turned to check and smiled when she saw Laura sleeping. Mr. Ramaschi was growing frustrated by the traffic's slow pace. He was eager to return to their house and get some sleep before another long day in his oil ministry office.

The convoy was six trucks long and in the lighter southbound traffic was proceeding briskly. The drivers and their companions, all young German soldiers, were thinking less about traffic and more about arriving in Bucharest early enough to get to a bistro for two or three steins of beer before reporting to their barracks.

Catherine was enjoying semi-reverie. For one evening at least, thoughts of political turmoil and military action were shoved to her mind's recesses. Alexandra was chatting happily, flitting from one topic to another – ballet, her friends and their romances, a book she was reading, her study of English that Catherine spoke fluently.

Halfway to Ploesti traffic had thinned, but Mr. Ramaschi found his car barely crawling behind a heavy farm wagon. "What in blazes is he doing on the road in the dark?" he grumbled to his wife. "I give farmers more sense than that. They should be in bed asleep."

His impatience amused Mrs. Ramaschi. "Perhaps he's not a farmer. Or if he is, maybe he's been doing day labor to supplement his income.

Perhaps hauling goods for the Germans. He might be as eager to get home as you are."

Mr. Ramaschi sighed. He knew his wife could be right. He merely grunted.

"Damn," he muttered, lips barely parting.

"Shush," his wife reprimanded softly. "You'll wake Laura."

His eyes rolled upward and his right foot depressed the accelerator and he swung left to pass. He was entering one of the road's few curves. As his car pulled abreast of the wagon, a high-set pair of fast-moving headlights nearly blinded him. Mr. Ramaschi had no time to swerve before hearing briefly the stomach-turning sound of metal crushing metal.

Catherine and Alexandra heard the crash. Moments later they saw the farm wagon, now stopped, and flames sprouting from a wrecked car. Singed hoses and belts were acridly scenting the air. Looming above the collapsed front of the car was a German Army truck; its driver and his companion were leaping out and down to the pocked pavement.

Catherine braked and she and Alexandra threw open the doors and went running toward the accident. Truck headlights were illuminating the devastation. Two soldiers were frantically trying to pull Mr. and Mrs. Ramaschi from the burning car. Catherine moved in closely and could see that both had suffered traumatic head injuries and were likely dead or mortally wounded. Her head shook sadly.

Alexandra peeked through a broken rear window and saw nothing. Then she heard a barely audible moan. She stepped closer still and looked down. Shaken, she stepped back and tugged at Catherine's left sleeve.

"Mother, there is someone in the back. Alive."

Catherine looked inside, saw the body in a fetal position and jerked the door handle. It was jammed. She saw soldiers running forward from the trailing trucks and beckoned them with a wave. Other soldiers were halting oncoming traffic.

By now soldiers had carried Mr. and Mrs. Ramaschi's bodies to the edge of the road and gently laid them side-by-side.

"Someone is inside," Catherine said, pointing.

Without a word one of the soldiers gripped the handle with his right hand, leaned his left shoulder against the door and pulled hard. It opened.

He then bent low, grasped Laura by her shoulders and began backing away. Catherine and Alexandra stepped past the soldier, crouched and supported Laura's torso and legs as they emerged.

Catherine was sitting beside the hospital bed when Laura awoke. Her head turned slowly toward Catherine.

"Where am I?"

"In Ploesti. In the hospital?"

"Who are you?"

"My name is Catherine."

"Why am I here? What happened?"

"An accident. You were bruised and shaken."

"I was sleeping. Was anybody else hurt?"

Catherine stood and stepped to the bedside. "Your parents, dear. I'm afraid...I'm afraid they couldn't be saved."

Laura stared and said nothing, struggling to comprehend. After a lengthy pause, "They are dead?"

Catherine nodded, reaching for Laura's hands and taking them in her own. Unless you have family who can care for you, she was thinking, Saint Catherine's Crib has a new resident.

CHAPTER 30

Rosalie Reynolds examined the invitation. Then she wrote on a slip of paper the names of the consulate's staff. Consul-General Kenneth Patton, Consul Clayson Aldridge, Vice-Consul Gordon Minnegerode, Vice-Consul Maurice Bernbaum, Assistant Trade Commissioner Charles Thompson and others, concluding with Joe Barton and herself. She paper-clipped the list to the invitation and then walked it to Patton's office to begin the routing.

Three days later Joe was standing at Rosalie's desk. "What can you tell me about this?" He was holding the invitation to a polo match for the coming Sunday on the large swath of green stretching between the Singapore Recreation Club and the Singapore Cricket Club. The complex lay a little more than a half mile north of the Union Building.

"Well, as you can see, it will be a match pitting the hometown Brits against a team of visiting Aussies. We're all invited. There will be a buffet brunch before the match and a reception afterward. All outdoors weather permitting. All in all, one of the perks that comes with a posting here."

"You've attended one before?"

"Yes."

"You going this time?"

"Wouldn't miss it. You?"

"I like horses and I like watching them run."

"Great. We can all stroll up to the grounds together. Except for Mr. Patton, of course."

"He'll be arriving from Spring Grove."

"Right. With his wife."

"I'm looking forward to it. Never seen a polo match."

"Joe, one more thing."

"Yes?"

"Buy a hat. A white one. You can go British and buy a pith. Or a straw boater. You'll see me under a white bonnet – with broad brims."

"The sun?"

"If you're hatless and not in the shade for a couple hours, you could boil water on your scalp."

The Singapore Recreation Club, built in 1883, was a two-story wood structure with broad staircases front and rear and surrounded by a veranda with drop-down shades to ward off the worst of the equatorial sunrays.

The Cricket Club, dating to 1852, was the more imposing edifice. Fortress-like, a gray granite façade. Four columns flanking the wide entrance. Ten more, shorter columns spanning the façade's second floor. Red tile roof. Palms, hedges and flowers surrounding the exterior. Inside, the ceilings were 12-feet high.

With no hint of rain in the day's forecast, the buffet was organized outside. Tables and chairs were arranged beneath huge umbrellas. Joe, wearing a white straw boater, let consular staff introduce him to their British hosts and the visiting Aussies.

After brunch guests positioned the chairs alongside the polo field that was 300 yards long and 200 yards wide. Joe and Rosalie sat beside each other. Two mounted teams of four each cantered their horses onto the field.

"Do you know why they call them polo ponies?" Joe asked.

"No idea," said Rosalie. "Maybe a result of the British penchant for understatement."

"Calling them ponies certainly qualifies as understatement," Joe said. "They all look like thoroughbreds. They could easily go nine hundred to a thousand pounds."

"And they're fast – as you will see," Rosalie added. "Matches are usually six or eight chukkers or periods. Seven minutes each. Because the Aussies have traveled so far today they're playing eight. You know, give the Down Under boys their money's worth."

"I see each player has a second horse – err, pony."

"Right, they alternate chukkers. There also will be a ten-minute halftime after the fourth chukker."

The match began and Joe thrilled to the action. The ponies were indeed fast. And maneuverable. Joe marveled at their ability to stop quickly and to turn, twist and regain stride with little loss of speed. He also much admired the horsemanship. The game was physical. Horses and riders were frequently bumping into each other, and there was the coordination required to lean low and strike the small ball – only three to three and a half inches in diameter – with a four-foot-long mallet while riding full tilt.

At half time the score was 2-2. "Lemonade or champagne, what's your pleasure, Joe?" Rosalie asked while rising from her chair.

"Lemonade. Where?"

"Under that tent," Rosalie answered, pointing to a large white tent near the Recreation Club.

"Iced, I hope," Joe smiled.

"At least tepid," Rosalie grinned.

The crowd gasped. The match was moving into the closing minute of the seventh chukker. Score: 3-3. Two horses, one from each team, collided near the Aussie goal. The Aussie pony pitched forward and rolled over his front legs. The rider, Lewis Jones, was ejected from his saddle as his pony collapsed and landed awkwardly. The pony was quick to regain its footing, but Jones was groaning while his left hand grasped his right forearm.

Rosalie could see blood oozing from between the fallen rider's fingers and dripping from his arm. She cringed.

"Looks bad," Joe murmured, rising from his chair. He hesitated then went running toward the injured rider. Rosalie, to her surprise, was following, only a few strides behind. Play had stopped and players from both teams dismounted and were clustering around Jones.

Joe knelt. "Let me look," he said to Jones. "Compound fracture." Showing through cracked skin was jagged white bone.

Next at the scene was a British doctor. A quick look and he was opening his black leather bag and reaching for cloth bandage. "We should get him to Singapore General. Can you stand?"

"Here, let me wrap his arm," said Rosalie, taking the bandage. Blood began staining her hands, but she worked steadily and undistracted.

When she was finished, the doctor used a metal clip to secure the bandage. "I don't know what you do, miss, but you've got the instincts of a fine nurse."

"Thank you," said Rosalie, face reddening.

Joe patted Rosalie's left shoulder and he and two other players helped Jones to his feet. He was able to leave the field unaided. Spectators were applauding.

"I guess that's the match," Aussie team captain Roger Willoughby said quietly. "Down a man. We'll concede the match to your lads."

"Let's call it a draw," British team captain Preston York replied graciously.

"You've no extra player?" Joe asked.

"Thanks for coming to our man's aid, sir. You too, miss. But no, we're just the four of us."

Joe surveyed the assemblage and pondered for a long moment. "This is the first polo match I've seen. But I can ride passably well."

Silence. Then Willoughby spoke. "You've been watching closely?" Joe nodded. "And you've seen what can happen to an experienced rider." Joe nodded again. Captain Willoughby's head shook in amazement. He looked at his two teammates. They shrugged their shoulders in an if-he's-crazy-enough-to-try-this-let-him-give-it-a-go gesture. Willoughby then addressed the British team. "Are you all right with this chap filling in?"

"Bloody foolish," Captain York said dismissively. But it was clear to all that Joe's quick action and attentiveness to the fallen rider had earned a measure of respect.

"Your name?" Willoughby asked.

"Joe Barton. I'm with the U.S. Consulate. Very junior position."

"Well, Joe Barton junior officer, it looks like the match will continue."

"I don't expect to show much skill with the mallet," Joe said, "but I think I can stay in the saddle for seven minutes. Barring a collision or loss of balance – or heart," he grinned semi-sheepishly. All smiled at the endearing self-deprecation.

Rosalie, hands dangling at her sides to prevent blood from staining her white dress, thought about saying, "Are you sure about this?" But she bit off the words. Rosalie was concerned about Joe's well being, but she also was curious. He'd never mentioned riding – not that unnatural given his posting on a smallish island but now he was about to mount a thoroughbred capable of accelerating to 30 mph.

"We won't ask you to change into a uniform," said Willoughby, "but you'll need to wear a helmet." He looked down at Joe's loafers. "And let's see if we can find a pair of boots that fit and fasten spurs."

Joe walked off the field with the seven players to secure helmet, boots and spurs. Rosalie, blood now drying on her hands, returned to her chair.

Consul-General Patton approached with a towel damp from dipping in the champagne tub. He offered it to Rosalie who began wiping her hands.

"What's going on?" he asked. "Where is Mr. Barton going with the players?"

"Sir," she replied, looking up at him, "I do think the best answer is, Just watch."

Minutes later Joe was riding with aplomb and aggressiveness that astonished the British spectators and his American colleagues alike – and that quickly earned admiration from the experienced players. His handling of the mount was generating assorted gasps, oohs and aahs from audience members – those whose jaws were no longer slack from seeing the white-clad American skillfully guiding a pony. When attempting to strike the ball with mallet, Joe was missing more often than connecting. But it was clear to all that he was relishing his mount's every stride, stop and change of direction. More than once he wanted to whoop his joy but refrained. During one long charge toward the British goal posts, Joe briefly found himself wishing that his former riding companions, Maureen Alston and Gabriella Balas, could be witnessing his polo baptism.

For Joe the seven minutes ended too quickly. At match's end the draw – 3-3 – was official. No concession. The two teams dismounted and began shaking hands as they walked their ponies toward the sideline. To Joe the scene had the welcome look and feel of the moments following a closely contested high school football game. Joe saw Rosalie waving – Were you ever a cheerleader? Joe wondered – and he saw Patton snap off a crisp salute.

Numerous spectators crowded around the players to offer congratulations.

"Champagne?" Willoughby asked. He pointed toward a large tent that covered a long table replete with small sandwiches, diced fruit and delicate pastries. At one end of the table were pitchers of lemonade and on the ground a large metal tub with champagne bottles waiting to be explosively uncorked.

"What would really hit the spot," Joe grinned, "would be a cold beer. But, yes thanks, champagne will do nicely."

British Captain York whispered in the ear of a teenage boy who went dashing toward the Recreation Club. Moments later before Joe could sip champagne, the sweating boy, short of breath, returned and sidled up to York.

"A toast," York announced grandly. "To our Australian guests and our American cowboy. And I do hope you take that as a compliment, Mr. Barton, because that is my intent."

Laughter all around.

"Compliment accepted," Joe smiled engagingly, "on behalf of all cowboys."

More laughter.

"But wait," said York. "No tippling quite yet." He raised his right hand high above his head. "Joe Barton, American tried and true, said he preferred beer to champagne and by jove he should have his beer." To loud applause the captain handed Joe a bottle of beer, cool, not cold, to the touch. "Bottle opener, anyone?"

The teenage boy tugged at York's sweat-glistened right arm. He was holding an opener. York held it high. "This lad has potential. His thinking was a step ahead of mine."

More laughter.

"Thank you," Joe said modestly. "Might I have the privilege of making a toast?"

Consul-General Patton and his staff, without exception, felt their chests swelling with pride.

"But of course," replied York. "Most appropriate."

"To the finest horsemen – and finest sportsmen – I've ever met or expect to meet."

Cheers erupted and the applause was sustained for a full 30 seconds.

As Rosalie joined in the applause, she was thinking the sender of those letters Joe receives from the Romanian embassy is one lucky woman.

"Mr. Barton," said York, "if ever we can return your favor, please do ask."

"Well, there is one thing," Joe said hesitantly.

"Name it." Captain York was beaming.

"As you now know, I like to ride. Perhaps sometime you'd let me take one of your ponies for a ride around the island."

"Any time, Mr. Barton, any time at all. Just come knocking at our stables. We'll leave word."

The next day, Monday, Joe decided to use his lunch hour to walk the mile southwest from Collyer Quay to Singapore General Hospital. He wanted to pay a visit to Lewis Jones, check on his injury and thank him for the use of his pony.

Joe made his way to the reception desk where he was directed to Jones' room on the second floor. On stepping out of the elevator, he saw a nurses' station and a sign, Maternity Ward. Joe approached the station where a nun was standing and checking a chart.

"May I help you?"

"Well, I'm here to see a Mr. Jones and was told second floor."

The nun smiled. "You are in the right place. We were overcrowded in the general wards but had empty beds here in maternity."

"Makes sense."

The nun had never heard an American speak, but the absence of a British or Australian accent and Joe's presence to see Lewis Jones caused her to ask, "Might you be the American who rode in Mr. Jones' place?"

"I plead guilty."

"Tales of your derring-do precede you, sir. Joseph Barton, isn't it?"

Joe blushed. "That's right. And you are…"

"Sister Regina."

CHAPTER 31

"I say, gentlemen, does this look at all like Gravesend? Or merry old England?" George Britton asked rhetorically.

"Except for the water, not quite," Malcolm Goode replied. "And even the water looks different. Less smudged, shall we say?"

"And more swimmable," added Oliver Needle. "Perhaps you'll try swimming it."

The "it" to which Oliver was referring was the Johor Strait.

The three soldiers, off duty and wearing civilian clothes, were chuckling at their bon mots.

"And there's a bridge," George said mirthfully. "Of a sort."

"Rather lacking the towers of London Bridge," Oliver added with faux pomposity before giving way to another chuckle.

The "bridge" to which Oliver was referring was in fact a low-profile causeway that at 3,465 feet spanned the strait separating Singapore island from the Malay peninsula. The causeway's construction had been feasible because of the strait's shallow depth, ranging from 45 to 75 feet at low tide. Construction had begun in 1919 and it opened on June 28, 1924. Initially it boasted two railway tracks, one each for freight and passenger trains. Later a roadway for vehicles was added. A causeway instead of a bridge was chosen because it was less expensive to build and maintain.

"As I didn't quite make it across the Thames," George said self-deprecatingly, "I think I might pass on this strait. But, gentlemen, I do think we might try our luck with some fishing. Let master fisherman Needle show his stuff here in the tropics. Salt water fishing here in the strait and fresh water in one of the reservoirs. Seletar, Bedok, MacRitchie – I hear they're all well-stocked. MacRitchie's not far from our barracks."

"Fishing," mused Oliver. "It might be the most excitement we'll have here."

"You'll have your own room upstairs. Next to Alexandra's," Catherine Caradja said to Laura Ramaschi. "I hope you'll be happy here."

"I'm sure I will be. I think I must pinch myself to really believe you have brought me into your home."

They were standing in the villa's foyer that opened onto several rooms and led to the staircase.

"You'll be kept busy. Helping keep our home clean. Feeding the chickens, collecting eggs. Checking on the sheep, moving them from the front pasture to others. I will pay you fairly."

"You needn't, you know."

"Actually, I must," Catherine smiled. "Work must be rewarded. I wouldn't have it any other way."

"Thank you again."

Laura wanted to hug Catherine but held back. Catherine, sensing the orphan's need for affection and reassurance, stepped forward and embraced her. She could feel Laura virtually melting against her chest.

Before Laura had been released from the hospital, Catherine and Alexandra had looked into her family situation. Laura's maternal grandmother was alive but aged. She had an aunt on her father's side, but she and her husband had four children, little money and were clearly reluctant to take on caring for another child. Catherine first thought of placing Laura in one of the Saint Catherine's Crib orphanages. But Alexandra then had said that having Laura in one of the bedrooms previously occupied by her deceased sisters would be a welcome change.

"If you would like to redecorate your new room, that would be fine," Catherine told Laura. "We want you to be absolutely comfortable with it."

"It is already feeling like home."

The baby was sucking contentedly and Maureen Alston Nelson was smiling. She had given birth to Corrine on April 1, 1941, or about 16 months after Maureen and Sam's wedding. Nursing Corrine hadn't come easily at first, but both daughter and mother now had the hang of providing and consuming nature's maternal food supply.

Maureen was in a reflective mood and her thoughts turned to Joe. I wonder if he ever thinks of me anymore. She was rocking gently back and forth in the wooden chair that was a prized family possession. More than 50 years had passed since Maureen's maternal grandfather had made it. Sam's a good husband, she reminded herself, and he helps with changing diapers and bathing Corrine after he gets home from work. And I know that Dad will see to it that Sam's career at the Mutual keeps going well. He's steady. And I know he'll never leave Shelby. But now and then – like right now – I ask myself if I'll ever get completely over Joe. Corrine had stopped sucking and Maureen shifted the baby to her left shoulder and began patting her back to generate a burp. I honestly don't know. He was my first love. My greatest, if I'm honest about it. Being with him was so exciting. So much fun. I loved laughing with him. Okay, Maureen, snap out of this, she commanded herself. Concentrate on the here and now. Got that? Good.

At her desk in the embassy, Gabriella was composing a cable.

Dear Ambassador Gunther,

Hope this finds you doing well. All fine here. Might be seeing you sooner than expected. Picture for Romania not promising. Feeling need to return Bucharest.

Sincerely,

Gabriella Balas

CHAPTER 32

Joe was walking north from Collyer Quay and thinking about home – Shelby – and Washington – Gabriella. It was a mid-November day in Singapore and Joe was dressed appropriately for an off-duty outing – white cotton pants, white shirt open at the neck and boater. He almost went sans socks but pulled on argyles. His loafers were brown.

If I was back in Ohio or D.C., he reminded himself, the air would probably have the feel of winter. Maybe some morning frost on the ground. I miss that. Here I'm in shirtsleeves – short ones. This will be my first Thanksgiving here. I wonder if the staff is planning anything special. If they are I can count on Rosalie to let me know. She's a heck of a woman. I'm a little surprised she's still single. Of course, look at me. Nobody forced me to come here. To leave Gabriella behind. I wouldn't be surprised if Rosalie left behind a broken heart. It's easy to imagine a man falling for her. I wonder if she'll stay single and make a career of the Foreign Service. Maybe I'll find a way to ask her. Without seeming overly nosey. Yeah, right. She's never asked me about Gabriella, and she sees all those envelopes from the Romanian embassy. She's no doubt curious but clearly respects my privacy. Restraint and discretion. Two more of her good qualities.

That conversation with self ended only when Joe arrived at the polo pony stables. He had phoned Preston York on Friday to ask whether the offer made after the polo match remained open indefinitely and if it was limited to a single outing. When Joe had mentioned a Sunday morning ride, York told him that a stable hand would be waiting to saddle the pony of his choice.

At the stables entrance Joe shook hands with Martin Sandler who led the way to the stalls. "We have lots of horses stabled here," the young man said. "It's a pleasure caring for them."

"Your duties?"

"The lot. Feeding, watering, grooming, exercising. Keep the tack clean. The pony stalls are down this way on the right.

"Why don't we go with Mr. York's? It's his offer."

"Good choice," Sandler said cheerily. With efficient movements, he blanketed, saddled and bridled the horse, a gelding.

"What's his name?" Joe asked.

"Colonizer." Joe's reaction was visceral. His head rocked back and then his lips pursed wryly. "Mr. York has a sense of whimsy"

"Evidently."

Colonizer was proving a boon companion. Joe was walking him placidly northwest on Upper Thompson Road. "I'd like to see the island's north shore, boy," Joe said aloud. "It's several miles but I know you're in excellent condition. We're in no hurry, are we? We'll take a look at the causeway and then start back. How does that sound? You should be back in your stall in time for evening chow."

The farther they proceeded from the city the more beautiful the island became. Long stretches of jungle greenery flanked the road. They passed small farms. The growing season here must be endless, Joe was thinking. And the livestock – mostly chickens and pigs – certainly look well fed. On the left Colonizer and Joe passed by Lower Peirce Reservoir.

The last road they traveled was Marsiling, and ahead Joe could see the blue of Johor Strait. "Almost there, boy," he murmured, stroking Colonizer's neck.

At the shoreline Joe looked left and saw the causeway. He also saw three men standing at the water's edge. They were wearing knee-length shorts, open neck shirts and straw hats with brims broader than his boater's. They had removed their shoes and socks that lay behind them. Parked at the roadside was a small truck. All three were holding fishing rods with reels, and Joe saw one of the men cast his line expertly. "He knows what he's doing, Colonizer. Let's take a closer look."

Oliver Needle was the first to notice Colonizer approaching. "Take a look," he said to George Britton and Malcolm Goode. "Wonder if he's one of our cavalry lads. I understand the Army still keeps a small contingent of horse."

"They can't stand up to tanks," George said thoughtfully, "but then they can go places tankers can only dream about. And horses don't burn petrol. Of course," he added whimsically, "their exhaust must be tidied up."

Malcolm rolled his eyes. "A weekend witticism from Mr. Britton."

"There's something odd about him," Oliver said. "He somehow doesn't look British."

"What do you mean?" George asked.

"I'm not certain. He just doesn't look like one of ours."

"Perhaps," George joshed, "we should ask him if he has a bearskin hat back at barracks."

As Colonizer neared the men, Joe raised his right hand to his boater's brim and tossed off a casual salute.

"There! See," said Oliver with a tone of vindication. "That's no British salute." Indeed, Joe's greeting had been the palm-down American-style salute, not the British palm-forward.

"Howdy." Joe smiled warmly.

"Need any more evidence?" Oliver nudged George with his right elbow.

"Hello."

"Any luck?"

George pointed to a covered, perforated metal bucket in the water. "Got a few."

Joe dismounted and stepped toward the men, right arm extended. "Joe Barton's my name."

"George Britton – East Surrey Regiment." He took Joe's hand and they shook briefly but firmly. "These are my friends – Oliver Needle and Malcolm Goode."

"Pleased to meet you," Joe said, shaking hands with each.

"Likewise, Mr. Barton," Oliver said. "Where are you quartered?"

"Collyer Quay."

"Not military?"

"No. Foreign Service."

"Long ride. Handsome horse."

"Belongs to one of your colonial officials. A polo player."

"You're an experienced rider," Oliver observed. "I could tell by the way you sat the horse. You were confident and comfortable."

"Thanks. Been riding for years. In the saddle and bareback as well."

"Bareback?" George said. "Sounds dicey."

"Not nearly as dangerous as living in England. I'm really sorry about what your countrymen are enduring. The bombings, the fires…"

"Frankly," said George, "we were a bit surprised to be sent out here. What with the Jerrys perched on the other side of the Channel. Maybe we'll get sent back. As it is we're so far from home and the war in Europe, well, we feel like we're beyond the shadows of war."

"Understandable," said Joe. "Let's hope it stays quiet here. And let's hope Hitler decides to stay on his side of the Channel."

"It appears he's given up invading us. Now he seems intent on bombing us into submission. But if he changes his mind, do you think America will come to our assistance?" George asked.

Joe shrugged. "If he does try jumping the Channel and gains a foothold, I'm afraid it would be too late."

"So true."

"I will tell you that opinion in America is divided. Some want to take on Hitler. After all, we are a nation of immigrants, and many are from countries Hitler has conquered. But others want no part of fighting another war in Europe."

"Isolationist. We've heard the term," George said. "And you? If you don't mind me asking?"

"Hitler needs to be stopped and his troops sent packing from occupied countries. If it were up to me, we'd be sending men and more equipment to England now."

"We appreciate your sentiments."

"Not at all. Well, gentlemen, we live in the here and now. So let's hope peace prevails in Singapore."

"Tis a slice of paradise," George smiled. He removed his hat and wiped his brow with a kerchief. "A decidedly warm and humid one. But when the sun is shining and the greenery glistening, the good Lord can't have painted many prettier pictures."

"Agreed. Well, I guess I should be starting back." Joe extended his right arm, and this time the shakes came faster and with noticeably more enthusiasm. "It's been a pleasure. Maybe our paths will cross again."

"Do you fish, Mr. Barton?" Oliver asked.

"Used to. It's been several years since I last baited a hook."

"From now on," Oliver said, "we'll bring an extra rod with us, just in case."

"Or you could alert me. Phone me at the consulate."

"You just might hear from us."

"If I do, call me Joe."

He inserted his left foot in the stirrup and sprang onto the saddle. He tossed off another salute and pulled on the reins. Colonizer pivoted and began heading back down Marsiling Road.

"First yank I've met," said Oliver. "Seems a decent chap."

"Let's hope more Americans begin thinking the way he does," George said pensively.

"Has an interesting face, don't you agree?" said Oliver.

"You mean his birthmark and scar?" George said. Oliver nodded. "He's not the kind of bloke who's easy to forget."

CHAPTER 33

At Grider Field south of Pine Bluff, Jeff Wolfrom was turning heads. Not with his flying which was fine but with his shooting ability that was exceptional. Jeff's accuracy with his late father's .22 caliber rifle had carried over to firing Browning machine guns – the kind used on U.S. Army Air Corps bombers. Jeff's mastery came despite the challenge of handling a Browning. His description: "It's like firing a horizontal jackhammer." In combat simulations Jeff had topped all other trainees.

"Son," a training officer gravely told Jeff, "your vision is keen. Keen enough to pilot. Your hand-eye coordination is superior. But your gunnery skills are truly remarkable. Best I've seen. I know your heart's been set on piloting, but we need crack gunners on our bomber crews. Keep enemy fighters at bay."

It was Monday afternoon, December 1. Jeff maintained eye contact with the officer. "Is this an order, sir?"

"Frankly, no. If you insisted, we would let you continue with pilot training. But as a gunner a crew would be depending on you to save their lives and their plane."

"So do you expect we'll be at war?"

"I'm not smart enough to know when but, yes, I think sooner or later America will take on Hitler."

Jeff sighed. "All right, sir. I'll do the Army's bidding."

In Hong Kong, west of the International Date Line, it was December 2. British intelligence officials based there were intercepting radio signals indicating that a Japanese attack – of some kind somewhere – was imminent. They felt certain the initial target would be in southern Asia and cabled London with their findings. London, preoccupied with continuing air raids on England and its war against the Germans in North Africa, pooh-poohed the possibility.

That same week British intelligence learned that Japanese troop transport vessels had been reported steaming south. They were sighted in the Gulf of Thailand – then called the Gulf of Siam since at that time Thailand was named Siam. The report put the fleet about 185 miles north of Kota Bahru, a Malay city just south of the Thai border on the long, narrow Malay peninsula.

Once again British officials discounted the report's significance. On December 8 – December 7 in the United States – Japanese forces would use Kota Bahru as a major landing site.

George Britton, Oliver Needle and Malcolm Goode had arranged another fishing outing, this one at MacRitchie Reservoir where their aim was fresh water catches. Once again they had the use of a small British Army truck – which they were finding easy to secure as long as they promised to share their watery harvest with a certain quartermaster officer.

The fourth rod they brought was being put to use by Joe Barton. George had phoned Joe who was eager to try his luck. Once again he had arrived on Colonizer and the ride northwest from the stables to MacRitchie Reservoir was much shorter – fewer than five miles – than had been the ride to the Johor Strait.

When Joe dismounted he was holding a brown leather satchel. He placed it on the ground in front of the three soldiers. "One of our fishing traditions calls for drinking beer." Joe bent down and opened the satchel. "Eight bottles. Two each."

"Well done," George said, beaming. "This is a tradition that might catch on among us Brits."

"I also brought some twine." He removed it from the satchel. "We'll tie it around the necks of the bottles and then place them in the water to get cooled. Better that way."

It was Sunday, December 7 in Singapore, still Saturday December 6 in Hawaii.

"I really appreciated your invitation," Joe told the three British soldiers. They were reclining on the reservoir's gently sloping banks. Shading them and surrounding the water was thick forest. The men were sipping their first beers. "Would you mind telling me a bit about yourselves? Why you joined the Army."

"Not all that much to tell," said George. "But if you insist on being bored, we'll accommodate you."

Hours later near five o'clock, the fishermen were pleased. Fourteen catches, cool beers, relaxed conversation and tree shade were forging bonds they all could feel and they felt good.

"You supplied the beer," said George. "We want you to take a few fish back. Put someone to work in your consulate's kitchen."

"That's not necessary," Joe replied.

"Of course it isn't," George smiled. "But you can't deny that some fried fresh fish would make a pleasant repast. We can use your twine. Tie it around the fish tails and you can hang them from your pommel. I don't think Colonizer will object too strenuously."

Laughter, the easy kind heard among friends, punctuated the outing.

"All right," Joe grinned. "Your argument is persuasive. When do you think we might do this again?"

That same afternoon, Lieutenant General Tomoyuki Yamashita, commanding the Japanese 25th Army, was standing on the bridge of the lead transport. He was sipping tea. "I have told Tokyo it will take us one hundred days to fight our way down the Malay peninsula, cross the Johor Strait and take Singapore. Our leadership was pleased with that assessment."

"As they should have been," said Yamashita's executive officer, Kuniaki Fusa. "That is a very ambitious timetable."

Yamashita smiled wryly. "What I didn't tell them is that it won't take us that long. Not nearly that long."

Fusa's eyes widened in surprise. "Why, sir?"

"It is always wiser to under promise and over deliver. I think we can do it in about seventy-five days. Perhaps eighty."

"Why are you so optimistic?"

"Arrogance. British arrogance. They see Asian peoples as inferior. Chinese, Indians, Malayans. No doubt they view Japanese the same way. No matter that our cultures are older and in many ways more advanced. Never mind that we have made much technological progress. Or that we Japanese defeated Russia early in this century and are overwhelming China as we speak. To the British we Asians are small, weak and incompetent."

"They hold us in contempt."

"Precisely."

One thought amused Fusa. Yes, Yamashita is short. But weak? He has the build of a water buffalo and the determination of a bulldog. His shaved head reflects a Samurai's fierceness. And incompetent? I almost feel sorry for the British.

CHAPTER 34

Sister Regina sat bolt upright. The explosions, one after another in rapid succession, puzzled her but only for fleeting moments. Lim Bo Seng was right, she recalled, her mind racing, the Japanese are attacking. She reached for the chain on the bedside reading lamp and pulled down. In the light, she blinked twice and looked at the clock. 3 a.m.

Nineteen hours. That was the time difference between Pearl Harbor and Singapore. Sunday, December 7 at 8 a.m. in Hawaii was 3 a.m. on Monday, December 8 in Singapore.

The other nuns were waking groggily, shuffling from their rooms, and Sister Regina quickly convened a meeting in their living room. "Pull yourselves together," she said briskly. "The patients must be frightened. As we are. Get to the hospital and comfort them. New mothers first. Bombs mean casualties so let's be sure everything is ready for emergency admittances."

"Who? Who is dropping bombs?" Sister Grace Ann asked dazedly.

"Japan, I feel sure."

"But why?"

Sister Regina remembered Lim's words. "They want to control Singapore's port facilities. They see them as key to controlling all of east Asia. Now, let's get across the drive and get busy."

City lights were on in Singapore, making the city an easy target for Japanese bombardiers. They faced no opposition, not in the air or from the ground. The city employee with the key to the master switches at the electric plant was watching a late movie in a neighborhood theater.

British radar operators had been tracking incoming planes, but it didn't occur to them that they might be enemy aircraft. Their assumption: British planes arriving at Sembawang Airfield on the island's north coast about four miles east of the causeway. In fact, the planes were long-range Japanese Mitsubishi G3Ms and G4Ms based in Japanese occupied Indochina.

Joe Barton and the consulate staff were jolted awake. He dressed quickly – the same clothes he'd worn fishing the day before – and exited his room. He saw Rosalie and others entering the hallway.

"Get downstairs fast," he shouted. "Get yourselves under a desk."

Rosalie, barefoot and still in a lightweight linen nightgown, went scampering for the staircase. She reached back and grabbed Joe's hand. "Come on," she urged him.

"Just a sec. Make sure everyone's up."

Moments later the staff all were accounted for on the ground floor. "Get under desks and stay away from windows," Joe said. "Broken glass could be as deadly as knives."

Joe then started toward the consulate entrance.

"Where are you going?" Rosalie called, her anxiety evident.

"To check on friends."

Joe was breathing hard when he arrived at Duane Hurd's sampan. He had completed the run – about six tenths of a mile – in little more than three minutes. "You awake?" he shouted down to the boat.

At the boat's stern Duane peeked from behind the canvass covering. "It isn't safe to be out, you know," he grinned. "This isn't a Chinese New Year fireworks show."

Joe placed hands on hips and sucked in air. "These have to be Japanese planes. I was afraid the waterfront would be a major target."

"Yes, but more likely Keppel Harbor than Marina Bay. That would be a better military target. But I'm touched by your concern. Has the consulate been hit?" Duane placed his hands on the promenade and vaulted up from his boat.

"Not when I left."

"The bombs seem to be falling everywhere. I need to check on my parents."

"Right." A pause, then an idea. "The polo ponies are stabled just a couple blocks from here. I'll borrow one and ride to your parents' house."

Duane nodded. "All right. I'll go to Collyer Quay. Wait for you outside the consulate."

"Okay."

"Joe."

"What?"

"This could be interesting. I'm sure the British brass expects to pummel the Japanese. Do you think they are too sure of themselves?"

With minutes after the first bombs detonated, Lieutenant General Sir Arthur E. Percival was telephoning Shenton Thomas. His wife Daisy, first to waken, took the call and roused her husband. Percival, trim and mustachioed, was general officer, commanding British and Australian forces in Singapore and on the Malayan peninsula. Thomas was colonial governor, a post he had occupied since 1934.

"These bombs are only a prelude," Percival told Thomas.

"You are expecting a naval attack?"

"Very likely. And possibly an amphibious assault."

"Well," Thomas said smugly, "I suppose you'll have to shove the little men off."

Aussie Major General Gordon Bennett, a wiry man, was equally dismissive. "Let the Japs come. They'll soon know my name, and we'll give the little fellows a flogging they won't forget." Bennett commanded the Australian 8th Division, and his men shared his confidence. Bennett reported to Percival whose boss was General Archibald Wavell, commander-in-chief, Far East. Both Percival and Wavell saw the threat more direly than Thomas and Bennett.

Aboard one of General Yamashita's transports, Etsuro Yamada, Kai Hata and Takuma Matsui were feeling anything but brash.

"An amphibious landing in the dark. Even if there's no shooting we could drown," Hata said quietly. The sound of their vessel plowing through the sea was doing little to assuage his worries.

"We have lived through much," Matsui added. "How much more?"

"You always think too much," Yamada chided him nervously. "Just follow orders."

"You know it's difficult for me to do some of the things you do," Matsui replied softly, his shoulders slumping forward, seeming to shrink his five feet seven inches to match Yamada's five feet five.

"You mean killing?"

"I can kill. In combat. You know that. But murder and rape? That's something else."

"The emperor demands it," Yamada said grimly.

"Really?"

"You doubt our emperor's commands. Remember, he is a deity."

"What I doubt are the ways his words are interpreted and passed along to us."

"You shouldn't trouble yourself with doubts."

By dawn Yamada, Hata and Matsui would be among 30,000 Japanese troops safely ashore at Kota Bahru. Why there? On the Malayan peninsula, it was the site of a British air base, and the Japanese quickly would over-run it.

Joe was comforting Colonizer with softly spoken words as they proceeded south toward Chinatown. Scattered bombs were detonating, startling both rider and horse. Several times Colonizer neighed and reared, testing Joe's horsemanship.

Joe kept the horse firmly reined while watching for craters and debris as they moved south on South Bridge Road. He saw few people in the street, and those who saw him were surprised by the apparition clip-clopping past on the rubble-strewn pavement.

Entering Chinatown Joe saw a shophouse on the street's west or right side explode in flames. Colonizer again reared in fright. Joe heard screams, winced, but kept moving. He turned Colonizer right into Pagoda Street and then quickly left on Tregganu Street. Here the darkness was unbroken, and Joe slowed the horse, not wanting to miss the Hurds' mint green shophouse.

He dismounted and walked slowly until recognizing their home. They must be awake, he told himself. No one could be sleeping through this.

Still grasping the reins with his left hand, he knocked lightly on the door.

A long minute passed and the door eased open.

"Mr. Hurd. It's me. Joe Barton. I came to see if you and Mrs. Hurd are all right."

The door opened wider. "Come in, please."

"Just a second. I rode a horse here. Let me tie him."

"Use the handle on our door."

Joe did so and stepped inside. "Let's leave the door open so the horse can see me."

He and Clayton Hurd shook hands. Su Mien was standing by a tea room table. She had lit two red candles. Clayton moved to her side. Joe bowed to her.

"What is happening?" Clayton asked.

"I think World War Two just arrived in Singapore. We won't know for sure till dawn, but I'm betting the Japanese are bombing us."

"Many innocent people are probably dying tonight," Su Mien said sadly.

"I've seen Duane. He is fine. He will be waiting for me on the quay at the U.S. Consulate."

"Thank you for coming," Su Mien said, voice unsteady. "We were so worried."

"Is it safe there?" Clayton asked.

"To be honest," said Joe, "I'm not sure if any place is safe tonight."

Two more explosions detonated, one clearly closer than the other, and all three flinched.

"Did you see any damage on your way here?" Su Mien asked.

"On South Bridge Road I saw some buildings burning." Joe chose to omit adding anything about victims' screams.

"I think we'll stay here," said Clayton.

"You could come with me. I could put you both on my horse and walk with you to our consulate."

"Thank you, Joe," Su Mien said gratefully. "But I agree with my husband. As you said, no place is really safe tonight. Please tell Duane we are fine and there is no need for him to come tonight."

Joe nodded. "All right. I will." He then looked around the room. "I would feel better if you stayed under a table or in a doorway. Until the bombing ends."

In the ghostly light from the flickering candles, Joe could see husband and wife smiling kindly. "We will take your advice, Joe."

"Good. Don't go outside unless your house is damaged or threatened by fire."

"We will stay inside."

Joe bowed. "I should be going." He turned toward the open door where he could see Colonizer fidgeting.

"Joe." It was Clayton's voice and Joe stopped and turned to face it. "You are a good man."

By dawn word of the Japanese landing at Kota Bahru had reached the East Surrey Regiment.

George Britton's reaction was predictably grim. "Gentlemen," he muttered to Oliver Needle and Malcolm Goode, "I think the war's shadow is about to reach us."

"Do you think the Japs can defeat our forces in Malaya?" Oliver asked, his thick eyebrows seeming to add weight to the question.

"I don't know. But it's not as if we Brits have never lost a battle or campaign. We've taken our bruisings in Afghanistan and South Africa. Not to mention a former colony called America. In Malaya, perhaps the Japs will have our lads outnumbered. Or out-tanked."

"If they do," Oliver asked pensively, "how long do you think our men in Malaya can hold on?"

"You mean if they can hold on at all?" George replied dubiously.

"You doubt our fighting ability?"

"Are you forgetting Dunkirk?"

"But those were Germans."

"And you're thinking the Japs aren't the measure of the Jerrys?"

"Do you?" Oliver asked.

"I know they defeated the Russkies and the Chinese," George said patiently. "We don't know how many of them will be pushing south. We don't know how much artillery they have or how many tanks. We learned earlier this morning about their bombers."

"So," said Malcolm, "we sit here and wait to find out."

George grinned. "If we are to use our fishing gear again, I think it will be north of the strait. No, I don't think we'll be afforded the luxury, so to speak, of sitting and waiting."

"You think," Malcolm said, "that we'll be aboard lorries crossing the causeway? Going to meet the Japs up north?"

"Precisely."

United States newspapers were emphasizing the Japanese attack on Pearl Harbor with huge front-page headlines, and radio networks were on the air with nearly continuous newscasts, most based on dispatches from Associated Press, United Press and International News Service. Scant attention in the west was being given to the virtually simultaneous Japanese assaults on Singapore, Malaya and Philippines. They were being covered almost as afterthoughts.

In Shelby that Sunday afternoon, Marie Hughes heard the radio bulletin. Moments later she slipped into a coat and pulled on black leather gloves. She stepped out onto the porch of her Grand Boulevard home, stood for a full minute and descended five wooden steps. She then walked slowly on the long, narrow cement walkway to the wider sidewalk paralleling the street. She turned and looked at her home. It was one of the smaller houses on Grand Boulevard, and her means were significantly more modest than most of its residents. But she loved it as she loved her neighborhood and its proximity to Seltzer Park. Only a row of houses immediately behind her backyard and Parkwood Drive beyond separated Miss Hughes' home from the park. As she stood facing her house, behind her on the narrow tree lawn was a green metal streetlight pole topped by a glass globe. She found the scene pleasing to eye and spirit.

As virtually always, beneath her coat Miss Hughes was wearing a dark dress – navy blue on this Sunday that had begun with church services – and a single strand of pearls. Her shoes were made for standing – which as a teacher she did much – and walking. They were black, sturdy with wide heels and laces.

Still facing the houses, she turned right, walked a short distance and then turned left and headed into Seltzer Park. Miss Hughes found the park a comforting oasis. A creek ran placidly through it and connected two sizable ponds. Ducks glided on their surfaces. An island sprouted in the larger pond and a small, white wooden footbridge connected it with the shore. Numerous tall shade trees graced the park.

She was thinking of boys she had taught who might have been stationed at Pearl Harbor, and in particular she was worrying about Joe Barton in Singapore. Joe, I hope you aren't regretting taking my advice to seek a life far beyond Shelby. Miss Hughes walked to the larger pond and stepped onto the small footbridge, slightly inclined to its center peak. The span was about 20 feet long. She crossed, stopped beside the island's lone tree and surveyed the water's still surface and the far shore. This small island feels so peaceful, she mused, so wonderfully tranquil and safe. I hope you can stay safe on your larger island, Joe. I am praying for your safety and that of my other boys in uniform.

Not far – about a quarter mile – from Seltzer Park on West Maxwell Drive, Maureen Nelson and her husband Sam also had heard the radio bulletins. Sam was stretched out on the living room floor, entertaining little Corrine with noisy plastic rattles and a spinning metal top.

Maureen was rocking gently in the old wooden chair and entertaining troubling thoughts. How will this war end? How will this war change my future? Will I still be a wife when it's over? Or a widow? My God, what a frightening thought. Alone with a child. What man would want us? I better not get pregnant again. I wonder if Dad can keep Sam out of the service? I wonder if Sam would let him try. And Joe, so far from home. I hope he can avoid danger. Sometimes I wish I could stop thinking about him. But I can't. I just can't.

On that Sunday afternoon in northern Virginia, across the Potomac River from Washington, Gabriella Balas was astride a spirited mare. She was riding along a quiet paved road and thinking alternately of Joe and her homeland. The air was just brisk enough for rider and horse to be expelling visible breaths.

A gleaming 1937 black Hudson Terraplane – dubbed so by aviatrix Amelia Earhart – with silver trim passed them and some 75 yards ahead pulled to roadside and stopped. Gabriella wondered if the car had died. Engine trouble? Broken fan belt? She continued riding until the mare was even with the car's driver.

He looked up, saw them and lowered the car window.

"Sir, are you all right? Are you having car problems?"

The man's head was shaking in dismay. "Have you heard? The news?" Before Gabriella could reply, the man continued. "I can't believe it. I… This is terrible."

"What, sir?"

"The Japanese have attacked Pearl Harbor. This morning."

"Pearl Harbor?"

"Our big naval base in Hawaii. Sounds like we've lost lots of ships, planes and men. My God, the Japanese could be steaming for California already."

Hawaii, Gabriella knew, was thousands of miles east of Singapore. If the Japanese take and occupy Hawaii, could Joe get back home? This war is spreading like a contagion. Come on, girl, I've got to get you back to your stables and get to the embassy and find out what's going on. Cables must be pouring in.

Gabriella tugged smartly on the reins, wheeling the mare to her left. Her booted feet kicked the horse's flanks, and she began galloping toward the stables.

In his home's spacious sitting room, Ion Antonescu was pacing excitedly. At 2 p.m. that Sunday in Washington, it was 9 p.m. in Romania. Word of Japan's attacks in the Pacific was welcome news for Antonescu and his cabinet – and to Hitler in Berlin. America will be certain to retaliate against Japan, Antonescu concluded quickly. That lessens our worries of the U.S. coming to Britain's defense and virtually eliminates any chance that America might try to liberate western Europe. This calls for a special nightcap. A celebratory toast. From a side table Antonescu picked up a bottle of his favorite plum brandy and poured generously. He sipped, smacked his lips, smiled and mused, I don't think brandy has ever tasted better.

In her manor house near Nedelea, Catherine Caradja's reaction was more measured. In her parlor she had been listening to the radio with daughter Alexandra and the newly arrived Laura Ramaschi.

"Japan," said Alexandra, "I know nothing about it. It must be powerful to be attacking the United States. Such a strong country. What do you think this means for us?"

All three were sitting on chairs positioned near the fireplace. Warming them were burning logs taken from the nearby, thickly forested Carpathian foothills.

"This could be good for Romania – or disastrous," Catherine began. "America is not interested in conquering and occupying other nations. Not permanently. Yes, it holds some lands taken during its war with Spain about forty years ago. But by and large Americans aren't colonizers. If America had any intention of trying to rescue France or the Low Countries, war with Japan will be a major distraction. Under no circumstance can I foresee America coming to Poland's aid. Or Russia's. There are Polish immigrants in America, but the distance is too long and obstacles too great and too many for America to fight in eastern Europe. I say this because I have lived in the West and have a feel for America's relations with France and the Low Countries. Without France, America probably wouldn't have won its independence from England. And America showed its willingness to help France in the First World War."

"How could Japan's attack on that place – Pearl Harbor – be disastrous for Romania?" Laura asked.

"Stupidity. Stupidity by Hitler. If he somehow does something to really provoke America, America might decide our oil fields and refineries would be too important – too tempting – to ignore. Hitler is already depending on them for much of his fuel. About one third, I'm told."

"What do you mean?" Laura asked. "What do you think America would do?"

"Bomb them. Bomb our oil fields. From the air."

On that Sunday Jeff Wolfrom was home from his training at Grider Field and was savoring a home-cooked supper with Iris Ann and eight of her boarders. It was a little after 6 p.m. Jeff was in uniform, trousers crisply creased, jacket pressed. The dinner table conversation was anything but jovial.

"Young man," said one of the boarders, a Union Pacific engineer and a World War I veteran, "you should be proud to be wearing that uniform."

"I am."

"Good."

"How do you think this dastardly Japanese sneak attack will affect you and your future?"

The engineer's question rattled Iris Ann and she nearly dropped her coffee cup. She had been asking herself the same question since hearing the first radio bulletin.

Jeff put down his dessert fork and picked up a napkin to dab at his lips. He was relishing consuming a slice of pie made from blackberries Iris Ann had canned in late summer. "I can't be sure, sir. We will probably have to rebuild our Pacific fleet before we can get back at Japan. And Japan seems like it's created a buffer zone by attacking the Philippines, Malaya and Singapore."

Listening to Jeff's words, Iris Ann was experiencing acute ambivalence. She was startled but pleasantly so by his thoughtful response. She was more than willing to credit his military training for adding to his maturity and wisdom. But she also sensed – to a far more worrisome degree – that he would in fact find himself high in the air and very much in harm's way. Briefly she wondered how many other American mothers were experiencing the same emotions at this very moment.

CHAPTER 35

"Are you sure, Sam? I mean, there is so much to think about."

"Honey, I spent the whole night staring at the ceiling," he replied. "It's the right thing to do. I hate the idea of being away from you and Corrine. Hate it. I know things could be hard for you. But I'm also thinking that your mom and dad will be more than willing to pitch in."

It was Monday morning, December 8, and they were sitting at their small kitchen table. Corrine was sleeping in her crib in her pink-walled bedroom. Maureen sighed. She knew Sam was right about her parents. And they would be proud of Sam for volunteering. A doubt was nagging at her, though. One man already had walked away from her and a second soon would. Maureen knew she was pretty, vivacious and intelligent, and she had returned to her pre-pregnancy weight. But, briefly, she questioned her charms.

"I'm proud of you, dear. I want you to know that." She pushed her chair back from the table and stood. She stepped to Sam's side, bent her five feet three inches forward and kissed his right cheek. "And I love you."

On that same day, Adolf Hitler did what Catherine Caradja regarded as utter stupidity. He declared war on the United States.

I have friends in England, France and Belgium, Catherine was reflecting, but I wish I had some – even just one – in America. I would love to learn first hand how ordinary Americans are viewing Japan's attacks and Hitler's foolishness.

I am Romanian, but I am thinking more like an American. Gabriella smiled and gently shook her head in amusement. She was at her desk in the embassy on that Monday. She picked up a fountain pen and began writing on paper embossed with Romania's crest.

December 8, 1941
Dear Joe,

You remember Alice Manescu, our embassy receptionist. She openly admits to having a love affair with America. Her "disease" must be contagious. I think I am having the same affair. No country is perfect, God knows that. But America is less imperfect than most and stands so strongly for what is good. How many other nations have a large statue that with open arms welcomes strangers from all over the world? And Americans are so friendly. Your Romanian gypsy has never felt belittled or threatened. Just the opposite. Americans have shown me amazing courtesies. Yes, I love your country. Which is not to say I no longer love Romania. I do and always will. But America occupies a large and warm spot in my heart and I want you to know that.

I know this letter will take ages to reach you and perhaps longer now that the Japanese are invading Malaya. Stay safe, Joe.

I love you.
Gabriella

The next day, December 9, in Singapore British officials took their first anti-Japanese action. They interned Japan's ambassador, Suermasa Okomoto, and other Japanese officials and civilians – mostly merchants and traders – at Changi Prison at the island's eastern end. Later they would be released and deported to India.

CHAPTER 36

The consulate staff was a disheveled group. It was 6:30 a.m. and none had managed more than a catnap since the bombs began falling three and a half hours earlier. Joe, with his birthmark and scar, a day's growth of stubble and hair in need of washing, had the look of a back alley thug. All save Consul-General Kenneth Patton were gathered near Rosalie's reception desk. He had not yet arrived from his Spring Grove cottage. He hadn't phoned, but the hour was early and no one could be sure that his phone line was intact – unless someone tried reaching him and that could wait a while longer.

"For the time being," Consul Clayson Aldridge said, "it might be best to stay put and see what the morning brings. Things are no doubt chaotic. We've received no cables from Washington. I do expect to receive queries from some if not all the American companies with operations here and throughout the region. If they can reach us. I doubt if we'll have many answers. I suggest that we all get a bite to eat and try to get a little sleep before things get hectic – if they do."

Joe pushed his right hand back through his dirty brown hair. "Sir, I think it might be wise to get a firsthand look at the damage, at least here in the center of town and down at the harbor." His words were holding everyone's attention. "With your permission I'd like to set out on foot, do a little reconnaissance. We'd be better able to answer questions and maybe cable a report to Washington."

All eyes shifted toward Aldridge for his reaction.

"Sharp thinking, Joe. Just be careful."

"Yes, sir." Then he grinned tiredly. "Before I head out I think I'll grab a quick cup of coffee. A little jolt of caffeine for fuel."

Rosalie nearly vaulted from her chair. "I'll get the coffee going straight away." A pause before she walked to the kitchen. "Joe, if it's okay with you and Mr. Aldridge, I'd like to go with you. Two pairs of eyes, you know. Just give me a few minutes to dress."

Bombs had exploded, streets were cratered, buildings had burned or been pocked by shrapnel, people had died, some slowly and horribly. In some neighborhoods, the smell of bloating corpses, quick to decay in the equatorial climate, was accenting the acrid odor of smoldering ruins.

Yet Joe and Rosalie saw British residents strolling streets, shopping and reading The Straits Times edition that was printed before the attack. Immersed in news of yesterday's now seemingly irrelevant happenings, they were sipping tea or coffee.

Rosalie pointed to cars parked in front of the Singapore Cricket Club, and Joe led the way. He wasn't a member but no one questioned his entrance or his presence inside. His renown gained on the polo grounds assured his welcome. He saw several British and other Europeans lounging on leather chairs and sofas. The early hour notwithstanding, they were sipping brandy and smoking cigars. One Englishman, attired in white - suit, shirt, shoes – accented by a blue- and black-striped regimental necktie and dark socks – proclaimed stoutly, "We'll hold out like Malta. After all, we are the Gibraltar of the East."

Joe turned toward Rosalie and rolled his eyes upward. The man was alluding to British-built defenses that included a large naval base, four airfields and impressive batteries of heavy artillery, all positioned to thwart amphibious landings on the island's east, west and south coasts. Fort Siloso on a small island just off Singapore island's south coast was a classic example. It bristled with large guns, howitzers and huge mortars dating to the 1860s. Such defenses along the north coast, separated from the Malayan peninsula by the narrow Johor Strait, were conspicuous by their absence.

Joe motioned to Rosalie to follow him outside.

"A trifle cocky, wouldn't you say?" she observed.

"I just might."

Later they found themselves walking past Cold Storage, a popular food emporium catering mainly to European and American ex-patriots. It was doing its usual brisk business, but nothing extraordinary. No customers rushing to stock up on staples. None asking for lanterns or gas lamps in case of power outages.

Heading south into Chinatown, Joe and Rosalie were picking their way through debris. Joe stubbed his right toe and began pitching forward.

Rosalie – nine inches shorter than Joe's six feet – grabbed his arm, and the 100-pound woman kept the 185-pound man from falling.

"Nice catch," Joe grinned. "I'm glad you're on our team."

They saw many Chinese venturing from their shophouses into the narrow, bomb-pocked streets where they were setting up charcoal burners and cast iron woks. Soon they were preparing fish on beds of bean sprouts and seaweed, rice blended with fish and vegetables, and noodles in rich, dark sauces. Others were using rubble as kindling to build cook fires above which they suspended cauldrons soon simmering with broth. The aromas became more enticing when they dropped in pork and water chestnut dumplings.

A Chinese woman saw Joe and Rosalie approaching slowly and beckoned to them in English. "Please, have something to eat."

Rosalie looked up at Joe. "It's getting on and we've had nothing to eat since dinner last night."

In Rosalie's tone Joe thought he detected a hint of a plea. His down-turned lips amounted to a shrug of agreement.

"Thank you, ma'am," Rosalie said. "We would be delighted to share your food."

The woman's warm smile conveyed her enthusiasm. She went scurrying into her blue-hued shophouse and emerged moments later with two bowls, a ladle, chopsticks and two soupspoons.

"I'm glad you accepted her invitation," said Joe as they continued walking south. "That was a darned sight better than we'd get today at the consulate."

"That's if the consulate cook even made it in today," said Rosalie. A few moments of silence. "While we're in Chinatown, do you want to check on the Hurds again?"

"Not now. I don't want to disturb them if they're sleeping."

Elsewhere on the island, Malays and Tamils were migrating from homes and shops to their mosques and temples to pray for their safety and that of fellow Singaporeans.

In Keppel Harbor Joe and Rosalie watched small bumboats making their usual runs, carrying goods to and from larger vessels resting at anchor. Flat-bottomed sampans were carrying their owners to favorite fishing spots.

Passing by schools, Joe and Rosalie saw students outside during recess, joyously playing tag. Inside, lesson plans for the day didn't include discussions of war and its possible consequences.

Returning that afternoon to Collyer Quay, Joe and Rosalie were walking in silence. Neither found it awkward. They were digesting all they had seen and heard.

Nearing their quay, Rosalie ended the silence. "A penny for your thoughts, Joe."

"Business as usual."

"We must be rubbing the same penny. That's what I was thinking."

"Not what I expected."

"Why are they so casual, so blasé?"

"Denial is probably part of the answer. Especially among the Brits. They can't accept that the nervy Japs would be attacking *their* island. Much less that they could actually conquer it."

"Arrogance," Rosalie muttered.

"That too. Plus maybe some shock that hasn't worn off."

"Yes and some stiff upper lip. A hallmark of our British friends. Not a bad trait," she quickly added.

"Another attack might have everyone seeing the situation for what it is," said Joe.

"That being?"

"Well, I don't think the Japanese would waste tons of bombs on a one-night raid. Pearl Harbor, yes, I can see that as a hit-and-run mission. Knock out our Pacific fleet and demolish our air corps. But Singapore? That's different. I think Japan wants our port, including dry docks. Plus the four airfields. I'm betting they see Singapore either as a southern buffer to their empire or a jumping off point for more conquests. Maybe right on down to Australia."

"So you expect an invasion."

"I do. And I'm guessing sooner rather than later, or the Japanese would hold off bombing us until they were ready to land troops here. Otherwise, why tip their hand early?"

"And us? Our staff? Do you think we'll stay or leave?"

"I think the answer to that will come after Mr. Patton talks to Washington."

CHAPTER 37

Prince of Wales, Repulse, Electra, Express, Tenedos and Vampire. The six ships were dubbed Force Z. They had arrived at Singapore's north shore naval base on December 2 to the huzzahs of British colonial officials and the cheers of seamen and civilians.

With Japan's army continuing to push south, the flotilla was regarded as a deterrent to possible aggression into Malaya. In addition to Japan's conquests in China, it now had invaded closer to Malaya in French Indochina (later Vietnam). Discounted by virtually every British naval officer and elected official was a central fact: before the vessels arrived, the aircraft carrier Indomitable that was to accompany them had run aground on November 3 at the entrance to Kingston Harbor in Jamaica. Once freed, the carrier had limped to Norfolk, Virginia for repairs that required 12 days. The ship was scratched from the mission that was to continue across the Atlantic, through the Mediterranean and then to Singapore. That loss meant that, in any combat, the other ships would be lacking close air cover.

Prince of Wales, completed in March 1941, was a major source of pride for the British Navy. At 35,000 tons she was smaller than new U.S., Japanese and German battleships that had been built in violation of naval treaties limiting such vessels to the Prince of Wales tonnage. But Prince of Wales at 745 feet long and 112 feet wide was modern, fast (capable of 32 miles per hour), maneuverable and bristled with rapid-firing weaponry. Three turrets, two forward and one aft, boasted 14-inch guns. Prince of Wales also was armed with 16 5.25-inch guns. Its defensive weapons included 32 two-pound "pom-pom" cannons and 16 .50-caliber anti-aircraft machine guns. Her crew totaled 1,612 men. By contrast, Repulse was a veteran cruiser – commissioned in 1916 – crewed by 1,309 men.

Commanding Prince of Wales was Captain John Leach. Commanding Force Z and aboard Prince of Wales was Admiral Sir Tom Phillips. Square jaw, penetrating eyes and years at sea lent him a rugged countenance that reinforced his reputation as a tough, old-fashioned "battlewagon admiral." Which made all the more implausible his nickname: Tom Thumb. Reason for the sobriquet: his bald head and short – five feet four inches – stature. Just one week previous to Force Z's arrival at Singapore, Phillips had been promoted to full admiral and named commander-in-chief, Eastern Fleet.

After landing at Kota Bahru and swiftly capturing the nearby British air base and its planes, General Yamashita's 30,000 men were granted a well-earned breather. Among troops lounging on a bluff overlooking the sea were Private Etsuro Yamada, Kai Hata and Takuma Matsui.

"So far so good," said Hata, stretching his arms out and behind his head and yawning. "The British barely resisted."

"That was the best part," agreed Matsui. "We had few deaths and only a few more injuries."

"The Chinese have been a more worthy enemy," Yamada observed, yawning and shaking his head. "I could use a nap."

"Do you think it's going to continue being this easy?" Matsui asked.

Their company commander, Lieutenant Haruo Wada, was walking among his troops. He overheard the three men talking. He said nothing. But pessimism was nagging him. We will all be lucky to survive this war, he was thinking. We have angered both the British and the Americans. How long can it be before they turn around and lash out at us? I know what I've heard. They have the better numbers. They have more raw materials, more factory capacity and more people and more men they can put under arms. I will keep those facts to myself for now. Let my men enjoy their success – while it lasts.

On December 8 at 5:35 p.m., Force Z began steaming north from Singapore. Its mission: intercept any Japanese transports sailing south and prevent them from landing their troops.

Force Z's presence in Singapore was no secret. Prime Minister Winston Churchill had announced publicly that Prince of Wales and Repulse were being sent to Singapore as a warning to Japan to stop their southern advance before reaching British-governed Malaya.

Admiral Phillips harbored misgivings about the operation. In an earlier discussion with General Douglas MacArthur and U.S. Admiral Thomas Hart, Phillips had told the pair his two capital ships possessed insufficient strength to tangle successfully in an all-out sea battle with a large Japanese fleet. Influencing Phillips' thinking was Prince of Wales' experience when newly commissioned. In the North Sea she had been part of the force that had hounded and attacked Germany's pride, the monster battleship Bismarck. On May 24, although Prince of Wales scored hits on the Bismarck which later was sunk by a pack of British vessels, the latter got the better of the former. A Bismarck hit to Prince of Wales' bridge forced her to retire from the battle and sulk her way home for repairs.

Prince of Wales enjoyed better luck during August 9-12 when she transported Churchill across the Atlantic to Newfoundland for the Atlantic Charter conference with Roosevelt – the first meeting between the leaders. Prince of Wales' good fortune continued while steaming through the Mediterranean. Near the British-held island fortress of Malta in late September, Prince of Wales successfully fended off attacking Italian planes.

Now as Prince of Wales pulled away from Singapore, Phillips and Leach were standing on the bridge. "Gestation for a baby is nine months," Leach said dryly. "Our gestation was twice that." He was alluding to the ship's launching in 1939 and her commissioning in March 1941. "It would seem, sir, that our first nine months outside the womb have been eventful."

Phillips chuckled. "Order a cake and let's hope we're able to celebrate our first birthday."

"With one large candle," Leach chortled. "Battleship gray of course."

"Champagne for the officers and men."

"Any doubts?" Leach asked soberly.

"Seas are calm today. Perhaps that's a good omen. But, yes, Captain, I have doubts. Which I expressed to MacArthur and Hart. The Japanese have far more warships in the Pacific than we do. But let me be clear. Doubts aside, I'm confident about this particular mission. We – our group – is after transports and I don't expect them to be heavily escorted. Certainly not by anything that can match our firepower."

"Attacks from the air?"

"There could be some. Possibly. But I expect we'll be out of range of any Japanese planes. But even if some managed to reach us, well, look around." Phillips half-turned and his left arm made a sweeping motion. "I don't see any Japanese aircraft penetrating our cannon and machine gun fire. It's fast, accurate and our men are well trained. And keep in mind, Captain, aircraft have never defeated a capital ship. Not one that is battle ready."

"Reassuring, Admiral."

"Our ships and our men have been battle hardened."

What was implicit in Phillips' assessment was the sentiment he shared with other British and American leaders: Japanese forces – land, sea, air – were inferior fighters. They weren't the measure – not physically, not intellectually, not strategically or tactically – of British and American warriors.

The Japanese were leaving nothing to chance. On hearing Churchill's announcement about Force Z's mission, Admiral Isoroku Yamamoto sent 36 Mitsubishi G4M bombers to reinforce Mitsubishi G3M bombers already based in nearby Indochina. The new contingent raised to more than 80 the total of high-level bombers and low-level torpedo bombers. They immediately began training for an assault on Force Z.

"This will be a test," Yamamoto said. "A stern test for us and for them. We will see who passes."

Leach and Phillips were sipping tea from large white mugs.

"I must say, Admiral," Leach said while looking straight beyond Prince of Wales' bow, "it would be still more comforting if we could be assured of air cover."

"Point conceded," Phillips replied, his eyes also fixed on the distant horizon.

"It was worrisome when the RAF told us, 'Regret fighter protection impossible.'"

"Well," Phillips said stoically, "we must go on without it."

The Royal Air Force did have fighters based at Singapore, but they were aging craft with insufficient range to provide an umbrella for a fleet steaming far to the north. Squadron 453 at Sembawang Airfield on Singapore island's north shore had relatively new Brewster Buffaloes. They were intended to provide close cover in the event of an attack. But design flaws had so severely hindered their performance during early test flights that they were deemed of questionable value.

The attitude of Captain William Tenant on Repulse differed. He had planned to ask Squadron 453 to keep six aircraft circling above him during daylight hours. Phillips denied his request. Squadron 488 of the Royal New Zealand Air Force, based in Malaya, tendered an offer of daytime air cover off the coast, but Phillips confidently declined.

The next morning at 7:13 a call came to the bridge where Leach and Phillips were sipping coffee. "Two Japanese reconnaissance aircraft overhead." The two commanders stepped outside and looked up. They said nothing.

Back on the bridge Phillips told Leach, "Tell all ships to be ready for defensive tactics."

At 2 p.m., Japanese submarine I-65 spotted Phillips' small fleet and radioed their position to the 22nd Air Flotilla headquarters of Admiral Jisaburo Ozawa. He didn't dither. Immediately he issued two orders. First he directed most of his warships in the area to escort the now empty transports north to Cam Ranh Bay in Indochina. Next he directed that some planes being loaded with bombs for a Day Two raid on Singapore instead be armed with torpedoes.

At 5:30 p.m., with sunset nearing, three Japanese seaplanes that had been catapulted from cruisers escorting the transports saw and shadowed

Phillips' vessels for an hour until nightfall. Phillips saw the planes but remained unaware of the submarine's surveillance.

Phillips found the planes' presence troubling. His confidence was ebbing and he made his own decision. "Contact the other ships," he told Leach. "We're turning back south."

"Aye, sir." Leach felt instant relief.

Phillips already had cleared the destroyer Tenedos to turn back because, negligently, she had loaded insufficient fuel. He also was thinking that changing course under cover of darkness might complicate more enemy detection and shadowing come dawn. In fact, after sunset Admiral Ozawa gave the green light for a night attack on Phillips' flotilla. But heavy cloud cover stymied the hunt, and the Japanese planes returned to their Indochina airfields. At one point that night, unbeknownst to either Phillips or Ozawa, their warships – Japan's numbered six cruisers and several destroyers – were only about five miles apart. Remarkably, Prince of Wales' radar did not pick up the Japanese vessels.

"Try catching some sleep," Phillips advised Captain Leach.

"And you, sir?"

"I'll stretch out in a bit."

Force Z's luck took a turn for the worse at 3:40 a.m. Japanese submarine I-58 spotted Force Z and, without seeking authorization, fired five torpedoes. All missed and the British didn't know they had been attacked. I-58 reported its sighting and assault to Ozawa's headquarters and again he reacted with dispatch.

"At zero six hundred hours," he ordered, "put ten bombers in the air and send them to the position reported by I-58." A pause. "Actually, send them south of that position. Let's assume the British are continuing their withdrawal."

Admiral Phillips napped but not for long. At 5 a.m., on December 10, he received a report of additional landings farther south at Kuantan or about half way between Kota Bahru and Singapore. Events began unfolding rapidly.

At 5:15 a.m., Prince of Wales spotters with powerful binoculars spotted objects on the southern horizon. Phillips, thinking they were enemy vessels, pursued – briefly. The objects turned out to be a large fishing trawler towing barges.

Phillips sighed and shook his head in exasperation. "Galling. Bloody galling."

"At least, sir," Leach said, trying to assuage his boss, "we didn't waste a lot of petrol. We're still headed to port."

At 6:30 a.m., Repulse reported bad news: Another plane – presumably Japanese – was shadowing the ships.

"Full alert, Captain," Phillips said, more with a hint of resignation than urgency.

"Right away, sir."

In the next moment, Phillips aggressive nature resurfaced. "Captain, get one of our own planes in the air."

At 7:18 a.m., Prince of Wales catapulted a reconnaissance aircraft – a Supermarine Walrus. It headed toward Kuantan and found no evidence of landings. After radioing back to Prince of Wales, the Walrus continued south to Singapore.

"Another rumor based on something other than verifiable fact," Phillips grumbled. "An age-old symptom of warfare. We Brits are not immune."

"Regrettably true, sir."

"Look, tell Express to veer closer to shore near Kuantan. Maybe it will see something our plane didn't."

Express investigated – and found nothing.

At 10:05 a.m., everything changed. On the bridge Captain Leach picked up his ringing phone. He listened a long moment and paled.

"Admiral. It's the Tenedos. She's being attacked. About one hundred forty miles south of us."

"Details?"

"Just a moment." Leach spoke into the phone. "What more can you tell us?" In another moment he lowered the phone to his side. "They say the attackers are nine twin-engine bombers."

In fact, the enemy craft were Mitsubishi G3Ms from Ozawa's base at Saigon. They each were armed with one 1,100-pound armor-piercing bomb. Their crews' combat inexperience then showed. They mistook elusive destroyer Tenedos for a battleship and missed with all their bombs.

At 10:15 a.m., more Japanese scout planes spotted Force Z and radioed its position.

At 11:13 a.m., the hell of war was unleashed on Force Z and her men. Klaxons began shrieking. Three waves of Japanese planes appeared high above the flotilla. Admiral Phillips didn't need to issue orders. Anti-aircraft crews, many bare-chested and sweating, on Prince of Wales, Repulse, Electra and Vampire all cut loose with cannon and ack-ack fire. Simultaneously, Leach and the other captains ordered evasive action and the vessels began zigzagging.

The first enemy wave included 25 high-level bombers. Seventeen dropped 1,100-pound bombs and eight dropped a pair of 550 pounders.

"Jesus!" Leach muttered fiercely, flinching as one of eight near misses sent up a towering geyser of seawater to starboard.

The first wave's 33 bombs scored just one hit – on Captain Tennant's Repulse. Damage was confined to a small fire and she powered on at 29 mph.

At 11:40 a.m., Leach muttered again, this time plaintively. "Dear Lord, please be with us."

Admiral Phillips said nothing. His jaws were locked tight and his eyes unwavering from the oncoming threat. The enemy's second wave was causing greater anxiety. At a distance its planes appeared as harmless dots. As the dots neared Force Z, they began taking shape. They swooped lower, like diving eagles, and seemed to be accelerating. As yet no markings were visible, but the men aboard Force Z ships needed no help identifying the menace.

Machine gun fire erupted from the wings of the oncoming planes, and Force Z answered in kind. Then, with deceptive laziness, long cylindrical objects dropped from the undersides of the Japanese planes. When the cylinders struck the surface, they splashed and dove but did not sink. They began knifing toward the British vessels. Force Z crewmen were watching the closing torpedoes with a range of reactions, some in fascination, others in awe and still more in terror. Moments later one of the lethal fishes struck Prince of Wales and detonated. The explosion flung pieces of metal and men in every direction. Primal screams were piercing the tropical air. Phillips and Leach were both rocked and reached out for the nearest handholds. They stayed on their feet.

In quick succession five more torpedoes plowed into Prince of Wales. More explosions brought more destruction and carnage, with men in the engine rooms and lower decks taking the early brunt. Cannons and anti-aircraft guns were booming, flames were sprouting, firemen were racing for hoses, men everywhere were shouting orders and, on Prince of Wales, screaming their agony as hot shrapnel sliced into their bodies and heat seared their flesh.

The battle had its land-based observers. When it began, Yamada, Hata and Matsui were boiling water for tea. High in the distance they could see planes dropping bombs. No signs of explosions followed.

"Practice?" Yamada asked.

"Can't tell," Matsui replied. "If it is, it seems like a big waste of ordnance."

Hata chuckled cynically. "As if our military hasn't wasted it before."

Then they saw other planes plummeting like hungry hawks diving for prey. When those metallic birds appeared poised to plunge into the sea, they seemed to defy gravity as they flattened out and went skimming only feet above the surface.

"What are those?" Hata asked, awestruck by the pilots' ability to wrestle their craft out of what looked like fatal dives.

"I'm not sure but if it's practice it's the most dangerous and expensive practice I've ever seen," said Matsui.

Moments later, beyond the horizon, clouds of black smoke began billowing skyward.

"Not practice," said Hata. "I think we might be witnessing history. I think one of our air fleets is attacking the enemy navy in the open sea – British or American. And if that smoke is any sign at all, we're winning."

Ozawa's bombers were winning. The last of the torpedoes to strike Prince of Wales left her in need of triage. It hit the young vessel's port side propeller shaft which was turning at maximum revolutions and helping power her at top speed – 32 mph. The shaft twisted, breaching the hull and rupturing the glands that prevented seawater from sluicing into Prince of Wales via the broad shaft tunnel. Within seconds she took on 2,400 tons of water and her speed dropped to 18 mph. Nearly instantly the engine room, boiler room, two machinery rooms, the port diesel dynamo room and other aft compartments were flooded and men were screaming in despair and drowning.

Phillips and Leach didn't need a detailed report on damage. Within minutes Prince of Wales was listing 11 degrees to port. That rendered useless her port guns as they couldn't be elevated sufficiently to fire effectively.

"Admiral –"

"Yes, I know, Captain. We need to think seriously about abandoning ship. We could go belly up."

Smoke was smudging their white uniforms, and balance was becoming precarious.

The sixth torpedo's effects rippled beyond the initial damage and flooding. Electrical power losses were crippling. Some of the gun turrets became inoperable. Pumps couldn't expel water fast enough to keep up with the flooding. Steering was hindered and internal communications were knocked out. Only the starboard engines were functioning, slowing the ship further to 15 mph. In short, Prince of Wales was fast becoming unmanageable.

"Admiral," Leach said grimly, "I'm calling for assistance."

"Go ahead."

It was 12:45 p.m. To his second in command, Leach said, "Ask Express to come along side. Prepare to take off our wounded first."

Phillips couldn't help pursing his lips and shaking his head in dismay. The Japanese pilots were proving far more skilled than he had imagined. His ships' defensive weaponry was proving alarmingly ineffective. And the absence of air cover was proving catastrophic. As the Prince of Wales list became more pronounced, Phillips coffee mug slid off a counter onto the deck at his feet. He didn't notice.

The crew of the Express was handling with remarkable aplomb the evacuation of the wounded. As it proceeded, Leach looked at his wristwatch. 1 p.m. He again turned to his second in command. "Pass the word. All hands abandon ship."

Leach was proud of his men. They were hustling but not panicking.

"Admiral, it's time."

"Not until all our men are off."

"Sir, I am imploring you. The fleet needs you. This war is just beginning."

"I appreciate the sentiment, Captain, but I'll leave when you leave." Both men knew what that meant; they would be the last two to depart.

Moments later, in a final convulsion, Prince of Wales began turning turtle. There were precious few seconds to react. Many of the most stoic of men still aboard Prince of Wales shouted and screamed reflexively. Others, equally terrified, uttered not a sound.

Phillips reached for Leach and the two men grasped hands. They slipped and fell. It was 1:18 p.m. As Prince of Wales rolled to port, she scraped Express, nearly taking the destroyer with her. Men aboard Express cringed in horror as several Prince of Wales crew were crushed between the ships.

Meanwhile, Repulse, under Captain Tennant, had been successfully dodging torpedoes – 19 of them. Her end began when a third wave of 26 torpedo bombers attacked simultaneously from several directions. Two torpedoes struck lethally. The first jammed Repulse's rudder, rendering her helpless to continue evading. Because 25-year-old Repulse didn't possess compartmentalization, she took on water fatally.

Captain Tennant immediately ordered the crew overboard. "Good luck and God be with you," he cried. Tennant was intending to go down with his ship, but several officers seized and forced him to leap into the sea. During a scant six minutes Repulse listed heavily to port, rolled over and sank.

Express continued picking up Prince of Wales survivors and Electra and Vampire began plucking Repulse crew from the sea. What spared the destroyers? Their smaller profile combined with superior speed and maneuverability. In total they rescued 2,081 men including Captain Tennant.

Losses. Of its 1,612 men, Prince of Wales lost 327. Because Repulse had less time to react, of her 1,309 men, 513 were killed. The Japanese lost three torpedo bombers.

December 11. The morning after the debacle, Churchill, while still in bed, took a call from Sir Dudley Pound, first sea lord. Said Pound, "Prime Minister, I have to report to you that the Prince of Wales and Repulse have both been sunk by the Japanese. We think by aircraft. Tom Phillips is drowned."

Churchill: "Are you sure it's true?"

Pound: "There is no doubt at all."

Later, in reflecting, Churchill lamented, "In all the war, I never received a more direct shock…As I turned over and twisted in bed, the full horror of the news sank in upon me. There were no British or American ships in the Indian Ocean or the Pacific except the American survivors of Pearl Harbor, who were hastening back to California. Over all this vast expanse of waters Japan was supreme, and we everywhere were weak and naked."

Churchill was looking at the global picture – Asia, America, Europe and his United Kingdom and its empire. A Repulse surviving officer, Lieutenant Tom Vigors, was seeing the situation more narrowly but no less astutely. He told a colleague, "I reckon this must have been the last battle in which navy reckoned they could get along without the RAF. A pretty damned costly way of learning."

Neither Churchill nor Vigors mentioned the locale that was most immediately affected by the sinking of Prince of Wales and Repulse: Singapore. With no capital ships in the vicinity the island – heretofore a naval bastion – had essentially been redefined as a land base.

CHAPTER 38

One after another, George Britton, Oliver Needle and Malcolm Goode along with other members of the East Surrey Regiment climbed into the rear of the canvas-topped truck.

"It would seem that today we switch from fishing to hunting," George said joylessly.

"Yes, but will we be predators or prey?" asked Malcolm, unconsciously fingering an earpiece of his glasses.

"Brilliant question," Oliver said. "But who can say? In this wretched weather I doubt if our RAF lads have been able to send up any recon."

"In other words," Malcolm grumbled, "we really have not a rat's ass idea of where the Japanese are."

"Only that they landed enough troops at Kota Bahru to flog our boys and capture many of them. Plus take our airfield," George said. "If the weather there is anything like here, they might be resting in British barracks and hangars."

The weather was dismal. Rain was beating a steady tattoo against the canvas a few feet above their helmets. The downpour had begun early the morning of the 9th and had continued unabated through the night and into the 10th. The ground's consistency was approximating that of a soaked sponge. Progress would be slow.

The long convoy was carrying the East Surreys across the Johor causeway and north to confront the Japanese – wherever they might be.

The gloom inside Singapore General Hospital matched the gray of the morning sky. Ordinarily Sister Grace Ann took comfort from the sound of falling rain. Its hypnotic effect freed her mind from concerns and often sparked creative thinking as with her ideas for annually celebrating the Christmas season.

This rain didn't provide its usual effect because the morning was unprecedented in the young nun's experience. Her first patient was a war casualty – a 12-year-old Chinese wisp of a girl whose right thigh and hip had been sliced by hot shrapnel during the December 8 raid. Gently, Grace Ann was changing the girl's dressings. She was groaning lowly, trying to be brave during Grace Ann's ministrations.

During the last 48 hours, Grace Ann had learned something about herself. To wit, she could be much tougher than she would have imagined. The ugly war wounds – flesh torn, holed and burned, innards exposed – that had been entering her ward were unsettling. But she had been able to overcome her initial queasiness. With newly arrived casualties she quickly was able to comfort and treat them with her customary brisk effervescence. Grace Ann's inner beauty was proving itself the equal of her stunning visage.

Elsewhere in the hospital nuns including Sisters Regina, Augusta and Caroline were busily ministering to casualties – checking IVs, emptying bed pans, sponge-bathing, sprinkling sulfa on wounds, changing dressings and bed linens and for the most part working without respite. The white aprons covering their light gray habits were stained with blood and clinging wartime hospital detritus.

"There you are," one of the nuns addressed Sister Regina. "You have a visitor in the lobby."

"Thank you."

A couple minutes later after descending steps and entering the lobby, she saw Lim Bo Seng wiping rain from his eyeglasses with a kerchief.

"Bo Seng, how nice to see you."

Positioning his glasses he smiled. "Good morning, Sister."

"What brings you here? Is your family all right?" she asked concernedly.

"Oh, yes. We are fine. All of us. I just wanted to see if you and your nurses needed anything. I knew you would be very busy."

"How very thoughtful of you. Especially in this rain. But I think we have everything we need."

"Good."

"Bo Seng, I can't help remembering your prediction about the Japanese. Now that they have attacked us, are you giving thought to evacuating your family?"

"Yes." Lim sighed resignedly and pursed his lips. "Choo Neo and I have discussed it. We are considering it. And I have taken a precautionary measure. I have paid the owner of a motor launch to have his boat available if needed."

"I'm glad. Where would you go?"

"Probably across the Malacca Strait to Sumatra first. After that, I'm not certain. You know, Sister, I also have my employees to worry about. If the Japanese do conquer Singapore and learn my employees worked for me, they could be persecuted. I couldn't take them all with me, and I expect most would want to stay in their homes with their families."

"Such difficult decisions for everyone. I shall keep all of them in my prayers."

"Now, Sister, let me ask you a question."

"Go ahead."

"Would you and your nuns leave with my family if it comes to that?"

Sister Regina smiled. "I plead guilty."

"To what?"

"To being too busy to think more about it."

In the hours after watching the sea battle, Takuma Matsui, Etsuro Yamada and Kai Hata were on the move. In rain so heavy it virtually eliminated vision, they and other members of their company were slogging their way across the peninsula. Their next objective – and that of the rest of General Yamashita's 25th Army – was to move quickly west to the peninsula's main north-south road and the coast beyond. They would then begin driving south. Yamashita's war plan was built on speed. His men would be pedaling bicycles and motoring in small boats along the west coast. The faster they moved the less time British and Australian forces would have to solidify their lines. Yamashita also regarded his plan as one that would minimize casualties. As much as possible he wanted to avoid mass infantry charges against fixed defenses. He also saw in speed another central advantage: His adversaries would struggle to estimate accurately the size of his invading army. He knew that British and Australian troops in Malaya outnumbered his 30,000 by about three to one. Well into the night of the 10th his men kept pushing through the jungle and across rivers and streams. On reaching the north-south road, 18,000 of them, including Matsui, Hata and Yamada, were exhausted. Nonetheless, they mounted and began pedaling south. Yamashita wanted them to advance a few miles before resting.

The East Surrey convoy stopped for the night about 60 miles north of the Johor Strait. A few of the soldiers who had jammed into the trucks considered themselves lucky. They were able to stretch out on the truck beds still protected by the canvas tops. Most, though, were forced to fend for themselves.

George Britton, Oliver Needle and Malcolm Goode were among many who sought shelter under the long, broad leaves of banana trees.

"Do you think it's possible for a body to melt?" Malcolm muttered dispiritedly.

"It might be a medical first," George chortled.

"I don't know what's worse," Malcolm groused, "the bloody rain or sweating beneath this rubber."

The men had no tents but were wearing hooded ponchos.

"You were right about one thing," Oliver said to George.

"That being?"

"You said the next time we fished it would be north of the strait. Of course as we've no rods the fish in the nearest pond or stream are quite safe."

"Too bad I wasn't wrong."

"I wonder if we'll ever dry out. I'll need a large towel just to dry my eyebrows."

"Didn't think soldiering could be this much fun, did you?" George teased. "But think of it this way, it will probably get much worse."

"I suppose you mean this bloody rain will match biblical proportions," Malcolm said cynically.

"I mean we've yet to meet the enemy."

Farther north on the peninsula, British troops who had met the enemy at Kota Bahru and been forced to retreat also were bivouacking for the night. Like the East Surreys many of them were seeking a modicum of cover beneath banana trees. In doing so they left their artillery pieces unmanned and unguarded. Reason: They thought the weather too inclement for the Japanese to continue advancing. As they would learn in the morning, their judgment was another costly mistake. Not only did they forfeit the artillery, most would be taken captive and struggle to survive the war in deadly POW camps.

Before December 10 ended, the British in Singapore were compelled to arrest one of their own. Captain Patrick Stanley Vaughan Heenan was born July 29, 1910, in New Zealand and moved in his youth to England. From 1923-1926 he boarded at Seven Oaks School in Kent. In 1927 he matriculated at Cheltenham College to prepare for a career in the military. Records show he was an inferior student with one faculty member describing Heenan as a "gloomy, resentful misfit disliked by other pupils." But he possessed an impressive physique and excelled at sports, in particular boxing.

After graduating Cheltenham at 19, Heenan joined Steel Brothers, a trading firm with interests in Asia. Still, he longed for military service and in 1932 became an officer in the Army Supplementary Reserve. In 1935 he achieved his goal when he was commissioned a lieutenant in the British Army. He was posted to India and assigned to the 16th Punjab Regiment. In 1941 Heenan's unit was sent to Malaya where he was transferred to the British Indian Army for training with its air liaison group. In June Heenan was assigned to Kedah in northern Malaya – in close proximity to where most British, Australian and New Zealand Air Force squadrons were based. It was there that Japanese military intelligence recruited Heenan to turn on his country.

He had begun using a radio to transmit sensitive information, including the locations and strength of the Allied airfields. Heenan's ruse: He used a Morse Code transmitter operated with an alphanumeric keyboard disguised as a typewriter. His transmissions assisted the Japanese in targeting objectives on their December 8 raids.

His treachery was uncovered on December 10.

"He isn't denying his guilt," General Percival said to his boss, General Wavell.

Wavell's head shook in dismay. "I'm tempted to order his immediate execution."

"He is fully deserving. But…"

"But we'll grant him due process. Schedule a court-martial."

CHAPTER 39

Catherine Caradja had listened to the announcement on her parlor radio. Now she was holding her daily newspaper and fixating on the front-page headline of the edition dated December 13. Daughter Alexandra and Laura Ramaschi were with her. All three were sipping tea from delicate china cups decorated gaily with red roses.

"Insanity," Catherine muttered. "It must be a contagious disease. First Hitler reaches a dubious conclusion: Since Japan has attacked the United States and the U.S. has declared war on Japan, he must declare war on America. Now that imbecile Antonescu also has declared war on America. Unadulterated idiocy."

"Perhaps," Laura speculated, "he did it to curry more favor with Hitler."

"Oh, no doubt about that," Catherine concurred disgustedly. "But since he already has all but handed our sovereignty to Hitler, why compound his generosity?"

"Maybe," Laura murmured, "he is a very insecure man."

Catherine's despair ebbed enough so that a small smile appeared. "You are wise beyond your years, Laura. Yes, Antonescu, for all his bluster and murderous tendencies, is insecure. And in my mind he has good reason to be. He already has plenty of enemies among his own people. Iron

Guardsmen for starters. Now he has made an enemy of the most powerful nation on earth."

In Bucharest, Ambassador Franklin Mott Gunther was distraught. Antonescu had not thought to send an emissary to alert Gunther of his intention. Gunther, like Catherine, had learned of Antonescu's war declaration via radio – in his case from an embassy staffer who had been listening and had rushed to the ambassador's office with the news.

Gunther had occupied his post for more than four years and had grown fond of Romania and its people. "It was bad enough," Gunther observed to his staffer, "that Antonescu all but extended an invitation to Hitler to send troops into Romania. And then handed management of the country to Gerstenberg. Now he takes the last step over the precipice and makes a mortal enemy of my country."

In Washington, Gabriella Balas sat at her desk, staring numbly at the communiqué. It tersely informed the embassy staff that it was now representing an enemy of their host country. Gabriella didn't shed tears easily, but on this occasion she couldn't stem the flow. She sniffled, then stood and walked to Alice Manescu's reception desk. Her friend was inconsolable.

"Antonescu has broken my heart." Alice struggled to get the words out amidst sobs. "I am now persona non grata in my wonderful adopted country."

Gabriella placed her right hand on Alice's left shoulder and patted. "I'm sorry, Alice. So very, very sorry." Then she bent low to kiss the tiny woman's cheek. Gabriella's tears dropped onto Alice's desk pad. Sadness was overwhelming her. She was weeping for her country, for her friends and for a love she sensed she would never see again. Gabriella dabbed her cheeks with fingertips, then straightened and returned to her desk. She sat and sniffled again. She considered writing a long letter – a love letter – to Joe Barton. It will take too long to get to Singapore, she thought, and I don't want him to receive tear-stained paper. I will cable him. Maybe he will see it right away and reply immediately.

13 December 1941
Dear Joe,
World gone mad. Must return to Romania. Stupidity reigns in Bucharest. Until now we have been in shadows of war. No longer. Always your Romanian gypsy.
Gabriella

Joe's return cable arrived within hours.

Dear Gypsy,
Cherry blossoms. May we see them bloom again together.
Joe

The trip was grueling but Gabriella was determined to return to Romania as quickly as possible. She had eschewed traveling with the rest of the embassy staff by ocean liner to Marseilles and then by train to Bucharest. A fast exchange of cables with her father, Cornel, and a wire transfer produced flight arrangements and the money to pay for them. Gabriella would hopscotch by air to New York, Newfoundland, Iceland, Ireland and Paris' Lebourget Airport – where Charles Lindberg had landed after his historic 1927 flight. She then would taxi to Gare de'l Est and entrain for Bucharest. She would arrive exhausted, but she would be where she felt a compelling need to be – home.

CHAPTER 40

The East Surreys were in trouble. General Yamashita's war plan was the proximate cause. His bicycle-mounted infantry along with troops in small boats were continually threatening to surround and cut off the British.

"Our training didn't include rapid retreat," Oliver Needle grumbled.

During the week since the regiment had departed their barracks and sped north, the troops had eaten little, rested less and shaved not at all.

"For the first time since becoming a British soldier," George Britton said dejectedly, "I am having serious doubts about the quality of our leadership. I've read enough of our history to know that our leaders aren't covering themselves with laurels of glory. At sea and on land, if we had a good plan, I've seen no evidence of it."

"The only thing that seems to be working," Malcolm Goode muttered, "is our rifles. Thank the Lord for small miracles. And keeping them clean and in working order in this infernal jungle is no mean task. That and keeping my glasses clean."

The rifles were Lee Enfield No. 1 Mk. IIIs. They had been designed and manufactured at the government-owned Royal Small Arms Factory in Enfield, England. The British Army side arm of choice was the Enfield No. Mk. 1 – a .38 caliber revolver. In recent days they had seen considerable use in a series of firefights best described as components of organized retreat – less charitably as British humiliation.

"Before you know it, George, you could be fishing again in the strait," said Oliver. "How long do you think we can hold off the Japs before we're back at the causeway?"

"At the rate we're retreating," George replied, "we could be toasting the new year back in Singapore. Not an especially cheering prospect."

Unbeknownst to the East Surreys and other British troops in Malaya, on Singapore island a resistance force was taking shape. Ironically, it required political accommodation.

Remarkably soon – December 18 – after the Japanese landing at Kota Bahru, British officials began recruiting European planters, miners and civil servants as well as Chinese the British believed could be trusted. The matter of trust wasn't trivial because the Chinese were members of the nascent Malaya Communist Party. But they knew Malaya, its people and terrain, and the British swallowed hard and invited them to join the hastily designated 101 Special Training School. Mutual hatred of the Japanese trumped bilateral antipathy. The 165 recruits received a crash course in stealth, weaponry, explosives and jungle survival techniques.

In short order they boarded small boats that carried them north up the west coast of the Malay peninsula where they were put ashore. Politics had been put aside during recruiting and training but was central to deployment; the Chinese communists were assigned locales where Communist Party membership was strongest. That doing so made sense militarily as well as politically was a bonus. Malayan Chinese were well aware of Japanese ill treatment of their brethren in China in general and of the rape of Nanking in particular and were eager to exact revenge.

Those initial resistance fighters formed the nucleus of what eventually became known as the Malayan People's Anti-Japanese Army. From the MPAJA's inception, challenges would test its mettle. Food, medicine, weapons, ammunition, communications, lack of working radios, training of new recruits and evading prowling Japanese patrols were ongoing problems. Most troubling were Japanese terror tactics that made Malayans of all races and ethnicities fearful of helping or openly sympathizing with the MPAJA.

Toward the end of December, Lieutenant Haruo Wada gathered his company in a jungle clearing near a small village in the foothills of Malaya's central mountain range. He raised his right arm and soldierly griping ceased abruptly.

"We have a special mission today," Wada began. "This new resistance movement is disrupting operations. They have felled trees that have hindered movement of our trucks, tanks and artillery. We are beginning to use precious resources – time and men – hunting them. Regimental headquarters wants us to send a strong message to the natives. Show any sympathy, provide any aid to these rebels and there will be severe punishment. There is a village only three kilometers from here. We will move in and torch it. It will be our first use of flame throwers so be careful where you are standing at all times. We will not kill fleeing civilians, not this time. But if any villager resists in any way, you are to execute him – or her – immediately." To Matsui, using flamethrowers and encouraging good judgment fell little short of an invitation to murder. "Form up," Wada ordered. "Column of twos."

Nuns didn't spend much time looking in mirrors. Their vows were of obedience, chastity and poverty. Adhering to those virtues inevitably led to embracing a fourth – modesty. When on December 21 Sister Grace Ann looked in the small bathroom mirror while brushing her teeth and readying herself for another long shift in the hospital, what struck her was not her beauty which eclipsed even that of the lovely Sister Regina. Vanity simply wasn't central to her persona. What she saw was haggardness born of physical and emotional fatigue. And if, the thought occurred to her, patients were seeing her as she now was seeing herself, the effect wasn't medicinally beneficial.

Grace Ann finished brushing and rinsed her mouth. Then she peered again at her reflection. An idea popped into her fertile mind and she brightened.

Sister Regina was listening indulgently. She had been laboring as long and hard as the other nuns and was equally dulled. This conversation with the creatively irrepressible Grace Ann was generating its usual effect: Regina's spirits were lightening.

"The props are outside and we don't need to rehearse," Grace Ann was saying. "That would take us away from our work too long. Well, perhaps a simple run-through, but that's all we would need."

Regina shook her head and smiled in open admiration of her younger colleague. "Your idea is wonderful and I'm certain our Lord concurs."

Beginning the next morning, squads of nuns entered all the hospital's wards with their 800 beds. A nun in each group was holding aloft one of the brightly painted figures from the crèche that had been set up on the hospital grounds.

When a squad reached the center of a ward it stopped. A nun then would make an announcement. Grace Ann did the honors for her group of five.

"As this year draws to a close, most of us have never seen such devastation and despair. We can't help thinking dark thoughts. It is only human to do so. Will our situation worsen? What will the future bring?" With her right hand, Grace Ann pointed to the figure of Mary, one of the wooden crèche pieces. She was depicted as wearing a blue robe with a white headscarf. "That is a likeness of Mary, mother of Jesus, from the nativity set that was on our lawn. Most of you here are not Christians. That matters not. What does matter is continuing to hope, to believe that we all will survive this nightmare and look forward to a future where we can pursue and fulfill our dreams." She had the rapt attention of patients who weren't blind to her beauty or deaf to the sincerity of her message. "We-" with her right arm in a sweeping motion she indicated her fellow nuns – "are keeping all of you – every one of you – in our nightly prayers. We are your nurses and we also are your petitioners to our Lord Jesus Christ." Several patients felt eyes moistening and throats constricting. "Before we continue with our work," Grace Ann said, "we would like to sing a hymn. It's a Christmas hymn but more importantly it's a hymn of hope."

Grace Ann motioned to her four colleagues. One continued to hold high the figure of Mary. Then all five began singing *O'Come All Ye Faithful*. Not a rousing rendition but a soft, lilting version that transcended language barriers. Even among patients who understood little or no English, few eyes remained dry.

CHAPTER 41

Tired though she was and feeling a strong need for a bath, Gabriella exited Bucharest's Gara de Nord train station and decided her first stop would be the United States Embassy. Afterward she would phone her father to arrange a ride north to their home in Ploesti.

As Gabriella's taxi was completing the one and a half-mile drive southeast to the embassy she couldn't help wondering what kind of reception awaited. The United States had not yet declared war on Romania, but would Antonescu's declaration have her feeling persona non grata as Alice Manescu had felt in Washington?

She saw the two Marines flanking the embassy entrance and waved timidly. In return they smiled. "Good afternoon, Miss Balas," one said warmly while pulling open the door for her.

"Good afternoon." A pause. "I'm surprised you're still here. I mean-"

"My tour of duty was nearly over, and I was ordered to stay on until the embassy had been evacuated."

"Is anyone still here? I mean, besides you two?"

"Not exactly," said the Marine.

"What do you mean?"

"Most of the staff have departed for the States, but Ambassador Gunther is still here technically."

"Technically? What does that mean?"

"I'm sorry to tell you, Miss, but Ambassador Gunther has had a heart attack."

"Oh, no! When? Where is he?"

"Two days ago, Miss. He's in the hospital. On Calea Floreasca."

Quickly Gabriella decided to walk to the hospital, about one mile north of the embassy. Doing so would give her time to sort her thoughts. "May I please leave my luggage inside?"

"Of course."

A nurse was leading Gabriella to Gunther's room.

"How is he?" She was holding a bouquet of red carnations purchased at a florist shop near the hospital.

"Not good, I am afraid."

Gabriella found it soothing to be conversing again in Latin-based Romanian. She cherished its soft rhythms.

"Here we are," said the nurse, pulling open the door. "He is sleeping. But you may feel free to sit with him."

Which is what Gabriella did. She used the time for reflection. On her friendship with Gunther. On friends she made on the embassy staff in Washington. On Joe. Will I ever see any of them again? Will I ever see the States again?

About 70 minutes after Gabriella's arrival, Gunther's eyes opened slowly. She stood and smiled.

"Gabriella." His voice was weak, barely a whisper.

"Mr. Ambassador. I am so sorry you are ill."

"Just back?"

"Yes, sir. Earlier this afternoon. One of the Marines told me you are here."

He nodded slightly. "It's so sad. No, not about me. Your country." His tongue licked his dry lips.

"Water, sir?"

"Yes, please."

Gabriella reached for a pitcher and poured a few ounces into a glass. She held it to his mouth and he sipped.

"How's that?"

"Better. Thank you." His voice seemed a little stronger.

"I brought these for you." She picked up the bouquet from the bedside table.

"They are beautiful. Thank you."

"You are welcome, sir. I can only begin to tell you how important our friendship is. You gave me opportunity. You let me grow. I am so grateful."

Gunther smiled. "Your ability. Your work ethic. They made it easy to let you spread your wings. And you flew. High and far. I am very proud of you."

"Thank you, sir."

"In my four and a half years here, I have come to respect and love your countrymen. My final prayer is for mercy for Romania."

Franklin Mott Gunther died that evening – December 22 – 10 days after Antonescu's war declaration. He was 56.

Later that night Gabriella was returning to the embassy, hoping it remained open. From half a block away in dim light, she was encouraged when she saw the U.S. flag at half-staff. Then she saw the Marines.

"I am glad you're still here."

"With Ambassador Gunther dead, we will be closing the embassy in the morning."

"Would you mind if I went inside? To collect my luggage. I would also like to take a last look around and send a cable."

"No problem, Miss."

Gabriella stopped briefly at the reception desk, letting memories come bubbling to the surface. She sighed deeply. Next she walked to her former small office and looked inside. I wonder who was its last occupant. Will she miss working here? Then she took a longer look at Gunther's office with its U.S. flag on a pole in the far corner. Lastly she made her way to the communications room. Her cable was brief:

22 December 1941

Dear Joe,
I am in tears. Ambassador Gunther died this evening. I was with him. He cared for Romania. Deeply. He was a good man.
Gabriella

CHAPTER 42

General Yamashita was of two minds. He had pledged to Tokyo leadership to conquer Malaya and Singapore within 100 days and in his mind was ahead of schedule. But he also was frustrated; British resistance had stiffened and was slowing the Japanese advance.

Johor Bahru was the southern most town on the Malay peninsula, and the East Surreys and other British troops were arrayed on a line about a dozen miles to the north. As night fell on December 31, the company including George Britton, Oliver Needle and Malcolm Goode was flanking the main road leading into Johor Bahru.

Lieutenant Haruo Wada called his men together in a small clearing. The night sky was clear but few stars could be seen above the thick jungle canopy. He delivered no impassioned speech. His men were seasoned combat veterans, and he was supremely confident in their determination and fighting ability. He presented their mission straightforwardly. "Tonight," he said, "our objective is to reach the outskirts of Johor Bahru. Our company has earned the privilege of leading the way, and once again we will use our bicycles to speed by the British. We will move out at two in the morning. Try to get a little rest."

Yamada, Hata and Matsui stretched out beneath a banana tree.

"We'd best check our rifles," said Hata.

"My mother would be proud of us," Matsui said, his sly grin not visible in the darkness.

"Why?" Hata asked.

"Because we keep our rifles as clean as she keeps her house."

All three men chuckled lowly.

A few minutes before two, the order came. It wasn't barked. Wada repeated it in a conversational tone as he walked among the 150 men in his company. "Everyone up," he said. "Fix bayonets and mount up."

His men responded efficiently, strapping their bayoneted rifles across their backs.

"Move out," Wada ordered.

George Britton and Malcolm Goode were taking a two-hour watch, one posted on either side of the road. About 20 minutes after two o'clock, Malcolm whispered urgently, "What's that?"

"Not sure," George answered, and both men strained to hear among the jungle's eerie night sounds. "Bicycle chains. Lots of them. Start waking the men on your side. Now. And tell them to fix bayonets. I'll do the same on my side. Hurry."

As George scrambled to rouse his fellow soldiers, starting with company commander Captain Brian Barnsworth, he couldn't help pondering the situation's irony. Clanking tank treads, whining incoming shells, whumping mortar launches. Those are sounds expected to cause fright. But bicycle chains? And yet, George mused, they've become as fearsome a sound as any of the others. Perhaps more so because of their threatening stealth and speed.

Lieutenant Wada looked back over his shoulder. "Pass the word," he whispered to the cyclist behind him. "Pick up the pace. No stragglers."

As fast as possible he wanted his men to blow by or through British defenses. If there was to be more fighting, he didn't want it to happen before reaching their objective: Johor.

"What do you think, George?" Captain Barnsworth asked. He and his men were crouched in shallow drainage ditches on either side of the unpaved road.

"Fire low, sir. Down bikes or men but cause a pile-up and stop them."

"Right."

"And fix bayonets."

"Right."

We are accumulating experience and wisdom, George was thinking, but will it be enough to stop the Japs? How many of us will survive this war? Or not?

"Here they come. Wait for my first shot," Barnsworth said, and word was passed rapidly back among the men in the ditches.

George tensed. The near panic of earlier skirmishes had diminished but fear of the unknown remained, and it was tightening British stomachs and grips on rifles.

Sweat was running freely down Takuma Matsui's face. His left hand reached up from the bike's handle grip and dabbed, once beneath each eye.

Captain Barnsworth squeezed off a shot from his Enfield revolver, triggering a fusillade of rifle fire.

Bullets tore through the spokes of Matsui's front wheel. He lost control and crashed into an adjacent bike. Both riders went toppling to the road.

Lieutenant Wada looked back and shouted, "Forward! Keep moving forward!"

Pedaling troops began maneuvering around the fallen riders. British rifle rounds continued slicing through the darkness. In the next sliver of time, Wada screamed primally, and his left hand reached reflexively for his right shoulder. His balance lost, down he went.

The advance stalled. Japanese troops dismounted, some scattering for roadside cover, others unslinging their Type 94 rifles and firing ineffectively into the night.

George saw an opportunity and on impulse vaulted from the ditch and went sprinting, bayonet poised, toward Wada. Eliminate their leader was the thought that struck him, and maybe the rest will fall back.

Matsui, on his knees, saw George's dark form closing. The Japanese soldier clenched his jaws, jerked his rifle from his back over his head and went scrambling toward Wada's side.

With George preparing to fire at point-blank range, Matsui raised up, slashing left to right. His bayonet sliced across George's chest, and the British private bellowed, spun and fell to his knees.

Barnsworth, Goode, Needle and other soldiers were out of the ditches, running forward and firing.

Matsui called for help and Hata, already dismounted, came racing forward. He and Matsui each roughly grasped one of Wada's armpits and began dragging him rearward.

Japanese rifles were returning British fire and Barnsworth shouted, "Get down! Stay low!"

Malcolm and Oliver dropped to either side of George, grabbed his upper arms, wrestled him to his feet and, bent low, hustled him back to a roadside ditch.

"Painful. Feels like a hundred bees have stung me across my chest. Bloody but not a serious wound," George said.

"Score one for the good guys," Oliver replied cheerily. "Soon we'll be fishing again." Then, turning serious, he added, "For once we held our own. No retreat last night."

"It was the chains," George said, half grinning, half grimacing. "The Japs need to grease their chains."

George was lying on a hospital tent cot, recovering from a medic's ministrations – quickly washing the long wound, sprinkling sulfa and wrapping a cloth bandage across the patient's chest and around his back.

"This might get you sent back to the island," said Oliver. "Or perhaps all the way to Gravesend."

"This scratch?"

"A nasty gash."

"I gather I will need a new shirt or a talented seamstress," George smiled through his pain. "Still, it should give me just a one-way ticket – back to the front. But at least I lived to greet the new year. No champagne, though, or even warm beer."

"Thank you," said Wada, "for saving my life. I am in your debt."

"Duty, sir, and an honor and a privilege," said Matsui.

Wada was lying on a thin blanket on the ground under a lean-to. "How many men did we lose?"

"Three killed, sir. Four wounded, including you. We recovered the bodies."

"The British are learning some lessons," Wada said admiringly. "They were smartly deployed and acted decisively. I think we took them for granted. Not again."

CHAPTER 43

Singapore, "Gibraltar of the East," might have withstood the enemy onslaught had the Japanese attacked as British officialdom had anticipated. With Singapore located in the southeast corner of the island, with miles of challenging terrain between the city and the Johor Strait and with hundreds more miles of jungle clogging the Malay peninsula, the British believed any attack would by necessity arrive sea borne. Hence, from the early 1930s, 15-inch guns, howitzers and machine gun bunkers had ringed Singapore and its port, ready to blast enemy warships and soldiers attempting amphibious landings. From December 8 onward many of those guns remained silent, and those pivoted to fire north proved largely ineffective.

The folly of this misguided deployment wasn't lost on Churchill. Commenting on the absence of fixed, stiff north shore defenses, he said acidly, "It's like launching a battleship without a bottom."

British weapons north of the strait that were continuing to sprout flames were mostly small-bore rifles, revolvers, sten guns, machine guns and light artillery pieces. The soldiers firing them were unrelentingly being pressured farther south. By mid-January Allied troops were backed against the strait, and a second Dunkirk was underway. This evacuation, though, was more complex; hordes of panicked civilian refugees were fleeing across the causeway and south to the city, quickly doubling Singapore's pre-war population of 550,000.

On January 22 relief began arriving. During the next three days some 40,000 Allied reinforcements arrived to buttress Singapore defenses. Most, though, were ill-trained raw recruits from Australia and India and inexperienced British soldiers diverted from Middle East outposts. Many Singaporean Chinese, having heard reports of Japanese depredations against mainland and Malayan Chinese, eagerly volunteered their services to Governor Shenton Thomas. As with the formation of the 101 Special Training School, these Chinese volunteers mixed loyalists and communists who put aside political differences to help repel a common enemy. Governor Thomas quickly authorized formation of the China National Council which put to work thousands building defensive works and undertaking other essential tasks such as finding shelter for refugees and organizing food stores.

When General Yamashita was informed of these developments, he merely smiled. He recognized that they might slow his progress, but he still held another trump card. Surprise, superior speed and maneuverability all had provided him with winning hands, and he hoped his remaining card would lead to gathering the entire pot.

As George Britton, Oliver Needle and Malcolm Goode were nearing the causeway's north end, intense enemy fire was their steady companion. It was January 31. The three men and Captain Barnsworth had volunteered to join other soldiers including two bagpipers for a particularly hazardous mission: serving as the rearguard for British combat engineers who would attempt to thwart the Japanese by rendering the causeway uncrossable.

Yamashita's men now having occupied Johor, the general was expansive. From his temporary headquarters in Johor's gray stone chief administrative building, he invited 40 fellow officers to a sake party to congratulate them on the successful advance. The menu adhered to tradition; dried cuttlefish and chestnuts accompanied the wine made from fermented rice. After pouring sake for all, Yamashita asked the officers to step outside. They faced northeast toward Tokyo, lifted their cups and toasted reverentially.

The nuns at Singapore General Hospital were not inclined to partying. They would have welcomed time for sleeping or even resting.

"My faith is strong," Sister Grace Ann was saying softly to Sister Regina as the pair were vigorously washing their hands with strong soap. "But I confess to having some serious worries."

Sister Regina paused from scrubbing and eyed her colleague. "Having faith doesn't mean not having very human feelings."

"Are you worried too?"

"Yes. For many reasons. Our patients. Especially young mothers and their newborns. The air raids are coming virtually every day, and I pray for no hits on our hospital. I worry for our beloved Singapore and its people of all races and religions."

"For us?" Grace Ann asked, looking down and resuming scrubbing.

"For our safety, yes," Regina acknowledged ruefully. "But let me ask you to keep that our secret. I would rather our nuns keep upper most in mind the welfare of our patients. I don't want them distracted by my worries."

"Of course." Grace Ann's respect for Regina was virtually boundless.

"Good," said Regina, reaching for a white towel.

"Sister Regina?"

"Yes"

"I am glad I'm not alone in my worries." She too began toweling her hands.

Regina straightened and pondered before voicing her next thought. "I'm glad I had someone to confide in. I am learning that courage doesn't always come easily."

They waited until the curtain of darkness descended. Then the rearguard began stepping onto the causeway and marching briskly toward its center. As quickly as possible, the British troops wanted to create greater distance between them and the encroaching Japanese. The engineers and supporting infantry were feeling a strong sense of urgency.

"Sitting ducks. That term somehow seems appropriate tonight," Malcolm muttered. He extracted his soiled kerchief from a pocket in his knee-length shorts and wiped his smudged glasses. "I guess I'd like to be able to see what hits me."

The causeway afforded no cover and precious little opportunity to create proper spacing among the men.

"Spread out," Barnsworth ordered. "Prone firing position."

His men obeyed, gingerly lowering themselves onto the railroad ties and the adjacent paved roadway for motor vehicles.

Teams of engineers began placing explosive charges. Their mission was to blow a gap about 60 yards long. The work required only minutes but seemed interminable to the infantrymen.

"Do you think the Japs know we're out here?" Malcolm asked George, lying on his belly on the opposite side of the tracks.

"They-" A flair exploded above them. "They will in a few moments," George said dryly.

"We're lighting fuses," shouted the engineers' commanding officer. "Everyone up and let's skedaddle."

The two pipers smartly led the way, skirling *Hielan Laddie*. George, Malcolm, Oliver and the other rear guardsmen pushed themselves to their feet, and pairs of boots began gallumping past the pipers and across the remainder of the causeway. They had run no farther than 100 feet when Japanese, their targets illuminated, cut loose with Type 99 rifles and light machine guns.

George heard a pair of screams. One came from a piper and the second, he realized, had erupted from his own mouth. "Fuck," he muttered as he fell to the pavement. "Not again."

Malcolm stopped and turned. "Hold on."

"No. Keep going. Get the bloody hell off."

Malcolm hesitated. "No bloody fucking way. Oliver! Anyone! Britton's down."

Within moments soldiers were aiding the downed piper, with one picking up his bagpipes. Two others dropped to either side of George. "My thigh. Right one."

They hoisted George to his feet, steadied themselves and began half-dragging their comrade toward the island. As they did so, Malcolm fired his remaining rounds, picked up George's Enfield and emptied it toward the Japanese. Calmly he reloaded his rifle and kept firing as he backed his way across the causeway. Two more flares exploded. He had not gone more than a few feet when the charges detonated. Malcolm stood transfixed, peering up through his glasses, as light from the flares showed ties, sections of rails and chunks of roadway being flung skyward. The remaining piper, seemingly impervious to the explosion and whining bullets, kept skirling.

In the next moment, Oliver felt a sharp sting. "Shit," he hissed, slapping his left hand against his left ear. When he pulled his hand away, it was dripping blood he couldn't see but could feel. He reached toward his ear again. "Jap bullet took a bite of my ear with it." He tried to ignore the dripping blood and wiped his hand against his knee-length shorts. "If that's the worst of it, I'm one lucky Tommy."

Now south of the causeway, Oliver found a stretcher. He and Malcolm steadied the canvas while two other soldiers eased George onto it. "Just a second," Oliver said, his ear still dripping red. He had both his and George's Enfields strapped to his back, and he shifted his shoulders, trying to reduce the discomfort. "All set."

"Sure?" Malcolm asked.

"Sure," Oliver grimaced and pushed aside the temptation to finger his wound. He and Malcolm lifted and began trudging south toward Alexandra Hospital on Alexandra Road. They were hoping to locate any vehicle – truck, car, ambulance. Otherwise they would be carrying their friend for 12 miles afoot. They desperately wanted to avoid that abhorrent possibility.

CHAPTER 44

Consul-General Kenneth Patton gathered the entire staff together in the Union Building's second floor conference room. It was 1:30 p.m. on February 1.

"I must admit, this is a meeting I'd never imagined having," Patton began. "Even when the Japanese landed at Kota Bahru, I didn't foresee them driving the British down the peninsula and back on to the island. I'm afraid I'm as guilty as anyone of underestimating Japanese fighting ability."

"Many share your guilt, sir," Joe Barton said somberly, "Americans as well as British and Aussies."

"Right," said Patton, pursing his lips and sadly shaking his head, "but that's small consolation. We need to deal with a new reality. I've been in touch with Washington. I recommended evacuation and Washington concurs. We'll make our way home. To the States."

"Right away, sir?" Rosalie asked. "The Japanese haven't crossed the strait, and the causeway has been blown."

"Does anyone in this room think that a ruptured causeway will stop the Japanese? Or even do much to impede their progress?" Silence for long moments. "I will tell you what I told Washington. I will no longer underestimate Japanese determination and skill. I'm convinced they will make short work of crossing the narrow strait. I've arranged a plane to take us out tomorrow. Predawn. To minimize the possibility of some marauding Japanese pilot using us for target practice. Our first destination will be Australia. Gather only the personal belongings you deem essential. We'll be using a DC-3 and cargo space is limited. Sorry but you'll have to leave heavy items and souvenirs behind."

"What about documents?" Joe asked.

"Good question. Mr. Aldridge will supervise sorting them – which papers to destroy and which ones we'll be taking with us. The ones to destroy we'll burn. Mr. Barton, would you be so kind as to locate a large drum or gas can? We'll use it as our incinerator. Set it up outside on the quay."

"Will do, sir."

"Good. Well," Patton sighed, "let's adjourn and begin making preparations." A pause. "Let me add that you have been a wonderful staff. A great team. I am proud of the work you've done. Most Americans know nothing of our little outpost. But the United States should be proud of your efforts. Thank you."

As the room was emptying, Joe hung back. He waited until he and Patton were alone. Patton eyed his young deputy assistant trade commissioner and smiled knowingly. "You've something to say in private?"

Joe nodded. "Yes, sir."

"You don't approve of my plan?"

"It's a good plan, sir."

"But..."

"But I have other plans."

"Do you mind sharing them?"

"I will locate a barrel or can and help with burning papers. I'll help in any other way I can. Beyond that my plans aren't fully formed. But I have friends here, and I'm not prepared to abandon them."

It was Patton's turn to nod again. "Admirable but foolish."

"That's probably what Miss Hughes would say."

"Who is Miss Hughes?"

"She's the reason I'm here."

Dusk was settling and Joe was on the quay, feeding documents to flames. Rosalie approached, carrying another armload. Joe turned and smiled. "A bonfire on a quay in Singapore. It almost sounds romantic."

"Almost romantic," Rosalie smiled, "but sadly so."

"Right. So, do you have your things packed?"

"Yes. But I've heard you don't." A pause. "There's this weird rumor going around. Any truth to it?"

Joe chuckled. "My secret's out."

"Was it supposed to be a secret?"

"Not really. I just didn't want to upset anyone. There's enough stress going around as it is."

"You're not the only one who's staying."

"What?" A pause. "Okay, not a particularly brilliant question. But then few would accuse me of being brilliant."

Rosalie chuckled in return. "You're funny. Anyway, I guess I know someone equally unbrilliant."

"For crying out loud, who?"

"You're looking at her. I'm staying too."

Joe bit off another What? before it could escape his lips. "For friends?"

"You could say that."

"I've never asked you about your personal life."

"Don't start now."

"Okay. But do you know how Mr. Patton regards my decision?"

"I can guess."

"What's your plan?"

"What's yours?"

"I want to be sure Duane Hurd and his parents are going to be all right. Then there are three British soldiers I want to check on."

"Your fishing buddies?"

"Right. And there's the nun I met at the hospital."

"Well, if you don't mind, I'll just tag along."

"And?"

"And what?"

"Is that all?"

"For now."

CHAPTER 45

Japan's aerial bombardment of Singapore was proving as regular and inescapable as the tides. Its bombers virtually owned the sky, and they arrived daily over the city, seldom impeded by Allied opposition of any sort.

General Yamashita stood hands on hips on the upper floor of the gray square tower of Johor's chief administration building. With powerful binoculars he focused on the causeway and its 60-yard breach. He turned to the commanding officer of the engineers' unit. Before Yamashita asked a question, the officer provided an answer: "Shouldn't be much of a problem, General. We have the expertise, and we can conscript the necessary labor. We'll work around the clock, and our air force" – he pointed toward bombers escorted by Zero fighters streaming south toward Singapore city – "will keep our workforce free from enemy planes – in the unlikely event any will dare to appear. They will also attack and destroy threatening enemy artillery positions."

"Very good. When will work commence?"

"Tonight or early tomorrow morning. We need only a few hours to move equipment and supplies to the causeway and round up a supplementary labor force."

"Who will volunteer?" Lieutenant Wada asked. For a long moment no one spoke. "I will, sir," said Takuma Matsui. Among the tallest of the soldiers in his company, Matsui had been a strong swimmer from early youth. Besides, he was thinking, it will feel good to shed this filthy uniform and let warm seawater cleanse my body – and purify my spirit.

He thus became a member of one of two four-man Japanese reconnaissance teams. All eight were volunteers. Their mission that night: swim the Johor Strait, stealthily scout British and Australian troop deployments and, undetected, swim back. If captured they would be shamed as they would have no means with which to end their lives. Of course, Matsui knew, if captured naked, he no doubt would be interrogated and executed as a spy. I am not eager to die, Matsui reflected as he stripped, not even in the service of our divine emperor. If he is truly divine. No one, not my parents or Shuri, knows I am skeptical about emperors and divinity. Heresy. That's how they would see it, and they would be appalled. If I ever voiced my doubts out loud while in the Army, my life would end quickly – probably with my head rolling on the ground. I could only hope that Lieutenant Wada would be my executioner and that his sword would be sharp. If our emperor were truly divine, our Army would suffer no losses. We would sweep aside all enemies without casualties. But if this mission succeeds tonight, it might save the lives of my fellow soldiers. Some of them anyway. Although some, many actually, deserve to die. Those who have raped and murdered. Like Kazuo Hoshi. I regret I had to kill him but don't regret that he is dead. I hope that young woman and her family survived.

Matsui looked at Etsuro Yamada and Kai Hata. In the starlight their faces seemed almost bright. They had not volunteered and Matsui didn't resent their choice. He and the other seven volunteers, all naked now, stood patiently while fellow soldiers blackened their bodies from faces to feet. They all looked at Lieutenant Wada who merely nodded. The eight separated into two teams and then spaced themselves widely. With no hesitation they stepped into the water of Johor Strait west of the causeway and began swimming south. Their breaststrokes were virtually soundless.

General Yamashita's confidence in his engineers was well placed. With conscripted Malay civilians – women as well as men – providing labor and working around the clock, the causeway breach was repaired by nightfall on February 4.

"You do not have to go. Nor do any of the other seven," Lieutenant Wada said somberly. "That is from General Yamashita himself."

"I've had a week to recover," Matsui replied.

The two men were standing near the waters of the strait, southwest of the causeway. They were alone.

"General Yamashita isn't thinking about you being rested. He values the information you brought back from the island, and he believes you have taken more than enough risk and made more than enough sacrifice." A pause. "For the record, I agree with him."

Matsui nodded. "I should remain with the other men in our company. I will go."

Wada smiled ruefully. "I thought you would. I sometimes think our Samurai traditions are a curse. They imprison our thinking. There is no way out."

"For most, that's true."

"Not all?"

"No."

"All right," Wada sighed. "That will be all." Matsui saluted and turned away to join his company. "Matsui."

"Yes, sir?" He stopped and pivoted toward Wada.

"Private Hoshi. I think I know what might have happened to him," Wada said softly. "There is no need to reply. Good luck, Private."

It was early evening on February 8, and Yamashita was ready to spring another surprise on the Allies. Beginning earlier in the day, his forces unleashed a furiously sustained artillery attack on Allied troops positioned in the Changi region along the island's northeast coast. British General Percival, perceiving the barrage as an attempt to soften Allied defenses prior to a mass landing, concentrated his forces there. We simply will not let the Japanese cross here, he thought.

Meanwhile, Yamashita and his planners were anticipating – correctly – that their diversion would leave weakened the island's northwest defenses. That would, they concluded, be especially true on and around Sarimbun Beach, about five miles west of the causeway. They also were taking advantage of what Matsui and the other seven reconnaissance volunteers had learned: streams and mangrove swamps provided gaps between Allied units – chiefly two Australian brigades, each fielding about 800 men and each deployed too thinly along fronts far too wide.

Leaving little to chance, Yamashita ordered a second artillery attack on Sarimbun Beach and surrounding areas. In addition he sent aloft Japanese aircraft – long-range Mitsubishi G3M Nells and G4M Bettys plus Zero fighters – to bomb and strafe the Allies.

Responding, the last remnants of Allied air forces – 10 Hawker Hurricanes – scrambled from Kallang Airfield, the only one of four Allied bases not within range of Japanese artillery. The other three bases - Tengah, Seletar and Sembawang – were located on the island's north coast and had been so cratered by Japanese artillery shells and aerial bombs as to be rendered useless. Many planes based at those fields had been destroyed on the ground.

Two of the 10 Hurricanes were piloted by Kenneth Draper and Randall Norton. Gamely they took on 84 Japanese planes. Remarkably, in their first sortie, Hurricane pilots shot down six enemy craft while losing only one. With dogfights rapidly consuming fuel, the remaining Hurricanes returned to Kallang, refueled and rose again. Draper and Norton were among them.

As the day wore on, Japanese planes were intensifying their attack on Kallang. They were determined to fatally pit Kallang's landing strips. General Percival then ordered the few remaining Allied planes, including those piloted by Draper and Norton, to safety across the Malacca Strait to Sumatra and the airfield at Palembang. They were the last Allied aircraft that would be seen over Singapore for more than the next three years. The Japanese now owned complete control of the skies.

At that same moment, Jeff Wolfrom was preparing to begin another afternoon of training at Pine Bluff's Grider Field. His proficiency as a gunner was becoming widespread knowledge at the base and was earning him respect. I can't help wondering, he mused, what it's really like to be in aerial combat. Flying through flak screens. Hearing bullets bounce off the

Plexiglas of a ball turret or pierce the skin of the fuselage. Or see another plane's fuel tanks explode. It doesn't sound much like glory.

Shortly after 8 p.m. on the 8th, Lieutenant Wada gathered his 150 men. Many were murmuring their dismay.

"These aren't exactly the large boats we used in our amphibious landing up north," Kai Hata grumbled. "And how many of us know anything about rowing? In the dark no less."

Before Wada could speak, Matsui observed calmly, "Motors make too much noise. Would you rather be shot out of the water or make it across in one piece in one of these?"

The "these" to which Matsui was referring were a seemingly endless row of frail collapsible boats. At precisely 8:30 p.m., 4,000 Japanese 25th Army troops pushed the tiny craft into the strait, scampered in and began rowing. Their objective was Sarimbun Beach – not a long stretch of white sand but an area bordered by jungle and marshes.

Coursing adrenalin was making the rowing easier than anticipated, and the soldiers were making quick work of the crossing. As the fleet and their crews were nearing the south shore, they heard an ominous whine followed by the inevitable whump. Moments later the sky brightened. A flare. Reflexively the rowing soldiers looked skyward. Within seconds fire began erupting from Aussie rifles and machine guns.

"Row harder!" Wada and his sergeants began shouting above the din. Wada was crouched in his boat's prow and was paddling fiercely. "Row faster!"

As Aussie bullets began pocking the strait's still waters and ripping into the boats and men, a ragged chorus of agonized screams began piercing the night air.

More flares were whitening the sky, the volume of Aussie fire was increasing, and the cries of those hit were strengthening the resolve of the oncoming Japanese.

This is not how I saw myself dying or want to die, Matsui thought fleetingly. Not drowning in this strait, not after swimming it twice. My body drifting out to sea. Shuri would never know my fate. Behind him he heard a scream. He glanced back and saw a soldier slumped over the craft's side. A reddish mass appeared where the left side of his face had been. Kai Hata, rowing abreast of the dead soldier, retched.

As the boats were nearing the shoreline, they began scraping bottom. Instantly soldiers, grateful for the feel of earth beneath them, began vaulting from the boats, firing as they ran ahead for the cover of mangrove trees that were growing right to the water's edge.

"This way!" Matsui shouted to Lieutenant Wada and others in the company. Remembering and putting to use his reconnaissance findings, Matsui began leading Wada's company into the mouth of a small stream. Men, panting from their rowing exertions, were struggling to keep their footing on slippery rocks. Minutes later, safely between units of Aussie defenders, Wada's men collapsed on the stream's gently sloping banks.

After catching their breaths, Matsui and Wada led their men on a flank attack against an Aussie company. The fighting, much of it close with point-blank shooting, bayonet thrusts and hand-to-hand combat, raged past midnight. Gradually the stubborn Aussies gave way. It was a scenario that played out repeatedly that night along the Sarimbun Beach front.

About 1 a.m. on the 9th, Yamashita landed more troops. Australian reserves were rushed in. Too late. By dawn one Aussie battalion had lost nearly half its men, and other units had been overrun or thrown up their arms in surrender. A few hours later the Japanese had taken Tengah Airfield. Only then did Percival realize the enormity of his misjudgment.

Once again Yamashita's forces had outsmarted and outsoldiered their smug opposition.

CHAPTER 46

The Allies' situation on Singapore island was deteriorating rapidly. On the evening of February 10, General Archibald Wavell, commander-in-chief, Far East, ordered the transfer of all remaining Allied air force personnel to the Dutch East Indies. From a practical standpoint the decision made sense. All four Singapore island airfields were no longer serviceable. From a symbolic perspective his decision was viewed dubiously. The symbolism wasn't lost on Churchill who immediately cabled Wavell:

I think you ought to realize the way we view the situation in Singapore. It was reported to the cabinet by the C.I.G.S. (Chief of the Imperial General Staff, General Alan Brooke) that Percival has over 100,000 men, of whom 33,000 are British and 17,000 Australian. It is doubtful whether the Japanese have as many in the whole Malay peninsula. In these circumstances the defenders must greatly outnumber Japanese forces who have crossed the straits, and in a well-contested battle they should destroy them. There must at this stage be no thought of saving the troops or sparing the population. The battle must be fought to the bitter end at all costs. The 18th Division has a chance to make its name in history. Commanders and senior officers should die with their troops. The honour of the British Empire and the British Army is at stake. I rely on you to show no mercy to weakness in any form. With the Russians fighting as they are and the Americans so stubborn at Luzon, the reputation of our country and our race is involved. It is expected that every unit will be brought into close contact with the enemy and fight it out.

Churchill's missive didn't dissuade Wavell from continuing with evacuating air force personnel. He did, however, tell Percival that Allied ground forces were to fight to the end and that there should be no surrender of Singapore.

In a key regard, Wavell was keeping his own counsel. His extensive military experience was telling him that Percival's only alternative to surrender was annihilation. Wavell was born on May 5, 1883, in Colchester.

He was the son of a major general and graduated from the Royal Military Academy at Sandhurst – first in his class. He was commissioned on May 8, 1901, and soon thereafter was initiated into combat in South Africa in the Second Boer War. He fought again in 1908 in a campaign in India where he had spent much of his youth.

A solidly built man of medium height, during World War I Wavell again saw combat, and in 1915 in the second battle of Ypres lost his left eye.

In July 1939 Wavell, his hair graying, was named commander-in-chief of the Middle East Command. In that role his forces defeated the Italians in North Africa in 1940.

In Singapore his pessimism was founded on his belief – mistaken as he soon would learn – that Churchill's assessment of enemy strength was wrong and that the Japanese vastly outnumbered the defending Allies. While it was clear to all that Japan ruled the skies, it was Churchill who was correctly estimating the size of Japan's invasion force relative to Allied troop strength.

Percival's mettle and that of other Allied senior officers was continuously being tested. Passing scores were few.

Kranji Beach was about three miles east of Sarimbun Beach or about two miles west of the causeway. Aussie Major General Gordon Bennett, who earlier had pledged "to give the little fellows a flogging they won't forget," ordered Brigadier Duncan Maxwell's 27th Brigade to stand firm amidst that jungle-covered shoreline. Which is precisely what Maxwell's men did – for a time. The Japanese' first assault on Kranji went badly. They were met with withering machine gun and mortar fire but also burning oil that Maxwell's men had sluiced into the strait. The Japanese suffered heavy casualties. Still they showed remarkable grit and were able to reach shore and establish a beachhead in the dense jungle.

That success enabled the Japanese to equip tanks with flotation devices and tow them across the strait to Kranji and onto roads leading inland.

Faced with mounting enemy pressure and worried that his forces would be surrounded, Maxwell discounted his brigade's early success and contravened Bennett's directive. He ordered his troops to withdraw. In effect, Maxwell's decision handed the Japanese control of all beaches west of the causeway. Worse, it gave Yamashita's troops opportunity to outflank retreating British forces farther south and west of the city. The noose was being tightened.

CHAPTER 47

On the morning of February 11, Captain Brian Barnsworth was standing atop Bukit Timah and looking north through binoculars. Next to him stood Private Malcolm Goode. They were wearing the standard British Army south Asian uniform – khaki shirt and shorts with knee-high socks.

"Did you ever imagine high ground so useless?" Malcolm asked. "Jungle-caped from bottom to near the top." The British had cleared the summit and used trunks of felled trees to construct breastworks of dubious height and strength.

"We'll have no clear field of fire," Brian agreed. "Unless the Japs accommodate by climbing the same path we did."

"Not too likely, sir. We might hear the Japs, but we won't see them till they're on us."

"Not a particularly comforting thought."

"Not when you consider all the jungle experience they've gained in Malaya and since crossing the strait."

"Of course," Brian mulled, "we're assuming the Japs will assault Bukit. They could try bypassing us – like they did in Malaya."

"Don't think so, sir. Not when they're getting this close to the city."

"I suppose not. Well, perhaps this is where we put a halt to their advance."

"Perhaps." A pause. "Do you think we can hold here?" Malcolm asked.

"Truthfully...I'm not certain, Goode. Our position here is stronger than it was north of the causeway. But we've suffered casualties, and our strength is terribly reduced. And of course the Japanese have more firepower."

"Sir?"

"Yes?"

"This is the highest I've ever been."

Brian lowered his binoculars and looked questioningly at Malcolm. "I'm not sure I catch your meaning."

"I grew up on the Thames at Gravesend. Not hill country. After school I enlisted and our training ground was largely flat."

"Same here," said Brian. "I grew up in Godalming – a village south of London. I went to Sandhurst and there were no heights approaching Bukit Timah's."

"In that regard, sir, I guess we are even."

"I'm thinking we're even in more ways than one." A pause. Now it was Malcolm's turn to cast a questioning look. "We've been through a lot together, Goode."

"That we have, sir. You know, in a way I wish my mates were still with us." Brian nodded his understanding. "Of course they're better off in hospital than here. Waiting for the Japs' next move."

The view from Private George Britton's window was soothingly pastoral. Trees, shrubs and flowers grew in profusion. Alexandra Hospital was a sprawling complex of structures along Alexandra Road about three miles west of the city center and just to the west of Bukit Chandu, a fortified hill. The hospital's administration building was a modest, single story while the ward buildings were three and four stories. They all boasted gleaming white exteriors and red tile roofs.

George shifted in a second floor bed and groaned lowly. Private Oliver Needle lay in an adjacent bed.

"I feel guilty," Oliver grumbled. "Your injuries make mine look like mere playground scrapes."

"You need to heal. And rest," George replied.

"I need to be with our regiment – or what's left of it."

The Japanese did not bypass Bukit Timah. Nor did they accord the British the favor of ascending the well-worn path to the summit. On the morning of February 11, Japanese artillery took aim at Bukit Timah and opened fire. Malcolm and Brian heard the whine of the first incoming shell and crouched low in their foxholes. The barrage quickly intensified. Within minutes both shrapnel and knife-like splinters from the jungle rain forest were inflicting bloody wounds.

"We need to get off the summit, sir," Malcolm shouted above the din to Brian. "The Japs have zeroed in on us, and we've no artillery to reply. The downslope will be safer."

"Agreed," Brian shouted. "Fall back!" he bellowed. "Fall back now!" Nearby troops spread the word and complied, retreating to the south slope. Troops on the north slope remained pinned down. Their mission was to halt any ascending Japanese. Chief reason: Much British Army food and supplies were stored there in caverns carved from the hill.

In the event of close contact, thick jungle growth would deny either side clear fields of fire. The Japanese, though, did hold three major advantages: they were experienced jungle fighters, uniformly they were in superior physical condition, and they were confident. Some of the British soldiers had tasted combat, but many more were untested.

"You hear that, don't you?" Oliver said to George.

"Not ours, I concede."

"Right. Jap artillery and it can't be more than a few miles north. I wonder what our exalted leaders are thinking – or doing."

Lieutenant General Percival and his cadre of brigadiers and other senior officers were huddled in a sprawling bombproof bunker situated some 30 feet beneath Fort Canning Hill. The bunker, to the immediate west of downtown Singapore, was serving its intended purpose as a command and communications center.

The mood was glum, bordering on funereal. In one room a harried telephone switchboard operator was taking incoming calls from units in the field and attempting to patch them through to Percival who was engaged in non-stop meetings. In another room three British officers sat at an elevated table overlooking a large tabletop map showing the deployment of both Allied and enemy units. Three other British soldiers stood on three sides of the table and used long thin poles to push coded wooden pieces that signified unit movements. With each nudging of the pieces it was clear that the Japanese were squeezing tighter the noose around Allied positions.

"George, I know you mean well, but I can't stay here any longer," said Oliver. "I'm checking myself out."

"Understood."

"I don't know if I can locate our lads, but I'm going to give it a go."

"Do be careful," George said concernedly. "There a war on, you know."

A slight pause, and then both men laughed at the absurdity of George's cautioning Oliver.

The British at Bukit Timah were astounded by the rapidity of the Japanese advance up the hill. Like the British, the Japanese wore beige uniforms. Unlike the British in their shorts, the Japanese wore full-length trousers, either tucked into calf-high brown boots or wrapped beneath canvas spats. Some of the Japanese troops were helmeted while others wore cloth caps. Virtually all were single-mindedly bent on pushing back enemy forces.

On the slopes of Bukit Timah they were besting the British, often in hand-to-hand combat. They were taking few prisoners, preferring to kill – they bayoneted the wounded to conserve ammunition – rather than slow their advance by looking after captives. Among the ascending Japanese were Etsuro Yamada, Kai Hata, Takuma Matsui and Lieutenant Haruo Wada.

Once commanding Bukit Timah's summit, the Japanese immediately began pursuing British troops down the steep south slope. Malcolm and Brian remained side by side, firing as they retreated through jungle so dense the sun's rays could barely penetrate the green canopy. Salty sweat was pouring down both the outside and inside surfaces of Malcolm's glasses, stinging his eyes. He refrained from removing the glasses, even for an instant.

"Humiliating, sir. We've done little but fall back for weeks. At the moment I'm nearly ashamed to be a British soldier."

"Many feel as you do, Goode. Let's all try to get off this hill alive and hope we can hold the line closer to the city."

"Hope. I'll concede it's important, but I'd rather see some sign that we've actually figured out a way to stop the Japs. They must have us vastly outnumbered."

In fact, unknown to Allies, their 100,000 men had the Japanese outnumbered by more than three to one.

From no more than 25 feet distant, Matsui glimpsed briefly an enemy captain's rank insignia. As quickly as it appeared it disappeared. Matsui leaned against a tree for support and waited, hoping to see additional movements. He brought his rifle to firing position, stock securely against his shoulder, forefinger poised on the trigger.

"Hold a steady line as we go down," Brian shouted to his men. They were struggling to maintain order and balance as they were backing down the steep hill. "Let's not open gaps for the Japs or get flanked." He looked left and right. "Good show. Keep our line even as best we can." With his left sleeve he wiped his perspiring forehead. Then he took another step downward, away from a wide tree trunk.

Matsui saw the movement and squeezed off a shot.

Singapore's defense wasn't confined to British and Australian troops. Malay and Indian contingents also were providing resistance across a wide front from northeast of the city to the far west.

At Pasir Panjang, a village about four miles west of the city center, the 1st Malaya Infantry Brigade was digging in. Crowning Pasir Panjang was Bukit Chandu, a forested hill and site of a major Allied ammunition store. Charged with defending Bukit Chandu was a Malayan platoon – 50 men – led by a young officer, 2nd Lieutenant Adnan Bin Saidi. On the evening of the 11th, he was checking a pair of mortar emplacements. Saidi had yet to see combat but was telling himself he would not falter. He was determined to demonstrate to his British colonial masters that he and his fellow Malayans were worthy of respect.

Malcolm heard a nearby "ungh" and turned to see Brian Barnsworth falling backward, red staining his uniform at the upper left chest. Malcolm dropped to his knees at the captain's side and saw his eyes rolling upward.

"Jesus," Malcolm hissed. Briefly he considered calling for a medic then quickly dismissed the thought. By the time a medic made his way across the forested slope and tended to the captain the Japanese would overrun them.

Instead, Malcolm slung his Lee Enfield over his right shoulder and across his back. He did likewise with Brian's rifle. Then he positioned himself above the captain's head, reached down, grasped Brian's armpits and began dragging him. "Sorry, Captain," Malcolm muttered, grunting from exertion, "I don't know if you can hear me but I've not the strength to carry you down this hill." This might be most senseless thing I've ever done, Malcolm told himself. If the captain isn't dead now, he could be within minutes. Or I could be shot. Easily since I have to stay in open spaces to keep dragging him. If only George or Oliver could see me now. We're a long way from Gravesend. Or maybe not.

On that same day, February 11, General Yamashita played his last trump card: He dispatched an invitation to General Percival to surrender. His communiqué read:

The Japanese commander to the British commander. In a spirit of chivalry we have the honor of advising your surrender. Your Army, founded on the traditional spirit of Great Britain, is defending Singapore which is completely isolated and raising the fame of Great Britain by the utmost exertions and heroic fighting. If on contrary you continue resistance as previously, it will be difficult to bear with patience from a humanitarian view and inevitably we must continue an intense attack against Singapore.

Percival, mindful of directions from Churchill and Wavell, chose not to reply. Nor did he convene a meeting of his senior officers. Yet he already had ordered reductions in rations of food and water for soldiers and civilians alike, and he was worried about dwindling ammunition stocks. The loss of Bukit Timah and MacRitchie Reservoir worsened Allied prospects, and Percival was becoming increasingly certain that a day of reckoning was nearing.

Among those opposed to surrendering were Duane Hurd and his parents. A central fact underscored their concern: Su Mien was Chinese. That Clayton and Duane shared African ancestry was worrisome, but they felt less threatened, thinking they might be able to pass as dark-complexioned Indians. That was particularly true for Duane.

Few if any in Singapore felt more threatened than Lim Bo Seng. With his reputation for supporting Chinese resistance and Japanese forces tightening the noose around Allied troops, both Lim and his wife Choo Neo knew that delaying action further would be dangerously tempting fate.

"You need to leave now," she was urging him. "Barring a miracle – divine intervention – the Japanese will soon conquer Singapore. And they will be hunting you down." They were sitting in Lim's company office on Telok Ayer, a north-south street on the eastern edge of Chinatown.

He nodded in resignation. "Some other Chinese community leaders are leaving today."

"You must go with them," Choo Neo said. "You must."

"Their boat is small."

"They will make room for you. Please go. The children and I will be all right."

"I wish I could be certain of that."

"If the situation becomes too dangerous, I have a plan for the children and me."

Lim smiled lovingly. "I'm not surprised." His petite wife, more than a head shorter than her husband, was easily his match in intellectual and spiritual strength and energy and he knew and relished that. Like Lim she wore glasses that tended to soften her features and mask inner toughness. "Can you bring the children here – within the hour? Take the older ones from school?"

"Yes."

"Good. I would like to explain the situation to them myself – and say goodbye." A pause. "I am feeling lonely already."

"I know."

"This could be –"

"Don't say it," Choo Neo interrupted. "Do not even think it."

Lim had in mind one more matter. After Choo Neo left his office, he hustled outside to his Ford. It was one he had purchased directly from the Ford Motor Company assembly plant on Upper Bukit Timah Road. He sped the one mile from his office to Singapore General Hospital.

"I owe you much," Lim told Sister Regina. "For the safe delivery of my children, your care of Choo Neo and for your counsel."

They were standing in the hospital's main lobby.

"May God continue to watch over you, Bo Seng." Sister Regina could feel a lump forming in her throat. "If I can manage to get away from here, I will look in on Choo Neo and the children."

"Thank you." Lim was tempted to reach out and grasp the nun's shoulders but refrained. Instead, he straightened, smiled gratefully and left.

Later that day, under cover of darkness and scant belongings, Lim and his fellow evacuees crowded into a tiny vessel powered by a sputtering outboard motor and crossed the Malacca Strait to Sumatra. Before long Lim would move on to India.

Later that night three people were sitting side by side. They had removed their shoes, and their bare feet were dangling from the promenade at Marina Bay. Duane Hurd and Joe Barton were flanking Rosalie Reynolds. Duane and Joe were thoughtfully puffing Lion Cities. Duane's sampan was anchored below.

"Do you mind?" Rosalie asked.

"What?" Duane replied.

"If I take a puff on your cigar. They smell nice and I'd like to see what they taste like."

Duane and Joe grinned. "Sure," Duane said, passing her the cigar.

Tentatively she placed it between her lips and peered up at Duane, the orange glow illuminating his dark features. "Here goes nothing," she shrugged. She drew on the cigar, held the smoke for long seconds, then gently blew it out. "Not bad." She grinned playfully, took a second puff and exhaled slowly. "But I don't think I'd like to try a whole one on an empty stomach."

Joe and Duane laughed and Rosalie joined them.

"Is there anything you won't try?" Joe asked.

"Haven't discovered it yet."

"Sure you don't want to evacuate with the rest of the staff?" Joe asked softly.

"I'm sure. Okay?"

"Okay." A pause. "What about your parents?" Joe asked Duane.

"My mother has agreed to leave," he replied. "Of course Father will go with her."

"Using your sampan?"

"Right. Across to Sumatra."

"Seaworthy?"

"If I set the right course and the waters are calm, yes."

"Then what?"

"I'm thinking of crossing back to Malaya and joining the Malayan People's Anti-Japanese Army. If they'll take a half-African."

"Think they'd take an all-white yankee?"

"Something to check out," Duane answered dryly. "The communists are teaming with the British and loyalist Chinese so why not a yank?"

"And a female one," Rosalie added in a tone subtly defiant, anticipating an objection.

"Whoa," Joe said. "I don't think so." He was thinking rapidly, wanting to nip in the bud Rosalie's gambit. "I'd feel much better if I knew you were watching over Duane's parents on Sumatra."

"Uh huh," Rosalie countered. "And do you think the Japanese will be content to let Sumatra go uncontested? Leave alone a nearby haven for trouble-making refugees from here?"

Silence.

"Well?" she persisted.

"It doesn't seem likely," Joe conceded.

"No, it doesn't. I don't think Duane's parents should regard Sumatra as anything but a temporary refuge." She looked up at Duane. Both he and Joe were admiring her military savvy. "I think you need to think about something longer term."

"Point taken," Duane said.

Silence ensued for the next couple minutes. Both men continued puffing on their cigars.

"You know," Duane said quietly, "we're all assuming the Japs are going to take over Singapore. I guess it does seem a safe assumption."

More long moments of silence then Rosalie spoke. "I know what you're thinking, Joe."

"You do?"

"You're trying to read my mind. You're asking, 'What's this little blond receptionist thinking anyway? Does she have any idea what she's letting herself in for?' Am I close?"

"Pretty close."

"Well, stop."

CHAPTER 48

For the 1ˢᵗ Malaya Infantry Brigade at Pasir Panjang and atop Bukit Chandu, the battle for Singapore began the night of February 12. This would be one engagement where, in fact, the Japanese outnumbered defenders – about 8,000 to 1,400. Moreover, Japanese infantry were enjoying the support of artillery and tanks.

Pasir Panjang and Bukit Chandu stood as the last defensive strong points west of the city. Stop the Japanese there, the Allies reckoned, and perhaps they could hold on until more reinforcements and supplies arrived. For the moment, the Allies had stabilized their line northeast of Singapore and took encouragement from that development.

Yamashita was anticipating another quick victory, one that would swing open the door to Singapore city. His successes penetrating down the Malay peninsula and the first few days on Singapore island had been so resoundingly rapid that his troops had outrun supply vehicles. Yamashita's men were low on everything except resolve. The general worried that if his counterpart Percival received accurate intelligence the latter would stiffen Allied resistance until more reinforcements arrived. To the proud Japanese commander, that was an unacceptable outcome.

Outside of Singapore, Lieutenant Adnan Bin Saidi's name was destined never to be mentioned with others in the pantheon of World War II heroes such as George Patton, Bernard Montgomery, Jimmy Doolittle or Audie Murphy. Yet few accomplished more with less in the face of overwhelming odds. If eyes can serve as a window into a person's psyche and soul, then Lieutenant Saidi's clearly revealed his mettle. They were black, penetrating and blazing with intensity. By dint of training, iron self-discipline, grit and an utter disregard for danger, Saidi and his platoon would earn a reputation for valor.

As was customary, the Japanese initiated their assault on Pasir Panjang and Bukit Chandu with a withering artillery barrage. The Malayans were well dug in, however, and incurred few casualties. Next the Japanese advanced with tanks and hurled a wave of infantry against the village defenses. The Malayans held firm and the Japanese backed off.

Against Saidi's hilltop platoon, the Japanese dispatched a wave of hardened troops up the slopes. "Don't waste ammunition firing down into the jungle," he counseled his 50. "Wait until the enemy closes in on the crest."

They didn't have long to wait. The seasoned Japanese energetically scaled the hill. Eerily, Saidi's men could hear the Japanese before they could see them. Still, they held their fire. As the first enemy troops neared the summit, Said shouted a simple command: "Now!"

His men skillfully rolled grenades among the enemy troops, began lobbing mortar shells down the slopes and opened fire with rifles and sub-machine guns. Throughout the engagement, Saidi remained in the open, moving among his men, firing and offering encouragement.

Japanese casualties began mounting quickly. Their wounded were moaning and crying piteously. Officers ordered retreat and troops withdrew to the hill's base.

Saidi removed a sweat-stained kerchief from a rear pocket, wiped his brow, inhaled deeply and then forcefully blew out his breath. "Good work, gentlemen. Brilliant actually."

Hours later the Japanese sent a second wave up the jungle-covered hill. Again Saidi's men drove them back.

February 13, 1942. The top headline on the front page of The Straits Times, the esteemed newspaper founded in 1845, read:

JAPANESE SUFFER HUGE CASUALTIES
IN SINGAPORE
R. (oyal) A. (rmy) GUNNERS STICK TO THEIR POSTS

Predawn that morning, however, saw hundreds of Singaporeans – whites, Chinese, Malays, Indians – chaotically trying to abandon the island. They had little faith that the Royal Army could stave off the menacing

Japanese. Those Singaporeans were frantic to avoid being taken captive by rapacious enemy troops. They saw the sea as their avenue of escape.

The Empire Star, owned by the Blue Star Line, was a 524-foot refrigerated cargo ship that had been launched in December 1935. As such ships went, it was fast and maneuverable. In addition to crew and cargo, it was designed to accommodate 23 passengers. Captaining it in 1942 was Selwyn Capon. On the morning of the 13th Captain Capon knew he would be vastly expanding that passenger capacity.

In the sisters' quarters, sitting on a rise across Hospital Drive from Singapore General Hospital, Sister Regina knocked on Sister Grace Ann's door. With Regina were Sisters Augusta and Caroline. Seconds later the door opened. Grace Ann was surprised to see three colleagues, her closest friends, standing there.

"I hadn't quite finished my devotional," Grace Ann said.

"I know," Regina replied. "Come with us."

"Where are we going?"

"There is a ship – the Empire Star – that began taking on evacuees last night. It is sailing today for Batavia." That city later would be renamed Jakarta and serve as Indonesia's capital.

"And we're getting onboard? Leaving?"

"You are," Regina replied as they walked down 12 steps to Hospital Drive and began the three-quarter-mile walk south to Keppel Harbor.

"Not you three? And what about all the other nuns?"

"Someone has to stay to work with the wounded."

"Why only you three and the others? Why not all of us?" Grace Ann asked, mystified at being singled out for evacuation.

"Because," Regina said calmly, eyes straight ahead, "you are the youngest."

"What does age have to do with this?" Grace Ann's tone suggested the first sign of indignation. "And you are only eight years older than I. Sister Caroline not that much."

"And because you are the prettiest and perhaps too much of a temptation for Japanese soldiers."

"Me the prettiest? You are beautiful – and not exactly ancient," the youngest sister said spunkily and much to the surprise of Regina, Augusta and Caroline. After all, nuns rarely argued with each other, never with superiors.

Sister Augusta, the oldest of the four, chancing a quick glance at her companions, couldn't refrain from smiling at this exchange.

"That's enough," Regina replied, not unkindly. Her words silenced Grace Ann, and the foursome continued striding purposefully. Minutes later they were nearing the dock and could see hundreds of panicked Singaporeans – men, women, children – swarming around the base of the vessel. Its tall, single stack bore a large blue star against a circular white background. Their desperation touched Captain Capon, a short, stumpy man with a bald head and warm smile. Supplicants clearly outnumbered berths.

"Look," said Grace Ann. "We are too late. There can't be space for me."

"I'm confident they'll take you on," Regina said, thinking it would take only a word or two with any senior officer to have her way.

"I'm not going," Grace Ann said, indignation now fully throated. "I refuse."

"You do remember the vows you took," Regina said congenially, eyes still focused on the scene before them.

"Of course."

"Obedience was one."

A thoughtful pause. "Yes, along with poverty and chastity. But," Grace Ann added, struggling to control her emotions, "there should have been another."

"Oh?"

"Loyalty."

"To God, of course."

"To each other. And to those in our care."

They had been proceeding at Sister Regina's customary pace – walking just short of breaking into a trot. All were sweating beneath their light gray habits and wimples. But now the senior sister slowed. She eyed her youngest colleague who didn't blink. Then she pointed to the Empire Star. "That ship could take you to safety. Eventually you could return home."

"My home in England, you mean," Grace Ann said, voice flattening. "I prefer staying at my home here – Singapore General."

Now Regina stopped. She faced Grace Ann. Augusta and Caroline deferentially stayed a couple steps behind. Regina reached out with her right hand and fingered the left sleeve of Grace Ann's habit. "I really don't know if this will offer you much protection. And," she said, voice lowering, "I'm not sure how much we can rely on God's cloak."

Grace Ann's right hand covered Regina's, still gripping her habit. "You might think me naïve. Or foolish. But I do understand my mission, and I do know where my heart is."

At 8:50 a.m., the Empire Star began easing away from the dock. On board were some 2,160 people – an approximation because amidst the tumult no accurate muster was recorded. It was known that the overcrowded ship had taken on 35 children and more than 160 women including 59 nurses. Grace Ann was not one of them.

Twenty minutes into Empire Star's voyage, the expected began – an attack by Japanese dive-bombers, six of them. They had been attacking all vessels of all sizes leaving Singapore, determined to prevent escape by anyone who might later prove a threat to Japanese rule. Several of those vessels were sunk.

Simultaneously, the Empire Star began taking evasive actions, and its contingent of Royal Air Force machine guns and gunners opened fire – with impressive effect. They brought down one dive-bomber, causing it to die in a fiery splash, and forced a second to break off its attack, smoke pouring from its tail.

The remaining four planes scored three hits that killed 14 passengers and seriously wounded 17 more. In a sense, the Empire Star and her passengers were lucky – numerous bombs narrowly missed the zigzagging ship, some by as few as 10 to 20 feet.

Intermittent aerial attacks continued for the next four hours, leaving passengers in an uninterrupted state of terror. The final attack began at 1:10 p.m. with nine dive-bombers hurtling out of the rich blue equatorial sky. Once again Captain Capon's officers and crew had the Empire Star running at maximum speed and twisting as sharply as possible.

From the first attack onward, the nurses onboard were dragging the wounded to safety, treating their injuries and offering comfort with soft assurances and murmured prayers.

The Empire Star reached Batavia and later Australia. On October 23, 1942, however, the ship, still under Captain Capon's command, again was targeted. Having returned to cargo-hauling duty and sailed from Liverpool, England, the Empire Star was torpedoed at 3:43 p.m. The resulting explosions killed four crewmen and caused the ship to list seriously to starboard. Others onboard escaped in three lifeboats – capacity 40 each – equipped with sails. Captain Capon directed all to head for the Azores. During the night, heavy winds whipped up the seas. At daybreak two lifeboats were within sight of each other – but not the one with Captain Capon. With 38 crew aboard it was never seen again.

Soon after the Empire Star had departed Singapore, the Vymer Brooke left with another large compliment of evacuees including 65 nurses, some secular, others religious. As the Vymer Brooke closed to within a half hour of reaching Sumatra, Japanese dive- bombers attacked and sank the ship. Twelve of the nurses drowned. The rest made it ashore on Banka Island, some after having spent 60 hours in the water. Newly arrived Japanese soldiers were waiting. They selected 22 of the nurses and ordered them into the sea where they were machine-gunned.

Only one, Sister Vivienne Bullwinkel, survived. She played dead in the water. Later, unable to survive in the jungle, Sister Vivienne surrendered and was interned with fellow nurses, first on Banka and later on Sumatra after the Japanese took control. Deplorable living conditions killed eight more nurses. Of the 65 aboard the Vymer Brooke, only 24 were liberated on September 16, 1945.

Before sunset on February 13, the Japanese again threw themselves against the Malay line at Pasir Panjang and again the Malays held firm. And the Japanese sent a third wave up Bukit Chandu. This time enough of their men cleared the crest to begin inflicting heavy casualties on the 50. Lieutenant Saidi was wounded but remained upright and encouraging, shouting himself hoarse. His men forced the Japanese to withdraw a third time.

Yamashita and his field commanders were feeling frustration and anger and didn't attempt to mask their fury. They knew their troops greatly outnumbered the Malays, and they simply weren't accustomed to defeat.

"We will attack again tomorrow," Yamashita thundered, "and we will succeed." For emphasis he pounded his right fist on the desk inside the manager's office at the Ford factory where he had moved his headquarters earlier that day.

Meanwhile, Saidi was concerned. His 50 had lost 13 killed and 11 more wounded. Ammunition was running low, and he knew sending men down the slope to unearth ammunition buried there would be condemning them to certain death. He and his troops would simply have to do their best with what they had left on the summit.

At Changi Prison at the island's eastern end, the cell door opened and a burly British military police sergeant, Ian Stoneleigh, was standing, hands on hips. The ends of his thick, graying mustache drooped below his lips. Stoneleigh, an eight-year veteran, stood six feet two inches, weighed 205 chiseled pounds and possessed arms that reflected having thrown countless hay bales in his youth on a West Sussex farm – where the two-story brick house dated to 1797, the stone and wood barn to about 1600 and the low-slung wood livestock shed to about 1550. His voice resembled that of an echo ascending from the bottom of a large Scotch whisky barrel.

"Get up," he commanded the prisoner.

"Why?"

"Do as you are told. Come with me."

The sun was slipping beneath the western horizon, and darkness soon would be lowering the curtain on February 13.

As disgraced Captain Patrick Heenan slowly exited his cell, Sergeant Stoneleigh spun him around roughly and applied handcuffs.

"What are you doing? Where are you taking me?" Heenan felt anxiety tightening his chest.

"Quiet," the sergeant ordered. He began pushing Heenan down a corridor toward an exit. Observing guards said nothing. Nor did other prisoners. Outside, Stoneleigh grasped Heenan by his left shoulder and began leading him around behind the prison and east toward the shore. Heenan stubbed his right shoe against a tree root and stumbled forward, falling to his knees.

Without a word Stoneleigh lifted Heenan to his feet.

"I demand to know where you are taking me."

In the lowering light, the sergeant unclenched his jaws. "Has it occurred to you," he growled dismissively, "that you're not in position to demand anything? You've been court-martialed for spying for the enemy and you have been found guilty. Some would say you didn't deserve the trial. I am one of them. In wartime, a desperate time for your country, you betrayed it. You are an officer but not a gentleman. You are scum. Now keep going."

Heenan could hear the South China Sea lapping against the shore. Usually that sound was comforting. Tonight it was different.

"Sergeant, I don't know who ordered this, but it is clearly a violation of my rights. Stop now and return me to my cell."

The military policeman heard Heenan's pleading tone and wasn't moved. "How many British lives did your treachery cost? How many lads fell to your depredation?"

Heenan ignored the questions. "Sergeant, who ordered you to bring me here?"

Stoneleigh stopped just short of snorting cynically. "In the best tradition of the British Army I am following no orders but seeing an opportunity and seizing it."

They were at the shore now. Along this stretch no sandy beach lay at their feet. Instead, a sea wall rose four feet above the water at high tide.

"Remove my handcuffs. Please. Don't push me in handcuffed."

"Even at high tide the water here isn't deep enough to drown you. Sadly so. No, you wouldn't drown unless someone held you under, and I wouldn't soak myself for that pleasure."

"Then what-"

With a smooth, quick movement, Sergeant Stoneleigh unholstered his Enfield .38 revolver, placed the muzzle against the back of Heenan's head and squeezed the trigger. The surf, the gun's snout pressed against Heenan's head and the palm trees behind them all tended to muffle the report. Bits of brain and blood went spewing in the darkness as Heenan crumpled to the ground.

The sergeant bent low and wiped his gun's barrel against Heenan's prison uniform. Once, twice, three times. Then he holstered the weapon.

He inhaled the sea air deeply and held his breath for long seconds before blowing it out as if to cleanse his psyche. Stoneleigh was a stickler for discipline and he was keenly aware that he had violated both military and personal tenets – albeit with tacit approval from above. He reached down for Heenan's shoes, grasped them and dragged his corpse the remaining feet to the seawall. Then, unceremoniously, his brawny arms lifted Heenan by his right arm and leg and dumped him into the sea.

There would be no formal inquest, and the sergeant was never so much as questioned. He hadn't expected to be.

CHAPTER 49

February 14, 1942. The top headline on The Straits Times front page read:

CITY'S NEW DEFENCE LINE
HEAVIER BOMBING AND SHELLING

The story's first five paragraphs read:

Fighting in Singapore is now taking place on a line running from Ang Mo Kio Village, MacRitchie Reservoir and Pasir Panjang.

This is revealed in the official communiqué issued at 5:30 p.m. yesterday. The communiqué says:

"Severe enemy pressure has been maintained on the Western Front during the last 24 hours, and his attack is being supported by increased air and artillery support.

"Shelling today has been frequent on our forward areas and on Singapore town. He has also carried out low level dive bomb attacks on our forward areas, and there have been many high level attacks in the town area by large formations of aircraft.

"Fighting is now taking place about Ang Mo Kio Village, MacRitchie Reservoir and Pasir Panjang."

Another front-page headline that day read:

ALL EVACUATION SUSPENDED AS FROM TODAY

There followed a single-sentence proclamation: By order of the General Officer Commanding, Malaya all evacuation from Singapore is entirely suspended. This also applies to women and children.

The proclamation would be widely ignored.

For Saidi's men during the morning of the 14th, time seemed to have stopped. An eerie silence prevailed. They knew it would end, and more than one was wishing for action, not for the killing or dying but to extinguish uncertainty.

They got their wish in the afternoon. First came another artillery strike, directed at both Pasir Panjang and Bukit Chandu. This one was briefer; the Japanese too were concerned about conserving ordnance.

Next for Saidi and his men came the familiar sound of unseen enemy infantry ascending through the jungle. The arrival of wave number four was imminent. No commands were necessary, Saidi knew. Instead he spoke calmly to his remaining men. "I am proud of you. Each of you. The Malayan people are proud of you. They will know of your sacrifice. They will remember it." He saluted his men and they returned the gesture.

The Japanese had committed reserves to this assault, and they came pouring onto the crest. At first, Malayan grenades and return fire stopped the Japanese. This time, though, the Japanese didn't fall back and descend. In short order they renewed their assault with increased manpower and undiminished vigor.

Simultaneously, Saidi's men depleted their ammunition. Reluctantly they climbed from their foxholes, stepped away from their mortars and raised their arms in surrender.

The same scenario was playing out below at Pasir Panjang. Remaining Malay troops were reluctantly capitulating. Some, though, managed to slip away and headed toward nearby Alexandra Hospital.

Atop Bukit Chandu a Japanese captain, holding his Type 94 8mm pistol, was slowly approaching Lieutenant Saidi. Saidi bent forward and carefully laid his Lee Enfield on the dusty ground. The Japanese captain studied his adversary. He admired Saidi's courage and tenacity. He could see that Saidi had incurred several wounds, although none life threatening.

The captain turned away from Saidi and motioned for one of his men, a private, to come forward. The captain holstered his pistol and took the private's Type 99 rifle, bayonet fixed. He turned to face Saidi, hesitated momentarily, then thrust the long blade into Saidi's abdomen. The lieutenant clenched his jaws, muffling an erupting cry, and slowly collapsed to his knees. Other survivors looked on, horrified. The Japanese captain pulled back on the bayonet then thrust again, this time aiming higher.

Saidi, groaning, toppled onto his left side, hands clasped, blood seeping from both wounds. Combined with bleeding from his earlier injuries, much of Saidi's beige uniform was now reddened.

It was necessary, the captain was thinking. As a prisoner the lieutenant would be a leader – a troublemaker.

Forty-eight hours, that's how long it took the 8,000 to defeat the 1,400. Saidi wasn't the only survivor to be executed. Many on the summit and below at Pasin Panjang met the same fate. A few survivors were spared and soon would be interned as POWs.

As February 14 wore on, Allied troops fought on. Two were Privates Malcolm Goode and Oliver Needle, now fighting with separate units. More than one million people had crowded into the shrinking area still held by the Allies. Civilian casualties from air raids and artillery bombardments were exceeding 2,000 a day. Food and water supplies were dwindling fast as were ammunition stocks.

"They're killing them!" cried Sister Grace Ann. "This cannot be God's will."

"Let's go," Sister Regina replied, jaws clenched.

The two nuns, habits swirling, went scampering down the embankment from the nurses' quarters, ran across Hospital Drive and went sprinting toward the carnage.

The slaughter they were witnessing was triggered by a single death that morning. Yoong Tat Sin was a fourth-year medical student at the hospital's College of Medicine, housed on the grounds in an imposing, columned building. Japanese shelling injured Yoong while he was helping at the Tan Took Hospital on Balestier Road, three miles to the north. He received first aid to staunch bleeding and was rushed back to Singapore General for emergency surgery.

Yoong died soon after arriving. That same evening his friends, including some 25 fellow medical students, decided to give Yoong a proper burial on the hospital grounds. They chose to convert one of several trenches dug earlier for air raid protection into a grave. As they were working, a Japanese artillery spotter saw them while scanning the area with binoculars from high ground to the north. With his guidance, Japanese gunners began lobbing shells at the defenseless students. Amidst explosions, flying shrapnel and screams, some students went dashing for cover in the hospital. Others leaped into the trenches and Yoong's grave.

The last of the incoming shells detonated as the two nuns were nearing the students. The blast's shock wave lifted Regina and spun here around. She landed supine, blood staining the front of her wimple. Grace Ann dove into Yoong's grave. Moments later, face, habit and wimple smudged, Grace Ann climbed from the grave and rushed toward Regina. The elder nun was on her hands and knees. Blood was dripping from her forehead onto the ground. A small piece of shrapnel had sliced her wimple and grazed her just below her hairline.

She looked up and forced a small smile. "I'm all right – I think. Tend to the wounded." Then she vomited.

"Don't try to stand," Grace Ann cautioned. "Sit." She reached into a pocket, removed a white kerchief and handed it to Regina. Then, gently, Grace Ann removed Regina's wimple. "Hold this against your wound."

Eleven of the students were killed, three injured. Two days later the dead would be buried in the trenches.

Alexandra Hospital was Singapore's British military hospital and stood at 378 Alexandra Road, not far from the base of Bukit Chandu. That close proximity contributed to the fate of the hospital and its staff and patients, including Private George Britton and Captain Brian Barnsworth.

About 1 p.m. on the 14th, some 100 Japanese soldiers began approaching the hospital that had opened barely four years earlier in 1938. The administration building was a single floor, about 60 feet long and 25 feet deep. It was white with a red tile roof. The white ward buildings and operating theaters were two floors with doors opening onto verandas bordered by three-railing banisters. The roofs were red tile. Occupying the grounds were shade trees including towering banyans plus palms, shrubs, flowers and lush greenery. They symbolized life and created a sense of serenity.

The mood of the oncoming Japanese was belligerent. Most of the troops were fatigued, nearly spent, from their exertions in the unexpectedly difficult taking of Bukit Chandu. In need of rest the troops were anticipating quickly and easily seizing control of the hospital and then lounging on its grounds.

Unbeknown to the advancing Japanese, remnants of the 1st Malaya Infantry Brigade had retreated through the hospital grounds and had set up machine guns on the verandas of both floors to cover their withdrawal.

The hundreds of patients included survivors of the Prince of Wales and Repulse, the fighting at Sarimbun and Kranji Beaches and the defense of Bukit Timah.

On learning of the approaching Japanese, Brian Barnsworth, his chest and shoulder heavily bandaged, eased from his bed, slowly exited the room and stepped onto the second floor veranda. What now? he wondered. Why would the Japs care about this hospital? Unless of course they think the wounded could somehow prove troublesome. Brian then noticed a manned machine gun emplacement farther down the veranda. Still weak from his wound, he shuffled toward the two-man crew and said, "Get that bloody gun out of here. Fire that and you will be inviting the Japanese to fire on staff and patients."

The gunner looked up. Brian's tone suggested a man accustomed to authority. But bandages and pajama bottoms included no rank insignia. "No disrespect intended, but who are you to be giving orders?"

"Captain Brian Barnsworth, East Surreys."

The Malayan gunner stood and saluted. "We held on for two days at Pasir Panjang, sir. Lost most of our men. Killed or executed. We are of a mind to surprise the Japs and kill a few of the bastards before falling back again."

The Japanese were now about 200 yards from the entrance to the hospital complex. They were walking single file and were led by a soldier holding aloft the rising sun flag. They were wearing camouflage green uniforms and steel helmets adorned with twigs and leaves. They were holding at the ready rifles with bayonets fixed and sub-machine guns.

Brian watched as a British lieutenant emerged from the administration building. He was holding aloft a white flag fashioned from part of a bed sheet he had tied to a crutch. The lieutenant began striding toward the Japanese. The soldier carrying the rising sun flag stopped. Another soldier stepped forward. Another minute – an eternity it seemed to Brian – elapsed. The British lieutenant stopped about six feet from the two Japanese. He spoke the word hospital, turned and pointed toward the complex clearly marked with large red crosses. As he turned again to face the Japanese, the second soldier abruptly bayoneted him. "Unnh." The bed sheet flag fell with the mortally wounded lieutenant.

In the next instant shots rang out from the hospital, kicking up dust in front of the Japanese. Brian, appalled by the murder, immediately sensed greater disaster unfolding. He shuffled to the nearest stairs and began descending.

Because of overcrowding, George Britton's makeshift bed was positioned with four others beneath the large dining room table in a second floor ward. An orderly was placing bread loaves on the table.

The Japanese broke from their single file and began fanning out and rushing forward. Captain J.F. Bartlett of the Royal Army Medical Corps went running forward to intercept the lead enemy troops. He raised his arms to signal peaceful intent and pointed to the red crosses on his uniform. The first Japanese soldier raised his rifle and at point-blank range fired at

Bartlett. Somehow the shot missed. Bartlett didn't wait for a second shot; he went scampering back and dived into a ward office – just as a grenade exploded behind him.

The camouflaged Japanese were opening fire and seeking cover amidst the greenery. One with field glasses was surveying the complex for machine gun locations.

From a second floor window Major J.W.D. Bull held up a red cross flag. The response was a shot that whizzed past his left ear and thudded into a wall.

Captain Barnsworth, sweating and laboring, was edging his way to the rear of the grounds. His wound was leaking. He was hoping to elude the Japanese and make his way east to Singapore city. He also was hoping the stitches binding his wound would hold. Behind him he heard cacophonous shouting and screaming in Japanese, English and Chinese.

Advancing Japanese soldiers were heaving grenades and concentrating their fire on the Malayan machine guns. Within 30 minutes Japanese troops had killed or wounded the remaining Malays and begun entering the hospital buildings. They were shooting or bayoneting virtually everyone who moved.

George Britton offered a brief prayer and girded himself for death. Ironic, he thought, I'm from Gravesend, and I'll be killed and likely left to rot or tossed into a mass grave. He glanced left and right at the other four soldiers lying beneath the large table. They returned his looks with silence and slight shrugs of resignation.

By now at least 50 doctors, nurses and patients lay dead or dying. They included three patients – bayoneted – who had been sedated and were undergoing surgery.

An artillery shell crashed into the end of a ward. Doors and windows blew apart and dust clouded the air. Some 20 men dashed from the building. Most were cut down but five managed to escape into the greenery. Later that afternoon they were captured and would be among the survivors.

George heard the shouts and footsteps nearing and he tensed. Eight Japanese burst into the dining room. Hungrily they eyed the bread. The orderly was sent from the room. The Japanese began gathering the loaves. A minute later they exited. Outside, George heard an anguished scream; one of the Japanese had bayoneted the orderly. George and the other four men under the table were that ward's only survivors.

Brian heard an angry shout. He recognized it as a command. He froze. He closed his eyes and tried to inhale deeply. Slowly he pivoted, his right hand pressed against his upper left chest. He didn't look down but could feel blood seeping through the dressing.

A dozen feet away a Japanese private was standing, bayonet poised to thrust. As slowly as possible, Brian removed his stained right hand from the dressing and raised it above his head. The soldier motioned him to begin returning to the hospital.

Dead at the hospital – doctors, nurses, orderlies, patients – totaled 250. The Japanese were permitting no medical activity.

CHAPTER 50

Sunday, February 15, 1942. The main headline on the front page of The Straits Times read:

STRONG JAP PRESSURE
Defence Stubbornly Maintained
VOLUNTEERS IN ACTION

The lead story's first paragraph read:

British, Australian, Indian and Malay troops and including now men of the Straits Settlements Volunteer Force are disputing every attempt by the Japanese to advance further towards the heart of Singapore town.

The story cited continuing air raids and artillery shelling but inexplicably included no mention of the hospital massacres at Singapore General or Alexandra. In the bottom left corner of the front page was this headline and brief article:

Lord Mayor's Message to Singapore

The following telegram has been received by his Excellency (Governor Shenton Thomas) from the Secretary of State for the Colonies to all those who are so gallantly and doggedly helping in the defence of Singapore.

"You are going through a great trial but I know you are doing everything you can and are resolved to continue to do so. I send to all of you my grateful thanks for your devoted assistance."

February 15 was Chinese New Year, but there was little cause to celebrate among Chinese – in China, Malaya or Singapore.

At 9:30 a.m., General Percival convened a conference in his Fort Canning bunker with 10 of his senior officers. All but two were brigadiers. One of the others was a major fluent in Japanese. The sole question up for discussion: keep defending or surrender?

Percival was standing at the middle of one side of the long conference table. Behind him was a wall map. White coffee mugs and notebooks were scattered on the table. To Percival's right at one end of the table was a clock.

One of the brigadiers placed his helmet on the table. Percival opened the proceedings by reminding the group of directives from Churchill and Wavell to keep fighting to the last man. None present supported that denouement.

Percival next suggested a counterattack. Its goal: retake MacRitchie Reservoir and food depots near Bukit Timah and drive the enemy's artillery from heights outside the city. That possibility too was rejected – unanimously. With ammunition running perilously low and still holding to the false notion that Allied troops were outnumbered, the defeatist brigadiers saw no reasonable choice but surrender.

Percival acquiesced. Only details needed finalizing, and they were worked out quickly.

Percival and his staff selected a delegation to meet with General Yamashita at his Ford factory headquarters, six miles northwest of Fort Canning on Upper Bukit Timah Road. Three men – one of Percival's senior staff officers, Singapore's colonial secretary and an interpreter – rode in a car flying a union jack and white flag of truce.

The factory office building was one and two stories. Topping the one-story portion was a familiar script *Ford* sign. Capping the two-story part was a flagpole – now flying the rising sun. Behind the offices were four long vehicle assembly bays. Percival's delegation entered through double doors – rich wood framing two high glass panels.

Yamashita was displeased by the delegation's makeup. "They are much too junior in rank," he muttered to an aide. The three were sent back to Fort Canning with a directive: Percival himself must represent the Allies. He could, if he chose, bring with him staff members.

During the next few hours Yamashita learned of the massacre at Alexandra Hospital. Angered, he dispatched Lieutenant General Mataguchi

Renya to visit the hospital with explicit instructions. On arrival General Renya and aides proceeded to the ward where most of the murders were committed. He went to the bed of each survivor and saluted. His aides then used bayonets to open cans of fruit they had brought and then personally served to the patients.

During those same hours Percival directed his staff to destroy – before 4 p.m. – all secret documents, ciphers, codes, technical equipment and heavy guns.

About 4 p.m., Percival and three officers arrived at the Ford factory. They were stopped at the street before they could pull into the visitor parking lot. All four men were wearing shirts with long sleeves rolled above their elbows, shorts, knee-length socks and helmets. One carried the union jack and another a white flag. A Japanese officer greeted and led them toward the entrance.

Inside, Yamashita was seated not at the head but alongside the factory manager's conference table. Seated beside him on either side were two fellow officers. Eleven more crowded behind his side of the table. He motioned to Percival and his men to be seated.

After perfunctory introductions, Percival spoke first. "Let's discuss terms and conditions that will be acceptable to both sides." He purposely avoided uttering the word surrender.

To Yamashita, Percival still was exemplifying British arrogance. He felt heat building beneath his tunic and collar. "These are my terms," he nearly barked, twice thumping the table with his right fist for emphasis. Without consulting notes, he laid out his terms. "You will surrender unconditionally all military forces in the Singapore area and do so immediately." Percival blanched. Reflexively his left hand clenched and moved to cover his mouth. Yamashita continued. "All hostilities will cease at eight-thirty this evening. All of your troops will remain in their current positions until receiving further orders. All of your weapons, military equipment, ships, planes and secret documents are to be handed over to my forces intact." At this juncture Percival was hoping that his instructions given earlier in the afternoon as to destroying papers and heavy guns had been carried out. "To prevent looting, you may temporarily allow one thousand of your men to remain armed until replaced by mine." A brief pause. "One more term. Our national flag will be flown over Singapore's tallest building – the Cathay Building, I'm told – as soon as possible." Yamashita had firmly in mind maximizing the psychological impact of the surrender.

"We have no ships or operable planes in Singapore," Percival said, regaining composure.

"I accept that as truth," said Yamashita, "I will take personal responsibility for the lives of British and Australian troops as well as civilians remaining in Singapore."

"Chinese and Malays?" Percival asked. "Indians?"

"All." Yamashita then slid the surrender document across the table. "Sign at the bottom."

Percival glanced down at the single page. Adorning its top was the crest of the Supreme Allied Command, South East Asia. Was Yamashita, Percival wondered, rubbing it in, using British stationery? "Let me have until tomorrow morning to sign. I would like to discuss your terms with my full staff and Governor Thomas."

Again Yamashita thumped the table. "No. Absolutely not. You must sign now."

Percival, an expressionless face masking humiliation, picked up the proffered pen and signed. It was 5:15 p.m.

Immediately afterward, Yamashita watched as his 15 Japanese officers escorted the four British outside. In front of the factory, the 19 men arranged themselves abreast for a photo. Percival's shame was bottomless.

Later, after the war, Yamashita revealed that he had denied Percival overnight to sign the surrender because "I was afraid in my heart they would discover that our forces were much less than theirs." Yamashita's final trump card – his monumental bluff – had clinched the victory.

CHAPTER 51

As word of Percival's capitulation spread, individuals wasted little time taking action.

Choo Neo phoned a friend. "It's no longer safe for my children. The Japanese know who I am and soon will find us. We need to leave."

Within an hour she and her seven children, the oldest 11, the youngest still in her arms, were at Marina Bay near the mouth of the Singapore River. Gingerly they descended a godown into a small boat powered by an aging outboard motor. One crewman sat on a short bench at the prow. The family occupied the next four benches, sharing the rear one with the motorman. Darkness was falling as the motor sputtered to life. Destination: St. John's Island, four miles south and the home of a cousin.

From Duane Hurd's sampan in Marina Bay he and Joe Barton set out afoot toward Su Mien and Clayton's shophouse on Trengganu Street.

"How long do you think we have?" Duane asked.

"It can't be long before the Japanese are controlling the streets. We need to get your parents to the sampan tonight."

A gentle rain began falling as a squad of eight Japanese entered Chinatown from the west. At the point was Lieutenant Haruo Wada. Among his men were Etsuro Yamada, Kai Hata and Takuma Matsui.

Though tired, they were exultant. Their orders: begin relieving the first of the 1,000 armed British troops and detain anyone else seen attempting to flee. Though not explicitly instructed, they felt empowered to react forcefully to any disobedience or resistance they might encounter.

In the nurses' quarters at Singapore General Hospital, Sister Regina called together nuns in the living room. They were watching her expectantly.

"We should be ready for the Japanese to arrive at any time," she began. "Follow their orders. Don't resist. Don't question. We've now seen for ourselves their depravity. They have no qualms about slaughtering innocents." Beneath Regina's wimple, her forehead wound was scabbing over. One of the nuns could be heard whimpering. Sister Grace Ann reached out to her and placed a comforting palm on her colleague's folded hands. "We will ask our Lord to see us through this safely. And we will ask for his mercy on our patients and doctors and staff. Let us begin by saying a rosary together."

The small boat had barely cleared the marina when Choo Neo and her children and crew heard the roar of bombers. They looked up into the rain and saw the first bomb fall from the lead plane's belly.

Moments later, terrifying explosions sent skyward geysers of seawater. Six of the children screamed. The seventh, the youngest, snugly in Choo Neo's arms, began wailing.

When the second plane dropped its load, the two crewmen dived overboard and began swimming back to shore.

"Come back!" Choo Neo shouted. They ignored her.

Then came more nearby splashes and explosions that roiled the water and rocked the boat.

"Here!" she cried to her 11-year-old son Leong Geok. "You hold the baby." She handed off her toddler and took the boat's tiller. Through rain-streaked glasses she kept the boat on a southerly bearing.

Lieutenant Wada's squad was entering the west end of Banda Street, about 300 yards from the Hurds' shophouse on Trengganu Street.

"Should we fix bayonets?" Private Hata asked.

Lieutenant Wada considered the question. "Just to be safe, yes."

Joe and Duane entered Trengganu from the east end off Pagoda Street. At the Hurds', Duane rapped the door only once before pushing it open. Su Mien was pouring tea for two British officers who seemed indifferent to the surrender and unfolding chaos. They looked questioningly at the odd pair – the exotic-looking dark man and his white companion.

Duane and Joe strode past the officers to the room's rear. Moments later, Su Mien joined them.

"Mother," Duane whispered, "the British have surrendered. You and Father must leave. Where is he?"

"Upstairs."

"Go up now. Tell him we are here and that we must leave now. It is far too dangerous for you. A Chinese. Go up now. Or would you like me to tell him?"

"No, I will. But my customers."

"All right. Go talk to them. Tell them your husband is ill and you need to go to him. Tell them they can leave payment on the table."

"Lord, please keep us safe," Choo Neo murmured. By now, splashing water had drenched her and the children. Salt water was dripping from their matted hair and cascading down their faces.

"When are they going to stop?" Leong Geok shouted above the din of roaring aircraft engines, the rumbling outboard motor and shrieking younger siblings.

"Any minute now," Choo Neo replied, squinting through her water-spotted glasses. Never had the lowering curtain of darkness seemed so welcome.

Darkness was equally welcomed by Australian Major General Gordon Bennett. That evening he handed command of his 8th Division to a brigadier and, then with other senior staff, commandeered a small boat and escaped across the Malacca Strait. This was the same general who had pledged to "give the little men a flogging they will not forget." His flight forever smudged his reputation. He eventually made his way back to Australia.

Darkness of a different hue was falling at Alexandra Hospital. A contingent of victorious Japanese went marching into the largest ward building. They forced 200 men – hospital staff and walking wounded – outside. Some were swathed in bandages or hobbling on casts. One was Captain Brian Barnsworth.

The Japanese tied their hands behind them and then methodically lashed them together in groups of eight. They were ordered to remain quiet on pain of "severe punishment." The men had no reason to doubt their conquerors.

The Japanese began herding the men from the hospital grounds south toward the waterfront. They crossed railroad tracks and passed smoldering oil storage tanks. Men too weak to continue were permitted to lay their arms on the shoulders of the more able-bodied. But two who fell were quickly cut loose from others in their group, bayoneted and left for dead, their screams followed by piteous moaning.

Brian tried not to dwell on what horror might be awaiting them at the end of this trek. Instead, he tried only to concentrate on his next step and remaining upright.

About a quarter mile from the hospital the procession arrived at a row of warehouses. The 198 men were jammed into three small rooms measuring no more than 10 by 12 feet. Doors were barricaded and windows boarded over. There was virtually no ventilation.

Some men were able to free their hands and those of others but some remained bound. Men had no choice but to relieve themselves where they stood. All became thirsty, some severely dehydrated and delirious. If, Brian thought, the Japanese have motive for this inhumane treatment other than satiating sadistic lust, I cannot fathom it.

Near midnight, Brian, hands still tied, felt a tugging on his binding. It was a fellow patient slipping into unconsciousness. Brian and others bent their knees, trying to ease the man to the floor. He could die before morning and likely would, Brian realized.

Late that night, General Yamashita learned that some Japanese troops were looting Alexandra Hospital. He ordered them arrested and executed.

Joe and the Hurds exited the shophouse. Clayton turned and locked the door – an automatic but wasted effort, he thought. They began walking east on Tregganu. Simultaneously, Lieutenant Wada's squad entered the street from the west. They were too distant to hear the foursome's footsteps, and the night now was too black to see more than a few yards ahead.

In her small room in the nurses' quarters Sister Grace Ann was lying supine, hands clasped and resting on her stomach. She was wearing a light linen gown, a gift from her parents. She found herself wondering about the fates of people – particularly nurses – who had evacuated on the Empire Star and other vessels. "God, please grant them protection," she whispered. "And please see my colleagues and our patients and doctors safely through this ordeal. I ask nothing for myself except courage." Sleep, she knew, would be slow in coming, if it arrived at all.

CHAPTER 52

February 16, 1942, Monday. Governor Shenton Thomas and his wife Daisy were interned at Changi Prison. Soon, though, the governor, like Percival, would be transferred to a camp in Taiwan and later in Manchuria. Daisy remained in Singapore where she was moved from Changi to a detention camp on Sime Road.

Brian Barnsworth's nightmare didn't end with dawn. The Japanese unlocked one of the doors and ordered the room's occupants outside. Then a second door – the one to Brian's cramped room – was opened and about half the men ordered outside. Brian was not one of them.

To the 100 now outside a Japanese captain said in broken English: "We are taking you behind the lines. You will get water on the way."

The Japanese arranged the 100 in a column of twos and began marching them away. Prisoner hopes were rising, and Brian was beginning to think he and the others might survive their ordeal.

A few minutes later those hopes were obliterated. Brian and the others still incarcerated began hearing anguished screams punctuated by cries including "Oh, my God," "Mother," and "Don't, please don't." The cries ended soon enough. A little later the sight of a returning Japanese soldier wiping blood from his bayonet confirmed Brian's fears: the prisoners had been systematically massacred.

In central Singapore Japanese troops and tanks were forming for victory parades. Soon soldiers were marching smartly and tanks rumbling down Battery Road and through Fullerton Square near the Singapore River. A second procession saw proud Japanese troops marching down Orchard Road, the city's tree-lined high-end shopping mecca. Few residents were watching; they were too terrified to leave homes, shops and offices.

The 22-foot sampan was crowded with people and supplies. Beneath its canopy, Duane, Clayton, Su Mien, Joe and Rosalie huddled. To increase safety, Duane had moved and anchored the boat farther out in Marina Bay.

Rosalie whispered to Joe. "I need to pee, and I think I need help."

Joe grinned. "When nature calls on a boat, I do think men enjoy an advantage." He didn't whisper.

Rosalie reddened. "Thanks for nothing," she bridled.

He shrugged.

"My mother will have the same problem," Duane said helpfully. "I should have thought to bring aboard a chamber pot."

"Come on," Joe said. "Move to the back, lower your drawers and sit on the edge."

"I must admit," Rosalie said, her chagrin evident, "I didn't foresee this."

"Not to worry," Joe said with a measure of sympathy. "I'll hold your hands and I won't look down. Then scootch backward a little."

General Yamashita again moved his headquarters, this time to Raffles College in the city center. He ordered the city renamed Syonan – Japanese for Light-of-the-South. The kempetai or military police established their headquarters in the art deco YMCA on Stamford Road. Yamashita's 25th Army began using as its headquarters Bukit Timah.

That morning 15 Chinese, intent on raiding warehouses at Keppel Harbor before the Japanese could claim the goods, attacked enemy sentries with clubs. They soon were outmatched and attempted to escape. Eight were caught, charged with looting and decapitated immediately. Their heads were displayed on streets with signs warning other would-be looters of this fate. Later, during the long occupation, when Japanese troops looted homes and businesses, their crime was smilingly and euphemistically called "shopping."

Brian heard the key turn and tensed. In the next moment he inhaled and simultaneously shook his head and pursed his lips. After everything, he mused ruefully – Malaya, the causeway, Bukit Timah, the hospital, last night and this morning – you'd think death would be a welcome arrival. End the terror. Endure more pain but end the terror. Not so. I am not ready to die. I hope I can hold myself together.

He and the others inside the room were ordered out. Why comply? he thought. Because we are soldiers and used to obeying orders? Silly.

The third room also was unlocked and its occupants motioned to exit.

Outside the warehouse, those among the 100 still tied were unbound. Then they were formed in a column of twos. A heavy rain shower, a frequent winter occurrence, began pelting the prisoners and their guards. Prisoners rocked their heads back and parted their lips wide to let drops moisten parched mouths. The captors began marching them not closer to the waterfront but east toward the city. Brian was puzzled and not at all sure he should be relieved. He could see that his fellow POWs were equally confused.

Their march would be a long one – 15 miles – and would end at Changi Prison. Why 100 were executed and 100 spared Brian would never learn.

CHAPTER 53

February 18, 1942, Wednesday. The Reign of Terror began. That's how Japanese treatment of Singaporeans, in particular Chinese, soon would be known. It started with Sook Ching, a Chinese term meaning "purge through cleansing." The Japanese term was dai kengho or "great inspection." It would presage a brutal occupation.

"Come in, girls." Marie Hughes welcomed into her home three of her Shelby High School history students. She was smiling warmly. It was 4 p.m., the traditional time for high tea in England and her colonies. Miss Hughes didn't fancy herself an anglophile, but she frequently invited girls to her home for tea. She simply relished opening her home to their company. Her invitations were coveted. Vicki Wilson, Nancy Nixon and Patti Helms were today's guests.

As was Miss Hughes' custom, she was wearing a dark dress – blue – and a strand of pearls. Her long brown hair, increasingly streaked with gray, was gathered in a low bun.

Sometimes she served girls tea in her sunny kitchen and on other occasions, as with today, in her parlor, a darker room brightened with fresh flowers. In either case, the tea was poured in the same dainty china cups. Always served with the tea were thin cookies, fresh from Miss Hughes' oven.

In the early minutes the girls were reserved, voicing few thoughts. As Nancy would later reveal to Vicki and Patti, "My mother gave me specific instructions about posture and general decorum."

Miss Hughes suspected as much and didn't rush the girls into conversation. Instead, she chatted lightly, laughing at her own small jokes while making final preparations and allowing the girls to gradually become comfortable with a woman quite unlike their stoic classroom teacher.

Sitting on upholstered chairs, sipping sugared and creamed tea and nibbling cookies, the girls soon were relaxed and feeling at home with a woman Patti later came to call Aunt Marie.

Tea chats with Miss Hughes touched mostly on fashion trends, floral arranging, cooking, baking and doings at SHS and around town. Today, though, with a war commanding daily front-page headlines, she observed somberly, "You know, girls, many of the boys in your class soon will be in military uniforms. Some of my former students already are in the service. They enlisted soon after Pearl Harbor. I worry about them."

"It seems strange," Patti said softly, "that we can sit here and enjoy tea with you when our friends will probably be in danger. And we know that many people in places like Poland and England have been killed. France and Belgium and Holland too. So sad."

"Yes, Patti," Miss Hughes agreed. "And having tea together so peacefully, it's a reminder of the precious freedoms we as Americans enjoy and too often take for granted."

"I'm thinking of becoming a nurse," Patti said, glancing at both Vicki and Nancy and then again meeting Miss Hughes' steady gaze. "An Army or Navy nurse."

Miss Hughes' features seemed to soften even more. "That's very admirable, Patti. But you need to think it through very carefully because being a nurse in wartime can be very hazardous."

"I've talked about it with Mom and Dad and they're all right with it."

"Good. I'm glad you've discussed it with your parents. That's very mature." A pause. Her citing maturity caused Miss Hughes to think of one of her former students. "You know, one of my boys – er, a former student," Miss Hughes corrected herself, reddening and smiling and delighting in the girls who giggled, "is already in a dangerous place."

"Who?" asked Patti.

"Joe Barton."

"Oooh," Patti sighed. "When I was a little girl, I had a crush on him. He was so cute. Even with that birthmark and scar. Or," she mused, "maybe because of them."

"Did he know you had a crush on him?" Nancy asked.

"Oh no, of course not."

The girls laughed and Miss Hughes laughed with them. Their exchange had her beaming. "Joe's in Singapore now. Or was. I hope he evacuated before the British surrendered." Then her smile gave way to consternation.

"What's wrong?" Patti asked.

"I was just remembering," she sighed. "I encouraged Joe to look beyond Shelby for his future. He took my advice and now I worry that he took it too far."

"Miss Hughes," Patti said comfortingly, "you mustn't blame yourself if anything happens to Joe. You – we – can pray for his safety but don't feel guilty. Okay?"

Miss Hughes gazed affectionately at Patti. "Okay, dear," she smiled. But now her thoughts already were turning to another young man, a man for whom she had cared deeply and still missed terribly. *After this accursed war in Europe is over, I must visit his grave. More than ever I believe Joe was right. That would be the only way to close that chapter of my life.*

Masterminding Sook Ching was Colonel Masanohu Tsuji, the 25th Army's top planning and operations officer. He launched Sook Ching with three days of "mopping up operations" by the kempetai. Chiefly, that meant sending out 1,000 Japanese soldiers to hunt down, arrest and often summarily execute anyone known or thought to be harboring anti-Japanese sentiment. Central to "mopping up" was the "great inspection." All Chinese men between ages 18-50 were required to report immediately to screening centers. The screening could best be described as haphazard and capricious. Suspects? They included men who wore glasses, had soft hands (thought to be evidence of the educated), or could read or speak

English. Also targeted were journalists, teachers and former British civil servants. Some were imprisoned but most were executed – shot, beheaded or hanged. How many Chinese men met such fates? Estimates range from 25,000 to 40,000. No doubt many among the dead were killed by shellings and bombings. While the total murdered during Sook Ching would remain unclear, what is known with certainty is that, within days of this "purification by cleansing," thousands of Chinese women were looking forlornly for husbands, sons, brothers, grandfathers, uncles and cousins who would never again be seen or heard from.

While Chinese were singled out for the widest spread, most vicious treatments, other races and ethnicities weren't spared. Eurasians were ordered to go for screening at the Singapore Recreation Club. Most were then told to go home but some were interned at the Sime Road camp. Later, many of those would be sent to do slave labor throughout the Japanese empire. After the war, few would return to Singapore.

More than 3,500 white civilians – British and Australian mostly but also hundreds of American ex-patriots – were interned at Changi Prison which had been built to hold only 600. Some 50,000 British and Australian soldiers were incarcerated at Selerang, a 400-acre military base just a mile south of Changi. Among the POWs were George Britton and Brian Barnsworth, Oliver Needle and Malcolm Goode.

Many whites were released daily on work details to clear bomb debris and repair roads – in the stifling humidity and with little to eat or drink.

The Japanese assembled some 600 Malay and 45,000 Indian troops at Farrer Park, about midway between the city center and the Ford factory to the northwest. They were urged to transfer their allegiance from the British Raj to Emperor Hirohito. Most refused and that meant imprisonment for all and torture for many. To drive home their message about misplaced loyalty, the Japanese selected 80 Malay officers and 100 of their men, marched them off to the south and shot them. Witnessing the atrocity were Sisters Regina and Grace Ann, watching from high ground west of Singapore General Hospital.

"This cannot be God's will," Grace Ann murmured through streaming tears. "He cannot be condoning this." She pressed her right thumb and forefinger against the inside corners of her eyes to staunch the flow.

"We must remain faithful," Regina said softly, refraining from even hinting that recent events had rocked her own faith. "We must remain true to our calling."

"I will forever remain a nurse. A nun…I've always thought of my vows as a sacred and unbreakable bond with our Lord. But now…"

CHAPTER 54

"We need to leave the bay," Duane said. "I expect the Japanese to soon take stronger interest in the boats. They probably believe there are spies among us. Or saboteurs." His parents, Joe and Rosalie were listening attentively. It was late afternoon on February 20. "I think they'll be spreading word that the boat people are to come ashore or send a launch out to tell us themselves."

"I wouldn't expect them to be tolerant of laggards," Joe added dryly.

"And wouldn't we make an intriguing group of suspects?" Rosalie observed. "Americans who could have evacuated but didn't. A Chinese wife with a black husband. And Duane. And all together on a boat in the bay. We'd be lucky if they didn't shoot us all."

Joe nodded. "Succinctly put, Rosalie." Sometime, he thought, not for the first time, I'll have to ask you about your upbringing.

"No need to candycoat," she replied.

"We'll get underway after dark," said Duane.

"Our course?" Joe asked.

"Once we clear Marina Bay we'll row a mile or so before starting the motor. No need to attract Japanese bullets or bombs. Then we'll stay far enough from shore to put our motor outside their hearing. But not so far that we can't make shore if the sea turns nasty. We'll head west for Sumatra."

"How long a trip?" Rosalie asked. "Not that it really matters, I guess."

"You do see things the way they are," Duane smiled. "I should think fifteen hours at least. In calm seas." He didn't mention the obvious; his flat-bottomed sampan wasn't designed either for speed or navigating rough waters.

"Are you certain?"

"Our best information tells us that Lim evacuated with other Chinese community leaders before the surrender."

"Their destination?" asked kempetai chief Lieutenant Colonel Oishi Masayuki.

"Informants – not yet reliable – think it was Sumatra," replied his deputy, Major Jyo Tomatatsu.

"If that's accurate and if he stays there, then eventually we'll find him. It shouldn't be long before our forces invade Sumatra and make short work of the effort."

"Yes, sir."

"And what of his family? His children?" asked Masayuki.

"As best we can determine they didn't evacuate until after the surrender. We think they might have escaped to one of the small islands south of here."

"With children, the island would have to be inhabited." Masayuki studied the wall map behind him in his new YMCA office. "That likely would be Saint John's."

"We will investigate."

"Now to Lim's friends." The chief picked up a sheet of paper from the desk. He looked at the handwritten list of names. "Eliminate them." He handed the list to Tomatatsu.

The deputy knew better than to question the chief, but one name was troubling him. He pointed to it.

"Yes," said Masayuki. "Her too but be discreet."

The nuns not on duty in the hospital had finished their evening meal, washed and dried dished, cookware and utensils and completed a devotional. They were heading to their tiny rooms.

Sister Regina paused before reaching her door, and Sisters Grace Ann, Caroline and Augusta, trailing, stopped too. Regina turned to face them. "I'm not ready for my room. Yet I feel the need for more prayer. If you'll excuse me, I think I'll visit the chapel."

"I feel the same," said Grace Ann. "I'll go with you."

"Could you two abide companions in prayer?" Augusta asked, smiling warmly.

"By all means," Regina replied.

The four nuns turned back, passing through their kitchen, dining and living rooms to the small, spartan chapel at one end of their quarters.

The four-man detail was using a small truck for the short drive from kempetai headquarters to Singapore General. Two of the kempetai were in the cab, the others semi-reclining on the truck's bed, their torsos and heads resting against the cab's rear.

"How will we know which one is her?" the driver asked Captain Hisamatsu Haruji. "They all look so much alike."

"We'll ask," Haruji answered.

The sea was calm and the sky largely starlit. But cloud cover was closing in from the south.

"We'll have no trouble navigating," Duane said. "Plenty of light. Even with some overcast."

Rosalie grinned. "If you have the eyes of a cat."

"Experience does help, Miss Reynolds."

"Oh, pishtosh. It's Rosalie."

"Rosalie Pishtosh," Joe chimed in. "Seems very fitting."

Inside the chapel the four nuns were kneeling side by side. They were not praying in unison though. Each was concentrating on her own petitions and recitation. Rain began falling on the red tile roof, enhancing a sense of serenity.

The chapel door flung open. Startled, the nuns swung their heads to the rear. Four men, all wet from the rain, two more so than the other pair, came barging in. One was armed with a Type 94 8mm pistol and the other three with Type 99 6.5mm sub-machine guns. They were attired in typical Japanese Army uniforms, but each also wore an armband with Japanese characters for kempetai. In heavily accented English, Captain Haruji asked, "Which one of you is Sister Regina?"

Before Regina could reply, the quick-minded Grace Ann said, "I am," and began standing.

"Come with us," said the kempetai leader.

"Wait," Regina said, standing. "I'm the one you're looking for. I am Sister Regina."

The captain's eyes flashed anger. "We are not here for child's play. No games, no guessing."

Augusta spoke firmly. "I am Sister Regina."

The captain's jaws clenched. "Enough. All of you, come with us."

The nuns hesitated. Captain Haruji motioned his three men forward. One reached out, grabbed Grace Ann's right arm and jerked her from the pew to the aisle.

"Umbrellas," said Regina. "May we please take them?"

"No."

Rain had begun pitter-pattering the sampan's canvas top, but the motor's dull rumbling was muffling the sound. Duane was manning the tiller. His parents were huddled together near the prow. Joe and Rosalie were seated together near the sampan's middle.

"If you feel I'm being too nosey," Joe murmured, "just say so."

"Just say so," Rosalie shot back in a terse whisper. Then her voice softened. "I know what you want to know."

"You do?"

"You've been dying to learn my background."

"I'm a curious person."

"You are more than that, Joseph Barton."

"Why so secretive?"

"I think of it as privacy."

"Point made and taken."

Rosalie grinned and in the sampan's close confines Joe could see her sparkling teeth.

"I'm from Lynchburg, Virginia. Born in 1917."

"A year younger than I. No southern accent."

"I scrubbed it."

"Why? When?"

"Starting at the University of Virginia."

"Founded by Thomas Jefferson."

"A slaveholder to the end who bedded one of his slaves. Maybe raped her."

"Does that answer my Why?"

"In part," said Rosalie. "The rest of the answer is hometown attitude."

"Attitude?"

"My father wasn't a klansman, but that's where his sympathies were. Are."

"What does he do?"

"Minister. Baptist."

"Oh."

"Right. Ironic, you're thinking. A man of God who can't or won't see past skin color. He – uh – colored – no pun intended – my thinking on religion."

"Not among the true believers?"

"True. I've little good to say about religion or those who preach it from pulpits."

"I see...Your mother?"

"If I believed in saints, she would qualify."

"I take it that she sees things differently from your father."

"As our British friends might say, 'Spot on, old chap.'" A long pause. "No more questions?"

"Not tonight."

The kempetai herded the nuns from their quarters down the rise to Hospital Drive. They grasped the nuns' arms and helped them onto the truck bed. Two kempetai climbed aboard after them. Captain Haruji and his driver then entered the cab. The truck exited the hospital grounds and began moving west.

"I wish we could have left a note," Regina said. What she didn't voice was her thought that they wouldn't be returning.

"Where do you think they are taking us?" Caroline asked.

"I don't know," Regina replied. "I only know we are heading west."

Rain was quickly soaking through their habits and wimples.

"Soon," said Duane, "we'll be reaching the western end of the island. Then it's into the Malacca Strait."

"So far, so good," Rosalie said above the motor's hypnotic rumbling.

Duane looked skyward. Farther to the south he could see starlight. The rain should be stopping soon, he concluded silently. No wind kicking up waves. We should be all right.

The drive over darkened, rough roads had consumed an hour. The truck braked at the rear of a southwestern beach that jutted out into the strait.

"Do you think they are going to rape us?" Caroline murmured worriedly.

"No matter what happens," Regina replied, patting Caroline's left shoulder, "you'll still be a virgin in our Blessed Mother's eyes." She was thinking – had been thinking during the ride – that rape might not be the worst of their fates.

Captain Haruji and his driver exited the cab and strode to the truck's rear. The two guards lowered the gate and hopped down.

"Out," Haruji ordered.

Caroline was the first to reach the truck bed's drop-down gate. The rain was intensifying and she hesitated. A guard reached up, grabbed her left arm and jerked. She lunged forward, losing her balance as her black shoes touched the wet ground. Her knees buckled.

Grace Ann hopped down and stooped to help Caroline to her feet. Regina jumped down and turned to offer a hand to Augusta.

"That way," Haruji growled, gesturing toward the water. Of all the nights for lousy weather, he was thinking. I'd rather be back at the YMCA. If I'm going to be wet there, it means I'm showering or swimming in the pool.

Duane called for Joe to join him at the stern.

"What do you think?" Joe asked.

Duane squinted north through the rain. "Looks like a pair of headlights."

"They're not moving."

"Doesn't add up," said Duane. "Not on a night like this."

Regina sensed the kempetai were expecting the nuns to continue behaving like sheep – shepherded compliantly. "I must protest this treatment," she said firmly. "It is unprovoked and uncalled for." Her outburst startled the kempetai. "We are women of God, and we pose no threat to anyone, least of all you gentlemen."

Haruji quickly regained his sense of command and control. "Quiet, woman. You are not to speak again."

"You cannot muzzle me."

Haruji slapped her left cheek hard with his pistol. Regina rocked back, struck the truck's gate and toppled to the wet ground.

Caroline whimpered. A guard grabbed her wimple and pulled it back off her head, revealing closely cropped brown hair.

Grace Ann felt her terror giving way to blistering anger.

"Binoculars?" Joe asked. "You have any?"

"Telescope," Duane said. "Use it for stargazing. I'll get it."

In another few moments Joe was adjusting the scope.

"What is it?" Rosalie asked.

"Here," said Joe, "have a look."

"Robes," said Rosalie. "They look like women in robes. With headscarves. Muslims? And Japanese with guns. I count four women and four Japs."

"Let me have a look," said Duane.

"Wait a second," Rosalie said. "Those aren't robes and scarves. They're habits and wimples. Those are nuns."

"That's enough," Grace Ann said bitingly. "You are not to strike her again." She pointed to Regina. "Or her," she added, eyes blazing and pointing to Caroline.

One of the guards swung his rifle's butt, clubbing Grace Ann's left shoulder and sending her to the ground. Haruji kicked with his left boot, striking Grace Ann's nose. Nearly instantly blood was joining rain cascading down and off her chin.

"What do you think?" Duane asked, handing the scope to Joe. He put the glass to his right eye.

"Not good."

"Rosalie," Duane said, "I'm angling the sampan inland. Take the tiller and hold steady for the beach." Rosalie wanted to ask, What on earth are you doing? But she held the thought. The sampan was now about 200 yards from shore, heading north. "I'll be back in a moment." Duane then scurried forward.

The kempetai pulled Regina and Grace Ann to their feet and shoved them along with Caroline and Augusta toward the sea.

"They mean to kill us," Caroline said, her brown hair sopping and clinging to her head.

"Keep your faith," Regina said, rain clouding her vision. "Heaven will welcome you."

"Where did you get these?" Joe asked. He was referring to two British sten guns that Duane was holding.

"They weren't hard to come by. Just picked them up. Some belonged to soldiers who fell and others who ran."

"Some?" Joe asked.

"I also have another sten gun and a pair of Enfield revolvers."

"A veritable armory."

The sampan had closed to within 100 yards of shore. The rain was muffling the boat's rumbling engine.

The rain notwithstanding, the nuns now were close enough to the water to hear the surf.

"Dear Lord," Regina prayed aloud, "in this hour of need, we recommit our eternal souls to you and your mercy."

"Keep going," Haruji ordered. "Into the sea."

"How's your aim?" Duane asked.

"I've never even fired one of these. I've shot a twenty-two rifle, but I was a teenager, and I wasn't standing in a moving boat."

Duane released the safeties on both weapons. "Do your best. We'll wait till we get closer."

Rosalie looked up at the two men. You two are too much, she mused. I wish my father could see you shoulder to shoulder. Black and white. He would be appalled. Call it the devil's own handiwork.

Su Mien and Clayton were holding each other tightly.

"What if they see us coming? Or hear us?" Joe asked.

"I hope they do," Duane replied grimly.

They didn't.

At the water's edge the nuns hesitated. Blood continued running from Grace Ann's nose. Haruji extended his right arm and squeezed the trigger. The bullet tore into the sand at Grace Ann's feet. "Keep moving!" he barked.

The nuns waded into the surf. The water was warm.

"The bastards are going to murder them," Joe muttered.

"Wait till the nuns get farther out."

Seconds later, the surf had reached the nuns' knees. The three kempetai guards leveled their sub-machine guns. The sampan had closed to within 50 feet.

"Now," Duane said, "Squeeze the trigger. Don't jerk it."

Simultaneously, flames erupted from the snouts of the sten guns and the Type 99 sub-machine guns.

Amidst the crackle of gunfire Regina heard screams. Two were female, two male. Caroline was hit, Grace Ann too.

Two kempetai guards crumpled to the sand. Haruji pivoted left, looking for the fire's source. In the next sliver of time, two rounds thudded into his chest. He fell, dead before he hit the ground.

The fourth soldier turned and fired toward the sampan. Rosalie screamed and involuntarily released the tiller. Joe and Duane both squeezed off rounds at the guard. A bullet tore into his right eye, and he spun and fell face down.

"Shit!" That was the first word to escape Rosalie's mouth. Blood was mixing with rain on the back of her right hand. Ignoring the pain she regained control of the tiller.

"Head for the nuns!" Joe shouted.

Moments later Joe and Duane, still gripping the sten guns, jumped into the surf. Regina was on her knees, holding Caroline's head above the surface. Grace Ann lay face down. Joe grabbed her roughly and pulled her face clear of the water. From behind he tugged hard against her midsection. Her mouth gaped and water spilled out.

Regina looked at Joe, then Duane. "I would ask who you are, but at the moment that seems a trivial question."

Joe and Duane both grinned.

"We've met, Sister."

"What?"

"At the hospital."

"Duane," Joe said, "help me get this one onto the sampan."

Clayton moved to the stern. "Let me help." Duane and Joe lifted the young nun, their effort complicated by her soaked habit. They handed her to Clayton and Su Mien who knelt and cradled Grace Ann's head.

"Okay, Duane, help the good sister with the other one. I'll be back."

Rosalie watched Joe go wading ashore. Four kempetai were lying close together. With his right shoe, Joe nudged each. One of the guards

257

moaned. Joe pointed his sten gun down, finger poised on the trigger. Then he thought, No, you deserve a slow death.

CHAPTER 55

February 21, 1942

My Dearest Joe,

I read a small item in the paper about Singapore, and I worry for your safety. Did you leave before the surrender? Are you being detained by the Japanese? I am wondering if this letter will ever reach you. I think I will write this letter twice. I will send the first one to the U.S. Consulate in Singapore. I feel certain it is closed but someone – Japanese? – must be occupying the building and maybe they will hold it for you. I will send the second one to the U.S. State Department in Washington. At least they should know where you are. If the first one doesn't reach you, perhaps the second will – someday, somewhere.

Things in Romania are not good. So many of our young men have been conscripted and marched off to war – a war most do not want. I fear that too many of them will not return. Father and I are talking about possibilities, but they seem limited since Germany is in effect running our country. Dictator Antonescu is pathetic. He curries favor with the Nazis and all but extinguished our sovereignty. He has the respect of few if any Romanians. If his censors see this letter, I could be in trouble. But I am posting it anyway.

My biggest hope now is that one day you will be able to visit my country and see its beauty – from the Black Sea to the Carpathians. Of course I want you to see it with me. On horseback.

With much love from your Romanian gypsy,

Gabriella

"You said we met at the hospital," said Sister Regina.

"That's right."

"I'm sorry but I can't seem to recall."

"I'm your American polo player."

"Mr. Barton!"

"One and the same."

"Well, you seem to make a practice of riding to the rescue – an Aussie polo team and now us."

"In both cases, Sister, I didn't ride alone."

Sister Regina was on her knees between Sisters Caroline and Grace Ann. Both were lying supine, unconscious. Sister Augusta was kneeling near Grace Ann's head. Joe, Duane and Rosalie were hovering over them, while Clayton manned the tiller. Su Mien stood behind them.

"I need to see their wounds," Regina said, "but in this darkness..."

"I have a lantern," said Duane.

Clear-thinking Regina started to say Good but instead asked, "Won't lighting it jeopardize the safety of everyone?"

"Possibly," said Duane, "but not likely, not out here and not at night with clouds and rain. No Japanese planes are patrolling. A Japanese ship might spot the light, but we should take that chance. I'll get the lantern."

Two minutes later Duane had lit the lantern and was suspending it over the nuns from a metal support for the sampan's canvas top.

Regina first examined Grace Ann. The right side of her wimple was blood soaked. Gently Regina inserted her right fore and middle fingers beneath Grace Ann's chin at the back edge of the wimple. She pulled it forward and then up past Grace Ann's face and back. Grace Ann's close-cropped blond hair was matted and stained red.

"Mr. Barton, would you please lower the lantern? Hold it close to Sister Grace Ann's head."

Quickly Joe reached for the lantern, unhooked it from the support and carefully lowered it.

Regina's fingers were probing a wound above Grace Ann's left ear. "No bullet or fragment. It appears she was grazed. With God's mercy I think she will survive." At that moment a low moan emanated from Grace Ann. The small sound lifted spirits.

"Now, Mr. Barton, I need to examine Sister Caroline."

A hole in Caroline's habit and surrounding blood told Regina where to look first. "Please position the lantern over her chest."

"Here?"

"That's fine." Sister Regina futilely tried widening the hole by tugging at the sodden habit. "Mr. Hurd, I trust you have a knife onboard."

"Yes, Sister. I'll get it."

Moments later Sister Regina was deftly maneuvering the razor sharp six-inch blade Duane had used to gut and clean fish. "Lower the lantern a bit more, Mr. Barton." She began slicing the habit.

"I don't know if I should be watching this," Joe said awkwardly.

"We are nuns but also nurses. We've seen everything, Mr. Barton. Under the circumstances, I don't think Sister Caroline would object to you seeing her flesh. All right?"

"If you say so," Joe said, still not entirely convinced of the propriety of seeing what had been hidden by a habit.

"Steady, Mr. Barton."

Mere seconds later the rent habit was revealing a wound dangerously near Caroline's heart. Sister Regina's head shook. She put her ear to Caroline's chest and held her left wrist, feeling for a pulse. Caroline's breathing was shallow.

"Mr. Hurd, I need your knife again, and I need your help. Squeeze in here with me." Duane handed Regina the knife and knelt beside her. "All right, Mr. Hurd, gently – very gently – roll Sister Caroline onto her side."

All heard weeping. It was Rosalie. In the glow of the lantern, Joe saw her dabbing at tears.

Sister Regina again put the knife to work. She cut away a ragged section of the upper back of the habit. The exit wound was distressingly larger than the entry hole. "No bullet to remove. Good. But no sulfa to sprinkle in the wounds. No sterile bandages. She's lost blood, much of it." Regina's cool professionalism couldn't hide the sorrow in her voice. She inhaled deeply. She returned the knife to Duane. "Do you think we'll make land by morning?"

"I think so. Or soon after daybreak."

"Perhaps we can locate a doctor on Sumatra." That simple observation spoke volumes; there was nothing more Regina could do for Caroline.

"Mr. Barton," Regina said, "could you help me stand? Please? I've been kneeling so long my legs are cramped."

"Rosalie," Joe said softly, "take the lantern."

She swallowed, blinked away tears and took the lantern in her right hand.

Joe cupped Regina's right elbow and lifted. The nun straightened slowly. "Thank you." A brief pause. "Sister Augusta, could I ask you to kneel for a spell? Let me know straight away if there's any change."

"Of course, Sister."

"I'll stay with you," said Rosalie, still holding the lantern.

"Shifts, Sister?" Joe asked.

"I think yes, Mr. Barton. One hour."

"I will take the next shift," Su Mien murmured. Those were her first words during the ordeal.

"I'll hold the lantern," said Clayton.

"Then I'll relieve you at the tiller," said Duane.

Regina eased her way forward to the prow. She closed her eyes. Dear Lord, she prayed silently, show mercy on these two young angels. They are devoted to your service. She opened her eyes and looked out onto the strait's black waters. Then she leaned forward, opened her mouth wide and vomited.

General Archibald Wavell also was on the move that night. At Churchill's direction, he was preparing to vacate his commander-in-chief headquarters on Java, the large Dutch East Indies island south from Singapore across the Java Sea. He was being transferred to India where he would take responsibility for the defense of a single country, Burma. His February 10 transfer of all Allied air force personnel from Singapore to the Dutch East Indies had cost him Churchill's respect. In Churchill's mind the handsome, gray-haired solidly built general had displayed a startling absence of grace and courage under pressure. There was much Churchill could overlook but not that. Back in May 1940 as France was collapsing under the German onslaught, Churchill had shown his own mettle by flying three times to Paris to try to buck up French President Reynaud.

Sumatra's sandy coast brought not hope but grief. It was difficult to imagine two women more different in cultural heritage and global outlook than Su Mien Hurd and Rosalie Reynolds. Yet now they were united in grief and support for Sister Grace Ann. They were flanking her, each with an arm interlocking with one of the young nun's. Both were shorter than Grace Ann. Rosalie looked up at the head wound, now cleaned and creasing the short blond hair.

Sisters Regina and Augusta stood at the foot of the newly dug grave. Joe, Duane and Clayton had dug the grave soon after Duane had artfully beached the flat-bottomed sampan on Sumatra's eastern shore. They had performed their sad labor with shovels borrowed from a nearby fishing village.

Sister Augusta had suggested the gravesite – a 16-foot high promontory overlooking the beach and the Malacca Strait's azure waters. "It fits her disposition," Augusta had observed. "Sunny. She kept spirits soaring."

Regina had no missals or prayer books at the ready. Her eyes were closed, head bowed. She was speaking from the heart. "We regret, deeply, losing our dear angel, Caroline. But we are forever grateful that you have welcomed her into your heavenly embrace. There can be no more powerful evidence of your goodness than your messenger who was Caroline. Those of us who were closest to her, who knew her best, will cherish forever our memories of this chosen one. We ask you to give us the strength to carry on in a manner that would make her proud. We were sisters in caring for others, in our calling to serve you, in our faith. She will always be one of us, until the day when we can join her in your heavenly kingdom."

"Amen," murmured Rosalie.

Soft "Amens" echoed from the others.

Grace Ann unsteadily stepped to the grave's edge, still supported firmly by Rosalie and Su Mien. She inhaled the scent from purple bougainvillea and then let them fall onto Caroline's body, wrapped in a small canvas sail Joe had purchased from villagers for five United States dollars.

Regina nodded and Joe, Duane and Clayton began filling in the grave with the earth they had excavated. When finished, Duane spoke, "I didn't know this nun, your sister. But I admire the life she lived. Sometime, I can't say when, I will return here with a proper gravestone."

Rosalie brushed away a tear and said, "I will come with you."

CHAPTER 56

As word of Colonel Jimmy Doolittle's daring April 17 raid on Tokyo spread, it electrified the Allies. It stunned the Japanese. They had believed their homeland immune to Allied bombing. The 16-plane attack almost immediately caused Japan's military leaders, stung severely by Doolittle's "30 seconds over Tokyo," to begin pulling back forces from the farthest reaches of their empire to further strengthen defenses.

The raid thrilled Jeff Wolfrom. That it had cost the lives of seven of Doolittle's men did little to cool Jeff's ardor to begin striking enemy installations and planes from a gunner's position on a B-24.

News of the Doolittle raid began reaching Singaporeans who had evacuated to nearby Sumatra on April 21. Although descriptions were sketchy, they were heartening.

"It's difficult to believe," Joe observed, "that American planes bombed Tokyo barely more than four months after Japan's attacks on Pearl Harbor, Singapore, Malaya and the Philippines. The raid gives me hope that we can take on the Japanese and whip them."

"I agree," Rosalie said, "but we do have something more pressing to think about."

Joe and Rosalie were alone, standing on the sandy beach below their campsite. The sun was creeping above the eastern horizon.

"You mean the Japanese invading Sumatra."

"It's inevitable," said Rosalie. "They control Malaya to the north of Singapore, and they must want Sumatra as a buffer to the west. Or as a launch point for more conquest. In either case, what's to stop them? Besides, they know that lots of Singaporeans fled here. They'd love to get their hands on groups like ours."

"I think we should talk to Duane – and Sister Regina – about our next move."

"Sooner," Rosalie said grimly, "would be better than later."

Inside a tent that protected Jeff from the sun but did little to offer relief from the blistering heat, he picked up a yellow Number 2 pencil and a single sheet of paper and began writing to Iris Ann.

June 1, 1942

Dear Mother,

Egypt and Pine Bluff have something in common. Heat. But there is also a big difference. Egypt is dry. I wouldn't be surprised if the Egyptian language doesn't include a word for humidity. We are near Great Bitter Lake which is the port for the Suez Canal. We are actually at a British RAF training base. Some of our instructors are Brits. Many are vets of the Battle of Britain. Decent guys. We respect them. With all the ship traffic it doesn't seem fit for fishing or swimming. Besides it's salty. We're about 50 miles south of the Mediterranean. Rumor has it – and this might get censored – that we have a big mission coming up soon. Our base is at Fayid – the enemy knows we are here – which is only about two miles west of the lake. But even with the lake so close, there's not much green to be seen. What I see everywhere is sand, sand and more sand.

How are things at the boarding house? Heard any good stories or juicy rumors?

I really appreciate your letters. They take a while to catch up to me, but I read each one many times over.

Your devoted son and desert flyboy,
Jeff

June 5, 1942. The United States declared war on Romania. The declaration came nine months after Ion Antonescu had rashly declared war on the U.S. Why the delay? And why declare war on Romania at all? Its military forces posed no threat to America or its interests. No direct threat. But Ploesti's refineries were producing one-third of Hitler's high-octane aviation gasoline, panzer fuel and lubricants. They also were supplying fully half the oil that was keeping Rommel's tanks and supporting vehicles running on the sands of North Africa. By declaring war on Romania, the U.S. was engaging in a diplomatic nicety – legalizing any future bombing raids on Ploesti.

"Mr. Barton," said Sister Regina, "might I have a word with you? Privately?"

"Of course." Joe was sitting in the shade of a coconut palm tree, eyes closed, wondering how Marie Hughes would regard her former history student's predicament. He stood and stretched his six-foot frame.

Joe and Duane had chosen a campsite not far from the beach and Duane's sampan but far enough inland to enjoy the shade of trees. Joe had used more of his dollars to buy four tents and other camping necessities, including canned foods. He and Duane shared one tent, although Duane opted to spend some nights on his sampan. Su Mien and Clayton occupied the second tent, Regina and Augusta the third and Grace Ann and Rosalie shared the fourth.

Joe and Sister Regina strolled past the tree line to the rear of the beach.

"Mr. Barton, let me be direct. We are feeling a desperate need to bathe and do laundry. I'm saying we because Su Mien and Rosalie are feeling the same need. At first I thought we nuns could bathe and launder separately, but as we're all in this together, that didn't seem proper." Joe nodded assent. "The stream near our camp should suffice. The water is clear, fresh and running."

"All right," Joe replied casually, curiosity causing him to wonder where this private conversation was heading.

"We've no starch or iron so our habits will come out looking a trifle rumply I'm afraid."

"Sister," Joe smiled, "your goodness will still show clearly through the wrinkles in your habit."

Regina blushed and smiled demurely. "Thank you, Mr. Barton. At least we and our habits and under garments will be clean. You can't imagine, well...I'm of a mind to dispense with my wimple. The jungle humidity turns them into thermal baths. Grace Ann of necessity is going without one, and I'll suggest to Sister Augusta that we shed ours."

Joe grinned, his smile surrounded by stubble that grew thick between every two- or three-day shaves. "I do believe Sister Augusta will find favor with your suggestion. But why the need for this private conversation?"

"Well, while we are in that stream, bathing and laundering, we women would feel safer if you and Mr. Hurd were standing guard. Discreetly, of course."

"Discreetly, of course." Joe smiled. "We'll be at a distance, but close enough to serve as security."

Laughter was an unaccustomed sound since the group's arrival on Sumatra and Sister Caroline's death. Joe and Duane, barefoot, were leaning against a pair of palm trees, about 25 feet from the stream. Joe was unarmed but Duane had tucked a revolver and his knife between his belt and trousers. Not that he anticipated needing them. They were for show, the visible security Regina had sought.

"Cleanliness must be raising their spirits," Joe said, the women's laughter penetrating the thick vegetation. "And camaraderie."

"It's been easier for us," Duane observed. "We just go down to the beach at night, strip and wade into the strait."

"You and your father and I —" A shriek of terror stopped Joe in mid-sentence. A second shriek followed.

Alarmed, Joe and Duane went dashing along a narrow path through the jungle to the stream, about 20 feet wide. Five naked women were in the water, squatting to stay concealed to their necks. Sister Augusta was pointing to a water snake, about three feet long, swimming placidly between the women and the bank. Joe glanced at Duane, shrugged and waded into the stream. He reached out and grasped the snake behind its head.

"Poisonous?" Duane asked.

"Not sure," Joe replied.

"Give it to me."

Joe stepped back onto the bank and handed the squirming reptile to Duane. He squatted, loosed his knife and dispatched the snake with a swift slice.

"Ewww." It was Grace Ann.

"My sentiments exactly," Rosalie said disgustedly.

"Everyone all right?" Joe asked.

The women looked at each other. "So it would seem, Mr. Barton," Regina answered. "Once more you have ridden to the rescue, as it were." She laughed gaily, and her merriment proved contagious – and cathartic. Augusta, Grace Ann, Rosalie and Su Mien broke into a symphony of joyous laughter.

Then, on impulse Regina straightened and threw her arms skyward. The other women and Joe and Duane were gaping at her in wonder. Her breasts were small, brown nipples contrasting sharply with the whitest of flesh. "Modesty is not one of our vows," Regina said, water dripping from her ears, chin and nipples, hands now on slender hips, "but it's a virtue we take seriously. But we – Augusta, Grace Ann and I – are nurses and have seen countless anatomies. I was weary of squatting, of hiding." She looked around at her friends. "I guess today was my turn to show – and surprise – myself." She laughed again.

"Well," Rosalie said puckishly, straightening, "if you can put aside your modesty, so can I."

Augusta shrieked – a shriek that blended shock and glee – and covered her mouth but remained squatting, as did Grace Ann.

Now it was Joe who laughed – and shook his head. "This wasn't included in my Foreign Service training. I'll wait for you ladies – er, sisters and…" He threw up his arms as if in surrender, pivoted and began retreating with Duane through the jungle to his palm tree sentry post.

All five women began wading toward the bank.

"I am not sure I can quite believe what I just witnessed," Grace Ann smiled, reaching for her undergarments, suspended from low hanging tree branches.

"What you just witnessed," Rosalie said, hands pushing her wet blond hair away from her face, "was something not terribly nun-like but very human."

"Well put," Sister Regina said. "I never dreamed I could be that human."

CHAPTER 57

Little Eva was an ungainly lass. Indeed, she shared a nickname, Pregnant Cow, with others of her ilk. She was wider – 110 feet – than she was long – 67 feet. She was fat, weighing 60,000 pounds. Jeff Wolfrom loved her.

The B-24 – known as the Liberator when flown by Royal Air Force crews – was powered by four Pratt & Whitney 1,200 horsepower engines. Her top speed was 290 miles per hour, and she cruised at 215-225 mph. Her service ceiling was 28,000 feet. She carried a crew of 10 or 11 – pilot, co-pilot, navigator, radio operator, engineer, bombardier, top turret gunner, ball (bottom) turret gunner, tail turret gunner and two waist gunners – one of which on Little Eva was Jeff. He was grateful to be assigned that post; he could stand while the turret gunners had to sit or squat in spaces so cramped as to threaten cutting off circulation to their legs on long missions. To date, though, Jeff and his fellow crewmen had yet to taste combat; they had flown only training runs.

To Jeff and most airmen, Little Eva and other B-24s looked more like boxcars with appendages than flying machines. Their thin wings were set high and appeared incapable of bearing their weight. The wings alone, never mind the fat fuselage, looked capable of preventing the B-24 from anything more challenging than taxiing.

She was a fooler. Not only could Little Eva become airborne, she could fly faster and farther – 3,700 mile maximum range – and with a heavier bomb load than her acclaimed big sister, the B-17 Flying Fortress.

B-24s were reliable too. They could lose three engines, suffer numerous wounds from flak and opposing cannon and machine gun fire and remain aloft. Perhaps the most telling testament to their airworthiness: Winston Churchill used one as his personal plane.

"My Little Eva isn't perfect," Jeff had written Iris Ann, "but I'm glad she's my steady girl."

Jeff's aerial combat baptism came on June 11. Early that evening in a Quonset hut, a Royal Air Force officer, no stranger to air combat, briefed 13 American B-24 crews. The men, some shirtless, were sitting on wooden benches.

"The first plane will lift off at ten-thirty p.m.," the RAF officer began. "Thirteen aircraft. The last should be in the air by eleven p.m. Destination: Romania. Ploesti, to be precise. You've heard of it, I know. Think of Ploesti as Hitler's main petrol filling station. Huge oil refinery complex. Soon I'll show you slide photos. They're dated but they'll give you a good picture of your target. You will enjoy the element of surprise. Reason: You will have the privilege of flying the first American mission to Ploesti – indeed, gentlemen, the first American mission to any target anywhere in Europe. A remarkable honor."

To Jeff, Little Eva enjoyed an additional advantage; piloting her was a fellow native of Pine Bluff, Wilbur West.

"You know," Jeff said softly, "we might have the only Arkansas accents in Africa."

"Or at least," Wilbur smiled, "in east Africa. There might be some more of us Razorbacks in west Africa. There were lots of us at Grider Field."

As lift off neared, Jeff knew he should be feeling anxiety. Clearly, the rest of the crew was. Would their first combat mission be their last? Most were smoking cigarettes or chewing gum. Two were writing letters to wives. Jeff by contrast was experiencing anticipation. Is there something wrong with me? he wondered. Am I somehow less feeling than my friends? I don't think so. I think I'm feeling the fulfillment of a dream. Maybe once we're on our way I'll feel nervous or scared. But not now, not yet.

At 10 p.m., the 13 crews walked unhurriedly to their planes. Some were tossing cigarette butts on the ground. They climbed into their craft through a low aperture. Jeff moved slowly to his waist gun post. He passed his right hand lightly along the Browning machine gun's long barrel. His weapon's arsenal included 250 .50-caliber rounds. Jeff was trained to shoot in short bursts; long bursts against moving targets would be wasteful and overheat the gun's barrel.

Bolstering Jeff's confidence were the rehearsals. Fayid base personnel had constructed an amazingly accurate, full-scale replica of Ploesti and its surrounding oil complex. Little Eva had "attacked" the fake Ploesti several times.

The actual mission would prove far more arduous, testing Little Eva's endurance and her crew's mental toughness. From lift off at Fayid to Ploesti and back would cover 2,400 miles. They would cross the Mediterranean, skirt the Black Sea and then angle inland past Bucharest and the final 34 miles north to Ploesti. Moreover, the men knew the flight to target would be uncomfortable in the extreme. At 25,000 feet, the outside temperature would be about 40 degrees below zero. The crews wore felt boots – they also carried with them regulation brown leather boots in case they were downed and had to walk long distances – and heated flight suits. But the B-24s interior wasn't heated and lips would turn blue and noses would drip.

Little Eva was tenth in the lift-off queue. Her wheels went up at 10:47 p.m. Once all 13 B-24s were airborne in the Mediterranean blackness, their pilots found it impossible to maintain a tight formation. Their plan was to regroup at daybreak.

By four hours into the sortie, Little Eva and her flying partners were contracting the aerial equivalent of a winter cold. The frigid interior temperature was thickening their bombsights' machine oil. Their fuel transfer systems began freezing. On Little Eva, Jeff heard the malady's first worrisome symptom: an engine coughed and cut out. A worm of anxiety began crawling through his midsection. Soon, a second engine wheezed and shut down. Jeff's thought: I should have taken time to write one more letter to Mother. Moments later, a third engine gave up.

That night in their Sumatra camp, Joe and Duane convened a conference. They didn't try to mask the situation's urgency.

"The first Japanese troops have landed south of here," Joe said, opening the meeting. "It won't be long before the Japanese spread out and take control of the entire island." His small audience was listening attentively.

"That can't happen overnight, can it?" Sister Grace Ann asked.

"No," Joe answered. "Sumatra is a thousand miles from north to south."

"And east to west?" Grace Ann asked.

"Two hundred fifty miles at its widest point. But I don't expect Sumatra to offer resistance. It has no standing army. And I doubt if they want to unnecessarily anger the Japs. We really have no choice but to leave. And we've little choice but to cross the Malacca Strait to the Malay peninsula. Duane agrees his sampan can't try a longer journey over open water. That would mean south across the Java Sea." He paused.

"Go on," Sister Regina encouraged him.

Joe rubbed his scar. "Duane and I had agreed back in Singapore that we would attempt to join the MPAJA. We're still of a mind to try to locate them and offer our services."

"And," Rosalie interjected tartly, "I made it clear that I plan to join them."

Smiles – understanding ones – all around. The more the rest of the group was learning about Rosalie, the more respect she was earning.

"I would think," Sister Regina said evenly, "that a resistance force could use expert nursing skills."

"Seems a reasonable assumption, Sister."

"And besides, Mr. Barton, once in Malaya, you wouldn't dream of leaving us to our own devices, would you?"

"I believe your question was rhetorical, Sister."

"You believe correctly, Mr. Barton."

Appreciative chuckles from everyone.

Duane spoke. "Our plan – our hope – is to try to keep our group together. Frankly we don't know if that will be possible. My flesh tone – and Father's – could be a problem."

None disputed Duane's thinking.

"Mr. Hurd."

"Yes, Sister Regina?"

"I don't think writing a letter of recommendation for you would much influence the MPAJA. But I do think they will find favor with my report of your dispatching Japanese soldiers who were about to murder us – who did murder Sister Caroline."

Jeff's love for Little Eva notwithstanding, she was letting him down. The plane was shivering and losing altitude. She could remain aloft on a lone engine but not fully loaded and not for long.

In the cockpit, Wilbur West called navigator Charles Davis. "We can't make Ploesti. Not this way. We weren't given an alternative plan, but I have one in mind. Get us over Constanta as soon as possible." To his bombardier, sitting lower in the nose and in front of West, he said, "We'll unload there on the juiciest military targets."

Minutes later, Jeff felt Little Eva lighten and seemingly bounce higher. She was dumping her six 500-pound bombs on ships anchored at Constanta, Bucharest's Black Sea port.

West began turning Little Eva on a tight arc to the southeast.

Said Davis, "You know we don't have near enough fuel to make it back to Fayid."

Everyone else on board knew the same thing.

The sampan was making its way slowly northeast across the Malacca Strait. Duane was aiming to make land near Melaka, about 100 miles north of Singapore.

Joe was sitting next to Sister Regina. "I've been thinking," he murmured.

"Yes, Mr. Barton."

"We really have no idea what's going to happen in Malaya. I'm worried about our women."

"So am I."

"You nuns don't have civilian clothing, so I'm suggesting – recommending actually – that you resume wearing your wimples. They make you look, uh, less accessible."

"Point well made, Mr. Barton. We will do so. Even though Sister Grace Ann and her wimple have seen better days."

Before the Ploesti mission got underway, Washington had asked Moscow to permit Little Eva and her sister planes to land in the Soviet Union if for any reason one or more of the B-24s couldn't make the return trip to Fayid. The Kremlin, technically an ally and already detaining some of Jimmy Doolittle's men, didn't reply. The silence itself sent a strong message. Crews also had been warned not to make emergency landings in neutral Turkey where detention also seemed a likely result. Turkey would remain neutral until February 23, 1945, when it declared war on Germany and Japan.

"Turkey. How far to Ankara? Can we make it?" West asked.

"About three hundred and fifty miles and it would be close," Davis replied. A pause. "We could be interned."

"Right. But we would not be dead."

From Jeff's waist gunner port, he was looking down on mountainous Turkey. He smiled as he recalled Sunday school bible stories. I wonder if we're anywhere close to Mount Ararat. It would be neat to see it and maybe remains of Noah's ark."

Ankara, Turkey's capital, was ancient. In 1,200 B.C., the Hittites had called the city Ankuwash. In 1942 the city's population numbered about 200,000. Its elevation – 2,800 feet above sea level – meant a climate that brought cold, snowy winters and hot, dry summers. In July the average high was 82F and the low 55F – pleasantly cool for sleeping.

Little Eva's descent was steeper than normal. The lone working engine's sputtering provided Jeff the explanation. Little Eva was burning its last gallons of gas. Jeff braced himself.

Little Eva's prescribed landing speed was 95 mph. She was dropping at about 125 mph. Her tires smacked the runway hard, smoke billowed,

Little Eva bounced and Jeff could hear one or more tires blow. His hands gripped the Browning.

Wilbur West was using every sinew of arm and shoulder muscle to keep Little Eva running straight and her wings clear of the runway. With so little fuel remaining, West's chief worry wasn't an explosion and fire. What he was struggling to avoid was cartwheeling or somersaulting. His tight palms were sweating.

The runway's end was nearing and Little Eva was slowing. Jeff lowered his head and exhaled. Other crewmen were opening closed eyes, making the sign of the cross and unclenching fists.

As Jeff dropped out of the B-24's belly he walked to West and cuffed him on his back. "Nice work, Razorback."

To the crew's surprise the Ankara Airport manager was anything but neutral. As the men deplaned, he handed Davis a box of candy and invited the crew to the airport café. There they were treated to a breakfast of bread, goat cheese and strong coffee.

While eating, they watched three more planes land. Two were B-24s from their mission. The third was a Messerschmitt 109 that had been pursuing them from Constanta, albeit none too aggressively. Like Little Eva, the new three newcomers were out of fuel.

In the end, none of the 13 Ploesti planes was shot down and no crewmen were killed. Two aboard a B-24 that had landed at Istanbul had been wounded but not seriously by machine gun fire from a German fighter. The damage to Ploesti's oil complex: virtually none.

As Jeff was sipping coffee in the café, his thoughts turned to Iris Ann. Well, Mother, Turkey is a long way from Pine Bluff. And this bread and cheese is no match for your buttermilk pancakes. I wonder what's next for us. How long will the Turks keep us? Where will they put us? Will I fly again?

CHAPTER 58

Duane throttled back on the motor and guided the sampan artfully onto the beach. The sun was already several hours into its daily broiling of the Malayan peninsula. Immediately the group began unloading – tents, shovels, sten guns, revolvers, ammunition, the changes of clothes for Joe, Duane, his parents and Rosalie and the utensils and few tools that were always part of Duane's sampan "household."

It didn't take long for word of the strange group's arrival to reach MPAJA leaders. Soon, a contingent – 11 men – arrived at the beach. They greeted the newcomers warily. Not a surprise, given Rosalie's earlier prediction.

Conversing wasn't a problem. The MPAJA members were Singaporean Chinese, and most spoke English. Further smoothing the newcomers' way were Duane's weapons and Sister Regina's account of the nuns' rescue. She omitted few details and purposely let show her anger and sadness at Sister Caroline's murder. That the new arrivals had brought their own tents and equipment and money to buy food lent them additional credibility with the MPAJA.

Resistance members helped Joe and Duane's group select a campsite – a small clearing high on a jungle-covered ridge in the central Malayan mountains. Nearby was a major MPAJA camp. Between the two camps a swiftly descending stream provided drinking water. In the opposite direction from the camp, Joe and Duane had used borrowed machetes to hack a path about 75 feet long and then dug a narrow trench that was serving as a latrine.

That's where Joe was headed as the sun's first rays were poking through the jungle canopy. He stopped when he heard footsteps approaching on the narrow path. Around a bend came striding Sister Regina.

"Mother Nature waits for no one," she smiled. "Good morning, Mr. Barton."

"Good morning, Sister Regina. Sleep well?"

"Well enough. Although I confess to missing the sea breezes on Sumatra." She was wearing her habit but had not yet put on the wimple. "You?"

275

"I was awake part of the night," Joe said. "Thinking about friends. Wondering how they are doing. One is in Romania."

"I see. Mr. Barton, I've been doing some thinking myself."

"As you often do," Joe gently teased. "Do I sense another private conversation coming?"

"For so early in the morning your senses are quite sharp."

"I'm game, but can it wait until after my trip to the latrine?"

Sister Regina chuckled lowly. "I'll wait here." She leaned back against a large tree.

"You're a sight," Joe grinned on returning from the trench-as-toilet.

"How so?"

"Never in my wildest dreams would I have seen a nun on a jungle trail. When I tell Miss Hughes – she was my high school history teacher – she'll know I came a long way from Shelby, Ohio."

"Yes, well, almost from the moment I entered the convent I saw myself in Asia. But not in the jungle with an American."

Joe laughed. "You'll have your own stories to tell back in England."

"Speaking of England and America, if I'm remembering dates correctly, today is the third of July. That would make tomorrow your Independence Day – the day that commemorates your breaking away from my homeland's shackles."

"Does that bother you?"

"Gracious, no. I'm just wishing – praying – that nations under the heels of Hitler and Hirohito could themselves be independent. Free."

"Including England's colonies? Like Malaya?"

"By all means, Mr. Barton. I hold no brief for imperialism. We British have helped certain peoples prosper, but too often we've kept them colonial subservients after they are quite ready for freedom. Or, in fact, freedom regained."

To his surprise Joe felt a surge of affection, an urge to reach out, to embrace the lovely, wimpleless nun. Instead, he said only, "That day will come, Sister Regina. I'm sure of that. I'm not smart enough to know when, but it will happen. Freedom is too powerful a force to keep leashed forever."

Sister Regina smiled warmly. "Mr. Barton, another thought has been occupying my mind. About freedom of a sort."

"I take it that it's the thought that had you thinking about another private conversation."

"Quite. Well, it's this. Given these difficult circumstances, considering everything we have been through, I think we could – should – be less formal."

Joe dipped his head slightly to the left and shrugged. "How so?"

"Sister Regina. That is five syllables. Let's reduce them to two – or two and half if you will."

Joe grinned. "What sort of contraction do you have in mind?"

"Sister R. Like it?"

"I actually think it suits you to a 't' – or an 'r.'"

"Oh? Why is that?"

"You're hardly the doctrinally rigid nun that I'd perceived women of the cloth."

"Mr. Barton, I-"

"Joe. If I'm to call you Sister R, then you must agree to call me Joe."

"Touche. Joe, I was what you Americans call a tomboy. I once did my share of running, jumping and climbing."

"I'm trying to imagine that."

Sister R laughed. "Just try picturing me as a young girl without a habit. Come to think of it, you've already seen me without my habit or anything else."

"Only from the waist up and not an unpleasant sight."

"Barring another snake in a stream, that's likely as much as you'll see."

They both laughed.

"If I'm to call you Sister R, I'm thinking it would be wise to tell Sister Augusta and Grace Ann. I would prefer they not regard me as a cheeky yank."

"Consider it done."

CHAPTER 59

"Check. I think." Jeff Wolfrom was staring hard at the pieces – exquisitely carved from black and white stone – on the ornate chessboard.

Opposing – and mentoring – him was another interned flyer – a Russian. "Yes," said Captain Leonid Zanskov, rubbing black, rough stubble, "you have checked me. You are really improving your game." Jeff smiled dubiously. It was the captain's tone of voice that aroused his suspicion. "But there are still lessons to be learned. Check is not checkmate as I will soon show you."

Jeff, 19, looked up from the board at the captain who was 25. He couldn't refrain from grinning. "I've heard you Russians are pretty good at this game," he said in his soft Arkansas accent.

"And," said Captain Zanskov, "we are, as you say, pretty good as teachers. And good teachers do not lose on purpose to their pupils. That would be bad, you do not agree?"

The chess set was property of Best Hotel on Ataturk Boulevard, Ankara's high street. Given their plush accommodations, Jeff regarded the hotel as aptly named. The boulevard itself was inviting. The center island was about 40 feet wide and adorned with trees and flower gardens. The hotel was just down the street from the U.S. embassy.

Captain Zanskov was one of 30 Soviet flyers who were spending their internment in quarters and with treatment that had them in no hurry to be repatriated.

Jeff and 36 other B-24 crewmen from the Ploesti mission were residing in the Best. They represented three complete crews and part of a fourth that had landed between Ankara and Istanbul. Although the political alliance between the U.S. and Russia was tenuous and tense – Stalin already was agitating with President Roosevelt and Prime Minister Churchill for a western front to relieve pressure on the eastern front – genuine friendship had fast taken root among the two nations' detained airmen.

"Do you like learning this game?" Captain Zanskov asked.

"I do," Jeff replied. "It's war – strategy – without death. But what I really like about chess is that there's no luck involved."

"No luck?"

"Okay," said Jeff, "there's luck if one player – a rookie like me – makes a really bad move, and the other guy takes advantage. But I mean, you can't win by rolling dice or spinning a wheel or drawing an ace."

"Now I know your meaning," the captain said expansively, "and I agree. But one question: What is a rookie?"

"A beginner," Jeff smiled. "No experience." The board was set up in a corner of the lobby. "Tell me," said Jeff, "how long do you plan to stay here?"

The question diverted Zanskov's concentration from the game. His black eyes looked hard into Jeff's brown ones. "As long as they will let me. You?"

"Only as long as I have to."

"Why?"

"Freedom. It's what I'm used to. It's what I crave. Like my mother's cooking."

"Hah. Freedom. In Russia we are free to do only one thing."

"Just one? What's that?"

"Whatever Comrade Stalin wants."

After an early dinner on July 3, Jeff left the hotel for a stroll. After three weeks of detention, he had grown accustomed to the remarkable liberty given internees. They were free to come and go from morning to midnight. They were drawing full pay from a U.S. military attaché whose office was in the American embassy. Some of the men were involved in romantic dalliances with hotel staff and women they met in nearby bars. Others were employing prostitutes eager to sell their services to the well-compensated Americans, less so to the uncompensated Russians whose few rubles were less appealing.

The evening temperature was cooling quickly, and Jeff sucked in a deep breath. Apart from impatience he was feeling fortunate. Captain West had kept Little Eva and crew in one piece each. They were eating well and resting comfortably.

Strolling leisurely, Jeff turned left into a narrow side street. A couple minutes later, passing an alley on his left, something caught his eye. He stopped and backed a step. About 20 feet into the alley he saw a ragged bundle of brown that looked more like a burlap sack than apparel. He took a step to move on and then stopped. Slowly, he started toward the bundle. It had badly scuffed small shoes at one end and dirty black hair at the other. The bundle lay on a filthy pallet of corrugated cardboard and appeared lifeless. Jeff bent forward and with his right hand reached down and touched the bundle. No reaction. He applied gentle pressure to its center and the bundle stirred.

Jeff squatted beside it. Gently, he cupped the bundle's smudged, gaunt face by its chin and lifted it a couple inches. A little girl, Jeff could see. She can't be more than five or six years old, he judged. I've seen fence posts that were rounder and thicker. Poor thing.

Jeff stood and looked in both directions. No sign of pedestrians and certainly none of anyone who might care about the child. I'm not sure what I'm thinking is all that smart. Someone might actually come for her. Nah. No need to kid myself.

Jeff's right forefinger and thumb rubbed his chin. Then he wheeled, walked briskly back to the alley entrance and broke into a trot back to the hotel.

In the lobby he looked around. Behind the reception desk, he saw a pretty young woman. Her cheekbones were high and the tip of her nose hooked slightly to the left. The imperfection was scarcely noticeable except when seen straight on. Her black hair was bobbed in a way that complimented her features. He walked toward her. The woman was wearing a name pin that told Jeff she was Eren Colason.

"Ma'am, I'm Jeff Wolfrom. One of the Americans."

"Yes," the woman smiled kindly, "I know."

"You speak English."

"A little. It is necessary. Often we have guests who have business with American Embassy and banks."

"I see. Well, I saw something near the hotel. Could you come with me? It would just take a few minutes."

"What did you see?" The woman appeared to be nearly a match for Jeff's five feet seven inches.

"A person." Jeff paused, upper teeth scraping lower lip. "I'd like to show you. Can you get permission to come with me?"

"I have received many requests from other Americans and the Russians. But not to leave the hotel."

Jeff felt himself reddening. "This is not, uh, like that. Okay?"

Eren Colason studied the young American. Something about him suggested trust – trustworthiness. "Just one minute, please." She turned away and disappeared into an office.

Ten minutes later Eren stood beside Jeff, peering down at the sleeping child. "She has no home."

"I thought so."

"Yes, her parents – if she has alive parents – they are too poor to feed her. To care. Please excuse my poor English."

"Your English is fine. Better than many Americans, trust me.'

"I do."

Jeff eyed her and smiled thinly. "Okay. Good. Now, what do we do with her?"

"Do?"

"Yes. Of course. We can't leave her here."

Eren's eyes closed and her lips pursed. "You are kind man. But do? There are many like her in Ankara."

Jeff sighed. "She is the one I found. I cannot leave her here. I can't. Look, will I be breaking any Turkish law if I pick her up?"

"I do not think so."

"Okay." Jeff squatted, maneuvered his hands beneath the child and lifted. "I think I've picked up heavier watermelons." He turned and began carrying her toward the hotel.

"What is your plan?"

Jeff shrugged. "I'm making it up as I go along."

Eren chuckled. "You are strange."

At the hotel, Eren pulled open the lobby door. Jeff stepped inside. "Can you go up to my room?"

She nodded. "I will go. Come." And she led the way to the elevator and up to the fourth floor.

Moments later, inside Jeff's room, the girl's eyes opened as Jeff placed her on the bed. "Don't be afraid," Jeff said soothingly. Then to Eren he said, "Can you tell her where she is? And not to be afraid? And ask her name."

The little girl inched away. "Don't be afraid, sweetie," Eren said in familiar Turkish. "This man wants to help you. All right? What is your name?"

The girl's eyes narrowed. After a long pause that reflected both suspicion and fear, she said barely audibly, "Natasha."

"My, what a lovely name. What is your surname?" For a long moment the child's eyes seemed to be looking inward, searching for an answer. "Mori."

"Natasha Mori," Eren smiled. "That's a very nice name." Jeff didn't understand the words but needed no translation. "Mr. Wolfrom," Eren said, switching to English, "what is next to do?"

"First, call me Jeff. Please. Like I said, I'm making this plan up as we go."

"We?"

Jeff allowed himself a light chuckle. "I think I just made you part of my plan. The girl needs a bath. I'll start the water. You get her out of that rag of a dress and anything under it. Hell - heck – I'm not even sure what color it's supposed to be."

"How's it going?" Jeff asked from inside the bathroom. He tested the water for warmth.

"Very good," Eren replied. "Jeff, she is only a child. You may come out."

"Are you sure?"

"Yes." Eren took Natasha's right hand and led her past Jeff into the bathroom. A few minutes later Jeff pushed open the door. Big dark eyes were staring up at him from the tub. Eren was kneeling, gently washing the child's torso.

"Hello, little one," he said. "Does that feel good? Eren, when you've finished and dried her, let's wrap her in another towel and put her in a chair. Okay?"

"Okay. Okay is very good English word."

"Very good American word," Jeff teased. "I want you to take her clothes downstairs."

"To the laundry."

"To the furnace. Burn them." Then he removed his wallet from a hip pocket and extracted 30 dollars. "Here."

"That will buy many new clothing," Eren said. "I can shop in the morning."

"Good. And get her anything else she needs. But she must be hungry. Would you ask the chef to make something a girl – maybe six years old – would enjoy? In the States, that might be peanut butter and grape jelly. But in Turkey, I don't know."

"Peanut butter and grape jelly?" Eren's nose wrinkled.

"It's a sandwich. You'll have to try one sometime."

"I do not think so."

Jeff turned on the room's bulky brown radio. 9 p.m. Maybe I can find some music, he thought. Something to help Natasha sleep. She still was perched on one of the room's two blue upholstered chairs. Jeff twisted the tuning knob. To his surprise he found BBC news. He plopped down in the other chair and looked at Natasha. "Right now I'm plum outa plan. I wish I could talk to Mother. I guess I'll just have to sleep on this situation. Maybe I can get you to an orphanage – with Eren's help. Nice lady, don't you think?"

Natasha, expressionless, was staring at the strange man who spoke a strange language. He doesn't scare me, she thought. He is big but not mean.

Jeff removed his brown boots and wiggled his toes. Then he stretched his arms above his head. The radio newsman droned on with war reports. "Natasha," Jeff said, turning toward her. She was asleep. Jeff smiled affectionately. "Okay. Warm bath and a clean towel have done you in." He stood and pulled back the bedspread, blanket and sheet. Then he picked up Natasha, still cocooned in the large white bath towel, and laid her down. He pulled the covers to her chin.

Jeff stripped to his olive drab boxer shorts and t-shirt. "Chair or floor?" he muttered. He pulled the two chairs together, facing each other. He turned off the radio and lights and fastened the door's security chain. He sat on one and put his feet on the other. "Sleep well, little one."

Later, Jeff didn't know the time, he heard knocking. Momentarily, as his eyes opened, he was disoriented. His head shook. In the darkness he stood and edged to the door and looked through the peephole. His head shook again. It was Eren and she was standing next to a cot on wheels. Jeff released the security chain.

"Open," she whispered. Jeff complied. "Do not switch on light. Leave open the door so I can see." She maneuvered the cot to one side of the room and quietly lowered it. She pulled back a sheet and blue blanket. "Put Natasha on it."

Jeff gently pulled back the bed covers, lifted Natasha, laid her on the cot and pulled the sheet and blanket forward.

Eren saw the two chairs. She smiled wryly. "You get in the bed."

"You seem to have your own plan," Jeff whispered, then smiled. He lay down.

Eren closed the door and put the chain in place. "No chairs," she whispered. "Please, make room for me."

In the darkness, Jeff could see nothing. He moved a foot to his left. He felt a body sitting on the bed, then reclining.

"This is good plan, no?" murmured Eren, still fully dressed except for shoes she had just removed. "I will be here when Natasha wakes up. I can get her food. You also. Then I can shop for clothes. Try to sleep."

"Right." Mother will think I made this story up, Jeff mused. Soon he heard Eren's even breathing. He lay awake for hours, staring up at a ceiling he couldn't see, thinking thoughts he couldn't sort.

CHAPTER 60

July 4, 1942. Jeff awakened about 7 a.m. Eren was gone. He propped himself against pillows and found contentment in watching Natasha, still sleeping soundly.

At 7:30, Eren tapped the door. Jeff moved quickly to open it. Eren entered bearing croissants and pastries, goat's milk for Natasha and a pot of strong coffee from the hotel kitchen. The aromas roused Natasha from her slumber.

"Good morning, Natasha," Eren greeted her. During the night Natasha's bath towel had loosened. "Stand up, honey," Eren said in Turkish. She wrapped it around the girl and fastened it with a pair of safety pins. She then helped Natasha to one of the chairs and placed the milk and food on a low table in front of her. Eren looked at Jeff. "Please come and sit here," she said, gesturing to the second chair. "I am leaving but will return soon."

"Okay," Jeff nodded as Eren pulled open the door. "Thanks for helping with my plan." He grinned and she looked back over shoulder, smiling.

Natasha began eating, slowly, savoring each bite. Jeff stood, poured coffee and started sipping the rich brew. "You know," he said, smiling down at Natasha, "I am only nineteen. I'm trying to figure out if I should think of you as my little sister or my daughter. Maybe my niece. I guess it doesn't really matter. What am I going to do with you? That's the big question, and I still don't have an answer."

A little before 10 a.m., Eren knocked once and called out, "It is me."

Jeff opened the door. Eren was beaming. She was holding a cloth shopping bag and stepped quickly to the bed. "Look, Natasha. New clothes." She began removing each item from the bag, holding it up for Natasha, then laying it on the girl's cot. Two complete sets of clothes – undershirts, panties, dresses and socks plus a pair of black tie shoes that Eren hoped would fit well. She pointed at Jeff. "Your Uncle Jeff bought these for you. He gave me the money."

"What did you just say? I heard you say my name."

"I said to her you are generous man."

"Oh. Well, you didn't need to."

Eren grinned. "You are also, um, modest man."

"Uh huh. Look, if you don't mind, I'll go downstairs a while. You can have fun dressing her."

As the elevator door opened and Jeff stepped into the lobby, he was smiling inwardly. Mother would never believe all this. Not in a million years. *Hell, I'm not sure I do.*

"Hey, Jeff. Happy Fourth!" The voice belonged to his fellow Little Eva waist gunner, Holmes Fountaine.

"Same to you, Holmes." Jeff's greeting was flat.

"Anything wrong?"

"Nah."

"Man, I'm looking forward to tonight."

"Yeah, me too."

The two young airmen were alluding to an Independence Day party. American Ambassador Lawrence Steinhardt had invited the 37 Ploesti mission internees to the embassy for a gala dinner. A fireworks display would cap the evening.

Jeff continued toward the lobby exit.

"Hey, Jeff, wait up," Holmes said. Outside on Ataturk Boulevard, Holmes said, "Follow me."

"Where to?"

"Just across to the boulevard island."

"All right," Jeff responded unenthusiastically.

Near a flower garden, Holmes stopped. "This should do. I wanted to be sure we have privacy." A pause while he surveyed the area. "You ready to blow this joint?"

"What do you mean?"

"I mean scram. Charles Davis has met a Turk who is willing to help us escape."

"Where to? When? How?"

"To Syria. It's south of here and a French protectorate. An ally. As for when, Charles says soon. Not sure how. Only some of us can go at a time. Too risky for everyone at once. You want in on this, don't you? The first group?"

"Yeah. I guess."

During the remainder of the day, Jeff spent most of the time in his room, watching Natasha occupy herself with an illustrated children's book and a coloring book with crayons that Eren had bought during her lunch break. Occasionally Natasha looked up and smiled. A surge of affection warmed Jeff. He had the room's radio playing, not for listening but as background for pondering. *Getting out of here, that's what I've been wanting. But now the situation is complicated. I hate the idea of Natasha back in that alley. But even if I don't join the escape, who knows how long I'd be here? Until the war ends and who knows when that will be? Or until the Turks decide to stop interning us. That could be anytime, tomorrow, next week, next year. I can see Eren has taken a real shine to Natasha, but she's not married, and I don't see her taking on motherhood for a stranger. Boy, this is tough.*

"You sure?" Jeff asked. His watch was nearing 6 p.m.

"Yes," Eren smiled. "My work day is complete. I will stay with Natasha while you celebrate at the embassy party."

"Gentlemen," began Ambassador Steinhardt, "I know you would rather be someplace other than Turkey. At the same time I must tell you that my staff and I are honored to have you as our guests. Especially on Independence Day. We view you as genuine American heroes. Your mission delivered a strong message to Hitler. Thank you." He led a round of applause from embassy staffers. "As you can see – and smell – I've tried to approximate traditional Fourth of July fare for this occasion. With," he chortled self-deprecatingly, "only mixed success. Livestock here tends to sheep and goats, not cattle, so our cooks will be serving lamb burgers." Chuckles all around. "Corn is plentiful and you can smell some roasting. Umm, can hardly wait. So are potatoes so the menu includes potato salad. No baked beans though. Sorry about that omission. For dessert we'll have freshly made ice cream. The best in Ankara, I'm told. And, gentlemen, there is plenty to drink so please avail yourself. A major agricultural product here is tobacco, so after dinner you can light up some fine cigars to enjoy with your drinks. Now, if I may, I would like to offer a toast. To you courageous young men of the United States Army Air Corps, we thank you for defending freedoms that are precious to us all."

Jeff enjoyed the repast and the relaxed camaraderie. He drank beer with his meal and afterward tried a cigar. "Not bad" was his assessment. He alternated puffs on the cigar with sips of cognac Steinhardt urged him to sample. "A right fine combination, Mr. Ambassador."

As the fireworks were beginning, Jeff peeked at his watch. 9:35 p.m. He found an ashtray, put his cigar down and unobtrusively eased his way from the embassy.

Jeff turned the key in the hotel room door and entered quietly. Only dim light escaping from the cracked bathroom door was providing illumination.

"Hi," Eren whispered. She was sitting in a chair, still wearing her reception desk blouse and skirt. Her shoes were beside the chair. "You left party early."

"A little."

"You had good time, yes?" Jeff nodded. "But you worried about us."

"A little."

"You go take a bath."

"Okay."

Twenty minutes later Jeff emerged, feeling refreshed. Eren was in bed. "I am staying. Do you mind?"

He smiled. "You are worried about Natasha, right?"

"A little," she smiled puckishly. "It will be better this way, I think. In the morning I again can take care of things."

Jeff nodded. In t-shirt and shorts, he returned to the bathroom and switched off the light. Slowly he edged toward the bed. He paused to look at Natasha. He reached down and patted her left shoulder. Then he got in bed.

"Jeff, did you ever sleep with a woman?"

"You mean before last night?" he asked in his soft Arkansas drawl. In the darkness he was grinning.

"Yes, before last night."

"Once."

"Here in hotel?"

"In Egypt."

"Did you pay?"

"Yes."

"You do not pay me." She rolled toward Jeff and placed her head against his left shoulder. She laid her left arm across his chest. "Nice, no?"

"Very nice." He placed his left hand against her back. It was bare.

"I have no night gown in hotel."

"No, I don't suppose you would."

"It is warm so I do not need a gown."

Jeff smiled. A long pause. "Eren, how old are you?"

"Twenty-one." A longer pause. "Is age important? My age?"

"No."

"Good. You sleep."

"Right." The feel of Eren's naked form nestled against his t-shirt and shorts was promoting something other than sleep. "Eren, look, I didn't get much sleep at all last night. I really should get some tonight. Understand?"

"Yes."

"Okay." With his right hand, Jeff began gently pushing Eren away.

She resisted. "Jeff, I have new plan. I will help you sleep. But Natasha is close by, so no noise. Okay?"

"Yes. Have you ever slept with a man?"

"You mean before last night?" Jeff could sense she was grinning. "No. Is that all right?"

"Yes."

"But I know how these things are done. Mother tells me. Remember, no noise."

"Eren, why are you doing this?"

"Jeff, why are you doing for Natasha?"

"It seems like the right thing to do."

"My answer is the same."

"A rope?"

"Right, made from bed sheets. Lowered from Charles' window on the third floor," Holmes Fountaine replied.

"How many?" asked Jeff.

"Just you and me tonight."

"The others?"

"Two or three a night over the next three or so weeks."

"What time?"

"Zero two hundred hours."

Jeff looked at his watch. 11 a.m. His lips pursed. He and Holmes were standing by the same flower garden on the boulevard's island.

"What happens then?"

"According to Charles they put us on the Taurus Express for Syria. But no one wants to embarrass Turkish border agents, so we get off the train before reaching the border and someone escorts us into Syria."

Jeff nodded slightly. "What about our vacated rooms here?"

"Charles says the staff is being compensated to be discreet."

"As in mum's the word."

"Right."

"Who's paying for all of this?" Jeff asked.

"Not sure. Could be Turks sympathetic to the Allies. Or maybe our side. Remember what Ambassador Steinhardt called us? Genuine American heroes."

"Clothes?"

"We wear our uniforms. I know, I know. It means people are gonna be looking the other way."

Jeff's left hand scratched the back of his head. "Okay. Look, I got some things to take care of."

"Yeah," Holmes muttered. "There's this rumor that a certain lady has been visiting your room. Can she be trusted?"

"Yeah. And anything else you might be thinking, stop."

"It's your business, just as long as it doesn't screw up our plans."

Jeff sighed. "Yeah, plans."

Jeff waited until Eren was alone at the reception desk. "Can you come up to my room during your lunch break?"

"Of course. I was planning to."

"Sit down," Jeff said. "Please."

Eren sat and Natasha crawled onto her lap. A good sign, Jeff thought. She trusts Eren.

"Are you enjoying the books, sweetie?" Eren asked.

"Will you read to me?" Natasha asked shyly.

"Yes. But first I think Uncle Jeff wants to talk with me."

"Will you read to me after he talks?"

"Absolutely. I'll read the whole book."

Jeff enjoyed listening to their Turkish exchanges. He didn't try to figure out what they were saying. Instead, he took simple pleasure in the rhythm of the language.

"Jeff, you look – uh, I cannot find the right word. Not sure?"

"Not sure pretty much covers it. Actually there's only one thing I'm sure of. I'm leaving."

"Leaving?" Eren struggled to prevent rising anxiety from elevating her voice's pitch and worrying Natasha. "No more detained?"

"Someone – I'm not sure who – is helping us escape from Turkey. I'm supposed to leave tonight. After midnight. Two o'clock. Other guys will follow each night. I thought you might have been told."

She shook her head. "So that is the plan."

"Not the one I had in mind," Jeff said dejectedly.

Eren felt her eyes misting and quickly and repeatedly blinked away the first tears. She was determined not to upset Natasha whose eyes were fixated on Jeff's.

"After work I will stay with you until you leave. I need to be here if Natasha wakes up during the night." Jeff nodded. "There is more, Jeff. After we eat and before Natasha sleeps, you must tell her…tell her that you are a soldier and must go. It is right to do that."

Jeff sighed. Both hands covered his eyes and he pressed them hard. "I will tell her. And, uh, I have fifty-six dollars in my wallet."

"No need to pay."

"This is not…this is not for you. Okay? It's to take care of Natasha until you can find her a home. An orphanage."

Hours later, Natasha was weeping softly but made no move to leave Eren's lap. Her savior was deserting her. Soldier? That meant nothing to her.

"I think she loves you," Eren murmured.

"Do you think I should hug her?"

"Come. Take her from me. Hold her close. Let her feel your love. You do love her, yes?"

Jeff sniffled. "Yes."

292

Neither Jeff nor Eren was clothed. In the darkness they were lying side by side, both on their backs.

"People," Eren whispered, "they come into life and then they leave. Hotel guests. Businessmen. Friends. A little girl. It is natural. But sometimes it is sad. It hurts. You entered my life, Jeff. It is sad you are leaving. But I am glad you entered."

"I will never forget you." Jeff's throat had so thickened he nearly choked on the words. "Or Natasha. I do love her. And I…"

"You love me also."

"Yes."

"Good. I give myself to you so it is good you love me."

"An orphanage. What kind of one do you think she will get in?"

"I do not want you to worry about that. Please. I will be certain she receives good care. Like you say, trust me."

"I do."

"I know."

"Who will take care of her tomorrow while you're working?"

"I have friends. Do not worry."

"I don't have pictures of you and Natasha." Jeff whispered miserably.

"Do you need pictures to remember us?"

"No."

"Jeff?"

"What?"

"This older woman, she wants to give you her again, one more time."

After what he estimated had been several hours, Jeff eased from bed and tiptoed to the bathroom, closed the door and turned on the light to check his watch. A little after 1 a.m. – 0100 military time. He looked at the mirror and studied his image. *Not sure I like what I see.*

He cracked open the door just enough to squeeze through and let a narrow shaft of light enter the bedroom. As silently as possible he padded to the small table beside Natasha's cot. He picked up one of her children's books. Then he edged to the bedside table and found a pencil. He turned and slipped back into the bathroom. Jeff placed the book on the sink's edge and opened it. On the blank page he wrote:

July 6, 1942

To Natasha Mori-
Love always
Uncle Jeff Wolfrom and Aunt Eren Colason

Outside the bathroom, Jeff returned the book to the table and then retrieved his clothes and tiptoed back inside the bathroom to dress. A couple minutes later he switched off the light and opened the door. He paused to let his eyes adjust to the darkness. Then he reached back into the bathroom and switched on the light. This time he left the bathroom door open a little wider. He padded to the cot and looked down on Natasha. I'd love to hold you one more time, honey. Then he turned and spent a long moment peering at Eren. Three days. Only three days. You have given me a lifetime of memories. You were right. I won't need pictures to remember. Then he reached to release the security chain. He placed his right hand on the doorknob and turned it. The door opened.

"Jeff," Eren whispered hoarsely. "Goodbye."

CHAPTER 61

In mid-July in northern Sumatra, British intelligence agents contacted Lim Bo Seng. They asked him to journey with them to India and take on a leadership role in a resistance movement.

"Why did you select me?" Lim asked.

"Several reasons," answered the chief British operative. "You are Chinese. You have supported Chinese efforts to repel the Japanese in China, Malaya and Singapore. You also have experience as a leader – heading your successful company. In short, we believe we can trust you and that you would prove effective."

In India, Lim was introduced to his co-leader, Captain John Davis. Born in 1911, Davis was dark-haired, clean-shaven, square-jawed and handsome. More relevantly he was a veteran Federated Malay States British police officer who could speak Malay and Chinese. He also had proven elusive, evading the clutch of the Japanese after they invaded Malaya. Together he and Lim would head up what was dubbed Force 136.

Apart from Davis and British Captain Richard Broome, the force would consist of Chinese. This required Lim to sneak into China to recruit fellow Chinese to join the cause. They all returned to India where they endured rigorous physical training and received comprehensive instruction in communications, logistics, espionage, sabotage and guerilla warfare. Their aim was to infiltrate and establish operations in Malaya where they would coordinate with the MPAJA. Their ambitious, ultimate goal: re-take Malaya from the Japanese.

Lim wrote several letters to Choo Neo, hoping they would reach her on St. John's Island. He also kept a daily journal.

Another letter writer was Joe Barton. Already encamped in the Malayan mountains, he stored his missives to Gabriella Balas in a leather satchel. He was holding onto hope that one day he would return to the Union Building and post the letters to Romania.

As each Force 136 cell completed training, members were transported via British and Dutch submarines to Malayan coastal waters. From the submarines they rowed rubber dinghies to shore.

The first such group made their way inland and hacked a path into the mountains. High on a ridge and far from the nearest road, they began building a base camp. It included several barracks. Lumber in the thick jungle was abundant. For the time being, Lim and Davis remained in India where they continued to strengthen Force 136.

Following the brutal racial cleansing of Chinese males, the next few months of Japanese occupation in Singapore were difficult but bearable for POWs, civilian detainees and so-called "free" residents.

Initially, all civilian internees were incarcerated within Changi Prison. Military POWs were housed in nearby barracks. Prisoners – civilian and military alike – were put to work building new facilities, repairing existing ones and clearing bombing rubble.

At first, free Singapore residents could listen to radio. Via short wave they kept up with war developments. But from August 1942, as Japan began incurring defeats, short wave was banned, and residents were restricted to listening to Singapore stations – monitored closely by Japanese authorities. Newspapers in several languages continued to publish – all overseen by Japan's Propaganda Department.

Most civilian cars were confiscated. Those remaining in private hands were shared among friends. But getting gas quickly became problematic. Mechanics along with friendly Japanese soldiers provided pilfered petrol – often for a fee. For many drivers charcoal became a substitute fuel, and the city's trolleys were converted to run on charcoal. Horse-drawn carriages staged a comeback as did bullock carts. More bicycles took to the streets.

To help keep bored, homesick soldiers contented, the Japanese established what they dubbed comfort houses. Most of the women were imported from Korea which Japan had colonized in 1910. Some of the women were girls – Indonesian and Malayan – and some were very young. One comfort house adjoined an elementary school on Cairnhill Road, just north of toney Orchard Road. Some Japanese women also were conscripted, and the occupiers regarded them as higher class and thus reserved them for officers. Most Singaporeans saw the comfort houses for what they were – legalized military rape.

From the occupation's inception the Japanese began developing a system for keeping tabs on the populace. Organizing and overseeing this effort were the deservedly dreaded kempetai or military police. They were charged with thwarting and quashing any resistance and carried out their mission with gusto. Some kempetai wore plain clothes while others were outfitted in Japanese Army uniforms with a distinguishing white armband. They could be and often were heartless. Anyone suspected of subversion could expect to be tortured in a variety of ways: water forced into mouth and nose until unconscious; uncooked rice and then water pumped into stomach causing internal bleeding; burning breasts and genitals with hot irons and lighted cigarettes; jerking out fingernails with pliers; electric shocks; upside-down suspension; flogging and more. Detainees were kept in cramped, smelly cells on starvation rations.

What qualified as subversion? Virtually any affront, perceived or real. Suspects were regarded as guilty. Failure to bow to a Japanese soldier could be deemed worthy of beheading.

The kempetai issued every resident a census card that listed every occupant of a household. A copy was kept at the nearest police station. The kempetai and their Singaporean puppet police conducted surprise checks. Unlisted occupants and their hosts could be prosecuted – if they couldn't buy their way out of trouble with cash or sexual favors. Still, many brave residents of all ethnicities took to hiding young girls.

To foster snitching, the kempetai employed a neighborhood vigilance system. They divided neighborhoods into groups of 300 families that were further subdivided into 10-family groups. Overseers were recruited from among the local populace. Corruption – chiefly in the form of blackmail – was rampant, but it spared many individuals from torture, rape and execution.

The occupiers also tried marginally more subtle means of control. Chinese and English schools were pressured to teach in Japanese. The Japanese insisted that students listen to propaganda and sing Japanese patriotic songs. As a result, most parents kept their children at home. The Japanese offered free Japanese language classes at night and although bonuses and promotions were given to those who learned the language, few attended.

Everywhere in Singapore, from Changi Prison to other detention camps to Chinatown, food quickly started to become scarce, a situation that would worsen.

CHAPTER 62

The woman was young and walking briskly on the cobblestone sidewalk. She was pretty but unsmiling with dark eyes shifting furtively from side to side. She was dressed shabbily – a plain white cotton top and a frayed ankle-length skirt, blue with rows of white flowers fringed with faded green leaves. Both needed laundering. She was carrying a wicker basket.

From about 90 feet away on tree-shaded Colentina Street, Gabriella saw the woman approaching. It was about 3 p.m. The woman's appearance struck Gabriella as unusual, more like that of a poor, rural villager than that of a resident of relatively cosmopolitan, prosperous Ploesti.

The woman stopped in front of the city's central police station. Again, she looked about furtively. Gabriella slowed her pace. Then she watched, puzzled, as the woman turned toward the police station entrance. She bent forward and carefully placed the basket on the first of three stone steps. Then the woman straightened, saw Gabriella approaching, quickly pivoted and went scurrying away in the opposite direction.

Gabriella, curious, quickened her pace. In seconds she was peering down at the basket and its contents – a newborn. It was swaddled in what appeared to be a heavy cotton blue rag. The infant was sleeping.

Gabriella looked around and saw no one. Abandoned, Gabriella was thinking. But why? She picked up the basket and examined the baby's face. It was cherubic. Gabriella ascended the steps and carefully pushed open a heavy wooden door. Inside on her immediate left was a barred window. Behind it was sitting a gray-haired uniformed policeman. With sleepy eyes he saw Gabriella stepping toward his window.

"Yes, miss, what?" And then he saw the infant.

"A woman," said Gabriella, "I just saw a woman abandon this baby outside your station."

The policeman shook his head and stretched his face, yawning to shake off boredom. "Happens too often."

"What?"

"At least once a month. More often in the winter months."

"Why?"

"Poverty. Young parents, too poor to feed their young."

"I… It's hard to believe."

"How many rural villages have you seen?" The policeman didn't wait for an answer. "Food is often in short supply, and in winter starvation can become a frequent companion. That's the way it is."

Gabriella's lips pursed and her eyes saddened. "This baby. What will happen to it?"

"Not to worry."

"What? This little creature is helpless. Who will care for her? Or him?"

"We'll watch over it – him or her – for the time being."

"Here? In a police station?" The notion appalled and worried Gabriella.

"Put the basket over there." He was motioning toward a nearby vacant wooden desk. The policeman looked over his shoulder at a round wall clock. 3:07. "Come back here tomorrow if you'd like. Four o'clock. You'll see. Don't be late."

The next day Gabriella entered the police station at 3:45 p.m.

"You're early," said the policeman behind the barred window.

"I didn't want to be late. Although I've no idea for what. Where is the baby?"

"In an office back there."

"Should I wait here?"

"Suit yourself."

Gabriella paused, then turned and pushed open the heavy door. Better to wait outside, she thought. Though the day was sultry, the sunshine was far more welcoming than the dull gray of the police station interior.

She didn't have long to wait. A gleaming black 1939 Plymouth with white-wall tires pulled to a stop in front of the police station. The driver's side front door was the first to open and out stepped Princess Catherine Caradja. From the passenger side emerged Laura Ramaschi. The two glanced at Gabriella, Laura smiling thinly and briefly, but hurried past her and up the steps and through the door. *Are they who I'm waiting for?* Gabriella wondered. She shrugged and followed them inside.

The policeman behind the barred window immediately slid off his high stool and straightened.

"Where is the child?" Catherine asked in a tone that the policeman took accurately as more a demand than a query.

"Just one moment, Madam." He went walking toward the station's rear.

Catherine half-turned and saw Gabriella watching curiously.

"Yes?"

"I saw the baby abandoned here yesterday. When I voiced my concern, that policeman told me not to worry and invited me to return today at four."

"He was right. You've no need to worry. The child will be well cared for."

Gabriella remained silent for a long moment. She looked at Catherine's young companion and then back at the princess. Overcoming reserve, Gabriella asked, "Who are you?"

"Let me answer with a question," Catherine said, a trace of a smile showing. "Who are you?"

"My name is Gabriella Balas. My father is head of the petroleum industry ministry. I was with our embassy in Washington, D.C. before the war."

"You speak English?" Catherine asked.

"Yes."

"So do I." She and the girl both smiled. "Now I will answer your question."

CHAPTER 63

On August 16, 1942, the Japanese surprised all prisoners, military and civilian alike, by moving Australian Army officers ranked colonel or higher from Selarang Barracks north to Formosa – now Taiwan. The men were put on Japanese transports – where they hoped they wouldn't be bombed or torpedoed by Allied warships. Lieutenant Colonel Frederick "Black Jack" Gallaghan took command at Selarang. He was widely respected by fellow POWs.

"I don't know," whispered British Army Private Gordon Gurney. "It seems a trifle dicey."

"What about you?" Australian Army Corporal Rodney Brevington murmured.

"If we're going to escape," British Private Oliver Needle replied thoughtfully, "now would seem the time. The Japs have reduced our rations, and we're already beginning to lose weight. It won't be long before we'll not have the strength or stamina to give it a go." A pause and he smiled thinly. "I'm for trying."

"Good mate," Brevington said in his broad Down Under accent. "How about you two?" His question was directed at two other privates, Brit Peter York and Aussie Tom Browne.

"I'm for it," Browne whispered, his endorsement not so much enthusiastic as determined.

"I suppose you can count me in as well," said York.

"Planning to ask anyone else?" Oliver asked.

"More than five," Rodney replied, "could complicate matters. We're going to have to be able to move quickly, silently and as invisibly as possible."

"How do you see us pulling this off?" Oliver asked.

"I think our best advantage is being part of the same work detail." The five were members of a work crew that the Japanese had doing road repairs near Collyer Quay. Bombs, artillery shells and heavy tanks had torn up many of Singapore's paved streets and roads. "We wait until late afternoon, not long before the lorries come to collect us. That's when the guards are tired, hot and thirsty and as eager as we are to be trucked back to Selarang."

Selarang was a 400-acre British Army post where the Japanese were detaining thousands of POWs.

"Do we bribe the guards?" Peter asked.

"I think not," Rodney said. "I know they've taken bribes for certain favors, mostly extra food. But no one's tried an escape before, and that raises the stakes for everyone including our guards. They could be unwilling to risk being implicated in planning the first escape. If found out, it could be their heads separated from their shoulders."

"Agreed," Oliver said. "They're conditioned to think and behave like Samurai and to regard their emperor as a deity. But I don't sense any enthusiasm for sacrificing their lives for five of the king's own."

"Then what?" Peter asked.

"We need a spot of luck," Rodney replied. "Our work detail needs to be assigned again to work near the waterfront. As our shift is ending we slip away to the quay and hope some friendly Chinese will shelter us on their sampan till nightfall."

"Do we all move together?" Tom asked.

"No," Rodney replied. "That would add to the risk of being noticed. There are fifty of us in the detail. We try to stay separated during the day. On a signal from me we begin slipping away between buildings and make for the marina. No mass dash. One at a time." A pause. "Yes, there's risk. The guards might see us. Chinese might inform on us. But again, no one has tried it, and that might be the key to success."

Under the Geneva Convention, POWs were granted the right to escape and protection against punishment if recaptured. The Japanese had chosen not to abide by the accord and that refusal had dampened the ardor of many POWs to seek liberty. Add to that the Japanese penchant for inflicting punishments, often capriciously as well as viciously, and POW acceptance of confinement became understandable.

"If we make it onto sampans, what next?" Oliver asked.

"Tomorrow morning when we're loaded onto lorries, each of us brings a small cache of cigarettes. We know they're as good as cash with guards and many civilians. Hopefully their value will extend to boat people."

"If it does?" Gordon asked.

"After dark we'll see if they can get us to any small vessel with a motor. Then we would make for the Malayan coast. Perhaps hook up with a resistance group. Or maybe get us across the strait to Sumatra."

The next afternoon was typical of Singapore. The temperature had reached 90 degrees and the humidity had climbed higher. But the work detail assignment was the one the men were hoping for – road repairs near the waterfront. Six guards.

Late that afternoon, as planned, the men bided their time until the last 10 minutes before their shift would end. At a simple British style salute, palms out, tossed off casually by Rodney Brevington, Oliver, Tom, Peter and Gordon ducked behind parked vehicles and piles of rubble and began walking as nonchalantly as seemed wise toward the bay.

On reaching Collyer Quay separately, four of them turned right. Ahead of them to the south they saw Oliver entering the quay. Rodney gave him a half wave and Oliver nodded in return.

Just ahead of Rodney, Tom, Peter and Gordon on their left was Clifford Pier, a roofed walkway that jutted about 60 yards into Marina Bay. As usual, the water was teeming with sampans and bumboats. The men's plan: get out of sight onto the pier and try to persuade one or more small vessel owners to take them aboard.

In the next instant their plan began unraveling. As they turned to enter the pier, three Japanese soldiers, each carrying a Type 99 rifle, came walking leisurely off the pier. They were startled to see four soldiers of the British and Australian armies. Rodney, Tom, Peter and Gordon were equally stunned. Mutual moments of indecision ensued.

Then the Japanese – Etsuro Yamada, Kai Hata and Takuma Matsui – collected their wits and lowered their weapons. "Raise your arms," Yamada ordered, simultaneously gesturing with his rifle. The men hesitated. Yamada bellowed, "Raise your arms now!"

The four Allied soldiers did as ordered.

At that moment, Lieutenant Haruo Wada stepped out of the Union Building that had housed the U.S. Consulate and now was serving as an administrative building for the occupiers. Wada looked to his left and saw and heard the commotion at the entrance to the pier.

Oliver had only moments to choose: turn around, walk away and hope to shed his British Army uniform or try something – anything – to aid his colleagues.

Matsui saw another enemy soldier approaching Wada from behind but had no time to shout a warning. Wada felt Oliver's left arm coil around his neck and apply strong pressure. With his right hand, Oliver unholstered Wada's Type 94 8mm pistol and jammed the snout against Wada's temple. His unspoken message to Yamada, Hata and Matsui was clear: lower your rifles to the pavement or I'll blow your lieutenant's brains from here to Johor.

Yamada was uncertain but Wada quickly solved the private's dilemma. "No," he croaked through Oliver's chokehold.

Yamada, Hata and Matsui immediately raised their rifles to the shoulder-high firing position and took aim at their captives. Then, with his left hand, Yamada signaled to Oliver to lower the pistol and free the lieutenant.

Reluctantly, Oliver complied.

Back at the Selarang camp the five captured fugitives were standing before Commandant Colonel Fukunaga's desk. To their left stood Lieutenant Wada. Behind them stood their three captors. To their right a bi-lingual Japanese major was serving as translator.

Fukunaga listened patiently to Wada's account, stated modestly with no self-serving embellishments.

"What you did," Fukunaga said impassively, "was unprecedented. It is also deeply disturbing. Your attempted escape – foolish and failed as it was – could inspire other prisoners to try the same thing. That is unacceptable."

"Under the Geneva Convention," Rodney Brevington replied evenly, "prisoners have the right to try escaping. Some would say we have the obligation to do so."

"The Geneva Convention," Fukunaga responded dismissively, "suggests that war is some kind of gentlemanly contest. It is not. Its purpose is conquest. Enemy soldiers who become prisoners deserve neither honor nor respect. Yet to this point we have overseen you Australian and British with a light hand. We have left it to you to organize yourselves and conduct your own affairs, even permitting you entertainments. In other words, without any mandate or convention, we have granted you trust. You have violated that trust and I find that totally unacceptable."

Lieutenant Wada sensed what was coming and dreaded it.

"Your fellow prisoners must be deterred from following your example," Fukunaga said, voice flattening, "and with that in mind I will make my own example of you. My decision is simply this: you will be executed and immediately. I will accord you one final privilege; your executions will not be public."

The five blinked and blanched. A slight pause and Brevington spoke unwaveringly. "Sir, the escape was my idea and the plan was mine. Execute me – the leader. Spare these men. My death as the leader will provide the necessary deterrent."

Fukunaga was impressed but unmoved. He shook his head. "All of you must die."

"Please, sir, I beg you to be merciful." Rodney's sudden shift from reasoning to pleading surprised everyone. "Allow these men to return to the barracks. Let them share our failure. That will be deterrent enough. Please."

"No. Lieutenant Wada, because your men were alert to their flight and because you acted decisively, I am giving you the honor of carrying out the executions. Your three men will serve as escorts. Lieutenant Colonel Galleghan will go as witness. That is all."

Hands tied behind their backs, Rodney Brevington, Oliver Needle, Peter York, Tom Browne and Gordon Gurney were being escorted from Selarang to the nearby sea. No one – the five condemned men, Colonel Galleghan, Wada, his three men, the major serving as interpreter – seemed in a rush to end the episode. Time seemed to slow if not stop, and a full half hour passed before the party arrived at Singapore island's eastern shore. Ironically, the point where they stopped was almost precisely where British traitor Patrick Heenan met his end.

The scene seemed surreally idyllic. Ocean water lapping against the sea wall. Cloudless blue sky. A single squawk from a lone white gull.

"Arrange yourselves in a row and kneel," Wada ordered. "About six feet apart."

The men spaced themselves, and then Oliver Needle spoke. "No," he said quietly but firmly. "We will not kneel. We are soldiers, not supplicants."

On hearing the major's translation, reactions varied. Wada was understanding and sympathetic. Private Yamada was affronted. Hata was stunned. Matsui was remorseful.

"Then turn around," Wada directed.

Oliver's head shook. "No. As soldiers we will face our executioners."

His stand calmed the nerves of his colleagues. Corporal Brevington even managed an admiring smile. Tears were misting Colonel Galleghan's eyes.

At this development Wada's "honor" was plunging to new depths. He would have preferred to turn the matter over to his men. Yamada, he was certain, would suffer no qualms about shooting these men. Hata, probably the same. But Matsui? Wada entertained lingering suspicions about Matsui's possible involvement in Private Hoshi's disappearance in Nanking. Yes, Matsui might defer accepting such an "honor." Wada knew, though, that he had to shove aside his fantasizing. If he didn't personally carry out Fukunaga's verdict, the commandant no doubt would regard his delegating the execution as dishonorable and disgraceful. Wada's army career would be finished and quite likely his life.

Oliver sensed Wada's reluctance. "Get on with it, sir."

Wada nodded and unholstered his 8mm pistol, the one Oliver had held to his head on Collyer Quay. Wada stepped to Oliver's side, placed the gun's muzzle three inches from his temple and squeezed the trigger. In the stillness the shot startled all. Oliver crumpled, bits of bone, brain and blood scattering, some falling into the sea.

Matsui winced. This is not war, he told himself, this is murder. I am ashamed to be part of it.

Wada inhaled shallowly, then began moving from man to man. By the time he stood next to the sixth, Rodney, his hand was shaking so violently he feared missing even from mere inches. He closed his left hand over his right to steady it, then squeezed the trigger.

He now had but one shell remaining. Briefly he considered ending the dishonor he was bearing. Instead, he gathered himself and, jaws clenched, said, "Drop their bodies into the water."

CHAPTER 64

Princess Catherine Caradja's 1939 black Plymouth was virtually hurtling down the dirt road, kicking up pebbles and trailing a dense cloud of Romanian dust. She was returning to her estate near Nedelea from one of the orphanages comprising Saint Catherine's Crib. Beside her was Gabriella Balas.

"I've been thinking about you," said Catherine, eyes focused on the narrow, winding road.

"How so?"

Catherine slowed the car slightly and the jarring subsided. She looked at Gabriella appraisingly. "You are young and beautiful and well-traveled. You are well-connected."

"As are you."

Catherine returned her eyes to the road and laughed. "I know my age and what it has done to my beauty. And my connections could become disconnected without warning. Wars can do that. But you…you won't meet any eligible young men working with me. No savior. No lover."

"I understand."

"And that doesn't trouble you?"

"No."

A pause. Catherine didn't avert her eyes from the road, pitted and rutted from the wheels of heavy horse-drawn wagons. "Who is he?"

Gabriella pivoted slowly to face the princess. "We met in Washington."

"He is American?" Gabriella nodded. "Why are you here? Why did you return to Romania? Especially now. Why did you leave him?"

"He left me."

"A dunce!"

"Hardly. He is with America's State Department. A Foreign Service officer and he was posted to Singapore."

"When?"

"Late in 1940. December."

"He didn't leave before the Japanese takeover?"

"I'm not sure. In his last cable he said he felt an obligation to check on some local friends."

"Is he all right?"

"I don't know."

"But you are waiting and hoping."

"Praying too."

"He sounds like a man worth praying for."

Catherine shook her head and momentarily closed her eyes. We'll all be lucky to survive, she was thinking. Young and old. Pretty and homely. Romanians, Germans, Russians, Americans, the people of Singapore. Europe, Asia, awash in blood. How could man – men – be so utterly stupid and callous? God must despair.

Catherine collected herself and braked the car. She depressed the door handle and pushed. "Come," she commanded.

"Where?"

"There," she said, smiling and pointing at roadside bushes. "Blackberries. We must pick some and then you and I will bake pies."

CHAPTER 65

The Selarang prisoners' attempted escape changed the Japanese mood. Commandant Fukunaga summoned Lieutenant Colonel Galleghan to his office. "I have been thinking," Fukunaga began. He was sitting at his desk and had not invited Galleghan to sit. "I believe I have been too lenient, too trusting. It was a mistake. The escape attempt by your men demonstrated that. So, I want you and all other British and Australian prisoners to sign a pledge, a pledge that they will not try to escape." Galleghan sighed and nodded slightly, a movement that Fukunaga mistook for assent. "Good. I am glad you agree."

"I'm sorry, Colonel, but I don't. Signing such a pledge would not only trample our army's tradition, but it would be utterly humiliating. On behalf of our men, I must decline."

"Colonel Galleghan, must I remind you-"

"Colonel Fukunaga," Galleghan interrupted, knowing his impoliteness would offend the commandant, "my refusal is non-negotiable."

The next morning, September 2, Japanese guards herded all Changi-area British and Australian POWs – some 20,000 – into the dusty barracks square at Selarang. Once assembled, Fukunaga stepped up onto a platform. "Yesterday Lieutenant Colonel Galleghan refused a request. A quite reasonable request. I asked that he and all prisoners sign a pledge promising not to try to escape. He refused. He said he was refusing on behalf of all prisoners. His position is unreasonable. That is why you are here. I want you all to hear my request directly. Sign the pledge and you can continue to manage your affairs. Tend to your gardens. Have your entertainments. Run your own hospital at Roberts Barracks."

Fukunaga heard the chorus of buzzing among the prisoners. Men were sharing their whispered opposition. "No!" shouted one. "We will not sign."

Furious, Fukunaga stepped down. "Keep them standing here," he muttered angrily to a young officer. The aide knew better than to ask how long. Hours later, the weary prisoners were dismissed – but those housed in barracks outside the Selarang perimeter fence were told not to leave.

That meant thousands of men would be trying to sleep on floors and bare dusty ground.

The next morning, Fukunaga called for Galleghan. The result didn't differ. In the afternoon the 20,000 again were bunched into the square. Fukunaga again mounted the platform. Without preamble he declared, "I am ordering you to sign the pledge. Disobeying my order will lead to severe punishment."

A few moments of muffled conversing commenced, and then a voice shouted defiantly, "We are soldiers, not sheep."

Fukunaga dismounted the platform and gestured to his aide. He in turn motioned to a dozen guards positioned across the front of the assembled prisoners. Six guards stepped forward; each reached out and grabbed an Australian prisoner by an arm and pulled him from the rank.

It wasn't lost on Galleghan, an Australian, that only Aussies had been selected. Summarily, the six guards began marching the six prisoners from the barracks square and continued through the camp's main gate. They were escorted to the sea wall, lined up and shot. Four fell into the water. The remaining two corpses were kicked repeatedly until they toppled into the sea where all were left to decompose.

Still no one signed the pledge. Later that day, several of the assembled prisoners sickened. Galleghan worried that, confined to the square, an epidemic could take hold and spread easily, killing thousands of weakened men. He asked to meet with Fukunaga. Serious, protracted negotiations commenced.

On September 5, agreement was reached. The prisoners would sign the document, but Fukunaga would accede to three conditions: the sickened men would be released immediately to the Roberts Barracks hospital and be given medications, the pledge was being signed under duress and the men would regard it as non-binding. To Fukunaga, the accord was face-saving. To Galleghan and the 20,000, the pledge was a sham. When copies were circulated for signatures, many men treated the agreement as fraudulent and entered false names. Popular forgeries included Winston Churchill and Adolf Hitler.

The episode triggered a worsening of conditions for Changi-area prisoners. Food became a carrot, withholding it a stick. Work hard, prisoners were told, and you will eat. Fail to work hard or not at all and you will go hungry. The work was strenuous for the fit, deadly for the unfit. Men were ordered to the docks to unload supplies, including munitions. They were used to clean sewers damaged by falling Japanese bombs.

Diseases including malaria, dysentery and dermatitis spread. Medicine became virtually nonexistent. Increasingly, prisoners were dispatched to work as slave laborers on railway building projects in Burma and Thailand, to Borneo to mine copper and tin and to Japan to mine coal. At Changi, the departed were replaced by newly captured prisoners – soldiers, sailors, airmen – from several Allied nations, including the U.S. What became a way of life for all was sharing – food the most prized commodity – and thieving while on work parties – again with food the most frequently purloined treasure.

Meanwhile, the Japanese were stockpiling an unintended but inevitable commodity – simmering hatred.

CHAPTER 66

The Malayan People's Anti-Japanese Army, Force 136 members and Joe Barton and Duane Hurd's little group all were facing challenges: shortages of food, ammunition and medicine; communications hindered by uncooperative radios; and terror tactics by occupying Japanese. The latter – the Japanese often burned villages thought to harbor locals sympathetic to the MPAJA – made Malayans of all races and ethnicities fearful of aiding the resistance. Still, some courageous Malayan farmers followed the MPAJA into the mountain foothills where they cleared plots and grew vegetables to feed guerilla forces – as well as the Barton-Hurd group.

Joe and Duane's first action came when nearby MPAJA members invited them to join a sabotage mission. The MPAJA delegation numbered four. "Our plan for tonight is cutting a phone line and blowing a section of railroad track," said their leader, Sun Dexin. "We are thinking you might like to join us. We believe six are enough so that we can succeed."

Joe nodded. "What time?"

"After dark," Sun replied. "We will come for you."

"I want to go with you," Rosalie said.

The Chinese leader looked at her but said nothing. He shifted his gaze to Joe.

"I know you do, Rosalie, but I'm afraid not. He" – Joe gestured toward the resistance leader – "has said six will suffice."

"Seven is a lucky number," Rosalie countered, "at least in America. Besides, I didn't stay in Singapore and come with you to be a spectator."

Sun Dexin's expression, one of unadulterated wonder, clearly reflected his shock at hearing a woman so forcefully argue with a man. Her boldness was transmitting a cultural jolt. He was asking himself, *Are all American women so disrespectful?*

The leader's second shock came when Joe acquiesced. "All right, but you will agree to follow his orders."

"Agreed," Rosalie smiled.

Follow orders? Sun thought skeptically. *Her? At best she will slow us down, at worst she will be an outright liability. How can Barton tolerate her company?*

As the day's last light surrendered to mountain darkness, the four MPAJA men arrived at the Barton-Hurd camp.

"We're ready," said Joe. He and Duane each had tucked between their belts and trousers the Enfield .38 revolvers Duane had picked up in Singapore. Duane also had his sheathed fishing knife, and Joe had acquired, courtesy of the MPAJA, a knife with a slightly curved six-inch blade. It too was sheathed – thankfully, thought Joe. *I'd hate to slip and fall with this baby ready to slice open my thigh.* Rosalie also was carrying a .38 revolver. She had run a length of rope through the trigger guard and then knotted it – a secure square knot cinched snugly against her waist. She also had altered a skirt. With needle and thread she had converted the skirt into a pair of culottes.

"I'm all set," Rosalie said with a quiet confidence.

"All right," said Joe. Then to Sun, "Lead on, sir."

"Joe." It was Sister Regina. "I would say be careful, but that sounds so silly. But I will ask that you not take any unnecessary risks."

"Understood, Sister R."

"Duane, Rosalie. That applies to you as well," Regina added.

Their descent proceeded slowly. The trail down was narrow and twisting and slicked by an afternoon rain. By the time they reached bottom the only illumination was being provided by a glittering sea of stars and a half moon.

"This way," said Sun, pointing to his right or north. "A little farther up the tracks is a tree with branches that reach the telephone line. One of us will climb up and over and cut the line. Below we will set charges" – he pointed to a leather satchel containing tied clusters of four sticks of dynamite each – "and blow the tracks."

Thirty yards ahead, one of the MPAJA members stopped. He would serve as one of two sentries. After walking another 30 yards, the group halted.

"That is the tree." Sun pointed to a mature specimen with thick, spreading branches. One of the men resumed walking; he would serve as the second sentry.

Sun looked up at the tree branches and said to his remaining man, "Up you go."

"Wait," Rosalie said. "I'm shorter and lighter and I should be able to climb out farther and get closer to the line."

The leader eyed her. *Pushy, belligerent, but now she makes a good point.* "Here," he said, opening the satchel and extracting a pair of wire cutters. "Take this."

Rosalie took the tool, hesitated momentarily, then inserted it beneath her blouse. "Need to keep my hands free for climbing," she said dryly.

Joe and Duane smiled wryly. The Chinese leader scratched the back of his head.

"Okay," Rosalie said cheerily, "give me a boost, Joe."

Rosalie positioned herself beneath a large branch, and Joe placed his hands on her hips. "On three," Joe said. "Ready? One, two, three." He thrust upward and Rosalie, arms extended fully, grasped the branch. She pulled herself up with an ease that astonished the cell leader. Rosalie steadied herself for a moment and began ascending, gracefully for the most part.

Sun was impressed. "She climbs like a monkey."

"Perhaps she's a subspecies," Joe said casually. The leader looked at him dubiously. "Only kidding," Joe smiled. "As a child I think she probably had practice. Old skills remembered."

Within a few minutes Rosalie had reached the height of the wire and was easing her way out on the limb. Midway she paused to reach under her blouse to shift the wire cutter farther to her left side. She wanted to be able to reach it with her right hand.

Now she was within reach of the line and was retrieving the tool. In the next moment, the northern sentry came walking briskly, not noisily running, toward the group.

"Men coming," he whispered to Sun. "Japanese patrol, I think."

"How many?"

"Judging by footfalls, at least eight. Maybe ten or twelve."

Sun shook his head. "We don't have enough men or fire power to fight and win. And we are not here to die needlessly. We will move away from the tracks and hide until they pass. No noises. None at all. Mr. Barton, please tell your friend to stay still."

"I would prefer you call me Joe."

Sun smiled. Very American he was thinking. "You may call me Dexin."

Joe craned his neck, his face upturned. "Rosalie, can you hear me?" he whispered forcefully.

"Yes."

"Men coming along the tracks. Enemy soldiers, we think. Stay perfectly still."

"Okay." She felt the surge of adrenalin that had helped man escape danger since pre-history. But she had nowhere to run.

"Your other sentry?" Joe asked.

"He will hear them coming and hide. Now let's move."

Sun and his two fellow MPAJA members, Joe and Duane moved deliberately into the trackside jungle grasses that were high and wide with some seemingly as sharp as Joe's razor blade.

To Rosalie, stretched out on the branch, the wait seemed interminable. Then she heard the oncoming Japanese. Eight men. She watched them passing below on the rail bed. She felt sweat drops running down her face and worried that they might fall on the Japanese. As the last two men were moving by, the tree branch creaked. To Rosalie, in the stillness the eerie sound might as well have been a howitzer blast.

Below, one of the Japanese kidded a colleague, "Maybe a tiger."

A second soldier chuckled and joked, "Or a monkey."

The trek back up the mountain path had been slow and arduous. Starlight and moon glow were scarcely able to penetrate the jungle canopy. Before beginning the ascent, Rosalie had cut the phone wire and gingerly descended from her high perch. When she reached the branch from which she had begun her climb, she hung by her hands momentarily before releasing her grip. Joe broke her fall. The MPAJA members and Duane had set the charges with fuses long enough for the saboteurs to walk back along the tracks and locate the trail that would take them back to their lofty aeries before the ear-splitting explosion.

Entering the Barton-Hurd camp, exertion and humidity had drenched the climbers with salty sweat that was irritating their eyes. Joe, Duane and Rosalie bid farewell to Sun Dexin and his men.

Rosalie walked to the tent she shared with Sister Grace Ann. Duane started for the tent he shared with Joe. "You coming?" he asked.

"I'll be along in a few minutes." Joe sucked in a breath of clammy jungle air and thought, Miss Hughes, someday if I share this story with your students, they'll probably think I'm just a delusional old man making up a tall tale and passing it off as a saga of derring-do. And Gabriella, if I tell you this story while we are riding together, the horses will probably neigh their disbelief. What a night. Well, self, time to get some shuteye. Joe turned and took a couple steps toward his tent.

"Joe."

The whisper stopped him.

"It's me, Sister R. Over here."

She was standing off to the side of their campground.

Joe padded cautiously toward the voice. He finally got close enough to Regina to make out her form. She was wearing her light, beige nightgown and shoes.

"I couldn't sleep. Even up here I could hear the explosion. Like the crash of distant thunder. I prayed but admit I was concerned about you, Duane and Rosalie."

"We had a little unexpected excitement," Joe said. "I'll tell you and the others about it in the morning." He turned to go to his tent but stopped, looked back over his shoulder and said, "You'd make one heck of a good mother."

"Why do you say that?"

"Because you couldn't stop worrying about your kids."

CHAPTER 67

"We are all losing weight," Captain Brian Barnsworth said.

"Can't be helped," Private Malcolm Goode replied woodenly. He was sitting on a shipping crate beside one of the barracks inside the Selarang camp.

Brian was standing, hands clasped behind his back. "No, but you seem to be losing more than most. I'm told you are sharing your rations."

"Not much appetite."

"So it would appear. Look, I know it can be an intrusion to give advice where none is wanted."

Malcolm looked up. "But you are going to give some anyway." Brian smiled thinly. "This crate is large enough for two. If you're going to meddle, don't stand over me whilst doing so. Sit."

The captain unclasped his hands and sat next to the private. "Thank you."

Malcolm's bowed head stared at the dirt between his feet. "I'm listening."

"Right. Most of us are going to survive this war. Some won't. In many cases the difference will be will. So the question becomes, do you have it?"

"I'm not sure I want it. We were three together."

"You, Britton and Needle."

Malcolm nodded. "Now we are two. A pathetic two. Prisoners of these accursed Japs."

"You would be only one if not for you. You saved Britton's life on the causeway."

"That seems ancient history. Useless history."

"Not so. Britton has recovered from his wounds, as you know. He also has the will to endure."

"Says you."

"Says he."

"Oh? You've spoken to him? Captain to private?"

"Only yesterday."

"And he told you precisely what?"

"Precisely, he told me he intends to return to Gravesend and try swimming the Thames again. And precisely, he is relying on you to be rowing his escort boat."

Conditions in Singapore were worsening. As prisoners – both military and civilian – consumed diets that did little more than stave off starvation, pounds fell from frames, immune systems weakened and diseases and illnesses exacted a steadily increasing toll. Food stocks that the British had built were depleted within a few months after the surrender. The occupiers began encouraging both free locals and internees to become more self-sufficient by growing their own food. The Japanese viewed the food shortages to be so serious that they took to sponsoring the formation of agricultural settlements in Malaya that exported production to Singapore. Still, some prisoners continued perishing from chronic hunger. By war's end, starvation would claim about 850 Changi-area POWs.

Despite deprivations, numerous POWs not only refused to lose heart but their sense of spirituality deepened and flowered. One group built a chapel at Changi Prison. Its peaked roof rested on four wood posts. On three sides, no walls confined the large altar that was backed by a V-shaped partition. Stanley Warren, a British airman, painted a series of murals on the backdrop. A British soldier, Sergeant Harry Stodgen, crafted an intricate cross from an artillery shell casing that easily matched those adorning countless churches. Other prisoners affixed his creation to the front of the chapel roof.

CHAPTER 68

Atop a ridge north of Ploesti, Gabriella was sitting astride Rainbow. She now stabled her mare at Catherine Caradja's Nedelea estate. What she saw in the distance was disheartening. It was the work of Lieutenant General Alfred Gerstenberg. Hitler had assigned to Gerstenberg – who became Romania's de facto head of state – the defense of Ploesti's complex of oil refineries, storage tanks and distribution facilities. The appointment ranked among Hitler's very best personnel decisions. Gerstenberg was 48, short and red-haired. He was a bachelor and loved books and art. His army career began with the cavalry, but he saw the future clearly and became an aviator, flying combat missions during World War I. He did not join the Nazi Party.

Gerstenberg showed himself to be both a brilliant strategist and a masterful tactician. A workaholic, he took it upon himself to quickly become fluent in Romanian. Germany's ambassador to Bucharest wasn't. Gerstenberg thus was able to communicate directly with Antonescu – whom he disdained – as well as other government officials and military members.

A bullseye, Gabriella was musing dispiritedly, that's what my hometown has become. And General Gerstenberg, his plan has all but assured that any Allied attack on Ploesti will become a blood bath. My dear Joe, your Romanian gypsy fears for the future of her homeland more than ever.

It's ironic, isn't it? America could be Romania's savior and its destroyer. She pulled on Rainbow's reins, wheeling the horse to its right and began riding back to her new home. I told Princess Caradja we would be home by dinner time.

Gerstenberg's defensive scheme made extensive use of technology. It began with outlying radar installations. Given three small, fruitless Soviet raids in June 1941 and the equally small and futile February 1942 American mission, he was certain more and bigger Allied assaults were inevitable. He also believed that they would be launched from afar – North Africa or Russia. He wanted as much warning – and preparatory time – as possible.

On the ground, Gerstenberg wanted the best technical expertise available and got it. Communications specialists, civil engineers, aircraft mechanics, intelligence analysts.

For labor, he had at his disposal some 70,000 Russian POWs plus civilian refugees who became, in effect, slaves.

Gerstenberg was determined not only to inflict punishing casualties on attacking planes but also to assure that oil production and distribution would continue largely unabated. His cauldron of anti-aircraft firepower was unprecedented. At its core were batteries of the vaunted German 88mm artillery pieces. The guns were versatile; already they had served with deadly effectiveness in naval and tank battles as well as in anti-aircraft operations in Germany and other Nazi-held nations. Gerstenberg positioned 40 of the .88-caliber batteries in a ring around Ploesti. Positioned farther out were batteries of smaller-caliber anti-aircraft guns. Sprinkled around and among the batteries were hundreds of machine gun emplacements. Some were located in pits banked with sandbags. Others were mounted on roofs, in church bell towers and barn loft openings.

Still, Gerstenberg's thinking wasn't limited to waiting passively for attacking aircraft to come within range of ground defenses. He also had mustered a fleet of fighters that could be scrambled within minutes of the first reports of radar screen blips.

What if Allied raiders managed to penetrate Gerstenberg's wall of fire and bomb the oil complex? This contingency didn't escape Gerstenberg's strategizing. He assembled a firefighting brigade – recruited from Germany where they also were badly needed – numbering some 500 experienced men. Their capability included a radio-equipped vehicle that enabled instant communication with his air defense personnel.

Gerstenberg further strengthened reactive ability by ordering constructed a pipeline that connected the ring of refineries, storage tanks and distribution facilities. Because the new pipeline was built above ground, if damaged it could be repaired rapidly.

Gerstenberg wasn't as blindly arrogant as General Bennett had been in Singapore, but he was confident that he had created a fortress capable of repelling the most determined onslaught.

"Man, that was some movie," Jeff Wolfrom said, not trying to mask his amazement. He wasn't alluding to the latest Betty Grable film, cowboy saga or War Department propaganda production. Instead, he was reacting to one in a series of briefing films that depicted the Ploesti complex and what it would be like for attacking air crews. They were central to his ongoing Army Air Corps education.

After escaping from Turkey to Syria, he found himself not returning to Egypt but to Benghazi in Libya, nearly due south across the Mediterranean from Romania. Because Little Eva remained impounded in Ankara, Jeff now found himself teaming with men who would crew a B-24 christened Shoot, Fritz, You're Faded.

Before embarking on a Ploesti raid, Jeff and his mates were assigned another long-distance mission: traverse the Mediterranean and help soften defenses on Sicily before the Allied landing. Jeff and Generals George Patton and Bernard Montgomery would never meet, but his efforts and those of fellow airmen would aid the coming invasion by American and British troops.

In Benghazi, Gerstenberg's strategy counterpart was Colonel Jacob "Jake" Smart. He was charged with developing a bombing plan that would deliver a telling blow to Hitler's chief source of fuel. Smart was a tall, sandy-haired southerner who more relevantly had shown himself to be a crack pilot with a deep understanding of the capabilities of combat planes and the men who flew and crewed them. The more Smart learned about Ploesti – the oil complex's configuration and the Gerstenberg-designed defenses – the more he appreciated the difficulties that would be confronting American pilots and planes aiming for Gabriella's bullseye. Most Allied bombing targets heretofore had been concentrated – large manufacturing plants, rail and dockyards, enemy airbases and submarine pens. By contrast, the dozen Ploesti refineries were ringed widely around the city, about five miles in diameter. Errant bombs striking the city would waste ordnance and kill innocent civilians. In addition to the dozen refineries strung around the city like rosary beads, two more were located as many as 18 miles farther away.

If the planned big raid was to succeed, pilots and bombardiers needed to be topnotch aerial marksmen. They needed to be able to pinpoint and hit key facilities such as powerhouses and pumping stations within the sprawling complex.

Then there was the matter of casualties – American ones. The B-24s were going to have to fly 1,200 miles from Benghazi to Ploesti and then make the return trip. That meant plenty of time for the enemy to identify and intercept the oncoming fleet.

Smart's analysis led to a conclusion that to him offered four advantages – and that sent shivers up and down the spines of Jeff Wolfrom and other American flyers. The B-24s would make the entire run across the Mediterranean and north up the Black Sea coast at low altitude – as low as 50 feet off the "deck."

Smart's strategy would enable the B-24s to evade radar detection. In the event of enemy interdiction, the low altitude would limit attacking fighters to striking from above. No swooping below and slicing open the bellies of B-24s. American planes that were mortally hit would have a chance for a skidding landing. Near the Ploesti targets, Jeff and other gunners would have the opportunity to not only shoot at attacking fighters but also to fire at ground-based flak gun crews.

Strategy disadvantages? Colonel Smart was aware that the Royal Air Force had gained experience with low-level bombing raids. They bordered on disastrous. In a low-level attack on a U-boat engine-making plant in Augsburg, Germany, 12 British bombers went in. Only five returned. At low levels, room for correcting pilot error virtually disappeared. The blasts from bombs could damage and bring down the bombers. Propeller turbulence could lead to mid-air collisions. Flak gunners didn't need to calculate and adjust for altitudes; they could fire at point-blank range.

Jeff wasn't unmindful of those scenarios. During one rehearsal he watched two bombers collide and instantly plummet the 50 feet to the desert floor. Skidding landings? Of the 20 men aboard the two bombers, only two survived, and later they would make the Ploesti run.

Approval for Colonel Smart's strategy had to come from the very top. General Dwight Eisenhower okayed it.

Charged with carrying out Smart's strategy was Major General Louis Brereton. In assessing the mission's dangers, including enemy capabilities, Brereton seemed to have schooled with World War I generals who had ordered waves of their men "over the top" – rising from trenches and dashing en masse into withering machine gun fire. "We expect our losses to be fifty percent," Brereton said with an air of detachment, "but even if we lose everything we've sent but hit the target, it will be worth it." When word of Brereton's bluster reached the Benghazi airmen, Jeff spoke for virtually all: "I don't think the general has ever drunk so much as a quart of the milk of human kindness. My mother would give him a good what for."

CHAPTER 69

Depending on perspective, the news from Stalingrad in November 1942 was cause either for elation or dejection. Hitler's besieging forces included the Romanian 3rd Army under General Petre Dumitrescu. Russian defenders had stubbornly refused to yield, and now the energized Soviets were launching a massive counterattack.

"I wonder how many of my Saint Catherine's Crib boys are being slaughtered," Catherine Caradja said plaintively. "Hitler could care less, the mad sop that he is."

"Making matters worse," Gabriella observed thoughtfully, "is the fate of the Jews. I've heard that our army has continued murdering many Jews in territories in the east."

"A blot on our proud history," Catherine replied, anger rising and shoving aside pathos. "Antonescu must be removed."

"How?"

"I will find a way."

Sam Nelson's predeparture leave had expired, and he was bidding farewell to Maureen and their little daughter Corrine. The tearful goodbyes were being said at Shelby's small, yellow and black New York Central station. Corrine was too young to grasp the situation's gravity. She knew only that her parents were weeping, and that was enough to open her own tear ducts.

"Sam," Maureen said, nearly choking on the words, "I love you and I'll miss you terribly. Please be careful. Promise me."

"I promise." In his sharply creased dress uniform, Sam epitomized the courageous, optimistic young warrior heading off to Lord-only-knows-what threats to limbs and life.

The stack of the huge black locomotive, its coal tender emblazoned with New York Central Railroad, was belching smoke. The conductor was calling out, "All aboard. All aboard for New York City."

That would be Sam's embarkation point for England and eventually continental Europe.

Sam lifted Corrine from the blue and white stroller with colorful beads strung across the front of the small tray. He kissed both her cheeks. Still holding his daughter in his left arm, with his right he again drew Maureen close to this chest. They kissed, long and passionately.

Then Sam disengaged, put Corrine back in the stroller, turned and stepped aboard the train. Slowly the steel wheels struggled for traction on the steel rails. As the train pulled away, Maureen kept waving until the last car disappeared around the first bend.

Two men, she was reflecting sadly, both caught up in this goddamned war. Excuse me, Lord. My dear husband off to Europe. Joe Barton in Asia – somewhere. I still miss him.

It was mid-morning when Sun Dexin appeared in Joe and Duane's camp. "We have received word – radio – that a large Japanese supply convoy is heading south toward Johor and probably to Singapore. We have been told to ambush it. And to take as many supplies as we can carry."

"You would like our help?"

"Yes. This is a large operation. All of our men will take part. About forty of us."

"Duane?"

"Yes. Count me in."

"Rosalie?"

"Of course."

This time her intended participation met no objections from Sun or Joe.

"I would also like to accompany you." The voice belonged to Clayton Hurd.

"Father," Duane said worriedly, "I would feel much better if you stayed behind. As protection for Mother and the nuns."

"Son, I believe in this case my value would be greater with you."

"We'll be all right," said tiny Su Mien.

"I agree," said Sister Regina.

Duane merely nodded his resignation.

"What time?" Joe asked.

"We need to descend the mountain and get in position," said Sun. "It is November so darkness falls early. I think we all should plan to meet at the bottom at six-thirty."

"We'll be there."

After the resistance leader departed, Sister Regina spoke softly to Joe. "If I were a priest, I would bless you."

"If you told me you would be offering a prayer for our safety, I would regard that as a perfectly acceptable alternative."

"I'm no longer so certain of my heavenly connections." She was alluding to Sister Caroline's death in her arms. "But instead of a single prayer, how about an entire rosary? Said together by all three of us?"

"I would feel abundantly blessed."

The guerillas' mission was ambitious. The Japanese convoy was 22 trucks long. The lead truck, with no canvas top, was carrying 20 armed escorts. The next 20 trucks were carrying provisions – food, medical supplies, ammunition. The trailing truck was the second escort vehicle. They were moving at about 25mph and maintaining spacing of about 25 yards – roughly a 725-yard caravan.

The 44 guerillas were divided into two groups and positioned along both jungle- covered sides of the unpaved road. The first group's mission was to stop the lead truck and kill the escorts before they could take up defensive positions or mount a counterattack. The second group included Duane, Clayton and Rosalie. They would attack the trailing escort truck.

No prisoners were to be taken. This policy was not merely manifesting vengeful blood lust. Prisoners would have to be fed and guarded and would strain resources. If one or more were to escape captivity, the resistance cell would be obligated to move its campsite.

If some Japanese drivers or soldiers managed to escape the ambush by fleeing into the jungle, the guerillas wouldn't pursue. Reason: doing so would delay their ascent back to their camps and jeopardize security.

"I'll fire the first shot," Sun Dexin said. "I will aim for the radiator." Holding his British-supplied Enfield, Sun lowered himself until prone, steadiest of the firing positions. To Joe he said, "You aim for the headlights."

Joe knelt with one of Duane's sten guns and steadied himself. Then to all, Sun said, "Surround the first truck and keep shooting until all are dead – or not moving. One stay behind to finish off any wounded. The rest divide into two groups on either side of the road and run to the other trucks. Shoot drivers and their sidemen. We should meet our other group coming toward us. Questions?"

"Just one," said Joe. "What about the supplies?"

The leader nodded. "We'll take what we can carry and burn the rest."

"Duane," Rosalie whispered, "I don't know if I can do this. Kill I mean."

"You don't have to. Just stay here and wait."

They were lying hidden with the rest of their group in jungle grasses bordering the road.

"No, I'll stay with you."

"You don't have to shoot anyone. Look, none of this has been easy for me. If the Japanese didn't murder so casually, I'm not at all sure I could pull the trigger."

A pause. "Thank you."

"For what?"

"Confiding. Sharing."

Moments later, the first pair of headlights passed by Duane's concealed group. The pairs went by at approximately 25-yard intervals.

Farther down the road, the first headlights were approaching Sun's group. "Remember," he said, "I'll fire the first shot."

Another dozen seconds passed and the leader squeezed off a shot. Joe and the other MPAJA members opened fire. Scant moments later, steam from the punctured radiator was spewing from the grill, and the headlights were smashed and broken. When the driver was hit, the truck veered and struck a tree.

The resistance fighters proceeded as directed and went running to either side of the lead truck. Their attack plan proved lethal.

At the other end of the convoy, when the rear truck braked, Duane, Clayton and the MPAJA fighters rushed from the jungle grasses and opened fire on the vehicle's 20 passengers. Rosalie stepped out on the road but hung back. Instantly, Japanese soldiers were hit, screaming and dying. Two nearest the cab vaulted over the sides and were cut down virtually the instant their boots struck the road.

As with the resistance force at the convoy's front, Duane's group divided and began advancing on either side of the stopped line of trucks. Rosalie followed. Four trucks down the line, a sideman leaped from the cab, firing 6.5mm rounds from his sub-machine gun.

Duane screamed primally – twice, twisting and falling. Mere steps from behind him, Rosalie squeezed her sten gun's trigger, and three of the rounds ripped into the soldier's torso, flinging him backward.

Rosalie and Clayton rushed to Duane and dropped to their knees on either side of him. The other MPAJA men continued advancing, shooting and killing the vilified Japanese conquerors.

Blood was leaking from Duane in two places. Ahead, the rapid firing had ceased. Only occasional shots to finish off wounded enemy were heard. Four Japanese drivers and their sidemen, riding in the convoy's middle trucks, managed to leap down and flee into the jungle.

"I am sorry we have to put our true calling to work tonight," Sister Regina said somberly. "My prayers were not answered in full."

"What do you think, Sister?" Rosalie asked. She and Regina were kneeling on either side of Duane in the nuns' tent. Sister Grace Ann was standing, holding a lantern.

Joe, Su Mien, Clayton and Sister Augusta, hands folded in silent prayer, were standing outside.

"Thankfully the convoy had medical supplies," said Regina. "We've sprinkled strong doses of sulfa in his wounds. We've done our best to stop the bleeding. You might have saved his life, Rosalie, when you applied pressure." Regina was referring to a wound just below Duane's right shoulder. "It was very quick minded of you." Rosalie had cut away part of her blouse and wadded it as a pressure bandage. "The bullet should probably come out, but I am no surgeon."

"But you've watched surgeons, haven't you?"

"Yes, to be sure. But even if I were game to try, we would wait for morning light."

"You will try, though, if you think it necessary. Or advisable. Won't you?"

Sister Regina peered into Rosalie's eyes and saw deep concern. "Well, the medical supplies included ether. So when Duane regains consciousness we can put him back under, if surgery seems the proper action."

"What about his head wound?" Rosalie asked.

"Lower the lantern, please, Sister Grace Ann," Regina instructed. "Head wounds cause a lot of bleeding, but his seems superficial. It was enough to concuss him, but I think it less of a concern than the upper chest wound. We should watch him, though, through the night."

"Watch for what?" Rosalie asked.

"Convulsions. Swallowing his tongue. We wouldn't want him choking."

"I'll stay with him," Rosalie said.

"I too," said Grace Ann.

"All right. If you need relief-"

"The two of us can spell each other," Grace Ann said.

"Sleeping arrangements?" Rosalie asked.

"Sister Augusta and I can use your tent tonight."

Stepping outside the tent, Regina held her hands close to her eyes. Blood.

Joe was watching. "Clayton and I could use a bath," he said. Both men were muddied from their exertions on the road and helping bring Duane up the mountain path. "If you'd like to go with us to the stream, you can clean your hands. Then wait close by while we bathe."

Sister Regina smiled. "It's a deal. Isn't that an American saying?"

"Very American, Sister R," Joe smiled. "I might make you a yankee yet."

CHAPTER 70

"It is becoming very clear," Catherine Caradja was saying to her daughter Alexandra, Laura and Gabriella. "The Germans can't win and we will lose. The Russians trapped the German Sixth Army outside Stalingrad and now are pushing back. The Americans have all but defeated the Germans in North Africa, and I'm hearing that they – the Americans – are preparing to invade Sicily. Can it be long before they land in Italy? And it's just a matter of time before the Allies invade Western Europe. Hitler will be squeezed tighter than a sea lion in a shark's jaws."

"Mother," Alexandra asked, "why do you say we will lose?"

"Because our soldiers are being crushed in Russia, and it seems inevitable that we will be trading Nazism for communism."

"And," added Gabriella, "Stalin isn't likely to overlook the fact that Romania attacked Russia. It could be bad for us."

"Antonescu is as blithering as he is ambitious and ruthless," Catherine observed. "I don't see him applying nuanced statecraft to our dilemma – one of his making."

"What if King Michael was our actual leader?" Gabriella asked.

"He is a smart, strong and yet sensitive young man," Catherine replied thoughtfully. "He would make an infinitely better leader than Antonescu. But if Michael was to occupy the throne in fact, not merely in name, I fear he still would have to do Stalin's bidding."

The reunion was unplanned and unexpected which made it all the sweeter.

On May 23, 1943, a Dutch submarine brought Lim Bo Seng and Captain John Davis and five Force 136 agents from India to the Malayan peninsula's west coast. From the submarine, the seven men rowed ashore in a rubber dinghy.

During a meeting at Sun Dexin's compound, Lim heard mention of a group of nuns who also were nurses. Lim asked to be guided to their camp.

"Bo Seng!" Sister Regina's greeting surprised her as much as anyone else. Her joyous shriek was more akin that of an excited schoolgirl than a worldwise nun.

Lim extended his right hand, and Regina clasped it warmly in both of hers.

"I am so pleased to see you," Lim said, emotion thickening his voice. And then his eyes took in Sisters Augusta and Grace Ann and the other camp residents.

Still clutching Lim's hand, Sister Regina said, "I don't know if you've ever met my colleagues. Sister Augusta, Sister Grace Ann, this is my friend Lim Bo Seng."

Lim bowed. "It is my pleasure to meet you."

The nuns bowed in return. "Thank you," Sister Augusta said modestly. "We know your reputation and respect what you are doing."

"Lim," Regina said, "let me introduce you to our saviors. And," she smiled widely, "I mean that literally." She released her grip on Lim's right hand. "These two men spared us from certain death. This is Joe Barton and Duane Hurd."

"Gentlemen," Lim smiled genuinely, "I am only now making your acquaintance, and I am already grateful to you."

Lim and Joe reached for each other's right hand. They shook firmly, eyes locked on the other's, mutual respect obvious to all.

Then Lim turned and began to extend his right hand to Duane. He hesitated when he saw the sling stabilizing Duane's right shoulder and holding his arm close to his chest. Duane smiled and extended his left hand that Lim took with his right.

"I heard about you at Sun Dexin's compound," Lim said. "I am happy to see you are recovering from your wounds."

"Thanks to Sister Regina's ministrations," Duane said.

Lim smiled. "I know well of her nursing skills. My wife brought eight children into the world under Sister Regina's care."

"You should also know that she possesses surgery skills," Duane smiled. Lim's eyes widened in curiosity. "She very neatly removed the bullet." Duane pointed to his upper chest.

They released each other's hands.

"She is a remarkable nun," Lim said. "I can't say I am surprised."

Duane spoke. "I would like to introduce my parents."

Clayton and Su Mien stepped forward. Lim shook Clayton's hand and bowed respectfully to Su Mien.

"We probably will see little of each other," Lim said in his properly structured, precisely enunciated English. He and Sister Regina were standing at the camp's northern edge. "I must move widely to coordinate actions among all the cells. We have few working radios. Our Force One Thirty Six and the MPAJA must coordinate more closely if we are to become more effective."

"If the Japanese learn you are in Malaya, they are sure to hunt you," said Regina.

"No doubt," Lim sighed resignedly. "I might be running and hiding as much as coordinating."

"How is your family?" Regina asked. "I think about them often."

"I have had no direct contact with Choo Neo. But my sources say she and the children are safe."

"I will pray that remains the case."

"Thank you." A pause. "Sister, in my heart I believe the Japanese will be defeated but only at a great price. If something happens to me and it is at all possible for you to look in on my family, I would be grateful."

"I will keep praying for your safety, Bo Seng. But, yes, if something happens to you and I survive the war, I will do my best to honor your request. But my greatest hope is that we both can return to Singapore and greet your family there."

Rain was beginning to fall gently on the mountainside.

"Sister," Lim said, "I should leave before you are soaked. But tell me, how are you and the other sisters faring? It cannot be easy for you in this camp."

Sister Regina smiled tiredly. "We have been through much, and one day I shall tell you the story. But we are resilient – perhaps more so than we knew – and we are coping well. Oh," she chuckled weakly, "we also have learned to walk on mountainsides."

Lim smiled at her small joke. "Is there anything I can get for you?"

The rain was beginning to fall harder.

"I think not. The raid on the convoy replenished our food stock and gave us sorely needed medical supplies."

"Good." He held out his right hand and once again Regina enclosed it in both of hers. "May our Lord keep you and the others here in his care."

"Up here I feel safe."

The Chinese resistance fighters from the neighboring MPAJA compound came rushing breathlessly into the Barton-Hurd camp. Dusk was settling in. Joe, Duane, Rosalie, the nuns and Clayton and Su Mien were standing and chatting. None was eager for the close confines of a tent before time for sleep or prayer.

"Sun Dexin sent us. The Japanese have located us. Their troops are starting up the trail to our compound. Your camp too. Our sentries have relayed the information."

"How many?" Joe asked.

"We think at least fifty – a platoon – are coming for us. For you, a squad of eight or ten."

"Your plan?" Duane asked.

"We are not running away. We are deploying ourselves in the jungle around our compound's perimeter. Some of us in trees, others on the ground. And wait. Let them enter. We have enough men and guns."

"Can one of you stay with us?" Joe asked. "To escort our women higher up the mountain?"

"We both can stay," said the fighter. "That is Sun Dexin's wish. My friend here will go with your women. I will stay here with you."

"All right," said Joe. "If we use your plan – position ourselves in the jungle around the camp – four of us should be able to take on an enemy squad."

"Five of us," Rosalie said resolutely.

The MPAJA man, fully aware of Rosalie's exploits, grinned. "Five would be better."

"You don't have to be part of this," Duane said. "You don't need to prove your courage to us or anyone."

"I'm not doing this to test myself," Rosalie replied softly. "And it's not for revenge. I just feel a need to help."

Duane nodded his understanding. "Are you surprised the Japanese have located us?" He directed his question to Joe.

"Are you?"

"I suppose not," Duane said. "There are too many people willing to curry favor with the Japs."

That reality, Sister Regina was thinking, could pose the gravest threat to all of us including Lim.

Jeff Wolfrom was swimming in the Mediterranean's soothing waters. He was naked. With him and equally naked were generals and privates and virtually every rank in between. The sea provided a welcome respite from the blazing sands of their nearby Benghazi air base. Swimming – and attendant conversations, horseplay and laughter – snapped the boredom that plagued the B-24 crews between their bombing missions across the sea over Sicily. It was July 1943.

As Jeff was wading in the waist-high surf, he found this thoughts turning to Iris Ann. I've been gone a long time, he reflected. Too long. I wish I could be there to help Mother with chores. He cupped water in his hands and splashed his face. Then he threw his head back and laughed. I'm concerned about Mother, but she is probably worrying her head off about me. I'm sure she can't imagine me swimming in the Mediterranean. Nope, not in Pine Bluff. I'll have to write and tell her that life here isn't all that bad.

Jeff's pleasant reverie ended abruptly when he felt a familiar stab of longing. Eren and Natasha. A year. I hope Natasha is in a good orphanage. Probably isn't anything like heaven, but it's gotta be a sight better than that alley. Eren. Man, I miss her. Lots more than I would have guessed. If – when – I make it back to Pine Bluff, I doubt if I'll ever meet a girl – a woman – like her. Never. Mother would be fond of her, I'd bet. Both of 'em are strong women. Pretty too. I love that little bend in the tip of her nose. I should write to Eren. I really should. I guess I'm afraid if I do, I'll hear back that things didn't work out so well for Natasha. Well, I gotta do it anyway.

Jeff slowly waded from the surf. There was no need to towel off. The Mediterranean sun and sea breeze would dry him within minutes.

They numbered 10 and they were ascending slowly and quietly, not wanting to telegraph their approach. They knew the platoon making their way up to the MPAJA compound was moving at the same deliberate pace. Both attacking forces were hoping to take at least one prisoner for interrogation but were under no orders to do so. Killing all in the two camps would be acceptable.

"I have an idea," Joe said. "Before we take to the jungle, let's build a campfire."

"Give the place an unsuspecting look. Or one quickly vacated. Good thinking," said Duane.

Higher up the mountain the nuns and Su Mien were kneeling in prayer. They had brought with them two cloth sacks, one containing food, the other medical supplies. Sister Regina was praying fervently that the latter wouldn't be needed. Not tonight.

The Japanese point man, a sergeant, glimpsed orange flickering through the high jungle grasses. He raised his left hand, signaling the trailing men to stop. With a sweeping arm motion, he signaled them to fan out. The sergeant was confident but cautious. He waited patiently for his men to deploy in a line 20 yards on either side of the trail. Then simple waves from man to man launched the final advance.

The roar of gunfire erupted from the direction of the MPAJA compound, and the sergeant's confidence increased. The occupants of this camp would find the fire distracting and not be expecting an attack on their site.

Joe, Duane, Rosalie, Clayton and the MPAJA fighter were widely spaced in a half-moon around the camp's topside. All were kneeling and sweat born of heat and anxiety was pouring from foreheads and armpits. All were armed with British sten guns with Duane holding his in his left hand. Joe and Duane also carried their Enfield revolvers tucked between belts and trousers.

The Japanese eased from the jungle into the clearing and saw no one. Only the campfire. They must have heard or seen us approaching, the sergeant thought. He was disappointed. Tent flaps were open. Still, he motioned his men to check each. Nothing. He spat disgustedly into the campfire.

From the direction of the MPAJA compound came cacophonous shooting that told the sergeant a major firefight was underway. At that moment he wished he and his men were there, helping to defeat the local resistance. The sergeant's men joined him around the campfire.

"What now?" one of his men asked.

"Burn this camp and everything in it."

The soldiers looked around and one eyed a two-foot limb on the ground near the trail head. A torch-in-the-making, he thought. The soldier walked to the limb, picked it up and returned to the fire. He held the limb in the flames until it ignited. He turned away and took two steps toward the nuns' tent. In that same instant, flames shot from five muzzles.

At the sound of the new, closer gunfire, the nuns clutching black rosary beads crossed themselves. In a fluid motion, the crucifix at the end of each rosary touched forehead, breast, both shoulders and lips.

The combat was one-sided. The 10 Japanese, clustered around the campfire, made easy targets. Screams of pain and shock erupted from all of them before any could squeeze off a single retaliatory shot.

Meanwhile, the fearsome firefight at the MPAJA compound raged on.

Joe and Duane, revolvers drawn, led Clayton, Rosalie and the MPAJA man toward the bodies. One had fallen across the campfire, and the MPAJA man kicked it away. He then used his boots to stamp out the flames. "No need to foul the air with a burning corpse," he said grimly.

Three of the bodies moved slightly or moaned. With the campfire providing illumination and with no evident emotion, Joe and Duane fired point-blank until all motion stopped and all sounds were extinguished.

Simultaneously, the nearby firefight was winding down.

"I hope that we were victorious," said the MPAJA man. "I will check and let you know."

"Okay," Joe said. "We will not go for the women" – a pause while he glanced at Rosalie, her five feet three inches drenched and smudged – "the other women until you return."

CHAPTER 71

July 31, 1943, Saturday morning. Jeff and the crew of Shoot, Fritz, You're Faded were nervous. So were the crews of 177 other B-24s adorned with names such as Utah Man, Tupelo Lass, Hell's Wench, Queenie, Ole Irish, Thar She Blows, Jersey Bounce, Lucky and Pudgy. All had good reason to be edgy.

This morning's agenda had but one item: full dress rehearsal. They would be attacking a full-scale mockup of the Ploesti complex. They would be dropping live 100-pound bombs. They would be flying at 50 feet above the desert floor. Fifty feet. Jeff found it easy to imagine 712 roaring Pratt & Whitney engines and their propellers generating enough turbulence to whip up acres of sand and bring down aluminum birds. Or that could obstruct vision – with no time to correct when only 50 feet separated plane from planet earth. Jeff knew the Pratt & Whitney engines were designed to fly 300 hours between overhauls. He also knew that in the destructive desert grit they could go only 60 hours. In addition, he and other crewmen were mindful of rehearsal disasters that had been plaguing mission preparations from the war's start.

Hours later, the men were celebrating. The rehearsal had gone splendidly. An omen? If not, an encouraging harbinger.

That afternoon the crews gathered for a final briefing and pep talk from General Brereton. He was standing, shaded, on a covered stage. He was wearing Khakis – trousers, shirt and a creased overseas or, as men termed it, cunt cap. Flanking him on the stage were the U.S. and 9th Air Force flags. Behind and beside the stage waved the broad leaves of palm trees.

Some assembled crewmen, including Jeff, were fully uniformed while others were bare-chested. Some wore pith helmets, others billed caps while still others went hatless. Some were attentive. Others were bored and slumping listlessly. Many were too anxious to listen; they simply wanted to get on with Operation Tidal Wave.

"Gentlemen," Brereton began, hands clasped behind his back, "I am the only person I know of who has held a commission in both the Army and the Navy. I have seen the fleet steam up the Hudson and watched the corps of cadets pass in full-dress parade. These sights are soul-stirring.

But today, as I saw your hundred seventy-five four-engined bombers come roaring across the African desert at fifty feet altitude, bringing dust from the ground with your mighty roar, I enjoyed the great thrill of my entire life. Tomorrow when you advance across that captured country, you will tear the hearts out of them. You are going in low level to hit the oil refineries, not the houses, and leave your powerful impression on a great nation." General, Jeff was reflecting, who wrote this talk? I'm getting your message, even though it strikes me as a trifle garbled. Which great nation will be on the receiving end of our powerful impression? Romania? Germany? America? Brereton continued, "The roar of your engines in the heart of the enemy's conquest will sound in the ears of the Romanians – and, yes, the whole world! – long after the blasts of your bombs and fires have died away."

Jeff smiled inwardly. General, have you forgotten our Brownings? They're likely to raise a ruckus too. Jeff reacted skeptically when Brereton declared that Operation Tidal Wave would shorten the war by six months. Hmmm, Jeff mused, six months from when? I'm no military genius, but it seems to me that unless somebody knocks off Hitler, I'll be voting age before the war ends. Jeff would be turning 20 on August 12. Just barely more than a year and I can stick a ballot in a box.

That evening Jeff dashed off a quick missive to Iris Ann.

July 31, 1943

Dear Mother,

I've been doing plenty of flying and swimming. No, the swimming hasn't been accidental. Our plane has stayed right where she's supposed to be when she's not parked on the sand. But we're right close to the Mediterranean, and it makes a nice swimming hole. Bluer and warmer than the Arkansas River.

I hope you're not overworking yourself at 305 East Martin. Let your hired help keep picking up the slack as long as I'm away.

I'd tell you not to worry, but I know how much good that would do.

Well I have an early wake-up tomorrow – that's Sunday – so I'd better close.

Your devoted son,
Jeff

He was stretching out on his cot when a thought struck. He sat up, swinging his legs over the cot's edge. He reached for paper and pencil and began a second letter.

July 31, 1943

Dear Eren,

I apologize. I have thought often of writing to you, but didn't because I was too afraid. I should not have been but I was. Why? Because I was worried I might hear back from you that things are not so rosey for Natasha.

I have concluded that I did not have enough faith in you. Forgive me, please. I know you have been looking in on Natasha at the orphanage. When you see her next time, tell her Uncle Jeff has not forgotten her.

I am now in Africa – Libya – but am looking forward to the end of the war and returning to my hometown of Pine Bluff, Arkansas.

I know we will never see each other again. I am not even sure you will receive this letter. Are you still working at the hotel? I do not have a home address for you. So maybe you will never see this letter. But if you do, maybe you can read it to Natasha. Of course, you would have to translate it into Turkish, and my writing might defy translation. Ha Ha.

Let me close this way. My memories of you will last forever and always be sweet.

Sincerely, your American friend,
Jeff Wolfrom

August 1, 1943, Sunday morning. Market day in Ploesti. Gabriella was strolling among stalls and ox- and horse-drawn carts brimming with freshly harvested vegetables and fruits. She loved the profusion of colors – red tomatoes, red and yellow apples, yellow lemons, orange carrots, dark green beans, purple grapes, black and blue berries, light green corn husks with golden tassels. In addition, cheeses, chickens, sausages and freshly baked breads were tempting shoppers. Adding to the colors were market vendors – women in brightly embroidered skirts and old men in white shirts and black hats. Nearly overwhelming olfactory nerves were the enticing aromas. Gabriella even welcomed the smells of the farm animals.

She was carrying two large, brown cloth bags. Her aim: fill them with market goods and drive Catherine's borrowed Plymouth back to her Nedelea estate and help prepare a noon repast for the two of them plus Alexandra, Laura and a half-dozen children – four girls and two boys ages eight to 12 – invited from one of the St. Catherine's Crib orphanages.

Shortly after midnight, B-24 crews had begun boarding. On Shoot, Fritz, You're Faded co-pilot Ernest Poulsen gave each man an escape kit. Contents included a folded Balkans map, cash (U.S., Italian, Romanian), food and water purification tablets.

Weather – bad – was proving a complication. A fierce pre-dawn dust storm was blowing through Benghazi where not a drop of rain had fallen for four months. Postponing the mission was not seriously considered.

Walking, braced against the fierce wind, faces covered to protect from the scalding sand, were the crews. With few exceptions they were young, many like Jeff, not yet out of their teens.

Now aboard the 178 planes were 1,763 men. They came from all 48 states plus Washington, D.C. Two men hailed, one each, from Canada and England. The 712 engines had barely begun revving when the dust storm claimed a victim; one B-24 was forced to abort.

Wingo-Wango was the first to lift off. Others began going wheels up three at a time at two-minute intervals. It took an hour for all the B-24s to join formations that were circling at 2,000 feet. But well before the last plane went airborne, sand-scoured engines forced 10 more to abort.

Jeff's Shoot, Fritz, You're Faded was near the head of the long queue. Once in the air and headed north, Jeff looked down from his waist gunner's port. He grinned wryly. Well, he thought, at fifty feet, getting cold won't be a problem. No worries about iced engines and no being detained in Turkey.

The low altitude was central to inflicting surprise on General Gerstenberg's defenses and the oil complex. During the long flight across the Mediterranean and up the Black Sea coast, crewmen could talk with each other via a plane's intercom. But communications among the B-24s was forbidden. Strict radio silence would prevail. The Americans needn't have bothered. Unknown to Colonel Smart and the U.S. planning team, the Luftwaffe recently had installed a signal interception unit near Athens. Its skilled personnel had deciphered the Allied code and had been monitoring 9th Air Force messages.

Three hours into the flight, compromised engines and the low altitude claimed another victim. Slightly ahead and to his right Jeff watched – first baffled, then horrified – as lead plane Wingo-Wango began to struggle. Before long it was teeter tottering, its nose dropping and tail rising and then repeating the gyration ever more rapidly and violently. With radio silence honored, no distress call came from the stricken plane. With its tail down and the plane nearly vertical, Wingo-Wango flopped onto its back and dove those unforgiving 50 feet into the sea.

"Sweet Jesus," Jeff muttered. "How could that happen?" The only aircraft he could possibly imagine behaving in a way remotely resembling what he had just witnessed was one of his childhood balsa wood toy planes.

Against mission rules, another B-24 broke formation to look for Wingo-Wango survivors but none was seen. That search plane, having spent much of its fuel and unable to catch up to the air fleet, aborted and began returning to Benghazi. The Ploesti-bound armada now numbered 165. It plowed on.

Lunch, typically Army, was eaten on the fly. As noon approached, the airmen cracked open boxes of K-rations. They used heating vents to warm cans of bacon and eggs and chewed on hard biscuits. Mother, Jeff mused, might throw a hissy fit if she knew what the Army was feeding us. And this lemonade powder, I've tasted better rusty spring water. At least the coffee is hot. Good thing we got thermos bottles.

Lunch at Nedelea turned out to be a particularly festive affair. Gabriella had braked the Plymouth near the villa's wrap-around veranda. She exited the car and then reached back inside to remove the two stuffed bags. The orphans had heard her approaching, and they had leaped down the veranda's steps to help lug the groceries inside.

Catherine eyed Gabriella's colorful haul, took in the children's excitement and declared, "A picnic! That's what we need. We'll wash the vegetables and boil them. We'll wash the fruit and slice the cheese, salami and bread." Alexandra, Laura and Gabriella warmed to Catherine's idea as excitedly as the orphans. "We'll slice the lemons and make lemonade. Children, would you like to help?"

A chorus of exultant squeals and upraised arms provided the answer.

"Alexandra, Laura, Gabriella, you may supervise. I'll get some blankets from an upstairs closet. We'll spread them beneath the grove of trees across the stream." The grove wasn't far from the shaded site where Catherine's husband Constantin and daughters Marie and Irene were buried. "I see clouds far to the north over the mountains, but here there's not even a puff of white to be seen. A perfect day."

The B-24s began making their turn northwest from Constanta on the Black Sea coast. It was another 100 miles to Bucharest. Still at tree top altitude, they would skirt the capital and continue north the final 34 miles to Ploesti.

On the ground, the roar of the oncoming B-24s had Romanians craning their necks. The planes' closeness shocked but didn't frighten them. Another air raid test, they were thinking – and some were grumbling. "Whose damned fool idea was this?" an elderly man growled. "Disturbing the peace on Sunday. Shameful." Few noticed the white stars inside blue circles under the wings or on the passing 215 mph fuselages. Many waved gaily at the planes.

Jeff saw many picnickers and in a stream saw a dozen or more teenage girls frolicking naked. "Must be mighty hot down there," he muttered, smiling. "Wouldn't mind joining them." In a park near Bucharest he saw

Romanian and German soldiers lying with, below and on nubile young Romanian women. None seemed to be protesting. He smiled again and thought fleetingly of the only two women he'd bedded – the Egyptian prostitute and Eren Colason – and in both cases the women had initiated the proceedings.

In Pine Bluff, 9:30 p.m. was approaching. For Iris Ann the day – with lunch and supper for regular borders and Sunday guests – had been predictably busy and tiring. Her kitchen helpers had finished washing, drying and storing dinner and tableware as well as assorted pots, pans and baking tins. In the sitting room Iris Ann sank into an overstuffed chair. Next to her on a round lamp table rested her Farnsworth radio. She hesitated then turned it on. Doesn't really matter what's on, she mused, just some background noise will do. Something calming while I think about Jeff. Her eyes closed. Libya, so far away. Even with his letters I can barely picture what it's like.

About five minutes had elapsed when one of the boarders, a Cotton Belt railroad yard worker, entered the dimly lit room. "I hate to disturb you, Misses Wolfrom. Could you please give me a little time?" His politeness bordered on plaintiveness.

Iris Ann kept her eyes closed for a long moment before letting them open. She looked up. The man, mid-fifties, was freshly shaven and he was one of her regulars. She sighed deeply. "Okay." She held out her hands.

The man reached down and pulled gently, helping Iris Ann to her feet. No need to discuss price; her fee was firmly established.

A few minutes after the lead B-24s passed Bucharest, Gerstenberg's hell introduced itself to Operation Tidal Wave.

On the ground, anti-aircraft officers saw the first low-flying B-24s and began screaming to their crews to change fuse settings so their shells would detonate point-blank.

Jeff gulped when the sky seemed to blacken suddenly with exploding flak. Smoke was so dense that locating targets immediately became difficult.

General Gerstenberg, alerted to the armada's approach, had been riding to Bucharest. He told his driver to stop, turn around and hurry him back to his Ploesti command post. Better to be closer to the action, he concluded.

The first plane to drop bombs was Utah Man. Virtually simultaneously, one of its machine gunners destroyed a switching yard locomotive. But the plane took its share of flak and machine gun hits. Utah Man would survive the raid and return to Benghazi – with 367 holes in its fuselage and wings. The plane and its crew were among the lucky.

Jeff watched the first fatality unfold. The plane bore one of the unlikelier monickers – Euroclydon. Its bomb bay was hit and flames immediately began streaming back inside and outside the craft. The pilot managed to climb a little higher. That gave time for three of its crew to bail safely. A fourth, navigator Jesse Franks, bailed but was killed when his parachute failed to open from the low altitude. Seconds later, Euroclydon crashed, exploded and burned.

Jeff had another cause for concern – 100 tethered triple-finned barrage or blocking balloons. They were floating languidly – and lethally. Attached to their cables were contact explosives. Skillful piloting would be needed to elude the balloons and still pummel targets.

B-24s were taking hits by the second. Shards of aluminum and Plexiglas were slicing into crewmen. Men on fire were wailing their agony.

Whipping through the air near Nedelea were gales of laughter. The picnickers were delighting in their food and each other's company. Then came the first crashing booms, and the picnickers hushed. They gaped at rising plumes of black smoke. Catherine stood, strong face slightly elevated, and looked to the south. "This is no mock raid," she said gravely. "This is real, very real. There is only one question: Who is attacking us?"

Earlier that day, Father Ewald Wegener had said Mass in Ploesti. Afterward, he changed from his colorful vestments and black trousers to a military uniform. Father Wegener also was a corporal, a German Army medic in a transportation regiment that trucked oil to the Russian front. Before the war, he had been studying medicine in Vienna. After the Wehrmacht had marched into Austria, it conscripted Father Wegener.

As Shoot, Fritz, You're Faded neared its target, Jeff saw German soldiers running toward wooden barracks, seeking cover. One of tem was Father Wegener. Jeff squeezed the trigger on his Browning and strafed the building. Miraculously, inside the structure not one of his .50 caliber rounds struck an enemy.

Father Wegener rushed outside. In the next instant, he saw a refinery storage tank explode in a towering fireball. He went dashing toward it. Minutes later he was guiding wounded soldiers to the regimental infirmary. He treated injuries and administered last rites.

One of the B-24 co-pilots, witnessing the carnage around him, lost his nerve and began crying and babbling incoherently. The navigator reacted quickly. He jumped up, turned, moved behind the co-pilot, pulled him out of his seat and pinned him.

Jeff spotted flak guns pumping away from atop several buildings. His first brief burst sent a gun crew, their bodies torn apart, flying from a warehouse roof. He grimaced and blinked. His second short volley sent shattered bodies tumbling from a storage shed roof. Next he concentrated on a looming water tank where machine gunners were firing from the encircling catwalk.

Moments later, Jeff Wolfrom and Catherine Caradja saw the same sight. Chattanooga Choo Choo was peppered with flak and mortally wounded. Its pilot managed to bring the craft to a skidding stop, nose biting into a cornfield's earth, tail a dozen feet in the air. The plane didn't explode. And paradoxically Chattanooga Choo Choo's crew was incredibly lucky. They had landed on Catherine's estate.

All around Jeff, B-24s were falling prey to Gerstenberg's curtain of fire. He saw Sad Sack II burst into flames and go down. Another B-24 was hit, staggered, dropped its bombs and careened into a German flak battery. All 10 Americans died along with eight Germans. Another B-24 pilot drove his stricken craft into a refinery building. Simultaneously the building, plane and crew fireballed. In another bomber, razor-edged flak decapitated a gunner. A moment later, Jeff felt shells whizzing past his head. "Lord," he murmured, "close call. Too close."

By now, German and Romanian fighter planes were scrambling and intensifying pressure on the American fleet. B-24 gunners – waist, tail, top, ball turret – saw their overheated barrels turning red. A German fighter shot the left wing off a B-24, sending it and its crew to cartwheeling deaths.

A B-24, pocked and burning, crashed near the infirmary where Father Wegener was tending to wounded Germans. He rushed outside and saw dazed Americans stumbling away from the mangled fuselage. He paused briefly and then went running toward them. One of the Americans collapsed onto his belly. Father Wegener dashed to his side and knelt. Gently, he rolled the injured man onto his back. Shrapnel had torn three jagged holes in his torso.

"I am a priest," Father Wegener said in German. The American was uncomprehending. Then Father Wegener removed his helmet, slowly made the sign of the cross and pointed to himself. The injured airman smiled thinly, and the priest began saying the last rites.

Jeff felt Shoot, Fritz, You're Faded shudder and suspected the worst. Pilot Robert O'Reilly strained to keep the plane aloft. His efforts were futile.

All the picnickers were standing. The children were befuddled and awestruck. They'd never seen large aircraft, much less ones burning and smoking. Gabriella saw the white star insignia on Shoot, Fritz, You're Faded and murmured, "Americans." Alexandra and Laura, flanking her, looked at Gabriella wide-eyed. "Yes," she nodded, "Americans."

Catherine, an aviation enthusiast and knowledgeable about planes since her youth, noticed something other than the white stars. The stricken plane was streaming nearly clear liquid. "Petrol," she observed admiringly. "The pilot is dumping fuel to reduce the chance of explosion and fire."

O'Reilly soon would learn that, like Chattanooga Choo Choo, Shoot, Fritz, You're Faded was about to plow a new furrow in one of Princess Caradja's cornfields.

Jeff and his colleagues braced for what at best they knew would be a rough return to earth. At worst? They all had born witness to B-24 crewmen who had been transformed into human torches. "Here we go, Lord," Jeff muttered. "Please stay with me."

"Laura and Alexandra," Catherine instructed, "stay here with the girls. Boys, Gabriella, come with me. If they are Americans-"

"Let's go," Gabriella interjected.

The two women, one lithe at 28, the other big-framed at 50, and the two boys went racing for the 1939 black Plymouth. They heard the sound – stomach curdling – of an aluminum fuselage enduring more friction than any engineer expected one moving vehicle to withstand, much less to remain intact. The impact separated Jeff from the Browning. His arms flew up and back and he landed on a pair of long cartridge belts.

Catherine started the Plymouth down the dirt road, then veered sharply across the lush meadow that fronted the villa. Shoot, Fritz, You're Faded had crashed a scant mile from the manor house – and still well within her estate's borders.

"Are you sure they are Americans?" Catherine asked.

"Not the crew," Gabriella replied. "But, yes, the planes are."

"Russian crews?"

"Possibly. We know that America has been shipping weapons and vehicles to Russia."

The Plymouth was jarring its passengers as it hurtled across the meadow toward the cornfield.

"Frankly," said Catherine, "I hope they are Americans."

"Oh?"

"America is our enemy on a technicality. Russia is our blood enemy. We fought them in the Great War. We are fighting them now. The Russians are beasts. They are going to defeat the Germans, and they will be heartless masters."

The big bird skidded to a grinding halt, its nose crushed, its tail 10 feet off the ground.

As the Plymouth braked, Catherine and Gabriella stared in amazement. Jeff and seven other crewmen were stumbling out from the wreckage. But seven of her boys from the nearest orphanage already were clustered around the B-24. Quick thinking, they were spraying the plane with foam-filled canisters used to quench oil well fires. Wells on Catherine's estate were central to her wealth and ability to continue caring for some 3,000 orphans around the country. The nearest tool shed was a mere 100 yards distant from the downed B-24.

The women and boys pushed open the car doors and went running toward the men. Catherine paused and looked back over her left shoulder. She had heard – now saw – another car jolting across the meadow. It braked beside her Plymouth. As its four occupants exited, Catherine's jaws tightened.

One of the orphan boys came running to her. "Two dead Russians are in the airplane!" he cried.

She nodded and with Gabriella took two more steps toward the wreckage. She saw Jeff, hands on hips, bent forward, shoulders heaving.

"Young man," Catherine inquired, "are you Russian or American?"

The largely unaccented English startled Jeff. He straightened. "The latter."

Catherine whirled and shouted, "Lunt aviation Americani!" Catherine's pleasure surprised herself as much as anyone else.

Gabriella, a match for Jeff's five feet seven inches, placed her hands against his shoulders. "She is my friend, Princess Catherine Caradja. You have landed on her estate. My name is Gabriella Balas. I once was posted at our embassy in Washington, D.C."

Jeff removed his flight cap and looked hard into her brown eyes and saw compassion. "We need to help my buddies trapped in the plane."

Catherine, Gabriella and her orphan boys peered into the ruptured fuselage. They could see that flight engineer Frank Kees had been crushed to death by the collapsed top turret.

"Can you hear me?" Gabriella called to the second man who was trapped in the mangled nose section.

"Yes," croaked navigator Richard Britt. His eyes opened then closed. He was soaked with gasoline leaking from a ruptured tank.

"Boys," Catherine instructed in Romanian, "run to the tool shed. Bring back tools to free this brave aviator." She turned to see herself observed by the plane's survivors and four black-uniformed SS officers. "We will also free your dead companion and see that he receives a proper burial."

"Thank you, Ma'am," said a shaken and thoroughly drained Robert O'Reilly.

"I will also have a doctor examine you and your men."

"I do not think so," said the senior SS officer. "These men are our prisoners. We will send them to Germany."

Catherine's eyes narrowed. Her mind was churning. In meticulously enunciated German, she said, "You are mistaken. You will not take them. This is my property and they are my prisoners."

Jeff understood not a word but sensed Catherine was speaking in the crew's defense.

"These men," the SS officer sneered, "are sworn enemies of the Third Reich."

"And you," Catherine said, her voice lowering an octave and steeling, "are citing a fact that has no relevance to this situation. They" – with a slow sweeping motion of her right arm she embraced the flyers – "and their aircraft have landed on sovereign Romanian territory, territory belonging to a member of the royal family."

The SS officer felt heat rising from beneath his tunic. "You," he hissed, "are a relic that explains why our Reich rules your backward excuse for a nation. I could have you shot for insubordination."

Catherine was unblinking. "You could shoot me for any reason or no reason," she said with measured regal calm. "But let me ask: Are you enjoying occupation duty?"

Her question, posed congenially, surprised the officer. "It is acceptable," he conceded grudgingly.

"If you would like it to continue, you would change your tone."

The next morning Jeff and his mates met more royalty. King Michael came calling at Catherine's manor house. He wanted to see a downed B-24 and meet crewmen. Word had spread quickly about Chattanooga Choo Choo and Shoot, Fritz, You're Faded having crashed on Catherine's estate.

As introductions were being made, Jeff couldn't help contemplating the places he'd been and the people he'd met since leaving Arkansas.

King Michael with Jeff as his passenger drove his Austin-Healy to Shoot, Fritz, You're Faded. When he saw gas still trickling from tanks, he filled a container and then poured its contents into his car's tank. Jeff thought it an unwise decision but couldn't bring himself to offer unsolicited advice to a king.

Michael and Jeff got in the car but didn't get far before the engine quit. As Jeff had suspected, the aviation fuel was too rich for a car. Jeff covered his mouth with his right hand to keep from chuckling. Michael turned toward Jeff, saw that he was struggling to stifle mirth and laughed at himself.

Officially, both the Allies and the Axis saw Operation Tidal Wave as successful. Hitler phoned Gerstenberg to congratulate him. Roosevelt acknowledged heavy losses but added, "I am certain that the German or Japanese High Commands would cheerfully sacrifice tens of thousands of men to do the same amount of damage to us, if they could."

What was the damage? The German armed forces suffered a 30 percent reduction in their supply of oil. Temporarily. Within months the refinery complex was operating at 90 percent of capacity. To actually destroy the Ploesti complex would require another 22 bombing raids – all conducted at high altitudes.

What was the price of the August 1 low altitude raid? To Jeff, numbers and lasting horrific images provided the answer. Of the 164 B-24s that made it to Ploesti, 45 were shot down. Eight were interned in Turkey. Twenty-three landed safely at Allied airfields on the islands of Sicily, Malta and Cyprus. Of the 88 that returned to Benghazi, 55 had suffered damage. Casualty figures showed 446 airmen killed or missing and presumed dead, 54 wounded and 79 interned in Turkey. Those totals didn't include the wounded – 70 – in captivity in Romania as well as a small number in Bulgaria. Among the survivors were those lucky enough to fall beneath the long, protective wings of Catherine Caradja.

Gabriella Balas offered her own assessment from a different perspective. Few Romanian civilians – and none of Catherine's orphans – were killed. She likened the accuracy of the bombing – calling to mind her memories of America's capital – to dropping a baseball from the Washington Monument's observation deck more than 500 feet into the glove of a catcher.

She also was grateful to meet Jeff Wolfrom and his American colleagues.

CHAPTER 72

Jeff Wolfrom was experiencing a strong sense of déjà vu. Detention, he was reflecting, this is my second go-around. Turkey and Romania. One thing's the same; nice people in both places. One big difference, though. I don't see an early escape. The Turks definitely looked the other way when we skedaddled to Syria and that was French territory. The Romanians might like to, but I think they think they'd be pushing their luck with the Germans if they helped us get out of here. And besides, where would we go? Russia? Not likely. Not with the Russians shoving the Germans back this way. I just don't see a way out. Not before the war ends. And that's if we win. I think we'll whip Germany, but I'm not so sure about Japan. I just haven't heard enough about what's going on out there in the Pacific to get a good feel. Well, at least as prisons go, this place isn't all that bad.

Timisul de Jos was, in fact, not all that bad. Barbed wire surrounded the camp, but inside conditions were better than many POWs had experienced at their bases in the U.S., never mind abroad. The American officers were housed in what had been a three-story resort hotel in the Carpathian Mountains north of Sinaia or more than 70 miles north of Ploesti. The building boasted a dining room, two bathrooms, four lavatories and 14 bedrooms with comfortable mattresses. Outside were tennis courts and a small gymnasium with showers. Breathtaking vistas of the mountains, including spectacularly striated cliffs, enchanted the officers.

Jeff and the other enlisted men were housed nearby in two dormitories that were part of a private girls' school. No indoor toilets graced the buildings, but the rooms were comfortable.

Most importantly, the camp was overseen not by the SS or even the Wehrmacht but by Romanians. Moreover, a particular guest was seen often and invariably was welcome: Princess Catherine Caradja. Frequently arriving with her in the 1939 black Plymouth were daughter Alexandra, Laura Ramaschi and Gabriella Balas. To the prisoners, views of the young women easily matched their appreciation for the picturesque mountains. On one early visit to "my boys," Catherine brought a radio and map of Europe.

"Can you imagine the Nazis letting POWs have a radio and map?" gunner Louis Medeiros asked rhetorically.

"Some days," Jeff said semi-apologetically, "I almost feel guilty being called a prisoner. My mother would approve of the food, and we don't have to work. Heck, we get to play chess, cards and volleyball. The Romanians are even paying us what we'd be making in the Army. Their currency, of course, but it spends just fine up here."

The food was plentiful if not varied or particularly tasty. "It's at least as good as we were getting at Benghazi," was Jeff's appraisal.

When word reached nearby villagers that Americans with cash to spend were their new neighbors, private enterprise instincts surfaced quickly. They came calling with meat – pork, sausages, chicken, goose – fresh vegetables and fruit.

Red Cross parcels caught up with many of the men, and they shared generously with fellow POWs. Besides, there was no quicker way to earn enmity than to hoard.

Doing the camp's work were Russian prisoners. They served as cooks, dishwashers, medical orderlies, janitors and launderers.

Only the intellectually lazy became bored. Prisoners were allowed to bake and make wine. A professor from Bucharest accepted Catherine's invitation to come and teach Romanian. Every Sunday the men were allowed to exit the barbed wire enclosures to walk to a nearby church that offered both Catholic and Protestant services. Some self-proclaimed pious POWs attended both.

Visitors weren't limited to Catherine and her girls. Several Romanian government officials, sensing the shifting tides of war, began courting the prisoners to build relationships with men they thought would emerge as members of the winning side.

Still, for Jeff the incarceration stirred deeply felt longing. When black-haired young girls passed by, he couldn't help seeing in their dark eyes those of Eren and little Natasha.

Catherine Caradja's "family" was expanding and would continue doing so. In addition to the 3,000 orphans in her care, by war's end she would serve as guardian angel for more than 1,000 downed American flyers.

CHAPTER 73

Joe Barton stepped outside his and Duane's tent. His palms pressed against his closed eyes, rubbed and then passed back, brushing by his birthmark and scar. He stretched and rotated his head to loosen kinks. Dawn was breaking on the mountainside camp. The surrounding jungle was ending its slumber. Birds and monkeys were among creatures beginning to forage – some noisily – for their breakfast.

In the center of the campground, Sister Regina was squatting, building a small fire. She already was wearing her habit. Her wimpleless blond hair had grown below her ear lobes. She saw Joe and smiled.

After fending off the Japanese strike, corpses were dragged into the jungle and left to rot or serve as nourishment for scavengers. The soldiers' failure to return sent a signal to the enemy of lurking mountain dangers. The campers now felt secure making small fires during the daylight hours.

The altitude, the jungle-thick slopes and dry wood kept what little smoke rose from being seen far below.

"Good morning, Sister R," Joe said while walking toward the fire. "If you weren't a nun you'd make a dandy girl scout," he joshed.

"I could earn two merit badges. One for fire building and a second for coffee making."

Joe chuckled lowly. "Or a third for boiling water for British tea."

Sister Regina straightened and admired her handiwork. "I think I'll wait a few minutes before putting the pot over the fire. The rest of our little fraternity should be emerging soon from their canvas cocoons."

Joe smiled. "Feel like a little stroll over to the stream? Splash a little cool water on our faces."

"A little morning ablution sounds refreshing."

The stream was about 12 feet at its widest and four feet at its deepest. Its current was fast, reflecting its steeply sloping mountain course. At the water's edge Joe squatted, cupped water in his hands and brought them quickly to his face. Twice. "My eyes are about the only thing that dries out in this climate."

Sister Regina squatted beside him and twice splashed the cooling water against her face, still whitish after 18 months of camping. Then she bent farther forward until the water was coursing through her short blond hair. She rose up and shook her head. "Hair washing in jungle streams wasn't covered at the convent," she said dryly. Joe laughed. "Do you know what I hate most about this war?" she asked.

Both were letting the water run between their fingers.

"There's a lot to hate about it," Joe replied. He splashed his face a third time.

"True, but what I hate more than all else is the loss of innocence."

Joe stood and stretched again and Sister Regina, hair dripping water onto her habit, straightened beside him. "And trust," Joe added resignedly.

"Look at Sister Grace Ann. So young, so sweet. And yet she has seen a world where murder is not only commonplace but too often committed without consequence. I know she's having difficulty reconciling that with a compassionate God." A pause. "So am I."

"Innocence and trust lost. What about faith?"

"I still have mine – on most days."

"Sister Grace Ann. Augusta. What about them? Do they still have it?"

"I hope – pray – that their faith is intact and strong. They might waver from time to time, but that's only natural."

A long pause and a single tear escaped the duct beneath Regina's left eye.

"You know," Joe said sympathetically, "if you weren't a nun, I'd hold you."

"I'm a woman and I could stand being held." She sniffled and smiled demurely. "After all, Joe Barton, you've seen me as both a nun and a woman."

"No fear?" Joe asked.

"About what?"

"About what could happen between us?"

CHAPTER 74

In Shelby, Maureen Alston Nelson was sitting in her living room, hand stitching together two large pieces of red felt. Time was getting late – nearly 9 p.m. – and Corrine was sleeping in her wooden playpen in front of Maureen.

It was December 1943 and Maureen was softly humming *Jingle Bells*. She finished stitching, held up her creation for inspection and smiled. It was a large Christmas stocking. She put it on the adjacent lamp table and picked up a piece of white felt. Scissors in hand, Maureen cut out a large letter S. She stitched the S to the stocking. Next, she decided, I'll make one for Corrine – same size as Sam's – and then one for me. I'll have such fun shopping. I'll fill them with practical and silly things. No oranges, though. Whatever I put in Sam's will have to keep till he gets back from Europe.

Sister Grace Ann was fingering a black-beaded rosary. It wasn't hers. It had belonged to Sister Caroline.

Sisters Grace Ann, Augusta and Regina were experiencing a sense of fulfillment. Increasingly they were being called to serve as nurses for the MPAJA members who were their mountainside patients. Resistance missions often meant injuries – cuts, abrasions, gunshot wounds. The nuns were patching, stitching and performing occasional surgeries.

"A farthing for your thoughts," Regina said to Grace Ann.

She pushed her hands back through her lengthening blond hair. "We didn't do anything to celebrate Christmas last year. I realize this war doesn't inspire much celebrating, but I feel an urge to do something to lift spirits – and perhaps remember Sister Caroline."

"Any ideas?"

"Not yet, but I am thinking it should be something simple…and elegant."

"Your creative powers will shine brightly as always."

Sister Regina was right. They did. December was monsoon season in Malaya. That meant gale force winds and drenching rains that transformed the mountain campgrounds and paths into the tropical equivalent of the Rockefeller Center ice rink. Slipping and sliding, if not skating, were orders of the day. The hostile weather and ground conditions virtually eliminated an outdoor symbol of the Christmas season. And, Sister Grace Ann was reflecting, she wanted to create something festive and memorable that would appeal to the entire group, not only Christians.

Her fertile mind hatched a concept. She asked Rosalie, her tentmate, if she objected to her idea.

"Not at all," Rosalie replied. "I love it."

The two young women gathered numerous small rocks. Then they scrounged among supplies captured on MPAJA raids. They found what they were looking for.

A week before Christmas they invited their campmates into their tent. At the far end on a small rectangular table they had fashioned an altar. Two relatively straight limbs, lashed together with a vine, formed a cross about 18 inches high and 12 inches wide. Holding it upright was a cluster of the small rocks. Draped over the horizontal limb was Sister Caroline's rosary. Flanking the cross were nine candles – a mix of red and white and one for each group member plus Sister Caroline. Holding the candles upright were more of the small rocks.

As the invited group made its way into the tent, no explanations were required. What was needed were handkerchiefs or tissues.

"We'll burn the candles just a little each day," said Sister Grace Ann, "so they last the season."

During the next few days, Chinese visitors began trickling into the Barton-Hurd camp. Curious, they were from the neighboring MPAJA compound. Word had reached them about the holiday season memorial. To a man they were touched by the humble tribute to spiritual life and undaunted courage.

On Christmas Eve at Changi, Brian Barnsworth and Malcolm Goode made their way to the camp chapel. It was packed. It was quiet. Men of all faiths were offering silent prayers and reflections. Malcolm was pleased to see George Britton among the supplicants. He wished that Oliver Needle, their master fisherman, could be there with them. Or maybe, Malcolm smiled slightly, you are.

On the mountain road to Timisul de Jos, Catherine's black Plymouth was leading a small caravan. Two small trucks, one belonging to her estate and the other driven by King Michael, were following. They were delivering to "her boys" Christmas hams, sweet potatoes, apples that had been stored in a cool cellar, freshly baked breads and pastries, and bottles of plum brandy.

Riding with Catherine was Laura Ramaschi. Driving the first truck was Alexandra and riding in the second truck with King Michael was Gabriella. Without exception the surprise feast they were about to spring on Catherine's "boys" had them tingling with anticipation. On the move with gifts, Gabriella was musing happily, just like Saint Nicholas – or as Joe knows him, Santa Claus.

Some civilians in Singapore also were on the move. Worsening food shortages had led the Japanese to begin evacuating some residents to places in the empire where food was more plentiful. Many POWs also had been transported to other corners of the empire, but not for humanitarian reasons. They were needed as slave labor.

CHAPTER 75

Chua Koon Eng was a fisherman on Malaya's western coast. He was ordinary in every regard. But because he made his living on the sea, the kempetai suspected that he and other fishermen might be aware of – or complicit in – movements of Force 136 agents.

The Japanese already had begun stopping, boarding and inspecting vessels – cargo ships and trawlers – off the west coast. On March 24 the kempetai arrested Chua.

Force 136 leaders Lim Bo Seng and Captain John Davis had their espionage network in place and operating. They worked from bases in Ipoh – about 350 miles north of Singapore – Lumut and Pangkor Island. Ipoh was a tin mining center and had been a major British colonial administration headquarters. The Japanese had been occupying Ipoh since December 15, 1941. From those bases Lim, Davis and fellow agents frequently updated and instructed resistance bands, including Dexin Sun's.

As covers, Force 136 agents using fake documents often passed themselves off as shop assistants or clerks. Some opened their own shops as fronts. They tried to get as close as possible to locals who had business dealings with Japanese authorities or leaders of Japanese-sponsored organizations set up to help the occupiers maintain control. To communicate, agents used messages written on tiny scraps of paper and inserted in Colgate toothpaste tubes or salted fish.

Japanese checkpoints were numerous, and Lim and Force 136 agents usually drove alone in delivery trucks to allay kempetai suspicions. To reach resistance groups, Force 136 agents would park their vehicles well away from jungle camps and then hike to MPAJA meetings. Based on what Lim learned, he radioed reports to British headquarters in India.

In late March, feeling a need to check on espionage plans and actions in the Ipoh area, Lim entered the city posing as a traveling businessman.

Under none-too-gentle interrogation Chua Koon Eng revealed that a Force 136 agent had approached him and requested use of his fishing boat as part of the unit's communications network.

"What about Lim Bo Seng?" asked a kempetai interrogation officer.

"Who is he?"

The officer slapped Chua across both cheeks. "You admit to working with enemy agents and deny knowledge of their leader?" the officer asked incredulously. "We are many things but not fools."

"I am a fisherman. I work alone on Pangkor Island. When a stranger asks a question, I answer. But I do not ask more questions."

"For a simple fisherman," the officer sneered, "you are a clever fellow. So let me ask you a simple question – as a stranger might. Do you have a family?"

"Yes."

"Would you like to see them again? Alive?"

The Force 136 agent who had spoken with Chua was Li Han Kwang. He was quickly found and arrested. Under torture, Li confirmed his dealings with Chua. Li then feigned further cooperation with the kempetai.

Lim Bo Seng had rented a room in an old cottage near Gopeng, a small town 12 miles south of Ipoh. He knew the Japanese were increasing vigilance with beefed up forces and were closing in on fellow agents and perhaps himself. On one occasion a Japanese submarine intercepted a coded message transmitted from a fishing trawler to an Allied submarine. The kempetai began arresting and torturing more trawler owners.

In Ipoh, the kempetai raided a general store they had learned was a safe house for Force 136 agents. Several of the agents, hiding in a basement, managed to escape. One, Tan Chong Tee, was trailed by the kempetai but eluded them and returned to his room in the nearby Tong Ah Hotel. His intent: alert Lim to the escalating danger. He didn't have the opportunity. Four kempetai burst through his door and arrested him. In Cantonese, a language Tan was hoping none of the kempetai understood, he asked a hotel employee to warm Lim. The kempetai leader's response: he arrested the hotel employee.

Another hotel employee got word to Mo Ching, a Force 136 agent. Mo Ching rushed to alert Lim at the country cottage.

Lim felt the chill of terror. "We have to leave at once," he said.

"The kempetai are everywhere now," Mo Ching replied. "Maybe we should wait until morning. Let the Japanese search all night."

Lim sighed and nodded. "Perhaps you are right."

He wasn't. Early next morning Lim and Mo Ching drove away from the cottage in the latter's black sedan. They headed toward Gopeng but didn't proceed far before encountering a log and barbed wire roadblock manned by six Japanese soldiers. It was March 27, 1944.

Sister Regina was alone. She was kneeling beside the stream, praying. "Dear Lord," she murmured, "please have mercy on Lim Bo Seng. As you know he has become one of your true believers. And no one, not any general in the army, is more important than Bo Seng to shaking off the shackles of Japanese oppression. It is not his own small force that is so important. It is what Bo Seng symbolizes – undying hope and unbending resolve. He is a messenger of faith and determination. And if I may, Lord, let me add that as much as his countrymen need him so also do his wife Choo Neo and their children. Please keep Bo Seng safely in your protection."

Lim and Mo Ching were taken to a kempetai center at 7 Chairman Street in Ipoh. The facility was a white stucco, two-story office building with as steeply pitched red tile roof.

Lim was lashed to a wooden cross. Interrogation and torture commenced without delay. A kempetai officer beat Lim with a steel rod. Lim took blows to his abdomen, chest and face.

Eyes closed in an effort to quell his pain, Lim's words were barely audible. "I will not divulge information."

Next he was forced to watch as Mo Ching was brought into the interrogation chamber. Mo was lashed to two wooden beams that formed an X. Water from a hose was then forced into his mouth, causing his stomach to bloat alarmingly.

"You devils!" cried Lim through blood-crusted lips.

"This is just the beginning," the chief interrogator smiled benignly. "Watch."

"Let him go. Please," Lim pleaded.

The interrogator drove his right fist into Mo Ching's swollen belly. Water gushed from his mouth.

"Pump him with water again," the chief ordered his men.

"Stop, please," Lim begged.

"Well?" said the chief.

For days Lim uttered not a word. He was whipped relentlessly, his torso a mass of shredded skin and torn flesh. He endured the water torture. He watched as a fellow agent's hands were chopped off with a meat cleaver. He prayed for strength.

To his amazement, Lim and fellow Force 136 agents were transferred from the kempetai center to nearby Batu Gajah Prison. Each man was confined to a small cell. Each day they were fed only one meal – usually a few chunks of rotting sweet potatoes. Remarkably, though, conditions eased. In the mornings, inmates were permitted to empty their chamber pots and shower from a courtyard hose. Some of the guards were locals and sympathetic to the resistance. They permitted the inmates to talk among themselves.

Lim received a pleasant surprise when Tan Chong Tee was brought to the prison. They were allowed to converse.

"What is happening?" Tan asked. "Why are we still alive?"

"I'm not certain," Lim said, "but I think that some of the Japanese are beginning to realize the war is lost. They are starting to think about the consequences of their brutality."

"We could still die here," Tan said, "of starvation or malnutrition."

"We might," Lim smiled, his eyes still bright behind the eyeglasses that somehow had survived his ordeal. "But remember to not sell your soul by cooperating with the Japanese. We might not live to see our victory, but I believe it is inevitable. If we are to die here, it should be without regrets."

"I will remember that – sir."

CHAPTER 76

April 3, 1944

Dear Maureen, my love and mother of my daughter,

Things are really gathering steam here in Merry Old England. Everything points to invasion day coming soon. We have been practicing amphibious landings and infantry tactics. I can't tell you where our practice landings are being held, and I could only speculate where we will land in Europe. As you can imagine, facts like that are being closely guarded by General Eisenhower and his top brass.

I'm a really lucky guy. You're hands down the best. I want you to know that. I never dreamed I would have a wife who is so loving, beautiful and vivacious. And I'll bet Corrine takes right after you. I can hardly wait to see you both again. I carry the picture of you two at all times, but I am more than ready to see the real thing. That shouldn't be too long after we take care of business in Europe. That means whipping Hitler's butt and bringing freedom back to the countries he and his Nazis have occupied.

When you put Corrine to bed tonight, give her a couple extra squeezes from her dad. I can hardly wait to put my arms around you again.

Your loving husband always,

Sam

Romanians were angered and Jeff Wolfrom and his fellow POWs were worried. Both emotions were understandable.

On April 4, 1944, 230 B-24s climbed into the skies to launch another major raid. Central facts differentiated this mission from Operation Tidal Wave eight months earlier. This assault on Gerstenberg's defenses would be conducted not from 50 feet but from high altitude. Gerstenberg, ever the master strategist and man of action, had used the interlude since Operation Tidal Wave to install more guns, build additional radar stations and acquire thousands of smoke generators to shroud the refineries in thick cloaks of gray.

To foil his wide radar wall, B-24 bomb bays were carrying canisters loaded with countless metallic paper strips.

On this raid the B-24s first plastered Bucharest. A main target was the capital city's railroad yards. Timing couldn't have been more disastrous. Aboard waiting trains were hundreds of Romanians fleeing the oncoming, rapacious Russians. American bombs killed and wounded many unsuspecting innocents.

The fleet continued north but largely skirted Ploesti and continued another 66 miles to Brasov. The medieval city was founded by Teutonic knights in 1211. It was situated about 2,000 feet above sea level in the Carpathians. Soaring mountains framed Brasov on three sides. Sprouting in Brasov's center is Tampa, a 3,000-foot peak. One of the city's most notable structures is Biserica Neagra – the Black Church. It dates to 1477 and takes its name from smoke stains left by a fire in 1689. The city's spacious central plaza lies near Rope Street that, as the name suggests, is among the narrowest in Europe.

Brasov became an Allied bombing target because of its industrial importance. A factory there produced Romania's first fighter planes. When American-made bombs from American planes exploded in the town, more Romanians were killed and wounded.

When word of the civilian deaths reached Timisul de Jos, for the first time Romanian guards flashed anger at their American wards.

"Boy," Jeff confided to fellow gunner Louis Medeiros, "those guys are plenty p.o.'d at us."

"Don't think it would take much more news like this to really set them off."

"Can't hardly blame them. A lot of innocent men, women and children died in those trains. Even the folks in those factories were working there because they had no choice."

Batu Gajah Prison consisted of single-story white buildings with orange tile roofs surrounded by barbed wire fencing. Risking more torture, Lim Bo Seng protested ill-treatment of his fellow inmates. Inadequate food and sanitation were taking a toll on prisoners' health.

Sam Nelson was eager for this dry-run to begin. It meant the real thing was coming soon. He and fellow GIs had been told that these maneuvers were tantamount to a dress rehearsal for D-Day. The liberation of Europe and war's end seemed close at hand. That meant returning to the States and home. Sam knew such dry-runs could be hazardous. He had heard about the disaster that occurred when two American-crewed Dakota transports carrying members of the First Independent Polish Parachute Brigade collided over rural England during practice airdrops. All aboard both planes were killed.

The amphibious landing was scheduled to take place at Slapton Sands on England's South Devon coast on April 27-28, 1944. The exercise was massive. Thousands of GIs in Higgins landing craft would rush from the boats and go storming ashore.

German intelligence had learned about the rehearsal and set in motion its own plan.

"What do you think?" asked one of Sam's buddies, Ashford Tanner, a tall, soft-spoken Georgian who went by Ash. "Think it'll be anything like the real deal?"

Sam languidly stretched his five feet nine inches and chuckled. "Well, the boats will be the same. The pilots will drive them in like it was the real thing. We'll be in the water like the real thing. But…"

"But what?"

"But we won't have to be dodging German bullets."

German mid-size cruisers were steaming north-northeast through the Atlantic, and their crews were manning battle stations. Destination: the waters off Slapton Sands.

The Higgins boats were positioned next to their mother ships, and GIs were descending the rope ladders. It was nearing 5 a.m. when the pitching landing craft began approaching the beach.

"Shit," Sam muttered.

"What is it?" Ash asked.

"I'm getting seasick."

"Join the crowd."

Numerous men in the boats were vomiting, splattering each other and fouling the air. Leather combat boots were slipping as the boats bounced through choppy waters.

"Damn," Ash moaned, his stomach heaving. "This water's a darned sight rougher than it was in earlier rehearsals. Couldn't be much worse on D-Day. Whenever that turns out to be."

A ring of Allied warships was supposed to be providing protection for the landing boats. Their crews were not on full alert.

The oncoming German cruisers were racing at flank speed. They came slicing through the line of surprised Allied vessels and opened fire.

Sam and Ash looked at each other, stunned by the closeness of the first booming detonations. An explosion off their Higgins' starboard side rocked the boat and sent a shower of cold seawater cascading onto the men.

"Holy shit!" cried Ash. "They told us this would be a live-fire exercise, but that's more reality than I want or need."

Before Sam could reply, more shells began exploding. His buddies were shouting protests at what they perceived as top brass stupidity.

"Man, somebody could get hurt," Ash spat.

"I have a sick feeling," said Sam, "and it's not seasickness."

"What do you mean?"

"I mean I don't think those shells are part of this rehearsal."

"Huh?"

"I don't think they're ours."

The German guns began scoring numerous hits. Pieces of American men and metal soon were sinking to the Channel's bottom. Another shell narrowly missed Sam and Ash's boat but exploded near enough to rupture the small craft. It immediately began taking on water that was mixing with the blood of soldiers sliced by shrapnel.

"Oh, my God!" Ash cried. "I'm not a strong swimmer to begin with. I don't think I can make it to shore with this rifle and gear."

"Dump the rifle," Sam shouted above the din. "Your helmet too. Stay with me."

In the next instant, the Higgins was foundering and Ash and Sam were in the water.

The German operation was hit-and-run. The cruisers wasted no time in reversing course and retreating to the open sea. Meanwhile, six landing craft were sunk and six more damaged. Some 750 Allied soldiers were killed and another 300 wounded.

The next Allied air assault on Ploesti was the biggest yet. A fleet of 485 bombers – combining B-24s and B-17 Flying Fortresses – struck Ploesti in early May. It was another high-level mission, and the bombardiers proved remarkably accurate. Civilian casualties were few. One result: another attitudinal shift at Timisul de Jos. POWs again enjoyed the good graces of their Romanian overseers.

Nineteen attacking bombers had been shot down, and their surviving crews were incarcerated in Bucharest. Once more Catherine Caradja's wings hovered protectively, keeping the downed airmen out of German hands.

Maureen was standing in the living room, holding Corrine. She had just changed the child's diaper and was about to turn on the radio for the latest news. The day was warm and the heavy storm door was open. About 1:30 that afternoon, through the screen door, Maureen heard a car door close. When she looked through the living room window, an elderly man was approaching and holding a small envelope. She recognized the man as Timothy Sullivan, the local Western Union messenger.

He was walking slowly toward the steps. In the first moments, Maureen was puzzled. In the next moment, cold, unspeakable dread gripped and shook her. Tears began to cloud her blue eyes. Corrine, sensing her mother's distress, began whining. When knuckles tapped gently against the screen doorframe, Maureen's body stopped shaking and froze. Then, stiffly, she began shuffling toward the door. No words were spoken. With Mr. Sullivan watching, Maureen opened the envelope.

The first tears came slowly. They quickly became a torrent. Miss Hughes didn't reach for a kerchief. Her trembling hands were holding the newly delivered edition of *The Shelby Daily Globe.* The front-page headline screamed: Local Soldier Killed in England.

One of my boys, Miss Hughes was grieving, the first one in this war to die in Europe. You were a fine student, Sam Nelson, a fine young man. And you leave behind a lovely young bride and a daughter who will grow up without your fatherly love and guidance. May our Lord keep you in his warm embrace.

Raids on Ploesti continued. They kept Catherine Caradja's mothering instincts finely tuned. During one attack she watched two airmen jump from a crippled B-17 over her Nedelea estate. One's parachute was burning and he was plummeting at accelerating speed. Catherine winced, knowing that death was awaiting his meeting with earth. She and Gabriella went dashing to the Plymouth and sped to the cornfield where the two parachutes had fallen. Joe, Gabriella was wishing fervently, wherever you are, I hope you're not taking unnecessary risks.

CHAPTER 77

By mid-May Lim Bo Seng knew he was seriously ill. His stools were laced with blood and mucus, and he was losing strength. In Batu Gajah Prison Lim had seen enough sickness to be reasonably certain of his self-diagnosis: dysentery.

The disease had been the scourge of armies and prisons for millennia. Contaminated food and poor sanitation were the disease's breeding grounds. People living in close quarters in tropical climates were especially vulnerable.

Sweat was drenching Lim. Freedom and family, he reminded himself, those are my foremost reasons for enduring. My faith is my personal pillar. I will be eternally grateful to Sister Regina for her shining example.

Word of Lim's deteriorating health spread quickly among Force 136 agents and MPAJA units. When it reached the Barton-Hurd camp, Sisters Regina, Augusta and Grace Ann prayed often for Lim's recovery. Su Mien joined them regularly. Rosalie, still uncertain about God and religion, sometimes envied the nuns for their faith.

Eventually, word reached Choo Neo who feared the worst and struggled with how many details to confide to their children.

A day later Lim awoke, his bare torso glistening in a sheen of sweat. His infrequent bowel movements had become excruciating as inflammation of the colon worsened. The Japanese provided no medical treatment. Prison officials were content to let Lim's suffering endure.

Lim tried to eat what little food was offered but his appetite was waning. Dear Lord, he prayed silently behind closed eyelids, I have asked for little. The truth is, my wants have been few. I was blessed with wonderful parents. I was doubly blessed when Choo Neo entered my life. My successful company allowed me to care well for our children. It allowed me to help others – my employees and the people of China in their misery, misery inflicted by the Japanese. You tell us to love our enemies, but in truth I cannot find it in my heart to love or forgive the Japanese. I hope you will forgive me for that failure. I now ask for only one favor: Please let me survive dysentery so that I might see freedom return to my family and all my people – in Singapore, Malaya and China. Wherever the Japanese rule.

Catherine Caradja and her companions – daughter Alexandra, Laura and Gabriella – were tingling with excitement. Catherine was testing her Plymouth's limits on the winding, ever ascending road from Nedelea to Timisul de Jos. They had news, big news, and they were eager to share it with "her boys."

"Hitler must be shitting in his trousers," the stout woman chortled. Catherine seldom uttered vulgarities, but that one had escaped naturally. The young women laughed heartily.

"Stalin," Gabriella added, "might be peeing his trousers from excitement." More laughter.

What had the car's occupants in spirits soaring higher than the Carpathian's looming peaks was the news that earlier that day – June 6 – the Allies had landed on France's Normandy coast.

"The Americans," Catherine exulted, "when they began bombing us, I knew it was only a matter of time before their soldiers crossed the Channel from England. It is a great country with a great leader – not like that murdering Hitler or our own lunatic Antonescu." Catherine quieted as her mind once again shifted to thinking how she might hasten Antonescu's permanent exit from the Royal Palace. An idea was beginning to take shape.

News of D-Day left Marie Hughes experiencing ambivalence. After U.S. troops had been nipping at the fringes of Hitler's empire in North Africa, Sicily and southern Italy, she was pleased to learn that the American Army had teamed with British, Canadian and Free French forces to stab at the heart of his most prized seizure – France. But that same initiative was tearing at her own heart; she wondered whether a second Belleau Wood might be fought – and extinguish the lives of more young men, including perhaps some of her boys. Miss Hughes decided it was an occasion for another solitary stroll through Seltzer Park and a visit to the small island in the large pond.

The news was slower – by three days – to reach MPAJA compounds, but once it did Dexin Sun himself delivered it to the Barton-Hurd camp.

"Will this not slow the Allied advances in the Pacific?" Sun asked Joe. "That would be very bad."

"It could," Joe replied after a contemplative pause, "but I don't think so. Churchill, DeGaulle and Stalin all have been pestering Roosevelt to create a second front in Europe. But I don't think FDR – Roosevelt – would have agreed if he hadn't concluded America has the necessary manpower, weapons and manufacturing capacity to successfully wage two wars."

"I hope your assessment is the right one," Sun said. "Sometime I would like to visit your great country."

"I left out one key ingredient," Joe observed, "and it might be the most important one. I'm talking about the will of the American people – civilians as well as soldiers – to defeat the forces of tyranny in both Asia and Europe."

Will wasn't enough for Lim Bo Seng to fight off the massive infection. Nor was prayer. During his final days fever and delirium were consuming him. In lucid moments Lim knew death was nearing. He lay shirtless on the floor, his chest and back crisscrossed with scars from beatings at kempetai headquarters. He was given no food, water or medicine. In the early morning hours of June 29, 1944, Lim's moaning ceased and he passed away. He was buried, still wearing his glasses, behind the prison in an unmarked grave.

Senior Japanese leaders knew immediately they had made Lim a martyr. Earlier in the war they would have given his death little thought. Now it worried them. They weren't blind to the war's shifting tides and what defeat might bode. The next day a visiting general berated and slapped the prison warden for letting Lim die. One immediate result: prisoners were given better food and a modicum of medical treatment.

Two weeks later, July 15, 607 American bombers launched yet another raid on the Ploesti oil complex. Gerstenberg's wall of fire continued to inflict casualties, and with increasing élan Catherine continued swooping in to rescue downed pilots and keep them from the grasp of the SS.

CHAPTER 78

Mail call. Jeff's eyes widened in surprise. The envelope was postmarked November 22, 1943. Eight months, he marveled. The Pony Express would've got it to me faster. Of course, he reconsidered, eyes closing in contemplation, the letter probably passed through countless hands in countless places – and on how many continents? Heck, he smiled wryly, it might even have gone through Pine Bluff. But what was intriguing him was the envelope's origin: Turkey, Ankara.

21 November 1943

Dear Jeff,

This letter is my first that I am writing in English. You can tell, I am sure. Haha.

Your letter to me was sweet. Thank you.

Natasha is in good care. But not in a orphanage. My dear mother would not hear of placing this dear girl there. She – mother – regards Natasha as her granddaughter.

My job at the hotel is good but not so exciting anymore. You gave me an excellent adventure. I think often about our time together.

If you receive this letter, I hope it arrives to find you safe. I pray for the war to end soon.

Eren Colason

Ending the war was foremost on Catherine's mind. More narrowly she was intent on ending Romania's ties with Hitler and Germany. With her customary verve she was ascending the stone steps of ornate Peles Castle near Sinaia. It was August 15.

King Michael himself greeted Catherine in the foyer. "I am privileged to have you pay a visit," he smiled warmly. They shook hands.

"You might not feel so privileged when you hear what I have to say," she said, her eyes and smile hinting at subterfuge.

"Oh?" His intelligent blue eyes suggested he already had grasped the purpose of Catherine's visit.

"I have been giving this much thought," she said.

"Please," the young king said, "come with me to my office."

Seated opposite each other across a white marble-topped coffee table, Catherine continued. "The risk to you would be great."

"And to you," Michael replied.

"But you are king, you are young and you represent hope for our country. Your loss would make mine appear trivial."

"Really? I know thousands of orphans and American airmen who might disagree. We both know what the fate of those children and young flyers would have been if not for your intervention."

"I am thinking of millions of Romanian fates. Those living now and those yet to be born."

Michael nodded. "If we are to work together perhaps we can improve their lot."

August 17, 1944. B-24s along with RAF Wellingtons and Halifaxes – 78 bombers in all – lifted off. Theirs would be the last of 22 high-altitude raids on Ploesti. The need had ended. Russia's Red Army was nearing Romania's eastern border and soon would be overrunning the country.

Once again Catherine saw parachutes descending over her estate. Both were afire. She and Gabriella hurried to the men. One had survived with minor injuries, but the other was wounded horribly, burned and blinded. They rushed him to a doctor. The airman died. As with one of his predecessors, the man was buried close to the graves of Catherine's husband and daughters. His death was among 2,829 casualties of Gerstenberg's Ploesti defenses that downed 324 U.S. and British bombers.

CHAPTER 79

Ion Antonescu picked up the ringing phone. "Yes," he snapped, "who is it?" His dictator's nerves were fraying as the Red Army continued driving relentlessly toward the Romanian frontier. In the coming crisis, he seldom stopped wondering how much support he could expect from Berlin. The stress was so continuous and intense that he often felt feverish.

"King Michael. I am here in my Royal Palace quarters."

"What do you want?"

"It is important. Too important to discuss by phone. Would you please come see me?"

Impudent twit. The closest you should come to me is Peles Castle. In other words, never. That was the reply Antonescu was sorely tempted to utter. He thought better of it as he contemplated a post-Nazi-controlled era. "When?"

"Now would be good."

It was Wednesday, August 23.

Catherine was busily working a phone in a room near Michael's Royal Palace quarters. Her calls were proving persuasive.

Michael masked his disdain and greeted Antonescu courteously. They were alone. Antonescu had been expecting discussion of military developments. Instead, Michael began by talking glibly about his extensive stamp collection. Antonescu's low esteem for the young king – a mere pretender in his eyes – was eroding by the second.

"Come with me," Michael said. "Let me show you some of my more valuable specimens."

Antonescu nodded and followed, his eyes rolling upward in disgust. A dilettante, he was thinking, I am using valuable time to satisfy the whims of a dilettante.

Michael led Antonescu into a large vault filled with glass cases displaying his prized numismatic collection. "Take a close look at these," Michael said proudly, pointing to a large case. "They are early American." He stepped away so that Antonescu could move closer. Then, Michael stepped farther away, slipped from the vault and used his considerable strength to close the heavy door. He quickly locked it.

Antonescu turned and felt anger surging. He pounded on the door. "Open it now!" he bellowed. "Open this instant or I will see you shot. I will shoot you myself."

Michael grinned and hurried to see Catherine. She was placing the black phone in its cradle.

"Antonescu is now our ex-prime minister," Michael said, barely able to contain his pleasure. "I have you to thank for giving me the necessary courage."

Catherine shook her head. "You had the courage. You only needed encouragement. The generals – our Romanian generals – are on their way here."

Next, Michael sent for Alfred Gerstenberg, Romania's de facto ruler. When the German general arrived and saw only Romanian generals with no sign of Antonescu, he knew instantly that his power had evaporated.

Michael continued distinguishing himself. With his generals observing, Michael and Gerstenberg quickly agreed on détente. Bucharest would be declared an open city – as would Paris two days later – and Romanian forces would permit Gerstenberg and his staff to leave the country unimpeded.

Next, escorted by generals, Michael walked to a nearby radio station. He announced Antonescu's capture, proclaimed Romania's loyalty to the Allies and formally surrendered to the Russians. His actions, however, did not preclude the Red Army from taking 130,000 Romanian soldiers prisoner and sending them to the Soviet Union where many would perish in POW camps.

Most Russian forces, intent on chasing retreating Germans, bypassed Bucharest. One road they were traveling would take advance units near Nedelea and farther into the Carpathians, right by Timisul de Jos.

A Red Army sergeant was driving a commandeered, open German staff car. With him were a lieutenant in the front seat and a private behind them. They were scouting, hunting for signs of retreating Germans when they saw Laura. She was wearing a white blouse and light blue, ankle-length skirt.

"I am hungry and from here she looks ripe," the sergeant said grimly. He slowed the car for a longer look. "If you have no objection, sir, I say we taste her."

"She looks appetizing," the lieutenant replied unsmilingly.

"She has the hair of a raven," the sergeant added, "and the body of a doe." He braked and the three men exited the car. Laura was about 50 yards away with her back to the roadside.

In the manor house kitchen Gabriella and Alexandra were discussing the good news phone call from Catherine and happily – almost giddily – preparing lunch. Laura was strolling through the meadow, occasionally skipping, admiring the fir tree-coated hills and murmuring to the sheep. The war is nearly over, she was exulting. The phone call from Catherine told us as much.

The lieutenant was wearing a sidearm and the sergeant and private each were carrying a PPsh, a sub-machine gun that held 71 rounds and fired at a rate of 800 rounds per minute. The faces of all three were heavily stubbled, and they stank of weeks in the field without a bath or shower.

In Laura's reverie she neither saw nor heard them – until they were about 20 paces away. She turned, expecting to see either Alexandra or Gabriella. When Laura saw the men she blanched and froze for a moment. Then a surge of adrenalin triggered her flee-from-danger instinct, a vestige of pre-historic man's genetic survival construct. Laura began running for the narrow stream and small wooden bridge that lay between her and the manor house, about 120 yards away.

The private saw her intended escape route and chose a pursuit angle that quickly cut her off. He tackled her and they both fell into the meadow's lush summer grass. That's when Laura screamed, "Help!"

Catherine and Alexandra eyed each other, dropped the knives and vegetables they were holding and went rushing through the house to the front door.

The lieutenant and sergeant caught up in mere seconds. Laura was squirming and the private slugged her high on her left jaw. He stood and pulled Laura, whoozy, to her feet.

Alexandra reached to push open the door to the veranda.

"Wait," Gabriella whispered.

The sergeant surveyed the property. He pointed to a stone barn across the stream and about 100 yards north of the manor house. "We'll take her there."

The lieutenant was mulling a different scenario. "No. Take her to the house. It's closer and cleaner. A thick mattress will be more comfortable than a filthy Romanian barn floor."

The private and sergeant, still holding their PPsh's, each gripped one of Laura's arms. Still dazed from the blow to her head, Laura shuffled along between the soldiers. Soon they were crossing the small bridge.

"They are bringing her here," Alexandra whispered. "What are they going to do?" Gabriella's reply was a cold stare. "Oh, oh, my God."

Gabriella took Alexandra's right arm. "Come. We need time to think." The two young women retreated through the house. They exited the rear door and flanked it, their backs pressed against the house.

Laura was regaining her senses as the soldiers half-dragged her up the steps onto the veranda. The lieutenant pulled open the door and they entered the foyer.

"There," the lieutenant said, pointing to the wide staircase. "Get her up to a bedroom." The private hesitated. "Remember," the officer half-growled, "what Romanians did to our people. They showed no conscience."

Laura again started resisting and the sergeant slapped her, a stinging blow that soon had blood trickling from her nose.

"Can you kill?" Gabriella asked Alexandra.

"I wouldn't have thought so."

They stepped back into the kitchen.

"Does your mother have guns in the house?" Alexandra shook her head. Gabriella walked to a knife rack. She selected two, each with a blade about eight inches. One was serrated. She handed that one to Alexandra.

The room was Catherine's and it was spacious. The four-poster bed reflected Catherine's decorating tastes. The posts were ornately carved, and the canopy was cream-colored with red roses and green leaves. A white-on-white floral-patterned spread covered the cotton sheets.

The sergeant threw Laura roughly onto the bed. Her long, curly black hair spread behind her head. "Rank enjoys privilege, Lieutenant."

"You saw her and it was your idea," the officer replied. "You get the first taste. Then I'll take my bite." He looked at the private. "You can share as well."

The lieutenant removed his belt with its holstered sidearm, a six-shot revolver. He looked around briefly and then laid it at the foot of the bed. The sergeant and private, flanking the bed, placed their PPsh's on side tables. On each was sitting a hurricane-style lamp with a floral-patterned globe.

Gabriella and Alexandra were inching their way up the staircase. Both were struggling to suppress fear. Gabriella was praying that their light footfalls wouldn't be answered by telltale creaking. Or that her pounding heart wouldn't explode through her chest.

"Your plan?" Alexandra whispered shakily. "We are only two to their three."

Gabriella shrugged nervously. "Surprise," she whispered. "If that isn't enough…"

Neither considered retreating and running for refuge in the nearby forest-shrouded hills.

The lieutenant and private pinned Laura's arms against the bed. Tears trickling from her luminescent, wide-set eyes and soft whimpers elicited no sympathy. Alexandra and Gabriella, she worried, I hope you have fled.

The sergeant climbed onto the bed. He knelt at Laura's feet and unbuttoned his trousers and underpants. The lieutenant reached out and pulled Laura's long skirt above her waist. The sergeant leaned forward and roughly pulled her cotton panties down and off. Then he forced her legs apart.

At the doorway Gabriella peeked in. Alexandra looked in after her. Trepidation instantly gave way to loathing and resolve.

The sergeant's right hand reached forward and groped Laura's labia. She shuddered and her eyes closed tightly. She tried closing her mind and nose to his stench. The sergeant hovered above for a few moments, then lowered himself and penetrated. Through clenched jaws, Laura groaned as her virginity was lost to a deep and painful thrust.

In the next instant the two young women flung themselves through the doorway. Gabriella vaulted onto the bed and plunged her knife deep into the sergeant's back. He howled then collapsed onto Laura. Simultaneously, Alexandra hurled herself onto the lieutenant. The impact knocked him against the headboard. With a swift motion Alexandra drew her right arm back, the knife's serrated blade slicing deeply into the officer's neck. In stunned surprise, quickly slipping into shock, he saw blood erupting from his severed artery.

The private still was gripping Laura's left hand. He gazed incredulously at the attackers. Blood seemed everywhere – gushing from the lieutenant, dripping from the sergeant and staining the bedspread between Laura's thighs.

Gabriella's left hand pushed down hard against the dying sergeant's back. Simultaneously, her right pulled hard and the bloody knife blade came free. Gabriella looked first at Alexandra; she was breathing hard and separating herself from the lieutenant, mere seconds from death. Then Gabriella swung her head to face the private. He saw the hatred in her eyes and knew he needed to act quickly. He released Laura's hand and without looking away from Gabriella reached behind for his PPsh. His fingers were fumbling for it.

Gabriella glanced back to her left, quickly found and picked up the lieutenant's holstered revolver. She dropped the knife and pulled the gun out. Gripping it with both hands she pointed it at the private. "Don't," she said in Romanian. "Don't," she repeated more forcefully, shaking her head. "Take your hand away from the gun." Slowly the private complied. "Raise your hands," Gabriella commanded, gesturing with the revolver.

"What are you going to do?" Alexandra asked. Blood still was dripping from the serrated blade in her hand. Gabriella's reply was a prolonged sigh. "If you don't shoot him," Alexandra said calmly, "what will we do with him?"

"I'm not sure."

"More Russians will be coming. We can't keep him here."

"You are right."

"He deserves to die."

"I know."

"If you don't kill him, Mother will."

At that observation, Gabriella smiled thinly. "Yes, she would."

"If you don't want to do it, I will."

The private, arms upraised, was sensing that Alexandra was posing his greater source of danger.

Gabriella began edging back away from the dead sergeant. Laura's eyes opened. Gabriella lowered the revolver slightly. The private's eyes shifted toward Alexandra. In that moment Gabriella elevated the revolver and squeezed the trigger. The shell's impact sent the private toppling backward from the bed. His left arm struck his PPsh and the lamp, sending both to the floor where the globe shattered.

Alexandra heard the private moaning. "He's not dead."

Gabriella eased off the bed and stood over the private. Blood was staining his uniform tunic midway between his chest and navel. His eyes were open and pleading silently. Gabriella bent low beside him and picked up the PPsh. She straightened and looked down pitilessly. "He will be soon."

Alexandra stood. She placed her knife on the floor and Gabriella did likewise with the two guns. Together they pulled the sergeant off Laura.

CHAPTER 80

Catherine knew there was precious little time to act. The detritus of carnage that she found on returning to her estate confirmed her worst fears about the invading Russians.

While Laura recovered from her ordeal, Gabriella and Alexandra first rolled the three corpses into the bloodstained bedspread and sheets. Next they dragged them downstairs and out onto the veranda. They then used a wheelbarrow to move the bodies, one at a time, into a copse far to the rear of the house. "They don't deserve graves," Alexandra said. "Let the wild boars dispose of them."

As quickly as possible Catherine contacted staff at all St. Catherine's Crib orphanages on the Soviets' lines of march and urged immediate evacuation until the danger had passed to the west. Meanwhile, she instructed, hide the children in the forests.

Next, her thoughts turned to her original boys, the prisoners at Timisul de Jos. "The Russians supposedly are allies of the Americans, but true friends? Can they be trusted even a little not to murder wantonly – regardless of military or political arrangements of convenience?" She was directing her assessment to Alexandra, Laura and Gabriella. "Then there are the retreating Germans. We can expect only the worst from them. I am driving up to Timisul, and I don't want to leave you here."

Not far from Nedelea Catherine encountered a Soviet-manned roadblock. Each man carried a PPsh. A Romanian-speaking Red Army officer ordered the four women from Catherine's Plymouth. She felt the bile of disgust tanging her throat as she guessed that the officer was a Romanian who had been captured by the Russians and had decided to defect. He scrutinized the Plymouth. He then ordered the four women back into the car – but not to drive on. Instead, he commanded Catherine to follow him to his command post. There a Soviet colonel made a quick decision: He would confiscate the Plymouth.

Catherine knew that rape and execution could be their fate but decided to press the matter. "I need this car to carry on conducting social services."

The colonel grinned snidely. "Spoils of war, dear lady. But I am not unreasonable. We will simply exchange cars." He pointed to his car – a decrepit 1926 Chrysler. Its color? Rust would best describe it.

Catherine coaxed the Chrysler on toward Timisul, increasingly mourning the loss of her beloved Plymouth with the passing of each tortured mile. "Money isn't the issue," she grumbled to the three young women who were suppressing smiles. "It's availability. Where in heaven's name am I going to find a decent, reliable car? Not in Romania."

At one point a slow-moving Russian tank column was clogging the main road. Catherine used narrow country lanes to detour. Farther on she encountered the rear of a horse-drawn convoy of Russian supply wagons. Their drivers and passengers were happily quaffing Romanian plum brandy. Her patience at low ebb, Catherine decided to try passing the plodding wagons, hoping not to meet any oncoming motorized vehicle. Her three passengers remained silent, not wanting to divert her attention from the narrow, twisting road.

At Timisul de Jos, a surprise greeted Catherine and her companions. The gates to both the officers' and enlisted men's quarters were open. GIs were roaming outside. The Romanian guards, fearing Russian retribution, · had fled.

To brake the coughing Chrysler, Catherine had to do little more than remove her shoe from the accelerator pedal. The four women exited – and Gabriella found herself doing something she'd not done before. She squealed. The proximate cause was recognizing Jeff Wolfrom.

On the road in front of the compound's gate they shook hands politely. "I'm sorry about the scream," Gabriella said, willing calm into her voice. "I didn't mean to embarrass you."

Jeff chuckled. "Not a bad reason to be embarrassed."

Gabriella's olive complexion tinged red. "I think that was a compliment."

"You think right. My southern upbringing all but demanded one. Chivalry lives."

"You look good."

"We've been treated well – thanks to Princess Caradja. We all – to a man – believe she is one helluva woman. If she ran for president of our country, she'd have all our votes."

Gabriella smiled warmly. "We need her here."

To Shoot, Fritz, You're Faded pilot Robert O'Reilly Catherine said, "The Russians might do you no harm. But I would feel much better if you left this camp. Until conditions are more stable."

O'Reilly smiled gratefully. "After all you've done for us, who am I to question your wisdom? Do you have someplace in mind?"

"Pietrosita. It is a small village deeper in the mountains. It is tiny but I think you and the men would be welcomed."

"I take it you know the people."

"Of course."

"How will we get there?"

"I've thought about that."

O'Reilly chortled. "Why am I not surprised?"

"I have money. Cash. Send some of your men to farms in the area. Negotiate for trucks."

Later that day seven wheezing, rickety farm trucks were following Catherine's complaining Chrysler. Misery was their companion. Rain was falling steadily on the men huddled under sodden blankets. Catherine worried that the narrow, winding mountain tracks might become impassable.

Arriving as darkness descended, Catherine, Alexandra, Laura, Gabriella and the American airmen were greeted cordially and invited to sleep in villagers' modest homes, some little more than hovels. Accommodations for most of the men were spaces on floors, some earthen. No one complained. This first taste of freedom after more than a year of confinement was being savored.

Dawn brought delights. Rain had surrendered to sunshine and smiling hosts led the men to the village park. It became quickly and abundantly clear that the village women had arisen early and begun culinary endeavors. The guests were directed to sit at tables groaning with roasted meats and corn on the cob, freshly baked bread, newly harvested melons and wine by the barrel.

Soon the air grew festive when local musicians began strumming balalaikas and guitars. Village girls and women of all ages began inviting the airmen to dance. None refused. The music was fast and infectious.

Gabriella stood and walked to Jeff. "Care to dance?"

He smiled and stood. "First time for anything," he answered, observing his fellow airmen trying inartistically to keep up with partners in their long, whirling skirts. "I did a little waltzing in high school but nothing like this."

After a few minutes most airmen were wheezing. Poor physical condition, full stomachs and folk dancing fueled an instant epidemic of shortness of breath.

"Enough," Jeff pleaded.

"Okay," Gabriella relented.

She took his hand and led him to the shade of a flowering tree. They sat at its base, backs resting against its massive trunk.

"How many of us are there here? I don't mean just here, but in Romania."

"Hundreds. Maybe a thousand or more. Most of you airmen are in Bucharest – watched and cared for by Romanians."

"Not Germans."

"Princess Caradja wouldn't hear of it."

"Do you miss Washington?" Gabriella nodded. "Friends there?"

"Of course."

"Anyone special?" Jeff's nosiness was surprising him but not off-putting Gabriella.

"A young man."

"Romanian or American?"

"American."

"Soldier?"

"No, he was a member of the Foreign Service."

"Was?"

"He was posted to Singapore, and I don't know where he is now."

"I see...Miss him?"

Gabriella nodded. "I do."

"How long since you've seen him?"

"More than two years. Closer to three."

"I'd say that fella's a lucky guy."

Joe Barton was perched on a large, gray boulder about 60 feet farther up the mountain from the camp. His knees were drawn to his chest and held there with clasped hands. Darkness had blackened the jungle. Joe could see just a few twinkling stars through the leafy canopy. He heard footsteps approaching lightly from below.

"Can you stand some company?" The voice was Rosalie's.

"It's a big boulder."

Rosalie's shortness proved no hindrance; she climbed gracefully onto the rock and duplicated Joe's knees-to-chest position. "How good is your imagination?" she asked.

"I don't know. Why do you ask?"

"Because mine is pretty vivid and I never imagined all of this. Never would have in a million years."

"You could've been home in the States long ago. Back to Lynchburg. Or Washington."

"And miss this?" Rosalie said incredulously. "I never imagined anything like this, but I wouldn't trade it for all those twinkling stars up there. Well," her next words slowed and softened, "except for the killing and dying. Watching – hearing – Sister Caroline take her last, shallow breath. I will never forget. But the rest – what an adventure. Of course, it would be nice if we lived through it," she smiled ruefully.

"And if we do survive?"

"Now there you go again, Mr. Barton. I tell you a little about myself and now you want to know more." Joe chuckled. "But I might surprise you."

Joe turned toward Rosalie. "Miss Reynolds, when I reflect on everything you've done these last three years and how you've done it, I don't think anything you'd do would be all that surprising."

"You never know."

On September 1, King Michael continued to demonstrate his decisiveness. He declared war on Germany, and he handed Antonescu over to the Soviets. A few Romanian pilots took to the air and began attacking Luftwaffe bombers and fighters and more than 100,000 German troops who were fleeing west. Other Romanians took over Gerstenberg's anti-aircraft guns and turned them loose on German planes that were intent on inflicting damage on open city Bucharest and its residents whom the Germans regarded as nothing better than feckless turncoats. German bombs killed and wounded not only Romanian civilians but also some interned American airmen.

Jeff 's next surprise was a big one – probably, he mused, his biggest ever.

A few days after leading the farm truck caravan to Pietrosita, Catherine returned. With her were Alexandra, Laura and Gabriella. "Boys," the robust princess declared, "you must get back in those trucks and follow me."

"Where to?" Jeff asked.

"To Bucharest."

"Why?"

"You'll see."

Soon the farm trucks were trailing Catherine south down the mountain road, past Timisul de Jos, through Ploesti and on toward the nation's capital. They weren't following the Chrysler, though. Through grateful King Michael's good graces, automotive availability had become a non-issue. Catherine now was piloting a gleaming black Packard from Michael's collection. She led the convoy to Popestii Airport, north of Bucharest and even closer to the city center than larger Otopeni Airport. There the Timisul de Jos contingent was awed to see an assemblage of some 1,500 U.S. airmen. They were standing in small groups, chatting collegially.

Catherine braked the Packard and the trucks pulled to a stop. The men began jumping off. Arrayed before them was an inspiring sight: a fleet of some 75 B-17 Flying Fortresses.

"What in the world?" Jeff stammered. "Why are they here? Where did they come from? Where are they going?"

Catherine's laughter was loud and infectious. Men felt compelled to laugh with her – and most did – even before hearing her answers to Jeff's questions. "Boys," she announced grandly, "you are looking at planes of the United States Fifteenth Air Force. They have come" – her voice faltered and she had to work at regaining composure – "to take you to Bella Italia." Her voice still cracking, she managed to add, "God be with you."

The impetus for the unprecedented large-scale rescue of Americans from deep behind lines was Lieutenant Colonel Jim Gunn. He had been shot down during the last of the American assaults on Ploesti. With King Michael's administration in place, Gunn petitioned for permission to radio 15th Air Force headquarters at Foggia. Permission granted. The 15th's commanding officer, concerned about intercepted radio transmissions, asked Gunn if he could arrange to fly to Italy to discuss his request. Who to turn to but Princess Caradja? She turned to her cousin, Constantine Cantacuzene. He happened to be a Romanian Air Force captain, and in short order was flying Gunn to Foggia in a captured German Me-109.

After discussions at Foggia, the 15th dispatched a reconnaissance flight to determine whether a mass aerial evacuation – one requiring a fleet of B-17s to fly some 550 miles behind enemy lines – could be accomplished safely. It was bad enough to lose a crew of 10 when a bomber was forced down. B-17s shot down while loaded not with bombs but American airmen would be a tragedy of epic scale.

Reconnaissance completed, subsequent preparations had been made quickly. The B-17s had been altered to accommodate 20 men each plus crew. Now at Popesti, the boarding process began. Catherine was weeping and so were more than a few of her boys. Many wanted to hug their savior-guardian angel but inhibitions of the day kept them from embracing a princess.

Gabriella saw Jeff in a line of men queuing to board a B-17. "Jeff," she called, "please wait a minute."

Jeff turned and stepped away from the line. He smiled as Gabriella came hurrying toward him.

"Could I ask you a favor?"

"Anything. Just name it."

Gabriella sucked in a breath and let it out slowly. "I know you will be in Italy for a while. But when the war ends and you are free to return home, well, on your way to Arkansas, would you please stop in Washington? Visit the State Department and ask about Joe Barton? Joseph Barton?"

"Ah, that's not all that big a favor. I'm happy to oblige."

"And perhaps send me a postcard?"

"Before I do that, I'll see if I can get a telegram to you."

"Oh, that would be wonderful."

Jeff's throat felt as though a vice was closing on it. "Like I said, that fella is a lucky guy. I hope he's okay."

"Thank you, Jeff."

"Now you take care of yourself."

"Okay."

Jeff turned to board the plane, then paused. "Oh, what the heck," he mumbled to himself. He pivoted and saw Gabriella still standing and watching. He stepped toward her, reached out and hugged hard. Gabriella's squeeze was just as hard. Not a word was spoken. None was needed.

CHAPTER 81

No one questioned the wisdom of King Michael's overthrow of Ion Antonescu. Had Antonescu remained in power, few doubted that Stalin in exacting retribution for Romania's attacking Russia would have unleashed an Armageddon on the much smaller nation. And while Stalin genuinely admired Michael's creative stealth and courage, the dictator was taking no chances on what future course Romania might take. Stalin wanted and demanded control.

He got it on September 12, 1944, when Romania and Russia signed an armistice. Michael shuddered at the terms – which Stalin had virtually dictated.

"This agreement – this document – is unacceptable," Michael had said to Lieutenant General Constantin Sanatescu whom he had newly appointed as prime minister. "It is tantamount to a capitulation."

"You have no choice," Sanatescu had replied. "Stalin will brook no actual sovereignty on his western border. We agree to his terms or he will turn his tanks on us."

Under the armistice terms Romania officially recognized its defeat by the Soviet Union. Romania was to be subject to occupation by Allied forces as represented by the Soviets. Romania ceded to Moscow control of news media, communications, mail services and civil administration.

"I fear our hopes of freedom are ended," Michael confided to Catherine and Gabriella.

"We will win our freedom," Catherine replied grimly. "It might take decades but we will prevail – and I will live to see it happen."

The armistice paved the way for the rise to power of Nicolae Ceausescu who had spent most of the World War II years as a political prisoner. His ascension began in 1944 when he was named secretary of the Union of Communist Youth.

On learning about the armistice, Jeff's reaction was one of gratitude. "Man, I'm glad we are in Italy or we could be interned by the Reds," he said to other liberated airmen. "And I'm thinking the Reds would be less hospitable than the Turks. And thanks to Princess Caradja, even as POWs we were treated pretty darned nice in Romania. Yeah, I know the Reds supposedly are our Allies, but I suspect their intentions after the war are different than ours."

Joseph Stalin, after seeing his nation at the brink of crushing defeat, was now lusting for conquest. In Singapore the attitude of Japanese officialdom contrasted sharply with that of Soviet expansionism. Japanese leaders saw their fortunes shifting inexorably from victory to vanquishment with increasing rapidity. They were now drafting locals to help build defenses for anticipated invasion by Allied forces. The Japanese oversaw conscripts digging trenches, stringing barbed wire, building pillboxes and boring caves in Bukit Timah. They forced 3,000 Singapore residents to begin building a new airstrip near the Changi-area prison complex. Here, as in their other Pacific strongholds, the Japanese were preparing to greet the Allies with unyielding defense.

Joe and Sister Regina were once again strolling toward the nearby stream to take morning ablution.

"From what we're hearing from the MPAJA our days in this camp are numbered," Joe said.

"So you really think the Japanese are losing?"

"Some of their leaders are in denial but, yes, it seems clear that the Allies now enjoy the upper hand."

"Well, Joe, you've certainly done your bit for the cause."

"A very small bit."

"Oh, no, more than that. Your actions have disrupted the Japanese. But I think just as importantly your efforts – your American presence – helped keep hope alive among the Malayan people. I don't mean only you, of course, but Duane and his father and Rosalie and Lim Bo Seng and Force 136 and the MPAJA. Without your work, think about how much stronger Japan's grip would have been. I feel quite sure the same could be said about resistance groups in other occupied nations in Asia and Europe."

Joe and Sister R reached the stream. As had become their early morning ritual, they squatted side by side, cupped the rapidly running water in their hands and splashed their faces three times. Then each gulped the cool water.

"I know you don't want to hear this, Joe, but to me and the other nuns you will always be a hero. You risked your life to save ours, not once but twice."

"I had plenty of help both times."

They both stood and shook water from their dangling hands.

"Your modesty and my gratitude were to be expected. But I am feeling other needs that were unexpected. Unprecedented for me, actually." Joe turned to face his friend. "I must admit, Joe, that they are more physical than mental or emotional."

"I think I'm glad to hear that."

"Because you're not in love with me."

"I probably could be. Very easily, actually," he smiled wryly.

"But you're still in love with Gabriella."

"At least with her memory."

"And I'm still in love with God."

"God knows what you've been through. I think an understanding God would understand your physical needs."

"I hope so. Especially if I were to give in to them."

King Michael would be the last monarch to lose his throne behind what would become known as the Iron Curtain. In addition to the September armistice, a harbinger of his political demise occurred in March 1945

when Moscow pressured him to appoint a new, pro-Soviet administration that would be dominated by the Romanian Communist Party. He was correctly assessing his future. On December 30, 1947, he would be forced at gunpoint to abdicate his throne and on January 30, 1948, to leave Romania. The communist government announced the monarchy's abolition.

CHAPTER 82

38 days: August 6 – September 12, 1945.

August 6: The Enola Gay, piloted by 29-year-old Paul Tibbets, dropped an atom bomb on Hiroshima.

August 9: A second such bomb was dropped on Nagasaki.

August 11: Singaporeans witnessed early signs of the coming surrender of the Japanese. That morning, the rising sun flag wasn't raised over schools when the opening bells rang. More remarkably, Japanese officials began uttering "Peace" and "Kudasai" (sorry) to Singaporeans. Some deigned to shake hands with Chinese residents and, shockingly, a few reached out to hug locals they had come to know.

August 15: In Tokyo, Emperor Hirohito stood before a radio microphone and announced his nation's surrender to the Allies. By this time the Barton-Hurd camp possessed a working radio, and the group listened to Hirohito's broadcast via short wave. Sister Augusta provided an approximate translation. "You see," she said jovially, "I'm still useful if only marginally so."

A subdued camp celebration ensued. It culminated with all paying their final respects before the in-tent memorial to Sister Caroline. The candles were allowed to burn until only stubs remained.

That night, Joe ascended to the large boulder he had taken to regarding as his own jungle chapel. For him there was something about sitting on the big rock that fostered reflection and tranquility. On this occasion he was reflecting on what he had witnessed during the last four and half years – courage, perseverance, death, faith, resourcefulness and more. He also was pondering his return to Singapore and what might happen afterward. He had been perched there about 20 minutes when Sister Regina approached.

"I've heard from Rosalie that you don't object to sharing your boulder occasionally," Sister R said. In the jungle blackness Joe could easily sense her good humor.

"I've not known Rosalie to exaggerate," Joe replied with equal levity. "Climb aboard."

Sister R's left hand hiked up her habit. Her right reached out and Joe took it and pulled. Three or so minutes of silence followed. Then Sister R murmured, "Are you thinking of her, Joe?"

"Yes. I don't know that she's ever seemed farther away than tonight. The world war is over – or nearly so – and yet we are still worlds apart."

"I pray – been praying – that she is all right."

Joe turned toward Sister R. On an impulse he leaned closer and kissed her left cheek. "The jungle made me do it," Joe joked but without apology.

"That was a chaste kiss, Joe," she smiled. "I can accept that." No reply. "What are you thinking, Joe?"

His lips pursed and eyebrows elevated. "As one of your fellow Brits might put it, a rather unchaste thought."

As Sister R was formulating her reply, she found herself swallowing. "If Hirohito is surrendering his empire, if I'm ever going to surrender to my feelings, this might be the time and place to do it." Tentatively she placed her hand on his shoulder.

"It would be memorable."

"It would be that and more."

August 28: Allied planes over Singapore dropped leaflets announcing the Japanese surrender and urging residents to remain calm while awaiting the arrival of British troops.

August 30: Etsuro Yamada, Kai Hata and Takuma Matsui watched the descending parachutes dispiritedly. British medical personnel and a contingent of soldiers serving as bodyguards were being dropped into prison camps. Japanese leaders had told their soldiers not to intervene.

August 31: British minesweepers appeared off Singapore and began clearing the surrounding waters.

September 2: The formal surrender of Japan took place on the deck of the USS Missouri in Tokyo Bay. Presiding was General Douglas

MacArthur. Among those MacArthur invited to sit at the surrender table was Lieutenant General Arthur E. Percival who in 1942 had surrendered Singapore to Japan.

In Singapore Japanese troops reacted variously to the surrender. Outside a small house on Hill Street that had been serving as their quarters, three Japanese soldiers were talking in subdued voices about the humiliating ceremony on the Missouri. They heard a single gunshot. A few minutes later came a second sharp report. Then a grenade blast.

"What do you think?" Etsuro Yamada asked.

"I think our fellow soldiers are choosing to die honorably," said Kai Hata. "We should too."

"I think we should sleep on it," said Takuma Matsui. "I hear that some of our officers are already beginning to prepare an internment camp for us on Jurong Island."

"Cowardly." Yamada spat on the street.

"Many of us," Matsui said calmly, "have girlfriends or wives or children back home. We would like to see them again – in this life."

Among the some 70,000 Japanese troops in Singapore, an estimated 10,000 committed suicide or lost their lives at the hands of vengeful MPAJA members. Many waited patiently at their posts or quarters for resolution of their status. Others used their swords to hack in frustration at banana and papaya trees. Still others took to burning incriminating files. A large number did march themselves to Jurong, a causeway-connected island just off Singapore's south coast where they hurriedly organized a detention camp.

September 5: British troops began landing in Singapore. They encountered no resistance.

Inside the Hill Street house, Yamada, Hata and Matsui sat in silence. They had watched the first British troops go marching by. Yamada was feeling swamped with shame. He studied a hand grenade. Hata and Matsui were watching from an adjoining room. Yamada pulled the pin and pressed it against his right temple. The explosion obliterated his head and blew out ground floor windows.

Hata stepped into the room and kicked at rubble. He removed a grenade from his webbed belt.

"No!" Matsui said sharply. "I do not believe there is honor in taking your own life. I know that goes against the Bushido code, but I believe that suicide has more to do with vanity and shame than honor."

"You are a good man," Hata said softly, "the best. And you always did think too much. Yamada told you that back in Nanking. And perhaps you have more to live for than we do." He smiled at his friend. A pause. Then he pulled the pin and held the grenade against his chest with both hands.

After the explosion Matsui looked thoughtfully at his own grenade. He removed it from his belt and held it with both hands. Then, carefully, he laid it down and walked outside. His lips pursed in relief, he began walking southwest toward Jurong Island. Shattered glass was crunching beneath his boots. His thoughts were ones of hope – of again seeing Shuri and his family.

Fears of mass murder at Changi-area and other prison camps proved unfounded. "I thought Changi might be my burial site," George Britton said to Malcolm Goode. "Now I know it can be Gravesend – but not anytime soon." Japanese overseers simply handed over the camps to those who had been prisoners. They saw no dishonor in doing so because they were merely obeying a new imperial order. American detainees were the first to exit Changi.

September 6: Some 34,000 military and civilian detainees were freed. At Sime Road camp, Daisy Thomas, wife of pre-war Governor Shenton Thomas, raised a union jack – the same one that previously had flown over the governor's residence.

September 7: Joe Barton, the Hurds – Duane, Clayton, Su Mien – Rosalie Reynolds and Sisters Regina, Augusta and Grace Ann all boarded a motor launch for the return from Malaya to Singapore. On landing, the entire group's first stop was the nurses' quarters at Singapore General Hospital.

That night, Joe and Sister R were strolling the hospital grounds. They paused beneath an umbrella tree, so named for the way its branches spread. In the faint glow of lights from hospital rooms, their lips met and held for long moments.

"I don't believe that was a chaste kiss," Sister R smiled, her voice tremulous.

"I guess it wasn't intended to be."

"My body is telling me things I shouldn't be hearing. We'd better stop with that one, or my vow of chastity might be history."

"Is that the way you want your history remembered?"

"Until now I would have said yes. Now I'm not so sure."

"I thought your certainty was going to surrender that night on the boulder."

"For a minute, I did too."

Joe took her hands in his. A long silence ensued.

"What are you thinking, Joe?"

"If it's only going to happen once, I'm thinking how wonderful it would be to make love to a wonderful woman."

"Even one you're not in love with?"

It didn't occur to Joe to be less than honest with Sister R. "Yes."

September 12: At 10:30 a.m., Lord Louis Mountbatten came striding south on St. Andrew's Road toward the steps of the handsomely columned Municipal Building. Mountbatten was dressed as the quintessence of virtue – in all white – hat, uniform and shoes. His mission – represent and sign for the Allies at the imminent surrender ceremony. Among invitees was Joe Barton in his role as a consular officer and U.S. representative. Joe put in a quick and persuasive word – "She's my consular colleague" – with a Mountbatten aide, and Rosalie was permitted to witness the surrender.

Moments later, the Japanese delegation came walking toward the Municipal Building. Flanking them – and serving as a de facto security detail – were Allied officers. At 11 a.m., General Seishiro Itagaki signed the surrender document. His right hand fingers were trembling slightly. The ceremony lasted nine minutes. Mountbatten then curtly ordered the Japanese to leave the building.

A crowd was gathered outside. Among the deliriously happy throng were the Hurds and the three nuns.

When Mountbatten emerged, Royal Marines atop the building raised a union jack – the same one the British had carried to their surrender at the Ford Factory on February 15, 1942. A Royal Marine band then struck up *God Save The King*.

When Joe and Rosalie descended the steps, hugs awaited them, both from their friends and strangers.

"I feel like I'm home," Sister Grace Ann said dreamily. "I'm thousands of miles from England, but I do feel at home today."

CHAPTER 83

With the war over, soldiers were heading homeward. To Jeff Wolfrom's surprise he was ambivalent about returning to 305 East Martin in Pine Bluff. He now had accumulated enough rotation points to qualify for discharge. But like many GIs his wartime experiences had altered youthful perceptions and plans. Still at Foggia, Jeff picked up a pen and wrote to Iris Ann.

September 13, 1945

Dear Mother,

This will be my last letter from Italy. It's such a beautiful country. You'd love all the mountains, and I've got to admit these Italians know a thing or three about cooking and baking. If I stayed here much longer I'd be a tubby.

I am almost ready to head for home. My duffel bag is pretty much packed. I plan to make two stops along the way. The first one is Ankara, Turkey. From here in Italy it isn't all that far. Just across the Adriatic Sea, Greece and the Aegean Sea. I've already made arrangements to get there. I'm catching rides with some Air Corps guys who are hauling supplies to Ankara. It took the Turks a good while to make up their minds, but earlier this year – February – they finally gave up their neutrality and signed on with the Allies. Anyway there's someone I want to look up in Ankara. I'll tell you more when I see you.

My second stop will be in Washington, D.C. I agreed to do a favor for a friend. Look somebody up. I'm not sure how long these stops are gonna be or how they will turn out. I guess I should say that I think Pine Bluff might seem kinda small after everywhere I've been and everything I've seen and learned. Some of those lessons might have taken hold. So I guess what I'm saying is that I'm not sure if I'll be spending the rest of my life in Pine Bluff.

I've got a lot to sort out, and I hope you understand.

Your loving son always,
Jeff

"Do you think we'll ever see each other again?" Joe asked plaintively. It was mid-afternoon.

Duane's head rocked back and his eyes closed in concentration. "I don't think so. Not if you stay with the Foreign Service. You won't be posted to Singapore again."

Duane and Joe were standing on the promenade where they had first met soon after Joe's arrival in December 1940.

"How about after I retire?" Joe said, semi-joshing.

Duane laughed heartily. "You're making a big assumption."

"That being?"

"That I'll still be alive and kicking when you call it quits."

Joe smiled. "At least we won't forget each other."

"I quite agree. You're a fine young man, Joe Barton. If your government gave a medal for loyalty, I would pin it on you myself."

Joe blushed and his throat thickened. "I've never met a finer man, Duane Hurd. Don't think I ever will."

Duane extended his right hand and Joe clasped it between both of his, holding it firmly. No more words were spoken.

They released their grip and Joe turned and began walking slowly back to the Union Building on Collyer Quay. He was weeping.

Rosalie was standing on the quay as Joe approached. Smoke was curling from a cigarette she was holding.

"You've never smoked before," Joe said, eyes still rimmed with red.

"You mean you've never seen me smoke," she corrected him impishly.

"Did you? I mean before we met?"

"No. And there you go again. Being nosey."

They both laughed.

"So, are you taking up smoking?"

"Nope. Just satisfying a sudden craving. Can't explain where it came from. Anyway, this damned thing doesn't have much taste. Nothing like that Lion City cigar Duane let me puff on a few years ago."

"You've been a trooper," Joe said.

"I have, haven't I? At times one filthy trooper. I wonder if my hair will ever be blond again." She laughed and tossed the butt into the water.

"So look, Rosalie. Let me be a little nosey about your future. What's next for you?"

"Duane might have something to say about that."

"What?" Joe's tone and widened eyes signaled his shock.

"Did all that gunfire make you go deaf?"

Joe laughed. "You caught me by surprise – again."

"We – Duane and I – had plenty of time to talk on the mountain."

"He didn't say anything to me about you two just now," Joe said faux accusatorily, pointing back toward the promenade.

"He left that for me. And I know what you're thinking, Mr. Barton."

"You do?"

"College girl, career woman. With an uneducated Asian-Negro. Can't possibly work."

"Actually I was thinking how lucky you two were to find each other."

"Really?"

"Really."

"You know, if Duane and I have a child, it could be the world's first trifecta baby – black, yellow, white all in one package."

"That would make one helluva package. And, Rosalie, I'm dead certain sure you'll make one hell of a wife and mother."

"I will, won't I?"

"I believe we can get you on the first evacuation ship headed to England. From there I should think you'd have no problem arranging transport to the States."

"I appreciate that, sir."

"Well, as the lone yankee consular officer who stuck it out here, we Brits owe you a measure of gratitude and respect." Colonel Carlton Waverly was speaking with Joe on Collyer Quay, outside the Union Building. Repatriation of Japanese troops was already being organized. "Moreover, in my short time here I've already heard of your heroics on the polo grounds."

Joe chuckled. "A few minutes on a polo pony have led to lasting infamy."

Colonel Waverly chortled. "You soon will be on your way to mastering British understatement." They shook hands. "Bon voyage, Mr. Barton."

"Right. Well, sir, I think I'd like to disembark a little sooner than England. Maybe in Lebanon after we pass through the Suez Canal. Or in Greece if that's possible. That would be better yet."

"Really? Why?"

"I'm thinking of visiting Romania."

"Of all the places on God's green earth…"

Joe grinned. "Actually it sounds pretty inviting to me."

"Bucharest?"

"Ploesti."

"My lord, is there anything left of that poor city?"

"I intend to find out."

"A personal interest?"

"You could say that."

EPILOGUE 1

If only Joe Barton could see me now, the small woman was thinking. He would probably be grinning. His old teacher taking the advice of her student.

Marie Hughes had disembarked at Marseille and by train traveled north to Paris, arriving at Gare de Lyon station, just a few blocks southeast of Notre Dame and only two blocks from the Seine. The trip was tiring but she was buoyant. It was the summer of 1947. She next had taxied to cavernous Gare de'l Est, bought a ticket, walked down Platform 9 and taken another train about 40 miles east to Belleau Wood. Now she was standing at the entrance to Aisne-Marne American Cemetery.

I think Joe was right, she thought. This visit has made my heart feel less heavy. Lighter. I'm fifty-six and this is the lightest it's felt in almost thirty years. Now I need to locate his grave to say goodbye. I don't think I'll weep, not even a little. I actually feel happy. I wonder if I'll ever see Joe again, to thank him.

EPILOGUE 2

In the early 2000s Romania authorized an international commission to study the country's role in the Holocaust. In 2004 Romania accepted and released the study's findings. The commission estimated that Ion Antonescu's regime had systematically murdered between 280,000 and 380,000 Jews in territories conquered by the Romanian Army as it proceeded eastward into Russia and Ukraine. Romanian troops were largely responsible for a massacre at Odessa in which more than 100,000 Jews were shot during the autumn of 1941.

The report concluded: "Of all the allies of Nazi Germany, Romania bears responsibility for the deaths of more Jews than any country other than Germany itself. The murders committed in Iasi, Odessa, Bogdanovka and Peciora, for example, were among the most hideous murders committed against the Jews anywhere during the Holocaust. Romania committed genocide against the Jews. The survival of Jews in some parts of the country (Romania) does not alter this reality."

Most Jews living within Romania's borders survived the Holocaust, albeit under harsh conditions.

As for Ion Antonescu, the Soviet Regime under Joseph Stalin executed him as a war criminal in 1946.

EPILOGUE 3

Catherine Caradja proved indomitable and tireless. In 1949 the communist regime nationalized her orphanages and St. Catherine's Crib Foundation. Facing prosecution from a government that feared her voice and courage, in 1952 she escaped – with help from her daughter Alexandra, who had fled to Paris in 1948, and France's secret services. Weeks later she arrived in Vienna.

Catherine soon resumed her charitable work and in 1954-1955 directed relief efforts for children in Algiers that had been shaken badly by an earthquake on September 9, 1954.

For the next year she traveled in western Europe, giving talks in France on "Life Behind the Iron Curtain" and speaking on the BBC in England. In December 1955 she received a visa, enabling her to immigrate to the U.S. Soon afterward her arresting visage was seen by millions of Americans on TV, beginning with Dave Garroway's morning show.

For the next 35 years she lived mostly in Comfort, a town in the Texas hill country. She resided briefly in Baltimore and Kansas City. She continued to travel and speak. Then she decided she again wanted to see "her boys." On August 28, 1972, more than 500 of "her boys" reunited with her in Dallas. Her reunions with the former POWs continued annually for many years, with Catherine as guest of honor and main speaker.

On August 27, 1976, during the U.S. bicentennial year, Catherine helped dedicate the Peace Monument at Valley Forge National Historical Park for the Freedoms Foundation which in January 1977 awarded her its George Washington Honor Medal.

The Romanian Revolution of 1989 culminated on Christmas Day when within the space of 24 hours dictator Nicolae Ceausescu and his wife Elena were arrested, tried, convicted and executed. Within weeks the new Romanian government returned to Catherine 20 acres of her estate near Nedelea. She couldn't resist the pull of her roots and in mid-year returned to her homeland, taking up residence in one of her former orphanages.

Catherine enjoyed her homecoming for nearly two years before dying on May 26, 1993, at age 100. Among those attending her memorial service were Gabriella Balas Barton and Jeff Wolfrom.

Catherine's youngest daughter, Alexandra, died in 1997, at 77.

EPILOGUE 4

In the aftermath of World War II, many observers concluded that King Michael's coup of Ion Antonescu had shortened the war by as many as six months and spared hundreds of thousands of lives. Soon after VE Day, President Harry Truman awarded Michael the highest degree (Chief Commander) of the Legion of Merit. Stalin decorated him with the Soviet Order of Victory "for the courageous act of the radical change in Romania's politics towards a breakup from Hitler's Germany and an alliance with the United Nations, at the moment when there was no clear sign yet of Germany's defeat." As of 2010, King Michael was the sole surviving recipient of the Soviet honor.

EPILOGUE 5

Singapore today isn't lacking for reminders of World War II and its devastation. A particularly touching reminder is one of the simplest. A painted wooden cross about four feet high is affixed to a 12-inch thick granite base. Trees shade the memorial at Singapore General Hospital near the spot where medical and dental students were slain on February 14, 1942. It pays tribute to the soldiers and civilians killed along College Road. A bronze plaque mounted on the base is inscribed: *Beneath this cross lie 94 British, 6 Malayan, 5 Indian, 2 Australian soldiers and 300 civilians of many races, victims of man's inhumanity to man, who perished in captivity in February 1942. The soldiers are commemorated by name at Kranji War Cemetery.*

EPILOGUE 6

Lim Bo Seng's legacy continues. After the war, he was disinterred from his Batu Gajah Prison grave and, after a hero's funeral, re-interred in Singapore on a hill overlooking MacRitchie Reservoir. In his euglogy, Richard Broome, one of Lim's Force 136 comrades, said, "He died so that Singapore and Malaya might be the home of free people who could once again enjoy peace, prosperity and happiness."

Today, an obelisk-style memorial to Lim sits in the shadows of Singapore skyscrapers near the north bank of the Singapore River – just steps away from the memorial to Sir Stamford Raffles at the site of his first landing on the island in 1819.

On the 50th anniversary of Singapore's liberation, 18 Force 136 veterans posed proudly for a photo in front of the Lim memorial.

Lim's widow, Gan Choo Neo, died September 25, 1979, at age 70 from cancer. His eldest son, Lim Leong Geok, died at age 72 on December 7, 2004.

EPILOGUE 7

Private Malcolm Goode and Captain Brian Barnsworth concluded that they had enough in common to go into business together. *Barnsworth & Goode* was a sporting goods shop specializing in fishing gear. The shop was located in Gravesend. The partnership endured until the men retired in 1990. Goode died in 2005 and Barnsworth in 2008. They are buried in the same graveyard with Pocahontas. Private George Britton attended both their funerals.

EPILOGUE 8

In early 1946 General Tomoyuki Yamashita was brought before a war crimes tribunal in the Philippines for atrocities committed by Japanese forces defending Manila from advancing American troops during the war's closing months. Ironically, Yamashita had ordered Manila abandoned as an open city, and he and his men had retreated to a mountain redoubt. But the Japanese Navy ignored his order and Japanese seamen proceeded to murder thousands of Manila residents along with internees. Had Yamashita not been tried in the Philippines he no doubt would have been tried in Singapore, even though after the Alexandra Hospital massacre he had ordered the perpetrating troops arrested and executed.

In his diary Yamashita had written, *I want troops to behave with dignity, but most of them do not seem to have the ability to do so. This is very important now that Japan is taking her place in the world. These men must be educated up to their new role in foreign countries."*

Yamashita never succeeded. Instead, the savagery and brutality of the Japanese soldier became enduringly infamous. The general was hanged on February 23, 1946.

EPILOGUE 9

Ashford Tanner stood gazing at the building that resembled a small castle or an imposing mansion. It was red brick, two high-ceilinged stories with a turret, steeply pitched roof and wide cement staircase. He was, in fact, looking at Grant School that had been built in 1896.

"Nothing like that in Douglasville," he mused aloud. He looked at his watch. "Kids should be coming out soon." Moments later a loud bell signaled day's end and chattering students began pouring outside. Ash waited patiently while incurious children rushed past him. It was mid-September 1945. Then he saw her descending the steps. He was certain it was she; he had seen her photo so many times. She was carrying a black leather purse in her right hand and file folders in her left.

"Maureen Nelson?" he said.

"Yes." She eyed him quizzically. Strangers in Shelby were few, even fewer standing outside her school.

"My name is Ash Tanner. You might not know the name. I was a friend of your husband." Maureen whitened as blood went rushing from her face. "Ma'am, are you all right?" Ash reached out, gently cupping Maureen's left elbow.

"I think so. I – This is a shock."

"I'm sure it is. Is there someplace we could sit? Besides these steps?"

"There's a bench at the rear corner – by the playground."

"Mr. Tanner-"

"Ash, please," he smiled. They were seated on the slatted wooden bench with iron armrests and legs.

"All right, Ash." She inhaled deeply, color returning to her face. "I'm Maureen. My husband. You were his friend. What brings you here?"

"Sam saved my life and I wanted you and your daughter to know that. I thought about writing but decided telling you in person might be better."

"This is very nice of you. Where is your home, Ash?"

"I'm headed there now. Georgia. A little burg name of Douglasville. About twenty miles west of Atlanta."

"This is quite a detour."

"Not so big. Not considering what Sam did for me."

Maureen swallowed. "How did it happen? I only know where and when he died."

Ash sighed and looked out across the stone-covered playground with its swings, slides and teeter totters. "We were rehearsing for D-Day. An amphibious landing. The Germans got wind of it and shelled our landing boats. Lots of men were killed. I don't swim well and Sam did. We ditched our rifles and helmets and he grabbed me by the chin and towed me to the shallows. I thought we were okay. We stood and then another shell burst and shrapnel hit Sam. I called for a medic who did his best but Sam was gone."

Maureen was blinking back tears. Ash waited patiently. "I'm so glad you came here to tell me. Thank you."

Ash shrugged. "Do you need a hand getting home?"

"I think I'll be all right, thank you."

"Okay. Well I guess I'd better get back to the train station."

"Ash, if you don't mind me asking, what are you planning to do when you get home?"

He smiled. "My parents have a grocery store. They would like me to get in the business and eventually take over."

"You don't sound terribly enthusiastic."

"I'm afraid I'm going to disappoint them. Because of what I saw in Europe – England, France, Germany – I'd like to become a teacher. That's what my heart is set on."

"What are you interested in teaching?"

"History. I think there's a lot youngsters should learn about."

Maureen experienced what she later would recall as an epiphany. "Ash, could you stay the night in Shelby?"

"Well…"

"I'd invite you to stay at my home, but you know…"

Ash chuckled. "Yes, I do. Appearances."

"But my parents, they would love to have you. Especially when I tell them your story. They have plenty of room."

"Ma'am, Maureen, why the invitation?"

She smiled. "There's someone I'd like you to meet. She's a high school history teacher. Marie Hughes. You'd like her and she you. I'm sure she'd love to talk with you about Europe and teaching history. Share her teaching methods."

"This is very nice of you."

"Considering what you've been through, it's nothing. And I'd like you to meet my daughter. Sam's daughter. She's too young to understand all this. But I'd like to get your picture with her. Me too."

"I would be honored."

A long pause. "Is your heart set on returning to Georgia?"

"At one time I wouldn't have hesitated to say yes. But after seeing a good bit of the States and a piece of Europe, I guess I'm open to possibilities."

ACKNOWLEDGEMENTS

Credit for details on Marie Hughes' teas goes to two of her invitees, **Nancy Nicholson Yoder** and **Pat Shedenhelm Papenbrock**, both graduates of Shelby High School. Nancy lives in New Jersey and, like Miss Hughes, became a history teacher. Pat, who became a nurse and lives in northeastern Ohio, was Miss Hughes' next door neighbor and thought of her as Aunt Marie. Pat still has – and wears – two silver and blue enamel scatter pins, gifts that Miss Hughes brought back from a visit to Scotland.

In July 1967, I first visited Pine Bluff, Arkansas with **Lynne Haley**, then my girlfriend and later to become my wife. Lynne's maternal grandparents, Frances Elizabeth Willard (Willard to her contemporaries and Munnie to her grandchildren) and John (DeeDee) Holmes, had operated a boarding house in Pine Bluff. As a young girl growing up there, Lynne and her sister, **Dianne Haley Vots**, helped Munnie with shopping for food, baking and collecting payments from boarders and drop-in diners. The character of Iris Ann Wolfrom is entirely fictional, but the street address and description of the house's interior and daily operations are based on Lynne's and Dianne's crystal clear memories as well as photos.

While **Natarajan "Prasad" Varaprasad** and I were classmates at Stanford, we never expected that, years later, we would be reuniting in his homeland of Singapore or that he would be providing invaluable research assistance for this book. At the time of my research visit to Singapore, Prasad was CEO of the National Library. Before my arrival, he suggested sites relevant to the book and asked two of his staff, **Mr. Yit Chin Chuan** and **Ms. Azizah Sidek**, to answer my questions. Both provided me with remarkably detailed replies. On my arrival Prasad thoughtfully handed me a letter of introduction that gave me access to the National Archives and then drove me to several sites on my list of historically relevant places. Chuan also drove me to several sites, and Azizah provided me with photocopies of the last three editions of *The Straits Times* published before the British surrender. Another member of Prasad's staff, **Mrs. Keat Fong Tan,** cheerfully booked my hotel reservations and furnished helpful logistical information on Singapore.

Another Stanford classmate who served as a driver and guide is **Oon Soo Khoo**, a semi-retired judge. He also introduced me to "hawker food" in Chinatown – a delightfully local dining experience.

Poh Hong Tan, another of my Stanford classmates, is a native Singaporean and a senior government official. Preceding my Singapore visit, she provided a map and guidebook. She also took my list of historically relevant sites, coordinated with Prasad and Oon Soo, and created an itinerary that enabled me to make the most of my time there. The itinerary included phone numbers for all my Singapore contacts. Poh Hong met me on arrival at Singapore's airport and thoughtfully provided a pre-paid cell phone to facilitate communications.

Before arriving in Singapore, I'd never met **Grace Thong**, yet her assistance proved invaluable. She works for a company I once worked for, and a mutual friend who knew of my pending visit to Singapore emailed Grace and asked if she would serve as a driver and guide. Quickly she replied in the affirmative. Grace proved a good sport; she drove me to the base of Bukit Timah and, despite a nagging foot injury, insisted on hiking with me to the summit. It was a steep and sweaty climb with monkeys foraging along the jungle trail. A bonus was having Grace's lovely daughter **Natasha** join us for a relaxing outdoor dinner on the north bank of the Singapore River.

Bill Miller is a friend – and world traveler – of the first rank. He has climbed and hiked mountains in Africa, Europe, North and South America, Asia, Australia and New Zealand. We first met in 1971. Bill lives in suburban Washington, D.C. and provided me with facts about the cherry trees that abound in Washington.

Alexandra Dinita and I first met and worked together more than a decade ago in Bucharest. During several visits to Romania, she organized itineraries that enabled me to see much of that lovely country – Ploesti, Peles Castle, Sinaia, Brasov and the stunning mountainscapes.

Poh Hong Tan

Prasad Varaprasad

Oon Soo Khoo and author

author and Grace Thong

ROSTER OF REAL-LIFE PEOPLE

Clayson Aldridge

Ion Antonescu

Captain J.F. Bartlett

Major General Gordon Bennett

Corporal Rodney Brevington

Private George Britton

Major J.W.D. Bull

Prime Minister Armand Calinescu

Captain Selwyn Capon

Princess Catherine Caradja

Irene Caradja

King Carol I

Nicolae Ceausescu

Mo Ching

Prince Radu Cretulescu

Charles Davis

Kenneth Draper

Queen Elena

Chua Koon Eng

Lieutenant Colonel Frederick Galleghan

General Alfred Gerstenberg

Ambassador Franklin Mott Gunther

Emperor Hirohito

Captain Patrick Heenan

General Seishiro Itagaki

Captain John Leach

Lim Bo Seng

Lim Loh

Virgil Madgearu

Lieutenant General Mataguchi Renya

Brigadier Duncan Maxwell

Prince Yasuhiko Asaka

Joseph Balestier

Maurice Bernbaum

Major General Louis Brereton

Richard Britt

Captain Richard Broome

Sister Vivienne Bullwinkel

Captain Constantine Cantacuzene

Alexandra Caradja

Prince Constantin Caradja

Marie Caradja

King Carol II

Chiang Kai-Shek

Prime Minister Winston Churchill

Princess Irina Cretulescu

Captain John Davis

General Petre Dumitrescu

Queen Elizabeth of Romania

Jesse Franks

Choo Neo Gan

Lieutenant Colonel Jim Gunn

Admiral Thomas Hart

Marie Hughes

Nicolae Iorga

Frank Kees

Li Han Kwang

Lim Leong Geok

General Douglas MacArthur

William McGuffey

Lieutenant Colonel Oishi Masayuki

Louis Medeiros

King Michael

Lord Louis Mountbatten

Ambassador Suermasa Okomoto

Admiral Jisaburo Ozawa

Lieutenant General Arthur E. Percival

Ernest Poulsen

Sir Stamford Raffles

Lieutenant General Constantin Sanatescu

Colonel Jacob Smart

Sergeant Harry Stodgen

Daisy Thomas

Charles Thompson

Colonel Masanohu Tsuji

Stanley Warren

Father Ewald Wegener

Admiral Isoroku Yamamoto

Yoong Tat Sin

Gordon Minnegerode

Randall Norton

Robert O'Reilly

Consul General Kenneth Patton

Admiral Sir Tom Phillips

Sir Dudley Pound

Lieutenant Adnan Bin Saidi

Horia Sima

Ambassador Lawrence Steinhardt

Captain William Tennant

Governor Shenton Thomas

Major Jyo Tomatatsu

Lieutenant Tom Vigors

General Archibald Wavell

Wilbur West

General Tomoyuki Yamashita

Tan Chong Tee

SOURCES

- American Heritage New History of World War II. C.L. Sulzberger
- Balkan Ghosts – a Journey Through History. Robert D. Kaplan
- Breaking The Tongue. Vyvyane Loh
- Dictator Style – Lifestyles of the World's Most Colorful Despots. Peter York
- In-person site visits:
  - Malaysia
  - Pine Bluff, Arkansas
  - Romania
  - Singapore
  - Washington, D.C.
- Insight Singapore. 2005
- Lee Kong Chian Reference Library of Singapore – National Library
- Lim Bo Seng – Singapore's Best-Known War Hero. Clara Show. 1998
- Ohio University – The Spirit of a Singular Place – 1804-2004. Betty Hollow
- Online articles – Romania
  - B-24s - uniforms
  - Brasov
  - Catherine Caradja
  - Constantin Caradja
  - Michael of Romania
  - Operation Tidal Wave
  - Peles Castle
  - Ploesti
  - Ploesti Air Raids
  - Romania in World War II
  - Sinaia
- Online articles – Singapore
  - Alexandra Massacre
  - Battle of Sarimbun Beach
  - Battle of Singapore
  - British Military Hospital

- o HMS Prince of Wales
- o HMS Prince of Wales (Battleship, 1941-1941)
- o Changi
- o Changi POW Camp
- o Changi Prison
- o Empire Star
- o Heroines of Empire Star
- o Lim Bo Seng
- o Malayan People's Anti-Japanese Army
- o Singapore in World War II
- o Singapore War Memorial
- o Sinking of Prince of Wales and Repulse
- Pine Bluff, Arkansas – a Visual History. 1992
- Ploesti – The Great Ground-Air Battle of 1 August 1943. James Dugan and Carroll Stewart
- Scarlet S yearbook. 1960
- Singapore & Malayan Directory for 1940
- Singapore National Library
- Singapore History Museum
- Straits Settlements Annual Report of the Public Works Department for the year 1939.
- The Eagle in the Lion City – America, Americans and Singapore. James Baker
- The Forgotten 500. Gregory Freeman
- The Straits Times. February 13, 1942
- The Straits Times. February 14, 1942
- The Straits Times. February 15, 1942
- The Straits Times. June 19, 2010
- The Syonan Years: Singapore Under Japanese Rule 1942-1945. Lee Geok Boi
- Time-Life History of World War II. 1989
- Treasures of Time. February/March 2003.
- Wonders of the World. 100 Great Man-Made Treasures of Civilization.

LaVergne, TN USA
11 November 2010
204388LV00002B/3/P